HOT WAX

ALSO BY M. L. RIO

Graveyard Shift
If We Were Villains

HOT WAX

M. L. Rio

WILDFIRE

First published in 2025 by Wildfire
An imprint of Headline Publishing Group Limited

5

Cataloguing in Publication Data is available from the British Library

Hardback ISBN 978 1 0354 2116 9
Trade Paperback ISBN 978 1 0354 2117 6

Offset in 10.92pt/16.12 pt ITC New Baskerville Std
by Six Red Marbles UK, Thetford, Norfolk

Printed and bound in Great Britain by Clays Ltd, Elcograf S.p.A.

MIX
Paper | Supporting
responsible forestry
FSC® C104740

Headline's policy is to use papers that are natural, renewable and recyclable
products and made from wood grown in well-managed forests and other
controlled sources. The logging and manufacturing processes are expected
to conform to the environmental regulations of the country of origin.

Headline Publishing Group Limited
An Hachette UK Company
Carmelite House
50 Victoria Embankment
London EC4Y 0DZ

The authorised representative in the EEA is Hachette Ireland,
8 Castlecourt Centre, Dublin 15, D15 XTP3, Ireland (email: info@hbgi.ie)

www.headline.co.uk
www.hachette.co.uk

For Gram, who really gets me
And for James, the Thelma to my Louise

PROLOGUE

STONE FRUIT

Suzanne burned rubber like she could outrun all the baggage, the
crates and cable trunks that crashed against the tailgate every time she
lurched into a higher gear, clumsy with the stick shift after all these years.
Her strange inheritance, a literal truckload of shit she'd already tried
to leave behind. At least her father left her half a pack of Marlboros,
smashed behind the driver's-side visor. He'd quit smoking six years ago,
or so he said, but must have started up again since then. It hurt not to
know when, not to know why. The cigarette lighter glared at her, an angry
red ember almost lost in the sea of buttons crowding the dashboard.
Suzanne lit up with a trembling hand and cranked the window down an
inch to let the smoke and the smell of him out, to let the darkness in.

Hellish humidity had chased her out of Miami, a malevolent yellow
moon bobbing like an angler's lure in the misty rearview. She hadn't
driven the Ranchero since she first learned to drive. Her fingers skittered over the dash, feeling for anything familiar to hold on to, but he
never could stop fucking with it, making modifications that were more
like mutations until the car was a rolling anachronism. Gil and the grip
of the tires had grabbed her from beyond the grave and hurled her
back to that blazing black summer, 1989.

They hadn't spoken since he quit smoking, but the world felt deadly
empty now that he was gone. She searched the FM band for some
kind of divine intervention, a sign or an answer to her ten thousand

questions. Why had he left her the little he had when they'd said so little to each other since they grew apart and she grew up? Her heart jumped at every voice that sounded like his, every colorful burst of Cubonics, every late-night DJ spinning lovesick lullabies, every rock and roller who'd ever met the devil at the crossroads.

Nothing but static in the midnight marshlands, or maybe it was just the antenna. She stayed off the interstate instinctively, though nobody would be looking for her yet, if they looked for her at all. Gil's death had thrown her a lifeline, at least—bought her a week to work out what to do and where to go and given her wheels to get there. The only thing Suzanne knew for certain was that she wasn't going home.

She'd been driving too fast and driving too long, sidewinding white-line hypnosis warping the highway, the wheels wandering underneath her. She tried to blink her eyes open wider, shifted against the seat. Might have imagined the whiff of bay rum and black coffee still clinging to the leather. She groped across the dashboard again, turning dials and twisting knobs at random, desperate for some other voice to fill her head until the tank was empty again.

The glove box fell open and she snatched her hand back, but not fast enough. She'd triggered one of Gil's mechanical booby traps and music came on, mid-verse, mid-song. A voice, *his* voice, older and softer, but still unmistakably him. The way he always sang scratch vocals, a rumble and hum thrumming low in his chest.

Ain't you done squeezin' me, baby
Can't get no blood from a stone
But I been bleeding, cream and peaches
Picking scabs and feeding leeches
'Til there ain't nothing left but the bones

Suzanne swerved off the road, tires squealing in the wet, swampy weeds. The song stuttered and hiccupped until the car stopped with a shocking jolt. She gagged against the pain in her chest, where the seat belt had snapped the wind out of her. She crumpled over the wheel, bent and shaking and blinded by the sting of tears. Cigarette burning a hole in the hem of her shorts until it rolled off onto the floor.

Gil laughed sadly at himself, or maybe her, the mess they'd made of everything together.

Ain't they still makin' to break me
Can't brew no soup from these bones
But the vultures are here
And the vultures are hungry
Wheelin' and waitin' and achin' to take me
Don't let 'em get me baby
Come on home

The tape hissed into silence. She raised her head, wiped her eyes, felt around for her cigarette. Instead her fingers scraped across something cool and flat. An old atlas.

Gil had installed a CD player but apparently hadn't bought a new road map for twenty-nine years, the pages still glued together by psychedelic smears of wax. As she thumbed through it, the names came back by twos and threes, jumbled up with destinations they traced the routes between. Midnight Blue from Nashville to Memphis. Apricot from Milwaukee to Minneapolis. The paper crackled between her fingers and the crayon crumbled away like old scabs as she spread the Southwest across her lap, following the path her own childish hand had traced through the desert to Las Vegas—a winding red ribbon of blood.

PART I

IMPERSONATOR

THE **A** SIDE

PAPA WAS A ROLLIN' STONE

1988. The scream of the telephone punctured Suzanne's slumber
like a balloon. She stirred where she lay, curled up on the sofa, dreams
infused with the opaque midnight noise of the street three stories
below. She and her parents lived in a one-bedroom on the top floor of
a crumbling brick rowhouse on the bad side of Baltimore, which didn't
seem to have a good side anymore. Already the wino who haunted the
bus stop was up and rattling his cup, accosting commuters in a guttural
grumble that pleaded and threatened in the same breath. The phone
screamed again, strident as the school bell or the wailing police sirens
that lit up the neighborhood like the Fourth of July every Saturday
night. Suzanne rolled over, buried her face in the pillow, turned her
back on the world.

The third time the phone rang, her mother's high heels answered,
smacking down the hallway. The shoes were a recent acquisition, a necessary evil since Nora took a second job at the Macy's jewelry counter.
The ringing stopped abruptly as she snatched the phone off the wall.
Suzanne could see her without opening her eyes, handset wedged
under one ear, cord tangling around her ankles as she crashed through
the kitchen, throwing things in her purse with one hand, throwing back
her coffee with the other.

"Good morning, asshole." The refrigerator door swung open, condiments rattling. "Sure I do when it's five a.m. and our daughter's still

asleep. Or did you forget about her, too?" A splatter of coffee hit the
sink, then a mug clattered into the basin. Suzanne squirmed into the
cushions. She didn't want to hear one half of the same conversation
she'd been hearing one half of for the last three years. "I don't care
where you are or why you're not here. You're not here." Nora's heels
halted their angry march across the kitchen. "*Skelly?*" Suzanne pulled
her head under the blankets. Even she knew not to say his name to
Nora. He was so often to blame for her father's broken promises, but
he was also the reason Gil had a new label and a new record deal, had a
fighting chance to crack the charts for the first time. "You know," Nora
said, "I used to worry about road wives, but you've already got one! And
her name is Eric fucking Skillman." She wrenched the window open,
whacked a pack of Camels against the heel of her palm.

Suzanne knew the whole sorry song and dance, the way most Mon-
day mornings went. Nora would flick her ash into the broken soap
dish on the windowsill, then exhale long and slow. She was a nice girl
before she met Gil Delgado. She used to laugh when she said that. She
still said it, but she'd stopped laughing. "No," she said. "Come and tell
her yourself. Coward." She slammed the phone down again. Her heels
banged on the tile until she crossed over onto the itchy brown carpet
that covered the living room floor like a layer of mulch. Suzanne stayed
perfectly motionless until she felt Nora's hand on her shoulder. "Suzanne, honey," she whispered. By some tacit agreement they still played
along, pretended Suzanne was still sleeping. "Get dressed and brush
your teeth, okay? We'll both have to catch the bus today."

The bus map was the first map Suzanne memorized. Nora had
spread it on the table before her first day at Macy's, took one of Suzanne's crayons from the mug on the counter, traced the route from
school to the mall in bright Lemon Yellow, then covered the page to
quiz her. *Where do you get on? Where do you get off? How many stops?* Unlike
the school bus, which went only to school and stopped only for children, the city bus spun colorful cobwebs from Park Heights to Pigtown.

Before long, the creases in the map made a grid like a chessboard that spanned the whole city, each important square and the ways between them shaded with crayon from the mug on the counter or the stash of points and stubs crammed in Suzanne's backpack.

The second map she memorized was the South Fork shopping mall directory, another geometric maze of colored blocks and polygons. The entrance closest to the bus stop was farthest from the Macy's, the most direct route between the two through the food court and up the escalator, then around the corner and down again before she got caught up in queues for the movie theater. If she ran fast enough, she could weave through shoes and cosmetics and handbags and emerge into the parking lot for her mother's 4:15 cigarette break. Nora would give Suzanne a dollar, more if she had it, ask *How was school?* then send her back inside to buy a Coke or a candy bar and find somewhere to sit and do her homework. Then Suzanne's time was her own until the time came to board the bus home.

For the first few weeks, South Fork was her own personal amusement park. She watched women in skirt suits with imposing shoulder pads climb on and off the tailor's stool, twirl like ballerinas or stretch their arms out like acrobats, reflections refracted in a dozen directions by the funhouse mirrors. She tried on discarded garments in fitting rooms in a solitary game of dress-up, hid inside racks of fur coats and stroked the sleeves as if they were still warm and breathing. She snuck into movies, usually with families with two or three children already in tow, parents and ushers unlikely to notice an extra. But it was the record store that sang like a siren—music trickling out into the tiled tributaries that carried shoppers from one errand, one distraction, one impulse purchase to the next. The sign drew Suzanne's eye every time she passed. MOST WANTED RECORDS, it said, and she wanted more than anything to go inside. Even when she saved her dollars and dimes, she never had enough to buy an 8-track or cassette, but the bigger problem was her father.

Gil was music in motion. Even when he wasn't onstage, singing his heart out for the few believers who bought a ticket and anyone else who wandered in looking for a drink or a smoke or a way to kill time, melody trailed behind him like exhaust. He hummed and whistled, tapped his fingers and toes, scrawled lyrics in the margins of every napkin he picked up to wipe his mouth. Even his speaking voice had a certain rhythm, the sonorous rumble of rumba and son, the fugitive consonants he left behind in Miami, after he left his parents behind in Havana, even younger then than Suzanne was now. His English was impeccable, his accent learned from the silver screen, grammar and vocabulary collected like loose change from the pages of the Bible and ten-cent paperbacks. He learned music just like he learned language— mostly through osmosis. Gil sucked up sound like a sponge and wrung it all out again as soon as he set foot behind the microphone.

But music soured whenever Gil was gone, and these days he was gone much more than he was home. As soon as the door closed behind him, Nora changed the station to talk radio or turned the receiver off. Without him, the too-small apartment was too quiet, too still. But *being gone is a good thing*, Gil reminded them; every night he spent on the road was a night he collected a paycheck—if people bought tickets and they didn't get stiffed and nothing broke down. Those nights were rarer still. But it wouldn't be like that forever. He was so sure. "Don't worry, babe," he said to Nora and to Suzanne when she was old enough to understand. "Someday I'm gonna be somebody. You won't be able to walk down the street without hearing my voice or my name, and every time somebody says, 'Hey, play that again,' it'll be money in the bank. Don't worry."

But Suzanne worried. Every time she walked by Most Wanted she strained her ear, hoping to hear his new band, Gil and the Kills. Once, she went inside because some other somebody sounded so much like him that her heart leapt out of her chest to beat between her eardrums. When she asked the first person she bumped into, "Who plays this song?" the girl shrugged and said, "Somebody I don't know," or maybe, "Somebody. I don't know." Suzanne was too confused and embarrassed to ask anyone else. Gil made it sound like being *somebody* meant being somebody everybody knew. She avoided the record store after that, resisted its gravitational tug.

Her favorite haunt was the hobby shop, where she'd fork over a few precious dollars for a fresh box of crayons when she was fresh out. The same cashier worked every afternoon, but unlike the salespeople every- where else, he was never too busy to say hello and didn't seem to mind if nobody bought anything. A coffeepot percolated constantly behind the counter, a smell she knew so well it smelled like home. Notes of Raw Umber, dark chocolate, and Gil. She'd started drinking coffee as soon as she stopped drinking milk. It was in her blood, he said, strong and dark and sweet. Nora didn't like it, insisted it would stunt her growth. She'd always been small for her age.

But her size had its upsides. With longer legs, she couldn't have curled up in her favorite corner, in the back of the store, the empty nook between the cameras and the model cars. She learned the names and decals of every candy-colored roadster, partial to the yellow ones that looked like Blondie—the big, roaring Ranchero that always whisked Gil away and brought him back again. She riffled through the rack of atlases with their squiggling rivers and county lines and country roads and the grid of creases that failed to fence them in. When she found a name that felt familiar, someplace Nora had mentioned, somewhere Gil was going, she'd follow every possible path back to Baltimore and wonder how long it took to drive four hundred miles home from Ohio.

She test-drove every car in her imagination, traveled every inch of the map. She took the red Mustang across the Golden Gate Bridge, the electric-blue Ferrari down the palm-lined streets of Palm Beach. In every daydream she carried a camera, just like Nora used to do. Nora had stopped taking photos like she'd stopped listening to music and laughing at her own jokes, but Suzanne still had the itch, snapping make-believe pictures for Rand McNally to print in next year's atlas. That was where the fantasy frayed. Toy cars wouldn't get her far, and all the cameras in the hobby shop were locked up behind glass—except one. There was a Polaroid 640, with a rainbow on the box. If she'd done the math right, and she saved all her snack money, she could buy it for her birthday.

When her birthday came, she piled coins and crumpled ones in front of the cashier. "There's enough," she promised. "I counted."

He looked puzzled. "What for?"

"For the camera." She stumbled over the words, realizing she'd never spoken it out loud, breathed that wish into existence. She wanted that rainbow, the Technicolor memories it promised. "The Polaroid. It's my birthday."

He smiled across the counter. "How old are you?"

"Ten."

"Congratulations! That's a big birthday. That 640 must have been waiting for you, but you'll need some film to go with it."

She hadn't thought of that. Didn't know the camera wouldn't come with everything you needed in the box. The cashier took a packet of film from the wire rack beside the counter. Polaroid 600. It had been there all along—right size, right shape.

"I can come back," she said, eyes already welling up. "In two weeks, I'll have—"

"Oh," he said. "Didn't I say? You get one pack for free if it's your birthday." Suzanne sniffed at him, suspicious. Nora had taught her to be wary of free-handed strangers. What might they expect in return? But the cashier didn't give her time to wonder. He pushed the box toward her. "Limited-time offer, so you'd better take it."

She didn't need telling twice. She ran all the way to Macy's, too excited to feel the pinch of last year's Keds, the sting of blisters on her heels that ruptured and peeled and split open again but never quite healed. She dodged around shoppers and security guards and was gasping by the time she stumbled past the fragrance counter. The jewelry section only made her dizzier, every display case a prismatic whirl. She crash-landed on a plinth where a mannequin wielded a Gucci umbrella as if it were a rapier. That was where they met at the end of each day— Nora had warned Suzanne not to come up to the counter, because it wasn't "a good place for children" and her manager disapproved.

Suzanne sat for a long time. She pulled the Polaroid out of her backpack and held it on her lap, precious as a first pet. She read the instructions, word for word, and didn't notice the passing of the first half hour. Then the store began to empty, women laden with shopping bags bustling toward the exit, bidding each other goodbye with quips about getting home before their husbands to hide the evidence and heat up dinner. Suzanne looked around for a clock and didn't find one, but when the doors swung open and shut, she craned her neck to see outside and knew by the sky—Carnation Pink and Indian Red—that Nora was late.

She returned the camera to the box, the box to her backpack, and clambered off the plinth. She inched between the display cases, searching for someone with a watch or a name tag to ask for the time, but the sales floor had emptied. The first person she happened across happened to be talking to her mother. He wore a blue shirt with a collar and shiny brown loafers with tassels on the toes. Tortoiseshell glasses perched on a square face with a friendly smile. Something he said made Nora laugh—a big, helpless belly laugh she tried to hide behind one hand. She only succeeded in smudging her lipstick, and then her mascara when she wiped her eyes. Nora never laughed like that, and she looked so beautiful Suzanne stopped to stare. The man was staring, too, staring at Nora like he'd never seen a woman before.

The prickling feeling from Suzanne's pinched toes crawled up the backs of her legs and then her spine and through the roots of her hair. Her face felt sunburned, heart throwing itself against her rib cage like it wanted to escape. She turned back the way she came, hugging her backpack and its precious cargo to her chest. Her sneakers squeaked through the hollow, empty store, but neither Nora nor the man seemed to hear.

The mall's walkways felt too wide without any other people on them. The lights were too bright, the air too cold, the music too quiet. Suzanne wandered the map she knew so well like a stranger, taking random turns and escalators, but she kept coming back to the same landing. The music was a little louder there. She realized the PA system had been shut off, and instead the sound was coming from Most Wanted. The security grille hadn't been lowered all the way. Feeling oddly defiant, she ducked underneath.

The only person inside was a chubby, gap-toothed stock boy. He had a wiry red beard, like Hägar the Horrible, and dozens of LPs in shrink wrap piled on the floor in front of him. He moved a price tag from the left corner of a record to the right, did the same to the record beneath, and the one beneath that, and the one beneath that. Suzanne watched him painstakingly move price tags from left to right five times and asked, "What are you doing?"

He jumped and clutched his heart. Suzanne noticed her own was no longer hammering, as if breaching the terra incognita of the record store had reset some sort of trip wire in her body.

"Jesus, kid, don't sneak up on somebody like that!"

"Sorry." She tilted her head to read the name tag he'd knocked askew. "Doug."

Doug scowled. "Do you have a parent somewhere?"

"My mom works at Macy's."

"Okay, well, you can't play in here."

"Can I help?"

"What?"

"Can I stay if I help?" She pointed at the LPs—a stack of shiny black squares, each with the scaly, hooked head of a buzzard peering out from the center. Skin a shocking shade of pink, the words *Hard Candy* dangling from its beak like roadkill. She knew that song, "Hard Candy." She'd heard it on the radio.

Doug started to say no but changed his mind halfway. "N— How old are you, eight?"

"I'm ten." She didn't say *Today*. Double digits or not, still small for her age.

"You know left and right?" He glanced at the Elvis Presley clock on the wall, hips ticking back and forth.

She wiggled her fingers. "Left-handed."

"Okay, so move the price tags from the left to the right, all right? Like how you read, left to right."

She set her backpack down and sat. "Why are we moving them left to right?"

"Because Billy is an idiot and he put them in the wrong corner, and corporate won't let us put them on the floor in the morning if the price tags are in the wrong corner, and if they're not on the floor in the morning there'll be hell to pay." He stabbed a sticker down and left a smudged thumbprint on the cellophane.

"What's corporate?" Suzanne asked.

"A pain in my fat ass. But they've put everybody else out of business, so, y'know, here we are, violating child labor laws so Babel Mouth can make another million bucks."

"Who's Babel Mouth?"

Doug turned one of the records over. "That," he said, "is Babel Mouth. Nicky and Vince DeWitt and their army of miscreants."

They were somebody, Suzanne thought. She'd heard their names before, but she'd never seen what they looked like. They wore a lot of dark eye makeup, which made their pale faces even paler. She thought the photo was in black and white, except that one of them was wearing lipstick, the same poisonous pink as the buzzard on the front. So that was what somebody looked like. She could have looked much longer, but Doug turned the record back over, resumed moving stickers.

Suzanne watched and learned that they didn't come off easily. She coaxed them loose corner by corner until they finally peeled free. Left to right, left to right, just like Elvis's hips. She bobbed her head to the bump of the bass from the speakers in the ceiling. "Is this Babel Mouth?" she said. "This song."

Doug snorted. "Definitely not. Why, you like it?"

Suzanne nodded yes.

"Never heard *Licensed to Ill* before? Never heard the Beastie Boys?" Suzanne shook her head no. A grin broke through the rootbound tangle of Doug's red beard. "Kid," he said, "I'm about to change your life."

THE **B** SIDE

WAKE UP, LITTLE SUSIE

The kick drum thumped through Suzanne's dreams, thumped be-tween her temples and behind both eyes. No, that was just the dia-bolical Florida sunshine and the 90-degree crick in her neck making themselves known. When the pounding didn't stop, she reached blindly for the Wayfarers hanging from the visor and pushed them onto her face before she even tried to open her eyes. Thanks to the tint on the lenses and the dirt on the window and the shrieking head-ache that had finally rounded the corner between her third and fourth cervical vertebrae and embedded itself in her brain, she was slow to realize someone was knocking on the glass and yelped "Mother*fucker*!" when she did.

"Sorry!" He jumped away from the car like she'd pulled a gun. The window was still cracked from her last stale cigarette. No hope he hadn't heard her. "Sorry! Just wanted to make sure you were all right. You've been—ah—you've been dozing there for a while."

She glanced around the mostly empty lot. Wondering all over again where the hell she was and how she wound up there. After she ran the car off the road, the engine refused to start again and she had to risk turning her phone on to call for a tow. She'd been stranded nearly a week by then but had yet to lay eyes on any of the other guests hid-ing out at the Sundew Value Inn. The kind of place she hadn't stayed in years. The kind of place you spent the night when you didn't care whether you woke up in the morning. The kind of place that catered to the kind of people who couldn't wait to disappear.

Suzanne's crackpot vanishing act was off to a very bad start. Hard to run away when the car wouldn't run. She kept climbing into the driver's seat hoping it would start again, as suddenly as it had stopped. She had no idea how to fix it, and neither did any of the half dozen mechanics she'd called, begged, bribed, even propositioned in a fit of desperation. "Lady, I'd like to help you," the last one said, rebuffing her clumsy advances, "but the best suggestion I can make is that you sell this thing." She would have sooner sold her soul but didn't think she'd find a taker. She must have fallen asleep in the driver's seat. Not for the first time that week.

"And you've been, what, just watching?" she asked, not-so-surreptitiously wiping drool from her chin. The guy didn't look the part of a peeping tom, not that she was much to peep at these days. She squinted for a better view through the murky window. To let the Ranchero get so dirty was sacrilege, but she didn't want to draw attention to herself, and Blondie was hardly inconspicuous.

"Well, yes," said her young voyeur. He might have been twenty-five, but the drooping eyes made him look older—not tired, like hers, glazed with rudely interrupted sleep, but somehow unrushed. Unhurried. "Or, no, not exactly," he decided, hearing how it sounded out loud. "I've been coveting your car." He gave her a shrug and a helpless grin, as if to say, *Sue me.*

"It's not for sale."

"Sounds like it's not running, either."

"How long did you say you've been stalking me?"

"Not stalking," he said. "I'm posted up at the RV lot on the other side of the station." He pointed toward the gas pumps and the tiny convenience store where she'd picked up her room key and a few emergency rations to hold her over until she figured out where to go and how to get there. There was a garage around back, where they'd towed her in the first place. "Not in the business of buying until I can get a little more work, and it sounds like you need a mechanic."

Suzanne let out a hollow laugh. "Tell me something I don't know."

"You're looking at one," he said. "A pretty good one."

She lowered the window another six inches to get a better look. Too-big, too-blue eyes shaded from the sun by too much brown hair. He wore a white undershirt streaked with grease and a pair of old Levi's, knees faded from rigid blue to a pale, soft parchment. His hands had slid out of sight in his back pockets, but his arms were modestly muscled, scored with scratches and scars that testified to time spent working with tools, with metal and heat. "How good?" she said.

"Good enough to know that's a '68 Ranchero GT with the 428 Cobra Jet engine, but someone's been mucking around with the factory settings." He peered in through the window with naked curiosity. "Whether that person was a genius or a lunatic . . ."

"That always was the question," Suzanne said, vaguely, to discourage further questions about Blondie's origins. She was more interested in the origins of the messianic young mechanic offering to save her from herself. "What's the going rate? I'm on a fixed income, so to speak." He'd admitted as much, so why shouldn't she? Nobody staying where the word "Value" was part of the appeal had any reason to pretend.

He considered the car. Walked around the front bumper, down the passenger side, and around the rear before coming up to her window again. "Looks to me like some genius or some lunatic put a trailer hitch on this thing. You'd have to be crazy to do a thing like that to a car like this, but . . ."

"But what?" She didn't know anything about tongue weights or towing capacity, though she'd heard all those words tossed around by the road crew, the same way they talked about amp wattage and audio chains. Always in that tone of surprise that Gil hadn't yet killed himself doing whatever he was trying to do.

"But I've got a trailer and nothing to hitch it to," the mechanic admitted. "If I could get this beauty running well enough to haul my ass to Georgia, I'd call us even."

She pretended to consider it. Considered him again. Wiser than his years, just like she used to be, before the years caught up to her. "Deal."

She stuck her hand out the window. It occurred to her to lie, to give him one of the fake names she'd been using since she left Alexandria, but she couldn't jinx the agreement, even if it was just a handshake. "I'm Suzanne."

"Simon," he said. His grip was surprisingly gentle, his palm so warm and callused that she didn't even feel at first that two of his fingers were missing.

Simon returned the following morning. Suzanne was as ready as she'd ever be to open the door to the tatty motel room where she'd been marinating in her own sweat. The window unit rattled and wheezed like a lifetime of chain-smoking but didn't do much to keep the room cool or dissipate the musty smell that clung to the curtains. Nobody was likely to notice the heat or the odor when facing the freakish flotsam that had taken over the room. A riot of satin and leather and feathers and sequins. She'd grouped Gil's things in three loose categories: musical junk, costume junk, and other junk. Nobody could accuse him of being sentimental. He had no memorabilia—no posters, no press clippings, no pictures. The only photos in the room were faded Polaroids Suzanne had taken herself. She stashed them out of sight in the mini fridge when she heard Simon knock. Who else? She hadn't made a point of making friends. The fewer people who remembered her being there, the better.

"Morning," he said. He looked half-asleep still, but she suspected that was just the droop of his eyelids, the slow-down tempo when he talked. She couldn't decide if it was magnetic or unnerving and stared at him stupidly for a moment before she remembered to reply.

"Morning." Not a *good* morning, just a morning. A statement of fact. "Um. Coffee?"

"If you've got it, you're a godsend," he said. She left the door hanging halfway open as she rooted around in the fridge, pushing the precious packet of Polaroids gingerly aside. Heat didn't do them—or her—any favors.

"It's iced." There was no ice, though. "Well, it's cold. For now." Half past nine and the sun was already beating down like it had a grudge against the world.

"Thanks." He took the cup she handed him, leaning into the room but not too bold about it. Peering around at her cabinet of curiosities. "Cool stuff."

"Long story." A lazy evasion, but that didn't make it less true. "Came with the car." She wanted him fixated on fixing Blondie. Wouldn't breathe any easier until she'd put another thousand miles behind her.

Simon slurped the coffee, the thumb of his three-fingered hand hooked in his front pocket. It looked like a traumatic injury, not a birth defect—the fourth and little fingers lopped off at the knuckle, skin puckered and pink. Suzanne pointedly did not stare. Bad memories lurking everywhere. She stared instead at the toolbox behind him. A sticker slapped on one side spelled the words LIFEBOAT SUPPLY CO. around the rim of an orange ring buoy. It struck her as a good omen; maybe he really was there to throw her a rope. She felt the knot of tension that had lived between her shoulder blades for the last few days—few weeks, few months, five years—loosen, just a little. "Anything else you can tell me about it?" he said. "The car."

Christ, the things she could tell him. About late nights and early mornings yawning on the bench seat beside Gil, the bump of the cable trunks against the back of the cab, the engine and the radio in electric harmony. Instead, she blurted out, "Her name is Blondie." Because what she really wanted to tell him was impossible to articulate. The car was more than a car.

A slow smile, slow as his eyes. "It suits her." The car was still dusty, still dirty, but still a splendid butter yellow somewhere underneath the grime. She had Florida plates, letters and numbers in ripe Kelly green, with two juicy oranges dangling suggestively between. The plates, the red taillights, the bright, long body of the car—Suzanne hated to see it languish in her lifeless corner of the world. Simon glanced over his shoulder like he couldn't keep his eyes off her, like he could see right through the dirt and dust, knew what was hiding there. "Hell of a car."

Suzanne ran one hand through her hair, only to realize how unkempt it was, how long it had been since she cut or washed it. She and Blondie both in desperate need of a buff and polish. "Mechanically, though, you know," she rambled on, "I have no idea. Can't tell you much about the mods. Never was a gearhead." Not entirely true. She knew cameras inside and out. She didn't care for the newer DSLRs and had left them behind without regret, the idea of photographing one more engagement or one more wedding or one more pregnancy announcement utterly repugnant.

"Here's hoping I can make heads or tails of it," Simon said. He looked back at her with another long slurp of coffee. "And get us both on the road."

She crossed her fingers behind her back. Handed him the keys.

Two hours later, he knocked again, or so she wrongly assumed. After stealing glances out the window—taking her turn as voyeur, paranoia and curiosity making her twitch the curtains back again and again to watch him work—she wrenched the door open too readily. Hard to say who was more startled, Suzanne or the girl standing on the other side. She resisted precise categorization—age, race, and intent all decidedly ambiguous. She wore her hair in tight, long braids tied into pigtails, a Peterbilt T-shirt scissored off at the waist, a skirt stitched together from old bandanas, and a pair of high-top Chuck Taylors with shark teeth drawn jaggedly across the toes in Sharpie. "Hi," she said. "I'm Phoebe. Simon said you might have coffee."

Suzanne peered past her to find Simon's head under the hood, a tattered white rag dangling from his back pocket like a flag of surrender. Phoebe followed her gaze and let her eyes wander back without urgency.

"And you're . . ." Suzanne said. Simon hadn't mentioned a girlfriend, and neither of them was wearing a ring. She rubbed automatically at the tender band of skin around her fourth finger, which hadn't seen the sun for a long time.

"Just another drifter," Phoebe said, that much ambiguous, too. Did she mean *Like Simon* or *Like you?* Suzanne shifted her feet, the heat more oppressive than a moment before. Phoebe was not beautiful, exactly, but striking—the way people described supermodels. Almond eyes, freckles like the speckles on a robin's egg, plump pout of a mouth and a gap between her front teeth. Suzanne often felt frumpy but never, until this moment of unavoidable comparison, *dumpy.* Simon looked up from the engine, gave her a three-fingered wave.

"Coffee," Suzanne said, still looking past Phoebe at him. Wondering what she'd gotten herself into. "Sure, okay. Come in." She opened the fridge, nudging the packet of Polaroids a little farther back on the shelf. Feeling like a worm under a rock suddenly exposed to the world. She reached around on the table for a clean cup. She'd been stealing them in stacks of two or three whenever she ducked into the gas station for provisions, trying not to think about the waste.

"Bless you." Phoebe clutched the cup and gulped it down with a desperation Suzanne recognized as bone-deep caffeine addiction. They had that much in common. She drank while the window unit rattled through the silence, blowing sour, steely whispers of air in from outside. Phoebe smacked her lips, a drop of sweat snaking down her neck. "God, that's good."

"Help yourself," Suzanne said. Hospitality had never been her strong suit, but she was strong on strong coffee. She didn't know what else to say, stifled by the heat and the thundering echo of Gil in the room. Every corner occupied by an artifact or fossil from an unknown chapter of his life. Some were almost self-explanatory—the Mojo Barbecue piggy bank stuffed with guitar picks, for instance—while others defied interpretation. She glanced at the enormous sawtooth spurs dangling from the bedpost, wishing she'd put them anywhere else.

"Wow," Phoebe said, inflection so perfectly neutral she could have meant *Wow, what a mess* or *Wow, what great stuff.* "What's all this?" She glanced in the closet, where Suzanne had hung the most delicate costumes—jackets with epaulettes and hypnotic embroidery, a velvet jumpsuit he'd only worn once, in what one reviewer described as a "misguided Mick Jagger moment." Gil was a lot of things but never a coward, whatever Nora said, and his failures were sometimes more spectacular than his triumphs, up until '89. No coming back from that year.

"Your guess is as good as mine," Suzanne admitted. "I don't know if it's worth keeping or selling or if it's just junk."

Phoebe bobbed her head, not quite a nod or shake but something in between. "Not always a lot of rhyme or reason to what appreciates over time." She picked out a silky black bomber jacket with a tiger on the back and tried it on. It worked surprisingly well with the skirt and the hungry hungry high-tops. She checked her reflection in the mirror, shrugged out of it again, and returned it to the hanger. Suzanne watched her with a pang of envy. How easily she handled his things.

"Sounds like something you know something about."

Phoebe's head bobbed again. "Maybe." She reached for a couple of necklaces hanging on a nail in the wall, and after a moment's consideration chose a long chain with a tarnished, pointed pendant. She gave Suzanne the same consideration, then twirled her finger. Suzanne turned obediently. Felt Phoebe brush her hair aside, shivered as the cool metal settled on the nape of her neck. She hadn't realized what it was until she saw it up close. The nose of a dart, or it had been once. "You should keep that," Phoebe said, turning her around again to face her reflection. The pendant pointed down into the crevice of her cleavage—still sharp as a needle. She hadn't worn it in twenty-nine years, tried not to touch it or even to think about it, but couldn't get rid of it, either. Just carried it around like a curse or a bad habit she couldn't break. "Looks just the right kind of blasphemous on you."

"Thanks," Suzanne said in a thick, throttled voice, unsure if that was a compliment.

Phoebe smiled, sort of, tongue pinched between her teeth. She resumed her prowl around the room. "Who threw it at you, some kind of musician?"

"Yeah," Suzanne said in that same sticky voice, and didn't say, *If you only knew.*

Phoebe picked up a stack of CDs and turned them sideways, scanning the spines. She pulled one out of the pile and held it up for Suzanne to see. Gil's teenaged mug shot grinned at her. "Shit, you could really get something for these." Phoebe showed her another. A Polaroid was just the right shape for a CD case. Two men with too-long hair staring out at her in miniature. *Unholy Relics.* The last Kills record, never even pressed on vinyl.

"Really?" Suzanne said. "I thought everybody forgot about them." Or hoped they had. The dart felt heavier around her neck, bristles of black fletching scraping her skin.

"Morbid fascination never goes out of fashion," Phoebe said. "It's a collectors' item now. If we were flush I'd make you an offer. Got a lot of inventory but nowhere to unload it, not while we're marooned in this wasteland."

"What kind of inventory?" Suzanne asked. Surprised she knew the album. Unusual for someone her age. Unusual for anyone anymore. "You sell . . . CDs?"

"CDs, sure. Cassettes and records, too. Clothes, kitsch, electronics, you name it. Come take a look sometime, maybe we can make a trade." She put the CDs back where she'd found them with palpable reluctance. "Don't want to let that killer get away. Promise not to sell it off to anyone else just yet, okay?"

Suzanne fumbled for a second cup to pour herself some coffee, just for something to do, somewhere to avert her eyes. Like Blondie, she would never sell the CDs but couldn't explain herself, either. "Sure," she said. "I won't."

When the door closed behind Phoebe and Suzanne returned the coffee to the fridge, the packet of Polaroids stopped her. The cassette hiding at the bottom of the envelope. She squatted down, afraid to remove it too far from the only cool, safe place in the room. Most of the photos she remembered, labeled in her girlish penmanship with the improbable places they were taken. Wild Bucks Tavern. Sunspot Studios. One in the back of a van, one in the back of a limo. Each dated between June and August of 1989, except the one she was looking for. There they were, Skelly and Gil. Faded by the years, but still the same two enfants terribles making faces at anyone who picked up *Holy Relics*. Gil with his come-hither grin, Skelly baring his teeth like a vampire scorched by the sunlight. Pinned on the wall behind them were a hundred other Polaroids of a hundred other young hooligans, but nobody worth remembering.

Her hair stood on end despite the heat. The dart a strangling weight around her neck. She slipped the photo out of sight at the back of the stack and flipped through the others. A dark woman with huge hair barely contained by her headphones. A big bald bearded guy balancing half a dozen donuts on top of his head. A man's right hand, holding the camera at a safe distance. Black bones tattooed on his pale, pearly skin, one sly gunmetal eye peering out at her between two skeletal fingers.

She pushed the rest of the Polaroids into the envelope without looking at them. There was only one other picture, taken with a different camera. Gil again, crazy brown curls tamed halfway with a liberal application of pomade, shirt open at the neck, white socks peeking out of black trousers. He perched on Blondie's tailgate with a banner strung behind him that said, in sloppy red paint, JUST MARRIED. She stared a long time, trying to find his eyes, but the photo was too dark.

She slid it back into the envelope, the envelope back into the fridge. Closed the door and looked around the room, at Gil's inhuman remains. Among them, the map she'd brought in from the car. Another souvenir of that ill-fated year, the same atlas she carried everywhere, as if it might lead them to treasure. She knew it was only fool's gold now, but Gil had thrown her a shovel, and she was going to dig.

Snapshot: Miami, 1976

It was after midnight when the backing band broke down their in-struments. Nobody wanted the party to end, but the boys had only been paid to play until then and roundly refused when Gil begged for an encore. Weddings were demeaning.

"No, I'm going home," the bass player said, swinging his guitar into the back of the ramshackle Fanta van they used to drive their gear to gigs since it turned up at the impound lot and Gil somehow got it running. "We did this as a favor to you, man."

"Wait, hold on—"

"I been holding on long enough! My old lady's going to murder me for getting home so late with so little to show for it."

He muscled past Gil and hauled the door shut. Then came the drummer, sucking on a bottle of Colt 45 that was almost empty, which meant he wasn't going anywhere before the liquor store. That didn't stop Gil from grabbing him by the lapels and trying to turn him around. "Listen, they're dying in there!"

The drummer jabbed him in the chest with both sticks. "You want to keep going? Go solo." He made a wide, windmilling gesture toward the doors they'd just come out of, where the music had taken a disappointing turn into the prerecorded. "Everybody knows that's what *you're* dying to do."

Gil mouthed at him, no lie at the ready. "I— No, come on! You got it all wrong, eh? I'm just some asshole doing stand-up without you guys."

The Fanta van belched out a cloud of exhaust. "Well, you finally figured it out," said the guitar player, reaching out the window to adjust the walleyed left mirror. "Dumb fucking wetback."

The door slammed and the van sprayed gravel, and Gil could only holler curses in their wake. He knew he'd never see them again; they'd never called him that to his face. He thumbed a cigarette out of the pack in his pocket, damp and crushed from two hours' gymnastics under the hot lights of the ballroom. He'd played there before, a few different times with a few different lineups. In a former life it had been a bingo hall, but it, like Gil, was clawing its way up in the world.

"Got a light?"

"*¡Coño!*" His feet went out from under him, creepers squealing in the Ranchero's empty bed, everything slick from the afternoon's rain or the evening's humidity. He fell hard on his ass, hands slipping along the tailgate as he pulled himself upright again. He was about to let fly another flood of profanity but found himself face-to-face with one of the more beautiful girls he'd ever seen outside the pages of a magazine. Hair the color of honey, one dark beauty mark above her slanting eyebrow. She wore a silver satin dress that swirled like mercury around her knees. "Sure, I've got a light," he said, blowing smoke away from her. "You got a name?"

She smiled around the filter of her unlit cigarette and said, "I'd be reckless to give it out to strangers." In one hand she held a tiny purse, and in the other a plastic champagne flute. "Who knows whether I'd ever get it back?"

"Ah! Lucky for us, I know just the solution."

She pretended to smoke the unlit cigarette, mirrored the turn of his head and blew her invisible smoke the opposite way. "Go on, then," she said, "solve my problems."

"Easy." He climbed over the tailgate with exaggerated panache.

"Marry a Cuban." He gestured to the sign sagging across the back bumper. "We all have four or five names to spare."

"You make an interesting . . . proposal."

"Say yes and make me the happiest man in Miami," he said, going down on one knee with the banner pulled across his chest like a pageant girl's sash. He cracked the hinge of his Zippo as if there were a diamond ring inside. "And I'll make you Doña Gilberto Francisco Delgado García."

"Only Miami?" She bent to let the tip of her cigarette kiss the flame, then offered a hand to help him up.

"Only for tonight," he told her, clinging to her fingers longer than he needed to. "Tomorrow the world." He slapped Blondie's chassis with a flat, open hand. His palm stung and the yellow paint sang. *Fresh as a fucking daisy, eh?* So the groom had said when he picked it up from the body shop. *That's a car for a girl,* ¡maricón! Of course it was, Gil told him. What's a car for if not to pick up a girl?

The girl in the silver satin, for instance.

"Is that your car?" she asked. "Looks like she's already spoken for."

"She's on loan to the groom." So he could drive his bride back to the honeymoon suite in style. "But she's all mine. Oughta be, after the work I've done on her." He'd earned her on his back in the shop, before he was even old enough to work. His father was dead and his mother was still in Havana, where she would die, too, more than likely. He used to feel a yearning for home, sharp as a knife in his guts, but home was so long ago now the wound had healed over, and he felt nothing for it anymore.

"So, which are you," she asked after another contemplative drag, "Johnny Burnette or Steve McQueen? Or is Gilberto Francisco Delgado García something in between?"

That she remembered his names—all four of them—was all the encouragement he needed. "Something in between," he echoed. "Yes, that might be me."

"Might be?"

"You tell me." He bent down to stub his cigarette out in the gravel and got an eyeful of her ankles. Hem swishing around her legs as she swayed to the music still spilling out from the ballroom. He straightened up and opened the driver's door. A precarious invitation to slide into the darkness inside. The beauty mark levitated, rising toward her hairline.

"A light is one thing," she said. "But climbing into cars with strange men? What would they say about me."

"If you told me your name, we wouldn't be strangers."

"Maybe I like my men strange." She finished off her champagne and handed him the empty flute. He held the door as she slipped past him—insubstantial as her quicksilver skirts except for a wisp of sweet, woody perfume. Gil looked both ways, back toward the ballroom and down the road where the rest of the band had disappeared, then climbed in behind her.

She sat a modest distance away—the long bench seat a virgin wilderness between them—one wrist dangling out the window. He had no idea what time it was by then. Time telescoped onstage, stretched and shrank with the music, moving like molasses one moment, like an avalanche the next. Never before this minute, this girl, had he wanted it to stand still. He turned the key in the ignition and the dashboard lit up like a fireworks display. Her head turned, the lights reflected in her eyes. Good. He intended to dazzle her.

"Push that button there," he said. "Just above your knee." Just to let her know he'd noticed the way that silver satin had crept an inch or two up her thigh. He wondered what had brought her there—or whom. She was too untouched by the sun to be a Florida native. The glove box fell open. "Now push that red button, there."

"Will I be ejected?" she asked, but curiosity had bested her already, the button sinking under her fingertip.

"Doña," he said, "you can ride beside me forever."

"Or at least until the groom needs the car."

"That's just for tonight," he told her. "Now he's a married man, he's in the market for a family car."

"And you're not?"

He laughed against the seats, breathed in the dusky smell of the leather, the shimmering scent of her. A heady cocktail, but one he could drink down like water. "Not exactly compatible with my lifestyle." No sense lying. "They make it look easy, like one big party—and maybe it is, when you've got a cushy deal with RCA and a private plane, but to get there, it's work. A lot of work for a lot of nothing for a long time, and no guarantees." Any girl who got mixed up with him had to know what she was getting herself into. Take me or leave me! Most of them left. He didn't want to scare this one away—even if she didn't seem the kind who scared so easy. "But maybe someday, when I've had a chance to be somebody, you know?"

"Yeah," she said, the word sinking low in her throat. "I do." Before he could ask what made her voice go so soulful, it jumped back up to the tip of her tongue. "Nothing's happening."

He grinned across the dark at her. "Push the white button. Then the blue."

He listened for the hiss, the click, then her own voice answered her, with the soft velvet fizz of the tape. *Or at least until the groom needs the car.* She looked back at him in surprise. Gratified, he went right on grinning.

That's just for tonight.

She stopped the tape. "You did this yourself? All the wiring and everything?"

"And everything." He ran one hand along the dash. Blondie was his first love, and whatever happened, whichever girls took him or left him, she would be the last.

"But what is this . . . for?"

"I get my best ideas when I'm driving. For songs, I mean. But I can't always pull over to write them down."

She shook her head. "Somewhere between Johnny Burnette and Steve McQueen."

"A guy could do worse." He shifted closer on the seat. "A girl could, too."

She flicked her ash out the window. "Probably."

Her ambivalence was thrilling. He had nothing he hadn't worked for. He could work to win her over. Earn her, too. "And what brings a girl like you to a wedding like this?" It was hard to imagine her in the conga line.

"Friends. I'm visiting for the summer."

"Just the summer?" he said, because it was already September. "And then what?"

"I'd like to see more of the world," she said with conspicuous nonchalance—as if it were a passing fancy. But he sensed that she wanted to see the world the same way he wanted to be somebody, nothing nonchalant about it. "I haven't ruled anything out."

"Even telling me your name?"

She laughed at that—a fantastic sound, high and clear as the cry of a bird. He wished she hadn't stopped the tape, so he could play it back over and over. "Since you're so damned persistent," she said, "I'll make you a trade." She flicked her cigarette away, opened her purse, and took out a pocket camera. "Let me take your picture, and I'll tell you my name."

"What do you want a photo of a stranger for?" he asked, but she had already opened the door, slid out of the car. He followed a half second behind, smoothing his hair, overthinking his posture. He checked the tiny flash of his reflection in the side mirror. Still learning how to hold himself, how to *look* like a rock star—not just sound like one.

"If I tell you my name, we won't be strangers," she reminded him, reaching for the banner, which hung like a loose tie over the tailgate. "Sit there." She pushed him gently, and the bumper hit the backs of his knees. He sat. Heart wild at the warmth of her hand through his shirt. "Good. Lift your chin."

"It's too dark."

"I like when the light isn't right. It's more real. Lift your chin."

He didn't, just so she'd lean in close again and do it for him. He caught another whiff of perfume clinging to her wrist. "Which are you," he said, "Cybill Shepherd or Annie Leibovitz?"

"I'm just Nora," she said, disappearing behind the little Instamatic, no wider than an 8-track tape. "Don't move."

THE **A** SIDE

RHYMIN & STEALIN

Suzanne tugged Doug's untucked shirt. "Rattail, red sweatshirt, cas-sette section." The favorite hunting ground of the light-fingered. Cas-settes were easy to slip out of sight.

"Roger." He glanced up from the register. "Trip him if he gets as far as clearance." His fingers didn't stop moving until the cash drawer crashed open, the clatter of coins lost in the hustle and bustle of Music Tuesday, when all the new releases hit the racks. Suzanne bobbed and weaved between shoppers, her size her secret weapon: everyone looked right over her head, but she was just the right height to watch their hands. She had learned from Doug what to look for—bulging pockets and gaping backpacks and a certain slouch shoplifters adopted when they were trying too hard to look at ease.

She had also learned, after a few weeks' practice, to enjoy the thrill of the hunt. Stalking her quarry from aisle to aisle only to pounce just before they reached the doors, thinking they were in the clear. She ducked behind the curtain of an empty listening booth and peered out, watching as Rattail lifted another cassette, sliding it up under the hem of his sweatshirt and into his back pocket. He grew bolder as he moved through the store, convinced of Doug's distraction. Suzanne chewed her lip, waiting for her moment. She counted two, three, four more cassettes squirreled away. Scanning him head to toe, she deduced he must be out of pockets and about to beat a hasty retreat. A blare of brass from the ceiling speakers told her Doug was ready to make the catch. "Your butt is mine!" she sang to herself as Rattail sidled through clearance and started for the exit. Suzanne tapped her foot along to the handclaps overhead until it was time to stick that foot out of the booth. She caught Rattail right in the ankles and watched in giggling paroxysms as he fell headlong into a Scorpions display. *Savage Amusement*, indeed.

Rattail clawed his hood away from his face to find Doug bending over him. "Think you're pretty bad, don'tcha?" he said. "Empty your pockets, shamone."

They frog-marched him over to the cash wrap, everyone in line happy to wait and watch as Doug set him up in front of the corkboard where repeat offenders were inducted to the Sticky Fingers Hall of Fame. Suzanne rooted around in her backpack for her camera.

"We are panopticon," Doug intoned.

"Panopticon sees all," Suzanne answered solemnly. "Smile!" The Polaroid flashed and spat out a fresh mug shot for the corkboard. They pinned it up and kicked him out and Doug did a bow for the rest of the patrons before peeling twenty dollars off his wallet for Suzanne. Because the manager deducted stolen merchandise from the paychecks of insufficiently vigilant cashiers, every time they bagged a bandit, he paid Suzanne half in cash for her help. Nine times out of ten, it went right back into the till. Her backpack bulged and sagged and threatened to pull her over backward, her precious pocket money traded for singles and cassettes and CDs she had no way to play because the stereo at home had no disc tray.

She'd sprawl on the floor, hours past bedtime when Nora was asleep, with Gil's earphones clamped on her head, studying the liner notes with a flashlight like a seminarian at scripture. Strawberry fields and marmalade skies, her insatiable hunger for music increasingly indistinguishable from more corporeal cravings since she started spending her lunch money at Most Wanted, too. Every tape she played, every record she spun, made her want more. She could wait, she told her growling stomach, to guzzle milk from the carton at home. She could wait, she told her watering mouth, until Nora brought something back from the hotel where she worked on weekends. Nora did not notice, subsisting on her own paltry diet of cheap smokes and cheap coffee, cheap shots of vodka choked down like castor oil, cheap shots taken at Gil, the Macy's manager, the landlord and the government and God. Anyone who'd ever built her hopes up, anyone who'd ever let her down. Occasionally she caught herself and stopped and said, "Don't listen to me, munchkin. Mama's tired, that's all." But music was forbidden during daylight hours by unspoken edict, and there was nothing else to listen to. Suzanne grew resentful of the silence. Resentful of Nora. Resentful of the long absences that made them curdle and sour.

"Pint Size!" Doug barked in passing, half an hour later, arms full of *Appetite for Destruction*. "Bus!" Suzanne glanced up at Elvis, hips aswing, arms ticking toward four o'clock. She grabbed her backpack and bolted. She could run from the record store to the jewelry counter in three minutes flat on a good day, if the mall wasn't too busy and she avoided the obstacle course of the food court, where she'd have to dodge toddlers escaped from their mothers, custodians mopping up spills, teenagers necking in the shade of plastic palm fronds by the fountain. She sprinted the length of the second floor, took a hairpin turn onto the escalator, and stopped to catch her breath for half a minute before zigzagging through menswear and intimates, hanging a left at handbags, and bursting out of the northwest exit, where Nora would be waiting barefoot on the asphalt if it was warm enough, pumps akimbo, heels as badly blistered as Suzanne's.

The door banged open and the wind pinned it against the wall. The northwest lot was farthest from the main entrance and usually empty, a concrete wasteland where Styrofoam McDonald's boxes scuttled around in crablike fits and starts. But not today.

Today, no Nora. No bus. Just Blondie.

The car was parked on a slant across three spaces, basking and rumbling like a big cat after a kill. Sunlight boomeranged off the side mirrors, the sizzle and crash of the stereo choked off by the breeze. Gil was home.

She ran to meet him, backpack banging against her legs. But when she saw him through the window, curling that unruly forelock around one finger, she felt a sharp pinch in her chest. He'd left her alone with Nora and the spiteful silence for more than a month. Longer than he'd ever left before. She opened the passenger door and a blast of AC blew her bangs out of her face.

"Hiya, kid. Gimme a kiss." Gil leaned across the seat to proffer one bristly cheek and a whiff of bay rum, peaches, and pomade. He'd been trying to quit smoking for two years to spare his voice and traded cases of Luckies for bulk bags of Chupa Chups to satisfy the oral fixation. Masticated lollipop sticks filled an empty coffee cup wedged between the dashboard and the windshield. Blondie made a lazy zigzag toward the exit, past the bus stop, commuters Suzanne dimly recognized watching the butter-yellow car slide by. Gil seemed not to notice her stiffness, the silence she'd learned by example. Tongue swapping the lollipop stick from one corner of his mouth to the other. The dark tortoiseshell shades didn't quite hide the bags under his eyes. "How was school?" he asked, like everything was normal. Like they did this every day.

"Where's Mom?" Suzanne answered. Tired of pretending, for him and for Nora.

"Wasn't feeling too good, so she came home early."

"What's wrong with her?"

Suzanne pried her sneakers off. No shoes on the dashboard. There was barely room for her bare feet, the dash so crowded with buttons and knobs it looked like a flying saucer on the inside. In the few free minutes he found between gigs, Gil still tooled around with the car. He'd somehow talked the label into an additional advance to put toward better audio; if they wanted the next LP on time but they also wanted him touring to support the last one, he'd have to listen to the mixes on the road. Even he couldn't quite believe he got away with that one, but he'd gotten most places he'd been in life by being doggedly persistent and diabolically persuasive. His charm worked on Suzanne as well as anyone; already she was beginning to thaw, to warm to his glow. Gil was all fire, but nobody smelled the brimstone yet.

Nobody but Nora, of course.

"Nothing's wrong with her," Gil said. He talked around the lollipop bulging in his cheek like a tumor. "She's just got a headache. Working too much and driving herself crazy when she's not." He drove with one eye on the road and one on the radio, jumping from station to station and track to track at dizzying speed.

"Is that why you're home, because Mom's gone crazy?"

"Don't you start now," Gil said. "I'm home because I want to be home, and I wasn't home sooner because the band and the label and King Louie needed me on the road." Louie, the almighty manager. Suzanne had never met him, but Gil made him sound like something between a gangster and a god. "It won't always be like this," he said, to himself as much as her. "We're moving up in the world, baby girl, but can't take my foot off the gas too soon. Don't you want your old man to be somebody?" He ruffled the overgrown Delgado curls falling in her eyes. She took more after him than Nora. When they were younger and more in love, Nora always said she fell for Gil because he had hair on his chest and eyelashes like a girl. "Stay sweet, *mi cafecita*," he said, batting those long eyelashes at Suzanne while he dug around in the bag of Chupa Chups with one hand. "You're too young to be bitter yet." Her favorite flavor was the most elusive, but he could always find it, that perfect swirl of chocolate and vanilla. It was a sucker and an ice-cream cone at once.

She took it grudgingly, nudged his hand off the stereo dials. "Go back. I like that song."

Gil looked at her sideways, with a frown and a grin that didn't agree. "Since when do you have opinions on Joy Division?"

She shrugged, sulky again despite the unknown pleasures she knew by heart by now. "I dunno. Recently." His naked skepticism rankled. Like he expected time to stand still and wait for him to come home to get going again.

Gil tongued his sucker over to the other side. "Well, I know that's not your mom's influence."

"I can talk to other people, can't I?"

The grin slipped, leaving the frown and the dark circles behind. "What's with the lip, kid? Not like you."

She bit down on the lollipop, but it wouldn't break—it just glued her molars together like rubber cement.

Gil turned the music down. Not like him. "Nora said you yelled at her."

"So? You yell at her. She yells at you. It's all you ever do."

"Grown-up married people yell sometimes," Gil said simply, pulling the lollipop out of his mouth, watching it glisten as he spun the stick in the sunlight. "When you have a husband of your own you can yell at him, too. But you can't yell at Nora. She's got a lot on her plate, and I need you to keep the peace when I'm away, okay?"

Suzanne glared at the ragtop Cavalier in front of them, which had left its blinker on for the last five minutes. "What about when you're not?"

Because things didn't get any easier when Gil came home anymore. Nora hated him for leaving but never seemed happy to have him back. Everything he did and said annoyed her, and when he left again her temper rebounded on Suzanne and her unavoidable resemblance. She couldn't help being half Delgado, and under Doug's tutelage had finally stopped trying. She flouted Nora's unspoken rules, listening to the radio in broad daylight on the living room rug. The rest of her musical treasure was stashed out of sight between the couch cushions, where only her small hands could reach, but she resented the charade. She wanted tapes and CDs. She wanted a car instead of the bus. She wanted to go somewhere besides school and South Fork and their ugly apartment where there was nothing to listen to but her grown-up married parents yelling at each other about being grown up, being married, being her parents.

So she yelled back. Not on purpose, really, and not a lot—just one lunatic outburst that caught her by surprise as much as Nora, who had abruptly unplugged the receiver to run the vacuum cleaner. *Hey! I was listening to that!* They stared at each other for a long time, neither knowing quite what to do, before Nora hollered back, *Don't you shout at me! If anybody shouts, I'll do the shouting, understand?* She'd exercised the right for most of the night, until the downstairs neighbors started banging a broom on the ceiling. Nora took the headset away, and there had been a tangible chill in the air ever since.

Gil chewed and swallowed what was left of the sucker and discarded the stick in the coffee cup with the old, habitual jab of extinguishing a cigarette. "You're right, you know?" he said, the question rhetorical, an idiolectic form of punctuation. "We shouldn't fight in front of you. Can't make any promises for your mom, but I won't yell at her if you won't yell at her. ¿*Comprende?*"

Suzanne still wanted to argue, but not with Gil, not while he was around, not while he was warming to a bargain. If he and Nora stopped yelling in front of her, they'd have to stop yelling at all. The apartment was too small to yell anywhere else. "Okay," she said, "*comprende.*"

He ruffled her hair. "That's my girl. Unwrap me one of those, eh? Chocolate if you can find it."

"Turn it up," she said, already digging for that elusive yin-yang wrapper.

The grin was back. "You got it, babe."

Outside their apartment, Gil fumbled through his pockets, looking for his keys, until Suzanne reached around him to try the handle. The door swung halfway open and halfway only. A fug of cigarette smoke diffused across the landing, mingling with the stink of the German neighbors stewing cabbage downstairs. Suzanne wondered whether they'd done it on purpose, as payback for the racket last week.

"What the hell?" Gil thrust his shoulder against the door, and something scraped across the floor on the other side. "Nora! What. The. Hell." The fourth thump of his shoulder bought them another six inches, and he forged ahead, bending his body around the doorjamb at an angle Mr. Fantastic might have envied. He'd always been limber. Suzanne followed, slight as his shadow.

Inside, smoke hung in a haze so dense it seemed solid. She blinked to clear her eyes until she recognized the furniture, everything knocked out of place. The sofa was blocking the door, one end swung around with such force that most of the cushions had tumbled off. "*Qué es esta mierda*," Gil choked, kicking through clutter in the kitchen to force a window open. Empty bottles and jars and cartons, discarded shoes, a bag of dirty laundry spilling its guts from a split in the canvas. "Did a bomb go off in here?"

A scream of laughter answered from the bedroom. "Don't I wish!"

Suzanne edged around the sofa. Her sheets had been torn off and hung twisted over one arm, like a half-shed snakeskin. With a dizzy, plunging feeling, she saw dozens of cassettes flung across the mangy rug. She scrambled around the coffee table, backpack slipping from her shoulder and bouncing down on the couch. Her precious dragon hoard had been dragged out and ransacked—naked tapes bucked from their cases, hinges bent or broken, J-cards crumpled, ribbons pulled loose from the reels. An ashtray had tumbled off the table, cold cinders and cigarette butts crushed into the carpet and the rollers of her Talking Heads, her Tina Turner, the precious MC5 Doug had given her from his own collection.

"Jesus," Gil said, "*Christ*. Nora!"

She appeared in the mouth of the hallway, empty-handed. She must have smoked the whole case, must have run out. Her hair stuck to her neck in dark, sweaty seams, mascara smeared around bloodshot, swollen eyes. The enormous *Jaws* tank top she only wore to bed or the beach had slipped off one shoulder, so the shark seemed about to bite her head off. Suzanne felt a savage surge of affection for it.

"Hi, honey," she said. "Welcome home."

"What the hell is going on?"

Nora's red eyes fastened on Suzanne's backpack. She grabbed it off the sofa, tore the zipper open, and turned it upside down. "Maybe Suzanne can tell me."

Cassettes crashed down on the cockeyed coffee table, cases springing open, ejecting their contents onto the carpet. The Sun 640 hit the floor with an ugly *thud*, and Suzanne stifled a shriek. Nora shook the bag until even her workbooks and crayons spilled out. Last came the bundle of fives and ones, rolled up neat as a pair of socks and bound with a tiny blue elastic she used to wear in her hair.

"Do you see this? Do you see all this *shit*?" Nora flung the money into the kitchen, aiming for the open window, but she threw like a drunk—hard and wide. It bounced off the refrigerator and rolled under the table, which only made her laugh again. She reached at random for a Stooges cassette and threw it at his chest. "Do you see it, Gil!"

"So she's got some new tapes! So what?"

"So what? *So what?* So, do the math! I know you're no good with numbers, but I know you know how much that many cassettes cost. And the camera? The CDs? The rest of it?" He hesitated, but Nora didn't wait for him to catch up. "More than I make in a week, and more than you've made in a year, but your daughter—"

"Oh, *now* she's mine? I thought I was barely a father— Make up your mind!"

Nora seized fistfuls of tapes and fired them at him as fast as she could. Her aim hadn't improved, but she had so much ammo that one or two missiles were bound to find their mark. "DOES THIS LOOK LIKE *MY DAUGHTER* TO YOU?" She shot a look at Suzanne for the first time since they walked in the door. "I didn't raise a thief. She's all yours."

It was Gil's turn to laugh. "This morning I'm absentee, but now I'm the bad influence." He swatted the Misfits out of the air before they hit him in the face. "Can't have it both ways!"

"Maybe if we had more, she wouldn't have to steal!"

Suzanne's face felt so hot it hurt, the smoke making her head swim. "I didn't steal anything!" she hollered, forgetting her promise, betraying their bargain, the words boiling up and over just like they had last week. "I didn't steal anything!"

But neither of them heard her over the storm brewing between them—Gil's hiss of derision, the crackle of Nora's crazed laughter.

"You want me home more, or you want me to bring home more? I can't do both!"

"Oh, but it's fine for *me* to do everything around here and work two jobs besides—"

"I can't do my work here! My work is on the road—"

"I didn't steal anything!"

"Work! You don't know a goddamn thing about work—"

"*That's* rich—I was in the body shop when you were still in charm school."

"I didn't steal anything!"

"We're not nineteen anymore! Will you grow up and give up this *nonsense?*"

"I never said I would! You knew—"

"Oh, spare me, yes, I know how badly you want to *be* somebody—"

"Not just somebody's husband or somebody's father—"

"You *are* somebody's husband and somebody's father and you're doing such a bang-up job your daughter is—"

"I didn't steal anything!"

The slap hit Suzanne so hard she staggered. Her lip split like a tomato skin, dribbling juice down her chin. She was pulled or pushed or simply stumbled into the smoky black oblivion of the hallway. A gaping door drew her into safer, smaller darkness. She could still fit, just barely, under the bottom shelf. Small for her age. Folded into the familiar scent of clean laundry, soured by a carton of Camels and cabbage brewing downstairs. Sheets and towels dampened the ruckus from the living room, the boom of the neighbors' broom handle banging on the floor. Snot and tears and a froth of coppery saliva dripped over her swollen lip and puddled in the hollow of her throat. She lay limp and still until the heat drained from her face, memory an incurious blank, not knowing or caring whose hand knocked her voice out of her mouth.

When she crawled out in the morning, Gil was gone again.

This time she didn't ask when he was coming back.

MATERIAL GIRLS

The Lifeboat, as they called it, was anchored on the far side of the filling station with a few dingy RVs for company. Sunshine zinged off the trailer's shiny aluminum siding, a lightning bolt in the blank concrete wash presided over by a faded neon palm tree supporting what might have been a monkey once but had lost all its color and taken on the smooth, featureless character of an extraterrestrial. Not unlike a flying saucer in its way, the Airstream looked from the outside to be occupied by some intelligent life-form doing an imprecise impression of humanity informed largely by last century's cultural detritus. A life-size version of the orange safety-ring sticker on Simon's toolbox hung on one side, but that wasn't the only pop of color. There were tiny window boxes sprouting herbs and flowers, purple paisley curtains, a whimsical flying pig weathervane mounted on the roof like a TV antenna.

"Our zip code is in the trash stratum," Phoebe explained, if that counted for an explanation. The weathervane leaned one way and then the other as the occupants inside shifted. A thatch of peeling bumper stickers crowded around the back plate, picked up in places as far-flung as Mesa Verde and Atlantic City. Bigfoot's silhouette. A Ross Perot campaign sticker. One in the shape of a dog bone asked WHAT WOULD SCOOBY DO? Inside was even more chaotic than the outside, even more chaotic than the jumble of Gil's things in Suzanne's motel room. They'd made a dent over the last week, she and Phoebe, but a lot still needed to go overboard if they were going to be seaworthy anytime soon. The Lifeboat existed in a perpetual cycle of accumulation and evacuation to maintain the delicate balance of stuff and nonsense that kept Phoebe's business afloat.

"It's a system," she said, showing Suzanne how they stored their cooking elements inside the tiny oven, the first aid and sewing kits tucked inside their oven mitts. "A whole ecosystem." Clothes were folded away in compartments under the cushions in the front lounge and the bed that took up the whole back end. A pile of comic books and magazines cluttered the windowsill, given up as soon as they'd been read to make room for something else. Anything that had served its purpose or lost its shine was put up for sale or barter at the next flea market, the next street fair, the next swap meet. Remarkably, Phoebe had no trouble keeping track of it all. When Suzanne asked, she shrugged and said, "Not a lot of space to misplace things." She smacked the wall and a linen rack slid out from some invisible slot in the paneling. "And we gutted the old girl ourselves. Staple your thumb to a sheet of ply and you won't soon forget what you were trying to fix there." She spoke as if she was always in a hurry to reach the end of each sentence—a habit at odds with the vestiges of a Mississippi accent rolling around the back of her mouth like a loose molar.

"What's all that?" Suzanne asked, watching her pull pouches of slippery green material off the rack.

"These," she said, "are stuff sacks for sleeping bags. But they'll squeeze the air out of just about anything you can think to cram in there."

The current project was the pile of clothes—some of Gil's and some from Phoebe's stash that she had callously pronounced "not worth their weight in towing capacity"—heaped like raked leaves on the floor. Which had also been chosen according to its "wear-to-weight" ratio: how long Phoebe thought it would last divided by how much it would cost them to carry in terms of displaced load. Linoleum, measured by this metric, was worth its weight in gold.

A different wear-to-weight ratio applied to Phoebe's "dressing spectrum," which involved a lot of complex calculations privileging body type and gender presentation as much as actual measurements. "You pick based not just on your shape but the way you want it to drape. Shape-n-drape. So, you're probably"—Phoebe's amber eyes climbed up and down Suzanne with sinuous patience, like a python climbing a tree—"thirty-six, twenty-eight, thirty-eight? If you were going for—not that you are—a pinup look, I'd size you down and cinch your waist in. If you wanted something more boyish, I'd size you up. Long muscle tank. Relaxed. Yeah. Something like that." She took a powder-blue tank with a high neck off the top of the pile. Splashed across the chest was a cartoon race car, above it looping red text said DAYTONA INTER-NATIONAL SPEEDWAY. "That was Simon's, but it's too small for his big, brawny shoulders now." The python circled Suzanne again. "Keep it," Phoebe said, "it's cool. It would look good on you."

Suzanne felt herself flush and blamed it on the heat. The Lifeboat's ancient AC unit was Simon and Phoebe's next fix. They had several on the go at once. And while Simon wasn't what she would call *brawny*, they both had a youthful virility she found unnerving. They ate very little and moved almost constantly. They sweated buckets, drank cheap Mexican beer like it was water, and smoked a careful ration of cigarettes they rolled themselves with just enough weed crumbled in "to keep things interesting." They talked at each other in disjointed fits and starts, through the open door or open windows, picking up abandoned bits of conversation as if no time had lapsed, breaking off mid-sentence when Blondie or the Lifeboat pulled their attention away. Suzanne was dumb in the face of their boisterous busyness. Dodging stabs of shame at her own sluggish momentum since she was—she hated the phrase for all it snidely insinuated—*their* age.

"Okay." Phoebe passed one compression sack to Suzanne. "Cram."

They elbowed their way out the door ten minutes later, arms achingly full. Suzanne blew fruitless raspberries at the lock of hair curling into her eye, wondering whether she'd remembered to put deodorant on that morning. Not that it mattered. Phoebe and Simon had been living like sardines for so long they didn't seem to care what sort of brine they swam in. She envied their ease in their bodies, while she was embarrassed by everything, feeling her age like an overripe avocado. Then admonishing herself for even having this thought because it probably made her a bad feminist. She could ask; Phoebe would know. Despite living so much off the beaten path, Phoebe was still very much online. "Enslaved like everyone," she said one day, scrolling her screen at mechanistic speed. "When we can't move merch, the feed keeps us fed." She crossed herself and rolled her eyes, posted a new photo to the grid.

Outside, Blondie yawned in the shade of the lot's only tree, where Simon had bribed a guy to tow her with a clasp knife and a stack of vintage *Playboys*. Suzanne wondered idly, angling for a glimpse between the pages, whether he had actually jerked off to those—or Phoebe had. It was unavoidable, thinking about that kind of thing when she was in the trailer, touching their unwashed clothes, sitting on their unmade bed, the smell of their skin in the sheets. Did they resent each other's closeness in the throbbing humid summer, or did they sleep like two salamanders in a slippery embrace? She'd never quite broken the habit of making field notes on other couples, searching for some solid confirmation of what was right, what was normal, what love should look like. She felt she was playacting for six years of marriage, before everything got so horribly real.

That world felt five hundred worlds away, there on the Panhandle at high noon. Simon's spine as he bent over the front bumper made a damp, dark ridge down the back of his shirt. He pulled his head out from under the hood, stuck it back in through the window. Twiddled a knob on the dashboard, then spied her through the dirty windshield. "This is like a Ford Frankenstein," he said, emerging again. "Your dad had a hell of an imagination. Half this stuff shouldn't work, but it does. Which makes it tough to know what's actually wrong." He was the first mechanic stimulated by the challenge more than dismayed. Slow eyes, slow smile. *Like a tortoise*, Phoebe had said. *He's slow as molasses, but he'll live forever.* Which didn't make sense, but also did.

"Okay, I'm trusting you," Suzanne said. Because she wanted to, and because *he* wanted to, because if he didn't fix it, then they were stuck there, too.

"Dunno if I'd go that far," Simon said. "I'm feeling around in the dark here. Literally." He clicked the small black flashlight that lived between his teeth while he was working. Nothing happened. "Got a good zap, does it look burned?" He stuck his tongue out and the pink of it surprised her—vital and visceral as a slab of prime rib.

"Never seen a healthier one." The tongue was a muscle, she remembered. She stared until it withdrew, watched it move behind his teeth.

"That's a relief, considering all the dental work we haven't had done."

"Speak for yourself," Phoebe said, staggering out of the Airstream, struggling to roll up the end of a belt that had escaped through the top of its sack. "I floss!"

"With what, your embroidery thread?"

They ribbed each other without mercy but never seemed to bruise. It was tempting but impossible to say they were just too young to have too much baggage. Simon had lost two fingers he was evidently born with, and Phoebe wasn't unmarked by life, either—her forearms bore the spider-bite scars of bad habits and stick-and-poke needlework. One of her front teeth was chipped, but at least she was flossing.

"Bring me back a couple of double-A batteries if you can?" Simon said, clicking the flashlight again.

"There's a headlamp under the sink," Phoebe told him, walking backward toward the highway. "But it probably needs batteries, too."

They stood on the side of the road for half an hour, each with one thumb out and a stuff sack slung over each shoulder. A man in a pickup full of cantaloupes stopped just long enough to let them climb over the tailgate. He dropped them in the nearest town large enough to warrant a dot on the map with a couple of melons and an injunction to "Take care now." Phoebe blew him a kiss as he drove off and hoisted her stuff sacks up onto her shoulders again. There was a consignment store, she said, in the far corner of the strip mall.

Suzanne left her at the counter to haggle and wandered through the wares, curious what there was to be had at Miss Kaminsky's Yesteryears. An accordioned field camera mounted on a dusty tripod drew her eye

like a magnet. A tag tied around the lens mount read BROKEN BUT STILL
TAKES INTERESTING PICTURES. Suzanne wanted to laugh, wanted to cry,
wanted to steal the tag and wear it on her wrist like a monogrammed
bracelet. She turned it over out of morbid curiosity, just to see the
price. She'd always favored analog photography, not just because she
couldn't afford anything better for most of her abortive career. Like her
mother, she'd lost interest somewhere along the line, too burdened or
too bored with life to want to preserve any part of it. She documented
strangers' milestones instead, dutifully made the moments they wanted
to remember look brighter, more beautiful, more like the movies than
they really were, all the while wondering whether the photos would be
unceremoniously dumped in the trash when the honeymoon was over,
the babies grew up, the family fell apart. But maybe they were better off
letting go; who could say? The number of zeroes on the tag still made
her look twice, but she didn't drop it like she might have done a few
weeks ago—reminding herself she didn't need to ask permission, didn't
have to justify a purchase from a joint checking account. She looked
back over her shoulder to see Phoebe still waxing poetic to the cashier,
who was half her height and twice her age and wore a crumpled frown
like she didn't know or care what "deadstock" meant.

Suzanne moved into the next room, which was crammed with chairs
and sofas upholstered in itchy green tweeds and mawkish pastels. She
sat in a lawn chair with so much give in the seat her ass sank to the floor
and her knees jutted up toward her chin. But a fringed beach umbrella
blocked the doorway to the other room, so she stayed where she was.
Her phone was a flat, hard slab like a poker plaque in her back pocket.
She'd seen them on a gaming table once, that same summer that felt
like a fever dream now, when she'd slipped under a velvet stanchion
and followed her curiosity into the high-stakes room. She'd made a bad
habit of that. Being beneath notice had its perks.

She sat on the phone for one minute, maybe two, counting backward through the days since she left Miami. What was she still waiting
for? Stalling wouldn't solve anything.

She squeezed the power button until the screen became a slightly brighter black, a gray circle turning like a microscopic hurricane at the center. Dimly, she could hear Phoebe and Miss Kaminsky arguing over whether a Prada handbag from 1994 qualified as "vintage." Feeling less "vintage" than obsolescent, Suzanne grimaced at the oversaturated splash screen and reached for the pair of cat-eyed sunglasses stashed in the lawn chair's cup holder. It took her a moment to remember where to find the icon for her new banking app, a moment longer to remember her new login, her new password. The savings account was empty, but the checking showed a balance in the thousands. There would be more; according to Louie, Gil's former manager and reluctant executor, there was still a steady stream of income from royalties and publishing credits. Phoebe evidently correct in her estimation that morbid fascination never went out of fashion. It had been enough for Gil to live on toward the end. It would be enough to keep Suzanne afloat until she figured out where she was going and what she was going to do when she got there.

Notifications started pouring in as the phone reached out to tap the network. Dozens of missed calls, all from the same number. Texts and emails, too. *Suzanne, please call me. Suzanne, where are you? Suzanne, what's wrong? Suzanne, I'm so worried about you. SUZANNE, WHAT THE HELL? SUZANNE, ANSWER ME. SUZANNE*— She knew it was cruel, knew she was a coward, knew it wasn't fair to leave like she'd left, to let him think the worst when she didn't reply, didn't pick up the phone, didn't come home.

She checked the time. Glanced at their shared calendar, where all his meetings were blocked off in blue. He had a presentation ending in ten minutes. No more time to waste. Phoebe was still busy with Miss Kaminsky. Suzanne called and listened to his phone ring two, three, four times, and breathed a sigh of relief when his voicemail answered. She took a deep breath and waited for the beep.

"Rob, I—" Her voice got stuck in her throat. "Shit," she said when she found it again. "This is hard." As if that surprised her. Like it would be so easy.

THE **B** SIDE

BUT I LOVE YOU, SUZANNE

Rob Gabbard reluctantly agreed to meet his brothers at an over-priced sports bar for the Nats game. "You cannot," Casey told him, already masticating cocktail peanuts over the phone, "spend one more night sitting around obsessing about Suzanne. It's pathetic." Casey, who'd married his college girlfriend two months after graduation and barreled merrily along into fatherhood and homeownership without so much as a backward glance or a bump in the road.

But because, yes, it was pathetic to sit around the house listening to that fucking voicemail over and over, Rob relented. He forced himself to get in the shower, but still it looped through his head.

Rob, I—

He made himself comb his hair, put a clean shirt on.

Shit. This is hard.

Was she even talking to him, or just rehearsing the idea out loud? Trying it out, to see how it sounded. He trudged down the stairs, climbed into the car with a stack of Suzanne's CDs under one arm— unable to leave her behind completely. She said she kept them because the sound quality was better than streaming. He didn't hear the difference, but he didn't know her music well enough to know what the difference might be.

Rob, I—

He heard it again, that long nothingness between him, her, and *Shit.*

This is hard. Then she rushed ahead like the best way to do it was to get it over with, tear off the bandage.

Listen, Rob. I'm sorry to leave like this, but I'm leaving. I mean really leaving. It's for the best for both of us, so let's just make it easy, huh? She almost laughed at that, like she wanted him to be in on the joke. Days later, he still hadn't slept and still didn't see what was funny. *I was all wrong for you from the start, and I think we both knew it. Sorry anyway. You can have everything. I'll be okay. And you will be, too. Take care of yourself. Bye.*

A whole marriage undone in less than a minute. He rubbed his fingertips into his eyes, feeling the grit under each lid. He couldn't listen to it again, but he couldn't unhear it, either. He pawed through the CDs instead. Some of the band names rang a bell, but most he had never heard or even heard of. Who the hell was Captain Beefheart? He started the car and cringed through one or two minutes of unbearable snarling noise before punching the off button. Wondering, not for the first time, whether Suzanne had a few more screws loose than he'd realized. Not just endearingly eccentric, but actually a little unhinged.

Casey had said so from the start: *You always had weird taste in women.* Casey, the connoisseur of "normal." Two kids, two cars, a backyard with a swing set and a labradoodle named Lucky who looked like a four-legged L'Oréal commercial. The name of the subdivision was Rose Hill; Brad still called it Stepford. But Brad had been married and divorced three times and had only a cat and a burgeoning beer gut to keep him warm at night now. Rob had hoped to find a middle ground between his brothers, but if he had to choose, he knew which example he'd rather follow.

They both beat him to the bar, because Brad had nowhere else to be, and Dana knew better than to expect Casey home on game nights.

"Doesn't she ever get tired of taking care of the kids?" Rob asked after a desultory sip of whatever beer Brad had ordered for all of them. The pitcher was already half-empty, and it was only the bottom of the third.

"She loves it." Casey tore into a chicken wing. Unlike Brad, he stayed trim doing endless yardwork on the weekends. They could have hired someone, but Casey took a perverse proprietary pride in maintaining the house the same way Dana maintained the kids. That was what his father had done, and he saw no reason to do it any differently. "They don't stay little for long, and soon as one gets too big to pick up, she starts to talk about more."

"More?" Brad was busy shredding a wilted stick of celery to ribbons, eyes glued to the TV above their heads. Nobody at the bar looked at each other. They all looked up, talked sideways, chewed and swallowed and belched automatically.

"Whatever makes her happy," Casey said. "She won't be fertile forever. Might as well enjoy it while we can."

"Sounds fuckin' exhausting, dude." Brad poured himself another pint.

Casey stretched, pushed his chest out. Lurid orange buffalo sauce stretching the corners of his mouth, like a circus clown. "You bet it is," he said. "When a 'window' opens up, y'know . . . we haven't had so much sex since college. But it's a lot more fun when you're not trying not to get pregnant."

Brad snorted into his beer and set it down again, five-o'clock shadow flecked with foam. Rob stared at the pitcher on the mound, watched him wind up and fire. Strike one. Trying not to think about his wife, all the sex they weren't having, and the babies they wouldn't have, either. She was still his wife, he reminded himself. It took more than a voicemail to dissolve a marriage. "Was she always like that?" he asked. "Dana. With the baby fever." He couldn't remember it clearly; they were all so young then. Young enough that when Casey told them Dana was pregnant the first time, Rob and Brad assumed it was an accident.

"Not always." Casey gnawed thoughtfully on a drumette. "When we got hitched, she was already working for the congressman. She wanted a career, not kids, or said she did."

"Yeah," Brad agreed. "That was Claudia." Wife Number One. "Changed her mind as soon as she met Stuart, though." They had three kids now, two boys and a girl. Claudia still sent Brad Christmas cards. She was vindictive like that.

"They all do, eventually." Casey jabbed Rob with his elbow. "Chin up."

"Sarah didn't," Brad pointed out. Wife Number Two.

"Well, Sarah was a secret dyke," said Casey. "Doesn't count."

"Lesbians have kids, too," Rob told him.

"Not on their own, they don't. See, that's just it—women want to be independent now. Like you're a bad feminist or whatever if you admit you need a man. Just like with sex, right? They gotta pretend not to want it, make you work for it."

"That was Megan," said Brad. Wife Number Three. The midlife-crisis wife. Too young, too green, too recently a youth-group Jesus freak. She cried the first time they fucked and had to kneel and beg God for forgiveness afterward. They were doomed before they even said "I do." Rob never wanted that. Never wanted to marry too young or too soon because he only wanted to get married once. "Hey, we're getting thirsty over here," Brad called to the bartender. Rob rarely had more than two drinks in an evening, but why not? He didn't even have a cat waiting up for him to stumble in.

"What made her change her mind?" he said, unable to stop picking the scab and let the subject drop. "Dana."

"Her sister had kids," Casey said. "It was like a switch flipped, soon as she held her nephew. And when the girl came along? Forget it. She was a goner."

Rob understood that better than he wanted to. He didn't have strong feelings about children or fatherhood before Casey started having babies. Children had softened his brother, who cried at their births, kissed their skinned knees, kept their pictures on his desk and in his wallet and on his phone. Rob wanted to love something that much. Holding his youngest nephew the first time, he felt a sudden, gut-wrenching envy. He wanted to say to Suzanne right there, right then—we could make such a beautiful human. But she was uneasy, avoided the baby, refused to hold it, insisting she didn't know how.

You can have everything, she said. Fucking liar.

"Suzanne doesn't have siblings," he said, without really meaning to say it out loud. Brad kept refilling his glass before he got to the bottom.

"That's exactly the problem," Casey said. "Doesn't have any siblings. Barely speaks to her parents. Her family's so fucked up it's completely warped her perspective."

Right again. Suzanne never talked much about her childhood, especially not the part before Nora married Nathan. Rob never met her real father, and now he never would.

"Sometimes I wonder if she was abused or something."

"You mean, like, sexually?" Casey tore his eyes away from the bullpen for the first time all night.

"I dunno." Rob shrugged. Hadn't really meant to say that, either. "Maybe."

"Is she weird about sex?"

"Not until recently."

"When you brought up the kids thing?"

"Uh-huh."

"Huh," Casey echoed. "Hate to say it, but you might be onto something." He sighed, grasped Rob's shoulder with inebriated sincerity. "I'm sorry, man. That's some heavy shit."

"What do I do?" Rob asked, more or less rhetorically. Neither of them had any experience with his particular conjugal dilemma. "How do you even start to move past that?"

"You smother her with love," said Brad. An unexpected suggestion, coming from him. Sentiment was never his strong suit. "Only thing that ever worked with Megan," he admitted when they looked at him strangely. "When she had one of her meltdowns, all that helped was to hold her and tell her I loved her and I didn't care what God thought about it."

"Exactly," Casey said, stabbing Rob in the chest with one finger. "That's all women really want. Never mind kids and careers and the rest of it. They just want to be loved. Trouble is, some of them don't know how."

It's best for the both of us, she'd said.

Bullshit. She'd never known what was good for her, never mind him.

"So, what?" Rob said. Angry as he was with her for leaving like she had, he reluctantly acknowledged that Casey and Brad might be right. Angry as he was, what he really wanted was to have his wife back, to bring her home and make her believe she belonged there. She'd moved so much throughout her life, she'd never belonged anywhere. She was forty and still froze up when anybody asked where she was from. "How am I supposed to change that?"

"You love her anyway," Casey said, "no matter how hard she makes it. Prove you won't give up." He smiled, that wide red buffalo grin. "She'll come around."

"Maybe," Rob said. But maybe not. Casey didn't know Suzanne well. Rob looked up as the bar erupted around him. He watched the small white orb of the baseball arc through the air, the runners round the bases as the announcer hollered, "And it's going, going, going— I don't believe it, it's gone!"

I'm sorry to leave like this, but I'm leaving. Let's just make it easy, huh?

Fuck that. She'd always made it hard to love her. Why should he make it easy to leave him? After everything he'd done for her. Rob could not—would not—give up. But if he was going to bring Suzanne home, he was going to have to go and find her first.

THE **A** SIDE

BABY, I'M A STAR

"Suzanne. Kiddo. Slow down." Gil squeezed Suzanne's hand as she dragged him toward the escalators. "Your old man is . . . well, he's old. By your standards."

"You're thirty-five," Suzanne said, which sounded old but not that old. Her grandmother was fifty-eight, and *her* mother was still alive—or so Nora told her.

"When did you get to be so good at math?" Gil asked, stepping onto the escalator just behind her. Eric Skillman followed at a noncommittal distance. The space between them didn't really matter; they were clearly part of a set. Nobody else at South Fork looked quite like them, which wasn't to say they looked much alike. Gil was svelte and sportive as an otter, flashing grins at everyone and checking his reflection in every hard surface. Skelly was utterly indifferent to his own reflection, a long, jagged streak like a crack in the glass of each storefront they passed. Ironically it was the same ineffable disinterest that piqued Gil's interest in the first place. He'd found him propping up the house band in some subterranean dive in Detroit, the first axman he'd seen in a long time equal to the task of carving through drunken pandemonium with a flick of the wrist. Gil summoned Louie at once to press-gang him into the new band they were putting together, like a modern-day Fagin dragging a street urchin out of the gutter. Skelly didn't need much convincing—he was too good for the gigs he was playing and too good for what those gigs were paying—but the gutter stuck to him like a second skin. Tattooed knucklebones dangled from his belt like an implicit threat. He still had his sunglasses on and a cigarette in his mouth, despite the NO SMOKING signs posted all over the place. One of his teeth glinted gold, like a pirate. He wore his hair longer than Nora, an artless black shag perpetually tangled in the half dozen chains around his neck. His whole body was made of sharp angles, rawboned and wiry, half a head taller than Gil. He had the longest fingers Suzanne had ever seen. That was why they called him "the Hands," among other things—sometimes Skelly, sometimes Killer, sometimes Strings. He was rarely ever "Eric," not even in the liner notes.

She tried not to stare, but no one else did. As their escalator went up, the one going down watched and whispered and pointed. One young mother turned her daughter around to face the other way. Gil pretended—exaggerating just enough that everybody knew he was pretending—not to notice. Skelly smoked and tapped his ash into the fountain below, which felt like the opposite of a wish somehow. "Boo," he said to the woman who'd turned her daughter away as the escalators carried them past each other—ships in the midafternoon.

"Strings," Gil said as they stepped off on the second floor, "let's not antagonize the local wildlife."

Skelly looked over the railing, down at the shoppers and custodians milling around the food court. "You call this life?"

"Maybe not the kind of low life you're used to," Gil said. "But I'm sure we could rustle some up. Suzanne, where do the dirtbags hang out around here?"

"Where we're going, I guess," she said, forcing herself to slow down. There was no reason to run, but she was used to it by now. Always careening down the walkways at top speed. She'd lost interest in the mall beyond Most Wanted. It wasn't exactly the Hells Angels killing time in there, but it was where the teenagers too cool to be seen slurping an Orange Julius tended to congregate, drawn to the record store by some centrifugal motion of popular culture. Suzanne had felt it herself and tried to resist for so long that once she gave in, she gave in completely.

Most Wanted owned her now, as much as—or more than—either of her parents did. Nora was always working or with Nathan: the smiling man from Macy's, the new man in her life. Suzanne had only met him once, and he'd never been invited over, supposedly to safeguard the stability of her home life—whatever that looked like. Suzanne suspected Nora was ashamed not to have a better home life and didn't want Nathan, with his collared shirts and tasseled loafers and nice, shiny watch, to see the way they lived.

Not much else had changed since the separation. Gil lived the way he always had, out of his car and out of a suitcase and out of reach nine times out of ten. He called Suzanne at random from pay phones and lunch counters when he knew Nora wouldn't be home. She'd finally agreed—out of exhaustion or desperation to spend some time alone with Nathan—to let Suzanne supervise herself most afternoons. She would be eleven before long, a teenager soon enough. Surely she'd survive a few hours alone in the apartment without an adult. Usually, though, Suzanne went straight to the mall as she always had. But having Gil and Skelly in tow—that changed everything.

"It's always busy on Tuesday," she explained. "I told Doug I wouldn't be gone long. He needs me, for tagging shoplifters."

"And your mom knows you're still doing this," Gil said. She was never "Nora" to him anymore, and he was never "Gil" to her. Just "your mom" and "your dad," like they had never met, didn't know each other's names, hadn't spent twelve tumultuous years together. "She's on board with it." They hadn't quite worked out how to collaborate on child-rearing. Not that that was new.

"Umm . . ."

Gil held up one hand. "Never mind. Don't tell me."

"Why?" This question from Skelly, lagging half a step behind as if Gil had told him to heel but he was only following orders so long as it served his interests. He hadn't once—so far as she could tell, which was difficult to do—looked at Suzanne. His mirrored aviators only reflected her blank face back at her.

"Plausible deniability," Gil said. "Actually"—he sent Skelly a look over his shoulder, significant but inscrutable—"that's not a bad line for a song." They were, Gil told Suzanne when he called to say they'd be kicking around town for one day, working up material for the next album. Gil was the principal songwriter, but Skelly's instrumentals had become so instrumental that his opinions couldn't be discounted. They, too, were still learning how to collaborate.

Skelly flicked his cigarette over the railing, not even looking to see where it landed. "Gil," he said, "nothing you've denied has ever been plausible."

Gil threw his head back and laughed—a sharp yip that made Suzanne think of hyenas. He looked a bit like one, with his toothy smile and the pile of burnt-caramel curls that rose like hackles from his forehead to the nape of his neck. He was handsome, she realized, looking up at him under the sunshine through the milky skylights. Like a movie star. White people were always surprised to hear him speak Spanish, befuddled by any deviation from their expectations of what a Latino should look like. "Oh, ¡perdóneme!" he'd say. "We can't all be Go Go Gomez." And as they scratched their heads, he'd roll his eyes—which were sometimes gray and sometimes amber, depending on the light.

Suzanne looked back at Skelly again. Not much beauty about him, with his uneven teeth and hollow cheeks. Pale skin stretched over jutting bones, a long scar trickling from behind his left ear to his Adam's apple, as if he'd been improperly beheaded and improbably survived. None of that mattered, though. Even beside Gil's pink of health—especially beside Gil's pink of health—Skelly's unapproachable presence splintered through the atmosphere like shrapnel. He finally caught Suzanne watching him, or she thought he did, mirrored eyes lingering too long to be looking past her or over her head, the way most grown-ups did.

"Nora will believe whatever she wants to believe," Gil said. "Plausible or not." He changed the subject abruptly. "This must be the place."

Suzanne knew the clamor of the record store by ear, the babble of customers' conversations like backing vocals for whatever album corporate dictated they play. Today, it was John Cougar Mellencamp—*Big Daddy*. She held fast to Gil's hand, liked being tethered to him by something more than DNA. Everything was easier when he had free rein to go about his fathering in his own way. So maybe Suzanne didn't have a representative in the PTA or Take Your Daughter to Work Day, but so what? She could take her father to work with her instead.

"This way." She led him toward the checkout counter, Skelly trailing at a pointless distance. The space between them only elongated their entrance, gave every head time to turn their way. Not so pointless after all, Suzanne decided, following the eyes that followed them through the store, every whisper flitting past her ear softly as a moth. Nearly a year trainspotting shoplifters and her senses were heightened automatically.

Today she didn't care about thieving. Even the likely suspects— she knew them on sight by now, recognized something shifty in their bearing that defied precise description—had stopped in their tracks to watch Gil and Skelly go by. Girls elbowed each other and tittered behind their hands, eyes alive with mischief. Boys stopped browsing and sniffed the air for whatever rakish danger had made all the girls go pink and silly like that. A dash of flash and a sliver of sleaze, according to Gil's secret recipe. But the Hands turned heads without much help from Gil.

"Dude," someone muttered. "Dude? I think that's Eric Skillman."

"Nuh-uh," his doubting friend replied. "What would he be doing *here*?"

Suzanne glowed in the overflow of their ragged, roguish glamor. But the only reaction she really cared about was Doug's. She hadn't told him who her father was, unsure whether Gil had become *somebody* yet, somebody Doug would know by name. A moment too late, she wondered why the whispering boys knew Skelly's name but not Gil's.

"And I'm telling *you*, used is used. What do you think we have listening stations for?" Doug demanded of the latest customer trying to return a used LP for a scratch in the wax. "Don't give me that customer-is-always-right BS. Let the buyer beware! What does that sign say? ALL USED VINYL FINAL SALE. Next!" He waved away any further objections. "Whattaya got? Next!"

"You must be the famous Doug."

Doug looked from Gil to Skelly and then down at Suzanne. He nudged his smudged glasses back up the bridge of his nose, blinking like he might be seeing things. A drop of sweat escaped from beneath his hatband and disappeared again in the red thatch of his beard. "Pint Size," he said to Suzanne, "I got a bone to pick with you."

"What?" She was still clinging to Gil's fingers, suddenly aware of how childish it must look. "I told you my dad was in town today."

"Ye-ah," Doug said with an exaggerated roll of the eyes. "But you didn't tell me that your dad is Gil Delgado." When his eyes came back down from orbit, they landed squarely on Gil. "Holy shit, man." He laughed, the red of his beard creeping up his cheeks like a fast-moving sunburn. "She said you were a musician, but never said who. Extremely cool to meet you." A line had formed behind them, but nobody seemed to be in a hurry. If they hadn't already been ogling Skelly and Gil, they were now. Gil was all grins, letting go of Suzanne to shake hands with Doug, still gamely pretending not to feel every eye on him. Skelly didn't pretend. He stared back from behind his shades with such inscrutable intensity it bordered on hostile. He never moved except to toy with his earring, a wickedly sharp fishhook poked right through the lobe, grazing his jaw every time he turned his head. Suzanne wondered whether that was how he got the scar on his neck.

"Pleased to meet the man continuing Suzanne's musical education," Gil said to Doug. "Great little place you got here."

"We do what we can, but—"

"Our hands are tied by the powers on high," Suzanne recited.

"Home office," Doug explained. "Wouldn't know a truly good tune if it kissed them on the mouth or bit them in the ass."

"But you do," Skelly said in a low monotone. Doug's ears, poking up from underneath his maroon Coors cap, went as red as his cheeks, as red as his beard. The contrast between them was even more dramatic than the contrast between Skelly and Gil, and decidedly not favorable to Doug. He rubbed at the back of his neck, as flushed and flustered now as the girls they'd passed on the way in, who were handing a compact back and forth and liberally reapplying lip gloss.

"Like to think so," Doug said. "See, I'm listening not just as a listener but as an engineer, because that's half the song—the mix, the production." His eyes flicked from Skelly to Gil and back again. "I mean, you two produced 'Bad Business' together, if I remember right. Part of what makes it such a great track is that pan through the bridge that makes it sound like the whole thing's about to go over backward before that solo comes in for the kill and it's just—BAM! Right in your face. Was that the Flying V? Monster midrange on that thing."

"Good ear," Gil said before Skelly could answer. He had that faraway look he sometimes wore when a lightbulb was sputtering on. "You dig the new stuff?"

"Oh. Yes. Hell yes. 'Bad Business' is a solid lead single, but I stayed for the B-side. 'New Blues'? They just don't make a dirty twelve-bar like they used to. You guys really know how to sling some sludge." Suzanne would never tire of their slang, the way they talked about music with all five senses, the way a word that sounded bad and mean in any other context was often the highest form of praise for a rock and roller. Some of Gil's smug pleasure spilled over onto her, because she'd brought them together, and there they were, just as impressed with each other as she knew they would be. She glanced at Skelly, who seemed to be reconsidering Doug until the girls with the compact finally drew his gaze by knocking a pile of Tom Petty cassettes off a display. One pinned her sticky lips together, shaking in a fit of silent laughter, while the other fluffed her hair as if to say, *Who, me?*

Gil ignored the girls completely. "What's your last name, Doug?"

"Sandusky."

"Doug Sandusky," Gil repeated. "Don't get me wrong, but you could do better than this."

Doug's red face got redder. "Sorry?"

Gil glanced around the store. "You attached to this job?"

"It keeps the lights on," Doug said. "Why?"

"Would you rather be a real sound man? Because ours just quit, and if you're a fast learner, you could have yourself a new job by June."

Skelly spoke again. His voice had none of Gil's sonorous resonance.

It was flat as a blade and cut through the conversation like so much soft butter. "Gil."

"Yes, Killer."

For a moment that lasted a moment too long, they just looked at each other. The look was hardly blank but charged with something volatile that pushed and pulled between them, a fluctuating magnetic polarity. Doug was still as a statue behind the register, as if he were afraid to move and risk waking himself from this strange, audacious dream. At long last, whatever tension had been building between Gil and Skelly went slack. Skelly turned away from everyone and everything. Taking that as acquiescence, Gil wasted no time.

"When can you start?"

"I will quit the minute this shift is over," Doug said.

Skelly sniffed but didn't look back. "Since we're getting ahead of ourselves." Doug's eagerness evidently did not impress him like it had Gil. Never mind that Gil had seen Skelly's potential and plucked him out of a bad situation in just the same way just a few short years ago.

"Can't promise hazard pay for putting up with him," Gil said, unfazed, "but I've been telling Louie and the label to put it in the budget for this tour."

"You see what I'm dealing with here?" Doug said. "We're so underfunded I've got a fourth grader working security." Gil and Doug seemed to remember at once that Suzanne was there, why they were even talking to each other in the first place.

"Don't let Lou hear you say that or he'll put her to work."

"I like work," Suzanne said. She knew he was only joking, but the idea of going on the road with the band made everything inside her light up like Inner Harbor. "When I grow up I want to be Bob Gruen."

Gil let out another hyenic laugh, and Doug said solemnly, "She does." He gestured at the Sticky Fingers Hall of Fame, where Suzanne's handiwork with the Sun 640 had made many a light-fingered mall rat almost famous.

Skelly's head turned their way again but angled down this time. Suzanne looked up at him and saw two of herself, shiny and gleaming where his eyes should have been. "Gil," he said, though she felt certain, for the second time, that he was actually looking at her, "you've got the weirdest kid I've ever met."

"Apple," he said easily. "Tree."

"Before you go," she said, sensing it was now or never, "can I take a photo?"

Gil was game; Gil always was. She expected Skelly to refuse, but he merely fingered his earring, waiting until she had Gil where she wanted him, with his back against the Sticky Fingers board and a copy of the first LP, holding it in just the same attitude that the younger him in the image held the letterboard that said *Impersonator*. She didn't know what to call Skelly, she'd heard so many names for him already, and got tongue-tied three times trying to talk to him. She gave up, took the crook of his elbow, and turned and tugged him until the sunlight through the window fell squarely on Gil but didn't touch him. They looked good like that, Skelly looming behind her father like a long black shadow. Up close, he smelled like leather, or his jacket did—gamy and animal. She backed away, raised the viewfinder to her eye, and took one careful breath. "Okay," she said, to herself as much as them. "Don't move."

GUILT

With Gil's old studio cans clamped on her head, Suzanne didn't hear the knocking at first. Only when the music faded out did she realize that pounding wasn't coming from the kick drum.

"What?" she hollered, rolling halfway out of bed. Without work, she'd reverted to her adolescent habit of lying around much too late. Not that her work had demanded early rising very often; as Rob had none too subtly pointed out, her "job" was more of a "hobby," since she didn't earn enough to live on—at his standard of living, anyway. That she'd managed just fine before meeting him was not what he wanted to hear in reply. What he wanted and what she wanted irreparably misaligned.

The pounding on the door persisted, which was just as well— wallowing would do her no good. She kicked the sweaty sheets away, the air conditioner whining uselessly in the window. The small charms of the Sundew Value Inn were wearing off.

"Simon." She didn't know who else she had expected, which made it that much more embarrassing to be standing there braless with tumultuous bedhead, wearing his hand-me-down shirt from the Daytona Speedway. It was long enough for a nightgown, and she hadn't thought twice about wearing it until he was standing there watching her wear it.

"Morning," he said, a smile hiding in one corner of his mouth. "Hope I didn't knock too early. Sorry—I've made a bad habit of that."

"No, no," she said. "Actually, I don't even know—what time is it?"

He looked up at the sky instead of his watch or his phone, like most people his age would have done. "Almost noon."

"Well, shit," she said. "Then what are you apologizing for?"

"Not waking you sooner," he said. "She's ready."

"Who's ready?"

He stepped aside. "Feast your eyes," he said, but she had to shield them first. Blondie had never had such a high shine—not for twenty-nine years, anyway. And she hadn't just been washed and waxed, she was *running*. Humming, mellow, butter yellow, spilling the Stones into the sizzling midday. Simon leaned on the passenger door, elbow perched on the side mirror. It reminded her of how Gil used to drive, fingertips kissing the wheel, one elbow bent on the ledge of the open window. Maybe that explained the urge to fling herself into his arms. She started out on blind barefoot instinct but yelped as soon as her foot touched the pavement and leapt back inside. She rammed her feet into a pair of flip-flops and stumbled into the shocking sunshine.

Echoes of coffee and smoke still clung to the seats, but the dust had been wiped from the dash, the lightboard dimly aglow. "She's ready?" Suzanne asked. "You're sure?"

"She's chomping at the bit," Simon said. "Get some real shoes. You should drive."

Simon had filled the tank with gas and the glove box with CDs and cassettes swiped from Phoebe's inventory. The seat vibrated against Suzanne's back, the gas pedal firm underfoot. That pair of familiar tortoiseshell Wayfarers still hung from the visor by one leg. They felt right on her face, though they should have been too big—a piece of her inheritance as much as anything. Phoebe had gone to haggle again with Miss Kaminsky, leaving them the afternoon to go "anywhere," Simon said. "We could go anywhere."

They went nowhere special, the destination meaningless. Suzanne had only driven the car from Miami to Tampa before it broke down, the weight of Gil's unfinished business like ten tons of lead in the bed. But now the tires gripped the road with lust instead of grim determination. The engine no longer growling through gritted teeth but thrumming at the touch of her toes on the gas. Hot air whipped through the cab, making even more of a mess of her hair than it already was. The car lunged ahead at the gentlest pressure on the pedal, like Suzanne was holding her back, reining her in. She fought the urge to push the speedometer past 80, past 90, past 100—not with Simon in the passenger seat. She'd promised herself, a long time ago after a very near miss, never to play so fast and loose with someone else's life, no matter how little she valued her own. If he felt any anxiety about her need for speed, it didn't show. He leaned back against the seat with one arm extended, hand skating over her shoulder each time he reached for a knob or a dial on the dashboard, explaining all he had and hadn't learned about Gil's strange operations on the car. But Suzanne didn't need to be told that Blondie was a miracle of unhinged engineering. Unlike everything else, the Ranchero felt rightfully hers. She gnawed at a bit of split skin on her sunburned lips.

"I forgot about this song!" Simon exclaimed. Suzanne jerked her head, the sunglasses slipping an inch down her nose. She'd slid back in time, across the bench, felt herself sitting where he sat now. Bare feet kicking out the open window at the flat yellow nothing of the Great Plains. When Gil's amber eyes were still black and Skelly's magic hands were mangled by bad odds or bad judgment or just some bad star hanging over all of them. Simon slapped his thigh with the rhythm, and Suzanne's heartbeat fell in line. She never had talent, not much of a voice or feel for an instrument, but she could always keep time. You needed that to take good pictures, of live performers or with something as slow as a Polaroid. Photographs captured the subject like a cat pounced on its prey: jump too late and you'd miss it, too soon and you'd scare it away.

Glancing down the seat at Simon, sitting where she had as a strip of a girl in his robust young man's body, she would have liked to capture him like that. Wearing whatever had survived Phoebe's fire sale, drumming on his knee with his three-fingered hand, singing along to "Hounds of Love" in some absurd falsetto. Young men now were different than when she'd been young, or at least she hoped they were.

Suzanne drove aimlessly for hours and could have driven hours more, so long as Simon seemed content to be her hostage. But when she saw the checkerboard sign sprout out of the pink muhly grass that waved along the roadside, she put her blinker on. They climbed out of the car and walked up to the window, where the cashier took their order with squinty, gum-chewing suspicion and shouted it over her shoulder to the cook. All in one breath, words glomming together. "Two with picklesandcheese, no onion on one no mayo ontheother, one largefry one cherryCoke one smallstrawberryshake."

"With two spoons, please," Simon said.

"Twospoons!" she hollered.

It was a drive-in with one picnic table overtaken by seagulls who looked none too friendly, decades of rust gnawing through the thermoplastic. They opted to eat in the car, a feast in Styrofoam and wax paper stuffed into a flimsy cardboard box between them. Suzanne sucked cola through a striped straw while Simon peered under each bun to decide "Yours" and "Mine." The fries lounged like sunbathers slathered in oil in a red-and-white paper tray. Suzanne salted them liberally and licked her fingertips—suddenly ravenous, suddenly realizing she'd left the motel without eating breakfast and it was nearly sundown now.

"Yours." She piled the mustard packets in front of Simon and kept the ketchup for herself. "Mine."

"Yours." He plucked a maraschino cherry off the top of the milkshake before digging into the cloud of whipped cream beneath. "Mine."

Suzanne put the cherry in her mouth, stem and all. She loved their color and their candy sweetness. She chewed and swallowed and worked the stem around until she stuck her tongue out again with a tight scarlet knot on the tip. "Ta-da."

Simon took the knotted stem. "A woman of many talents." He breathed into the shallow bowl of his plastic spoon and hung it on the tip of his nose. "Ta-da."

"What we have here," she said, "is a riveting double act." The spoon fell from his nose and clattered back into the box. She dipped into the whipped cream with the other one. "Open wide."

He opened his mouth, but the gob of whipped cream hit him right between the eyes with a small, wet *slap*. He squinted at her through the mess. "Naughty," he said, and reached for a fry. He dunked it in the shake and, with a flick of the wrist, gave her a strawberry mustache. She got a nose full of milkshake, which only made her laugh. Simon wiped whipped cream off his forehead and crumpled a napkin to dab the pink slush from her face. She squinched her eyes shut, feeling ten years old again, vivified by sugar and salt and the thrill of the drive, the coming sunset flaring off the mirrors. Feeling ten years old until she felt Simon's three fingers on the curve of her neck, his mouth on hers, his tongue a lick of whipped cream on her lips.

Surprise and desire like the zero-gravity drop from the top of a roller coaster. The huge, sudden force of longing melted her muscles like butter, left them dripping down her limbs. How many hours had she watched him sweating over the engine block, an idle daydream she didn't dare indulge because—

"Phoebe." She tried to push him back, but he was so still, so solid, that she pushed herself instead, scudding down the bench until her kneecap smacked against the driver's door. "What about Phoebe?" She felt sick, the milkshake a sticky aftertaste clinging to her tongue.

"Shit. I'm sorry," he said. Hands up again, like the day he first knocked on her window. "I got carried away—I should have explained."

"What?"

"I'm sorry," he said again. "I didn't mean to upset you."

Not upset but upended. Thrown head over heels and ass over elbow. Her appetite had gone into hiding. She couldn't look at him or the food. She said, for no reason, "We should go."

"All right," Simon said. Always so subdued, but more now than usual. She turned the engine on before either of them could say or do anything else, turned the music up too loud to talk, and drove too fast to think.

Dark, almost, by the time they returned. Suzanne said, pointedly, "You should get back to Phoebe," and left Simon in the car with the keys and Marianne Faithfull, making an unlikely comeback with sandpaper stuck in her throat. *I feel guilt, I feel bad, I feel blood, not enough.* Suzanne had spun *Broken English* so many times during her teenage flirtation with psychosis that the song had made a home in the marrow of her bones. She fumbled to unlock the door to her room and shut it out behind her.

But the door was already open, the lights were on, and the music did not stop.

"Whoa," Phoebe said, frowning at the walkie-talkie in her hands before looking up at Suzanne. "Hey, you're home." So odd the way she said that, like they lived there together. Maybe when you had no permanent address, wherever you stayed for more than a few days—and whoever you stayed there with—felt like home. Phoebe had certainly made herself comfortable, barefoot on the bed with an old cigar box full of tiny pliers and screwdrivers. Suzanne wasn't sure whether the bantam tool kit was hers or Gil's. She looked right there, in among his things, though most of what was left had been boxed up. "Sorry for letting myself in," she said. "I needed the shears and you left it unlocked."

"Were you packing?" The room was much less a mess than when Suzanne had gone.

"Just a bit," she said. "Getting everything stowed on the Lifeboat, it's a whole process. I get distracted by every little thing—like these walkie-talkies?" She held one up. That was where the music was coming from. Still Marianne Faithfull, still rasping along.

Suzanne stared at them, too much boiling in her brain to focus on anything but what was right in front of her. Phoebe. Marianne Faithfull. "What about them?"

"I've been trying to get a signal—wasn't sure they worked, worthless if they don't but not a bad finder's fee if they do—and nothing until just now."

"Just now, that song came on," Suzanne said. Except it wasn't that song anymore, but the next one on the album.

"Yeah." Phoebe twiddled the dial, turned it up. A synthesizer flitted back and forth, weightless as a water bug. *In a white suburban bedroom, in a white suburban town* . . . "I popped the other one open but can't figure out what's going on in there." She patted the mattress beside her and the tools rattled like sleigh bells in their box. "Come sit, I'll show you."

Thinking it would be more awkward not to, Suzanne sat. Tried to keep an inch or two between them.

"See, look at this." Phoebe turned one handset over to pluck at the wiring behind the speaker cone. "These are sixty years old, but some of the hardware looks newer." The pins and screws sparkled in the yellow lamplight. "Didn't Simon say he found a microphone wired into the glove box?"

"Oh," Suzanne said. "Yeah. My dad had a tape recorder in there."

Phoebe looked toward the door. "Oh shit," she said. "I think they're talking to the car. Like he wired it up for CB radio or FHSS or something." Yes. Of course he had. Suzanne had forgotten about that. It made more sense than most of Gil's automotive meddling, given how often he was leading a convoy once the band got off the ground. "I think we're hearing inside the car." Which meant Simon must still be sitting out there in the dark. Which meant maybe he could hear them, too. The music clicked off, as abruptly as it had come on in the room. Phoebe was still looking toward the door. "He was so excited this morning, that he finally got her going."

"What?"

"The car. He said you might go for a drive."

"Oh. Yes. We did." She was talking like a robot that hadn't mastered the messy ambiguities of human communication. Phoebe watched Suzanne, who didn't meet her eyes.

"Well, how was it?"

She couldn't lie. Wouldn't. "Phoebe—"

Phoebe heard the wrong chord in Suzanne's voice. No hiding from her. Her hand landed, light as a butterfly, on Suzanne's bare knee. "He really fumbled it, huh?" She said it like she knew, like she'd expected it. She could read Simon and Suzanne better than they read themselves, it seemed.

"I don't know— How was it supposed to go?"

"That depends, I suppose. Suze."

Tired of hiding, Suzanne finally looked her in the eye. No trace of unease in Phoebe's expression—just a sliver of a smile, just enough to give away the gap between her teeth.

"He's shy," she said. "He's no good at this. You wouldn't believe how I debased myself before he finally got the hint." She spoke about it so easily. "He wasn't even sure you liked him, but I was," Phoebe went on. Teasing now, but very gently. "Unless I'm wrong?"

"No," Suzanne said in a small, embarrassing squeak of a voice—like she was sixteen again, though she'd been less embarrassing then. "Not wrong."

"It's okay if it's too much, too," Phoebe said. "We just really like you."

"We?"

"Yeah, we." Phoebe tilted her head, smile turned on its side like a crescent moon. Suzanne stared at the dark space between her lips, the dark space between her teeth. "But it doesn't have to be *we* if that's not what you want. No jealousy—scout's honor." She held up three fingers. Just like Simon's.

"How does that work?" Suzanne asked. It ran contrary to everything she thought she knew about relationships—which wasn't much, or her marriage probably would have lasted longer. Or she would have known not to get married in the first place.

"It just does." Phoebe shrugged. "We don't have a lot, but love never runs out. There's enough for you, too, if you want." She leaned a little closer, kissed Suzanne's cheek. "Sleep on it. We've got a long drive tomorrow."

She stretched, straightened up. Suzanne stayed where she was, watched her pick up her shoes and walk barefoot out into the dusk. No sound of the engine before the door swung shut behind her. Suzanne sat there staring at the dead walkie-talkie until the dark outside held sway.

THE **B** SIDE

BACKSEAT NOTHING

The Prius was not a good car for a road trip, according to Suzanne, another firm conviction Rob didn't understand. It was safe, reliable, got great gas mileage. What more could you ask of a car you meant to drive long distances? He didn't understand the appeal of driving long distances just for the hell of it, either. Why not fly? The Prius was apparently why he didn't understand this: *It's fun to drive a long distance in a car that's fun to drive,* Suzanne had said, prompting some embarrassing midnight Google searches after the following conversation revealed that he did not know what "torque" was, how it differed from "horsepower," and that the Prius did not have enough of either to be considered "fun." His only defense was that driving and fun were mutually exclusive when you lived in a hundred-mile radius of the nation's capital, where traffic was oppressive, parking expensive, signage nonsensical, tickets inevitable and financially devastating. But the time had come to have a little more "fun."

Rob sold the Prius to a teenager bound for her freshman year at Swarthmore, thinking—a little sheepishly, watching her drive off—that yes, it did look a bit like the Little Tikes Cozy Coupe his nephews loved to run over the sprinkler heads, and yes, its engine did produce a high, girlish whine but not much in the way of power. Masculinity was supposedly "toxic" now, but maybe he'd overcorrected, veered too far in the other direction. Maybe his real mistake in his marriage was being too modern, too emasculated. Suzanne had walked right out without a backward glance, but maybe Casey was right and what she really wanted was to have to put up a fight.

Before Rob left town he stopped by the bank, took fifteen thousand out in cash, and took that plus the modest proceeds from the Prius to a house out in Reston with a black Dodge pickup parked in the driveway. For sale by owner, cash only. He had a few thousand left over. Driving-around money. Back at the house, he packed a suitcase, emptied the trash, then went through the rooms one by one—closing blinds and checking locks and making sure the lights were off. He stopped, automatically, in the doorway to Suzanne's office. She insisted on calling it a "studio," though he didn't see what the difference was. Another thing she never deigned to explain. Nothing in the house was louder than all the things she wouldn't talk about.

The room was always a wreck, her so-called studio. Books spilling out of the bookcase, CDs piled on top of the stereo, tripods and ring lights leaning drunkenly against the wall by the closet she used as a darkroom. Too much of a mess to know for certain what she'd taken with her, even after the last few nights he'd spent ransacking her drawers and dark corners for answers.

Rob felt suddenly exhausted. He fell into the desk chair. When had he last eaten? He made a note to check the pantry for granola bars. Suzanne had always been the one to buy snack food; she rarely ate real meals and seemed to resent his expectation that they eat together occasionally. Family dinners were a foreign concept. He almost laughed when he pulled her desk drawer open and saw the half-eaten bag of M&M's squirreled away in there—like she was hiding them from herself. Which was what she always seemed to be doing. She refused to be photographed, flinched if you pointed one of her cameras at her, as if she were in witness protection and trying to erase any evidence that she ever existed. But she left invisible fingerprints all over the house. All the photos were of him, but she'd been the one to take them—mostly posed beside peculiar exhibits at any of the dozen niche museums they'd poked around over the last two or three years.

She was working on a series that she never finished, and he tagged along when she let him. He loved those spontaneous day trips, giving in to her whims. Christmas villages, carousel horses, one especially incriminating Polaroid from a traveling gallery of sex toys dating back to the sixteenth century. Nothing he had any special interest in, but Suzanne was so goddamned *odd* that it was endlessly interesting just to watch her interact with the world. The studio was the only place she demanded total privacy. And up until she disappeared, he had respected that.

He picked up her wedding ring from where he'd found it the day before, in a shallow compartment of that middle drawer where someone more organized might have put pushpins or paper clips. He turned the thin gold band between his fingers, peering through the unblinking void at the center. When he first heard her voicemail, so artlessly improvised, he thought she must be having one of her infrequent freakouts—when for some inscrutable reason she went temporarily insane and temporarily deaf if he asked what in the hell was wrong. But the ring, tucked out of sight with her petty secret stash of candy, undid that assumption. She was planning to leave him before she even left.

He spun the ring on the desk like a quarter. A useless trick Brad had taught him when they were children. It whirled into an insubstantial sphere of gold, as if it might dissolve and disappear into thin air. After finding it, he'd turned the room over, taking inventory of everything left behind or taken along. Her handbag was gone, of course, but also her passport. She'd taken one battered old duffel bag and only the clothes that would fit inside it. There were a few empty slots on the bookshelf, but he couldn't guess which books had been there. The bottom shelf was the only one undisturbed. A dozen identical spines, blurred by a layer of dust, which might have been the only reason he even remembered the title: *Dust and Bones.* Suzanne's first and only photo book—another entry on the list of Unspeakable Things.

Rob slammed the spinning ring down on the desktop, pinned it there under his palm. When the quiet started to itch, he slipped it onto his little finger for safekeeping. Suzanne didn't play an instrument, but he always thought she should have—such delicate fingers. Bones like woodwinds. Bones like a bird.

Rob stood up from the chair. On his way out of the studio, he swept another stack of CDs off the receiver. When she didn't want to talk—which, of late, was always—he'd listen to the muffled music from upstairs as a sort of weather report on her mood. The volume alone could be a clue. He didn't know her music, but it wasn't too late to learn.

He threw his suitcase in the bed of the truck and the box of CDs in the passenger seat. He slammed the door and stared out the windshield for a moment, unaccustomed to riding so high. Their house looked different from that vantage point, dwarfed by the oak tree that dragged its branches across their bedroom window when it stormed. How stupidly proud he had been of that house when he bought it—the most concrete foothold he'd ever had on *success*, broadly defined. Before the flooded basement, the ant infestation, the other oak tree that fell on the garage, the HVAC that failed without fail every winter. Carrying Suzanne over the threshold—he'd insisted, against her vociferous protests, that chivalry wasn't dead to him yet—had given it a new kind of shine. It wasn't a bad investment, just a fixer-upper. A wife legitimized things in a way protracted bachelorhood did not. Someone was depending on him, which gave him the kind of purpose and direction his adolescence had lacked.

Depending on him sort of. That was part of the problem, he understood now. Suzanne had supported herself one way or another for most of her life, but only because her standard of living was so shockingly low. When they met she was thirtysomething and living in a microscopic studio above a pet shop in Columbia Heights that smelled like a birdcage and should have been condemned. None of her furniture matched and most of it had been handed down four or five times before arriving in her bedroom/office/kitchen/lounge. The apartment wasn't dirty—which would have been a deal-breaker—but looked like someone had dumped the contents of a junk shop in the middle of the floor and then shaken the room like a snow globe. Everything had a haphazard, accidental attitude, with the enormous exception of the stereo. It was much too big for the space it was in, gobbling up one whole wall. The equipment was shabby and outdated as anything else, but the records, CDs, and cassettes were fanatically organized. It was the only thing she talked about with unwavering certainty, so he let her talk about it long after he'd stopped really listening.

He popped the lid off the shoebox. Stuck to the face of the top jewel case was a Post-it note and two lines of Suzanne's scribbly shorthand: LOUIE C. $^5/_{23}$, TAMPA. If he didn't know her better, it wouldn't have been much to go on. But he'd cracked some of her ciphers over the years, knew $^5/_{23}$ wasn't a date but a cross street. She'd flown to Miami—which she never did if she could help it, which should have been his first hint that something was amiss. She hated air travel for its rigid efficiency: Point A to Point B, no stopping to sightsee. She hadn't mentioned Tampa, or anyone named Louie, which meant she must have been plotting this inglorious exodus for a while. She'd probably been ready to cut and run since the day they became man and wife.

I was all wrong for you from the start, and I think we both knew—

Rob jammed the key into the ignition. The engine roared to life, a big, snarling dog lunging against its chain. "Easy, girl," Rob told her, running one hand along the dash just to feel the vibrations. He peeled the Post-it off the plastic and stuck it to the windshield. If he drove like hell, he could get to Tampa by lunchtime tomorrow.

Easy.

THE **A** SIDE

IN FOR THE KILL

Suzanne was one of two children in attendance when Nora and Nathan tied the knot, after a courtship of indeterminate length. Nobody asked exactly when it started, collectively uncertain whether Gil was already gone or whether Nathan might have nudged him out the door. Suzanne didn't think so; he seemed entirely too innocent for that, with his square face and broad forehead and uncomplicated smile. He wore powder-blue button-downs and khaki slacks with pleats and matching socks. He liked *Cheers*, Steely Dan, and playing doubles at the tennis club. He didn't smoke, rarely drank, and never raised his voice. His only vice was Necco wafers.

The ceremony was held at a bed-and-breakfast in the Poconos on a sultry spring evening. The wedding party was small, the guest list short. The other kid was Nathan's godson, wrestled into a tiny tuxedo for his two minutes of fame as he toddled down the aisle with both rings in a basket and his mother following in a paroxysm of anxiety lest he drop it in the long grass of the terrace garden. Suzanne squirmed in an itchy eyelet dress cinched so tight around her waist that she could barely breathe. The first one she'd worn since her christening, and the last, if she got her way. She was so pink-cheeked from the sun and fatigued from lack of oxygen that she fell asleep in the cool, quiet dark of the coatroom and missed the cake she'd been promised for her participation.

She woke up in a trundle bed to the sound of her grandmother—who so detested Gil that she had never forgiven Suzanne for looking so much like him—snoring heavily. Disinclined to stick around and say goodbye, Suzanne thumped downstairs to the breakfast room with the suitcase she never unpacked and devoured Jordan almonds by the fistful while she watched the clock and watched the long gravel drive at the front of the inn.

It was after noon when she heard the Ranchero. She sat up straight in the window seat, forgetting the owner's desperate pleas to keep her hands off the glass. She hadn't seen Gil much lately—as wrapped up in his album release as Nora was in the nuptials. She'd confiscated the promotional copy he sent as soon as it arrived because "I don't care if he *is* your father, that should have a parental advisory label." So Suzanne counted down the days until the wedding, waiting for her chance to seize the record she thought of as her birthright, even though she'd never heard it. Doug had learned to say "No, not yet" instead of "Hello" when she arrived at Most Wanted, though he was just as eager as she was. He couldn't stop talking about the tour. Suzanne was silently sick with envy and begged him to tell her everything about every show; he pinkie-promised her he would.

Blondie emerged from the trees like a fish crawling out of the primordial slime, a higher life-form venturing into virgin territory. Suzanne bolted from the window seat, scattering almonds as she dragged her suitcase out the door. It bumped down the porch steps and fell over, but she left it where it landed. Gil was already out of the car, arms flung wide to catch her. He laughed in her ear, whirled her around in his cloud of coffee and cologne and rock and roll. Suzanne recognized the Pixies on the radio. Graciela climbed out of the passenger seat and watched them with a grin. She was the new tour manager and Gil's new girlfriend. She cut her curly black hair so short that her hoop earrings poked out underneath. She chewed gum nonstop, smacked and cracked it unabashedly. She always wore lipstick like cherry cola, she often wore Gil's aftershave, she never wore a bra. Everybody called her Gracie, but Suzanne understood why Gil called her *mi amor*. Suzanne was a little in love with her, too. Maybe she just wanted to *be* Gracie—or be somebody like her someday. One of the boys, one of the band, one of the crew.

"Hey there," she said as Gil swung Suzanne up onto the roof of the car to tie the shoelace that had come loose on her mad tear across the drive. "How was the wedding?"

"Too long," Suzanne said. "Can we go?"

Gracie laughed and snapped her gum. Bazooka pink today.

"If we don't tell your mom, she'll think you've been kidnapped," Gil said. "You want to run and find her?"

"No need." Gracie pointed toward the inn. With its dormer windows and scalloped shingles, it looked like a gingerbread house. Nathan and Nora emerged together, arm in arm.

"We heard some low-life greaser was making a racket out here," Nora said. They could joke about that kind of thing, now that they were no longer tied together by law or living space. "Had to talk Ms. Moultrie out of calling the cops."

Nathan picked up Suzanne's toppled suitcase and hefted it into the back of the car. The women embraced; the men shook hands.

"Congratulations," Gracie said. "Sorry we couldn't make the ceremony." Everyone knew they'd been invited as a courtesy and couldn't have come without Nora's mother making a scene. That the divorce proceedings had been more amicable than acrimonious was more than Gil deserved, maybe, even Suzanne could see that. But who was right and who was wrong mattered less when they could admit they just weren't right for each other and move on. She liked them better apart; they liked each other better that way.

"You certainly would have livened things up," Nathan said to Gil with a backward glance at the inn. "They run a very tight ship." He squinted up at Suzanne. "Was that you 'throwing almonds all over the rug'?"

"Not on purpose," Suzanne said, bouncing her heel against the window frame.

"You'd better get her out of here before old Miz Moultrie changes her mind about calling the law." Nathan winked and tugged her ankle.

"Got everything, kiddo?" Gil said.

Suzanne nodded and jumped down from the roof, trusting that someone would catch her. To her surprise it was Nora, who hugged her tight to her chest. "Be good," she said. "Be safe. You have the numbers where we'll be and you'll call me if you need anything." It wasn't a question. Suzanne squirmed, confused and embarrassed by the sudden show of concern. Yes, nine weeks would be the longest time they had ever spent apart, but it would also be the longest Nora and Nathan had ever been together without worrying about bedtimes or babysitters or whether breakfast would be awkward in the morning.

"You'll get her back in one piece," Gil said, "if you don't hug her head off first."

Nora let go, laughing and wiping her eyes. "I'm sorry, I'm being ridiculous."

"She's in good hands, babe," Gil said. He hadn't quite broken the habit of calling her that. Nathan and Gracie both pretended not to notice.

"Okay," Nora said, but her lip still trembled. She and Gil got along much better when they were apart, but unless she wanted to take Suzanne along on her honeymoon, he was going to have to learn to be a father and she was going to have to let him. Gracie made all the difference; she had four sisters, two with children Suzanne's age, and she'd promised Nora, one woman to another, that no matter where the tour took them, Suzanne would always be safe, always be taken care of.

But it was still Gil Nora turned to. Old habits died hard. She grabbed his fingers with both hands, like a trapeze flier afraid to let go. "I'm trusting you." Not *I trust you*, but *I'm trusting you*. As if it were a temporary condition, a trial run—which, in a way, it was.

"I know, babe," he said. "I know."

Suzanne sat between Gil and Gracie, with the Chupa Chups in her lap. They let her fiddle with every knob and dial, answered every question about every painstaking modification. Custom-fit car stereos had kept him afloat when the band was sinking, whichever band it was.

He'd played so many shows with so many unusual suspects that even he couldn't keep track of who played what in which lineup. But he was always the frontman; Gil played second fiddle to no one.

"Play the tape," Suzanne begged. "Play the tape!" He knew which tape she meant but laughed it off and promised her, "Later."

"Pleeeeeease?" She dragged the word out like she was pulling taffy—sticky and sweet and deceptively stubborn. "Pl*eeeeeeeeea*se?"

"Later, baby," Gracie said. "It'll be worth the wait."

They drove half an hour through winding hills, light splintered through the branches of the trees. Suzanne watched the road unfurl, emerging out of nothingness around each bend, as if Blondie's wheels summoned it from some chthonic place beneath the planet's crust. She sucked on a lemon lollipop and slipped her shoes off to dip her bare toes in the sunbeams pooling on the dashboard. She didn't realize she was drifting off to sleep until she woke up, nostrils flaring at the odor of benzene on the breeze.

Gil was gone from the driver's side, the car parked at one of two pumps outside a shack with a sign on the door that said SWANNBERG'S GENERAL STORE. In the passenger seat, Gracie pored over an atlas with a pencil between her teeth. Suzanne blinked against the sun, lower and larger in the sky than it was the last time she opened her eyes. The highways and byways came slowly into focus, familiar from the hours squandered in the hobby shop. Red *X*'s marked clusters of four or five cities in the Northeast, Midwest, Southwest—like dig sites on a treasure map.

"Where are we?" She rubbed the gum of sleep from her eyes.

Gracie took the pencil out of her mouth. "We're in the middle of nowhere, more or less."

"Show me."

"This is I-80." She pointed out a long blue squiggle inching eastward from the Poconos. "That's the interstate, so it goes across state borders. See?" The pencil followed a thin dotted line dividing Pennsylvania from New Jersey. "Even numbers run east–west. Odd numbers, north–south." She pointed out the nearest interchange, I-80 and I-95.

"What about these, with three numbers?"

"Those are beltways," Gracie explained. "They go around big cities." She traced the wobbling seismograph of 280.

"Like a belt?"

"Like a belt."

"What are those?" Suzanne pointed at the *X*'s clustered up and down the East Coast.

"Those," Gracie said, dimples deepening, "are the tour dates for the first leg."

"That's good, right? Ten shows in two weeks."

Gracie tucked Suzanne's hair behind her ear. "That's right," she said with a gleam in her eye Suzanne didn't yet know her well enough to recognize. "It's *very* good."

A cattail of bottle caps rattled against Swannberg's door. Gil walked smack into the sunlight, dark glasses catching the glare. A paper bag in the crook of each elbow, a coffee cup clutched in each hand. He passed everything in through the window before opening the door. "Did we have a nice nap?" he asked, and Suzanne's stomach snarled at the juicy, salty smells of french fries and ground beef. She hadn't eaten anything but lollipops and Jordan almonds all day. She sank her teeth into a cheeseburger so fast she swallowed wax paper.

"We're learning to read a map," Gracie said. "Suzanne's almost ready to take over as navigator."

"Never too young." Gil fired up the engine and slurped down some coffee. Black, two sugars too many. "What next?"

"Follow signs for 280," Gracie instructed. "And follow that to Jersey City."

Suzanne chewed and swallowed more carefully. Followed 280 across the atlas and frowned. "But that's east," she said. "Shouldn't we go south to get back to Baltimore?"

Gil tore into a burger one-handed, turned the music up. New York Dolls, still looking for a kiss. "Who said anything about Baltimore?"

It sounded like a trick question. ". . . Mom?"

He licked his fingertips, licked his lips, flicked one finger under her chin. "Then this will just have to be our secret."

Suzanne had never been to New York. The huge, filthy sprawl en-thralled her. She clambered across Gracie's lap to stare out the window as the brave new world went by, the dome of the sky dimming from burnt blood orange to dusky black. House lights going dark. The night swelled with sound and motion, the windshield like a Lite-Brite where the neon contrails of cars and food carts and club marquees made new constellations. Horns blared while noise and music poured out of open doorways. Gil swore in Spanish at lunatic drivers and reckless pedestrians, cable trunks crashing against the cab whenever he slammed on the brakes. But he was still drumming on the wheel, still singing along to the Pretenders on the stereo, still laughing around the lollipop stick that lived in the corner of his mouth, as if they were pieces moving on the board of some great elaborate game. *In the middle of life, in the middle of the road.*

"We're here," Gracie announced, though "here" seemed to be nowhere more specific than an alley too narrow to open the doors halfway.

"The paint, the paint, the paint," Gil chanted as they sidled out, moving in slow motion.

"You're late, you're late, you're late," Gracie answered. "I've got it, you go."

Gil tossed her the keys, grabbed Suzanne's hand, and ducked through a door marked NOT AN ENTRANCE.

Inside, everything was warm and dark and muffled, bass throbbing through the walls of hallways that bent at crazy angles under bare pipes and lightbulbs encrusted with mold. So many posters had been plastered on top of each other it was anybody's guess what color paint was underneath, the paper peeling off in hangnail strips, like the building was shedding its skin. Maps and blueprints came naturally to Suzanne, but she lost track of the NOT AN ENTRANCE they'd come in through in the dizzy maze of corridors and stairways to nowhere.

They stopped at a door painted dingy flamingo pink. A paper plate stuck to it with duct tape read, in a jagged hand, GIL AND THE KILLS. So this was "backstage"—as much a state of being as a physical space, where impatience, anxiety, and excitement prickled through the air like static electricity. The pink door opened into what appeared to be a walk-in closet for a traveling circus. Clothes and costumes and unlikely accoutrements hung from every hook and pipe and mirror. A table shoved against one wall was cluttered with takeout cartons, empty bottles, a tray of grapes going flaccid in the fug of body heat. Everything stank of sweat, cigarettes, and beer.

"I'm on my period again," announced a Black woman with enormous hair who was shaving her legs out of a popcorn bucket propped on a folding chair. "Why am I *always* on my period?"

"Better than the alternative!" barked the big bald bearded man doing chin-ups in the bathroom doorway. "Would you rather buy tampons or diapers?"

"I don't have a vagina," said a tall white guy with so much metal in his ears he could probably pick up a radio signal, "but I think once you reach the diaper stage you're back to buying tampons."

"Why don't you ask Dad?" the woman said, one heavily penciled eyebrow rising. "He'll clue you in."

"Look, he even brought the kids." This from the farthest corner of the room, where Skelly sprawled across a leatherette love seat with a lipstick-red Flying V cradled in his crotch. He wore a chambray shirt with both sleeves and most of the buttons torn off, the rungs of his rib cage making shadowed tiger stripes beneath. Thin as he was, cords of muscle moved up and down his arms as he bent and plucked and teased the strings. He strummed for a moment, then flipped the guitar over and played the other way. Suzanne stared, transfixed by the black bones inked on the backs of his hands. Like a dead man dancing the fretboard. She inched toward him without meaning to. The guitar wasn't plugged in, and she couldn't hear the music over the other voices in the room.

"Speak of the devil," said Gil. "Daddy's home."

"Your dinner got cold an hour ago!" The woman jumped up with one leg shaved, the other still slathered with Dial from the squeeze bottle hogging the vanity mirror. Only three bulbs worked anyway. "You get lost or what?"

"Hold up. No one tells me anything." The guy doing chin-ups dropped down from the doorframe, both hands raised like it was, in fact, a holdup. His palms were pink, with hard pale calluses. He must be the drummer, Suzanne decided. He looked about Gil's age, maybe older, with a jaw like a cinder block and threads of gray creeping into his beard. He nodded toward Gil's knees. "Who's this?"

"Who do you think?" Catching sight of Suzanne, the woman raised the other eyebrow. It seemed to be a talent, besides her official business as bass and backup vocals. She looked like Wonder Woman, if she'd been styled by Siouxsie Sioux. Wasp waist cinched into a slinky black bodysuit. Long, muscular legs under the film of suds. "Shit, Gil, Gracie said there was a family resemblance, but she's, like, a Xerox of you."

"It's creeping me out if I'm truthful," said the tall man who did not have a vagina. He didn't seem to be wearing a costume, so maybe he was a roadie.

"Later I'll explain how babies are made," Gil told him, and glanced down at Suzanne. "Seems you need no introduction, but go ahead, introduce yourself."

"I'm Suze . . ." Her voice died in her mouth as she looked around the room, shrinking under their undivided attention. "And you must be THE KILLS," she squeaked. They stared for a moment, then all started laughing at once. She didn't know why what she'd said was wrong, but the hot shock of embarrassment made her want to disappear behind Gil again.

"Must we, though?" said Skelly, the only person not to laugh, still turning the pegs and bending the strings. He'd already fired three guitar techs and driven two to quit, unable to rise to his standards or endure his blistering derision. They'd given up on hiring another one.

The bass player reached for the razor again. "Isn't it a little early in the evening for you to be this bitchy?"

"Hey," said the drummer. "Watch your mouth in front of present company."

"Delgado Junior?" Skelly said. "Surely she's heard worse."

"Sure, she can hear *you*." Wonder Woman smiled. "I'm Ruby, that's my lunk of a husband." She nodded toward the man with the big biceps and callused hands.

"Nash," he said. "We're the rhythm section." He clapped the tall guy on the shoulder and said, "Carney's merch and road crew."

"And Bad Attitude back there—he's the Hands." Ruby wiggled her fingers, nails lacquered black with bright yellow tips, like a French manicure done by a bumblebee.

The Hands looked up slowly, but the Hands kept strumming. "We've met."

Suzanne jumped when the door burst open, and there was Doug Sandusky, sweating and gasping and red to the roots of his hair. "Gil. About time." He crashed right into Suzanne and looked down to see what he'd tripped over. "Pint Size!" He seemed surprised to see her. "You're here."

"I'm here!" Suzanne said, beginning to believe it, something warm and golden swelling in her chest. All of them crushed together in the sweaty, scummy room.

"What's the weather report?" Carney said, nervously clicking the carabiner on his key ring. He had so many keys and hooks and tools hanging from his belt, she wondered how his pants stayed up. "Sounds like the opener's getting eaten alive."

Nobody answered, but the muffled noise from the ballroom made the crookedly incongruous chandelier shiver in its bracket. Goose bumps erupted up and down Suzanne's arms, though the room was still stifling. However many feet of concrete and noise-dampening egg crate were between them and the crowd, it didn't drown them out. All their voices swelled together in one voracious beastly roar.

"Thank you, Doomsayer," Ruby said to Carney, hands pressed together like a Buddhist monk. "Now get out and take Doug with you. Shoo."

Doug and Carney backed into the hall, and with them went the scattered funhouse energy that had ricocheted around the room before. "Fall in," Gil said, and the Kills closed in around him. Even Skelly stood up and joined the formation, one thumb hooked through his belt loop, the other bony elbow bent to rest on Ruby's shoulder. Suzanne disappeared into their peripheral vision with everything else outside the huddle.

"Don't let Carney spook you," Gil said, looking around the circle. Each of the Kills locked eyes with him, bodies turning and tightening, mirroring his every move—like a flock of birds or a pack of wolves. "They're only eating up the opener because they're hungry. And we *want* them hungry. We want them hungry for blood. Because we're about to do some righteous sonic violence, the likes of which they've never heard."

Nash bared his teeth and growled. Gil grabbed his head in both hands, foreheads smashed together. "WHAT ARE WE HERE TO DO?"

"VIOLENCE," Nash snarled.

Gil thumped him on the chest and turned to Ruby. There was a snap of skin on skin as they grasped hands. "WHAT ARE WE HERE TO DO?"

"RIOT!" she yowled, and Gil joined in, howling up at the chandelier until the crystals trembled. Nash pounded one fist into the opposite palm, big paw wrapped around his drumsticks.

Gil turned to Skelly. "What are we here to do?"

"Kill," Skelly said quietly. Suzanne leaned in, too, drawn like a moth to whatever it was, bright and smoldering between them.

Gil shoved him, hit his chest with both hands. "*What* are we here to do?"

"*Kill,*" Skelly said again, Ruby and Nash vibrating on either side of him. Or maybe that was the audience, thundering up through the floor.

Gil shoved Skelly harder. *"What are we here to do?"*

This time the Hands hit back, and he hit like a boxer, knucklebones landing two short, sharp blows to the meat of Gil's shoulders. *"KILL."*

Gil spun on his heel, hollered at all of them, *"WHAT ARE WE HERE TO DO?"*

"KILL!"

"WHAT THE FUCK ARE WE HERE TO DO?"

"KILL!"

He grabbed the strap of Skelly's guitar and yanked him so close their teeth or their cheekbones cracked together—Suzanne heard it from where she stood by the door. "Full tilt," Gil said. "To the motherfucking hilt." He looked up, grinned at the trembling crystals, stomped one foot, and screamed, "WHAT ARE WE HERE TO DO?"

They answered all together, in a wild, tumultuous shear that rang in Suzanne's ears for the next twenty-nine years.

KILL

KILL

KILL

KILL

KILL

PART 2

DON'T STOP THE ROT

Snapshot: Raleigh, 1995

Suzanne was not normally a nervous driver. The front seat felt more like her natural habitat than anywhere else, though she'd never had a car of her own. Even at seventeen she didn't need one, because her friend Melissa had a Volvo. Nobody called her Melissa and nobody called it a Volvo. Teachers called her Fessler and everybody else called her Big Fuss. The Volvo had once been a red 240, but after ten years oxidizing in the Great Dismal Swamp, before the Fesslers moved up in the world and down to the Research Triangle, it had faded to a fleshy pink and a vandal with a sense of humor had altered all the decals to say VULVA.

Suzanne glanced at the clock on the dash, which lit up only sporadically if the AC was running at the same time. It was already September but still hotter than hell and just as humid. She sweated in her shorts, watching the numbers stutter toward three o'clock. They were three hours from home, and Nathan and Nora would both be up by six thirty. They often went to bed before her "curfew" at midnight, which made it more or less optional, but if she and Fuss wanted to go to shows—and they wanted nothing more, wanted it like a drug they just couldn't quit—they had to be home by sunrise. So they climbed into the Vulva and drove hell for leather all the way to Washington and back just to see Fugazi.

Fuss had so mastered the fine art of rolling a joint in the crevice of the liner notes that she could do it at 85 miles an hour in the dim glow of the visor light. Like the pages of an old *Playboy*, her favorite CD booklets stuck stubbornly together. Though Suzanne had never enjoyed the woozy feeling of inebriation, she was, thanks to Fuss's finesse at blowing smoke into her mouth, learning to like marijuana. But they'd been kissing in cars and scummy underground clubs for nearly a year now, no longer needed the shotgunning charade.

That wasn't why Suzanne was nervous. Curfew had something to do with it, but that wasn't all. The car wandered across the centerline as she groped across the dashboard. She couldn't find the right button and kept hitting pause, play, pause, play, so Dead Moon stuttered and hiccupped through "Room 213."

"Christ, make up your mind," Fuss demanded, bracing herself against the glove box.

"Sorry," Suzanne said. "Don't like that song." Untrue, but there was no easy way to explain her tortured relationship to it—the neurotic, compulsive way she had played it until it was etched in her subconscious acetate, for reasons she preferred not to think about. *Something strange is going down in Room 213* . . . Through no fault of their own, some songs were psychically contaminated and couldn't be cured.

"Pick a song, pick a station, I really don't care so long as you stay there." Fuss smacked her hand away from the radio dial. Reflection steamed on the passenger window, freckles melting off her cheeks, tongue pinched between her teeth as she dabbed crumbs of kush off *Car Wheels on a Gravel Road*. They listened to everything, argued about all of it, made each other mixtapes on a weekly basis.

"—three thirty on Thursday night or Friday morning, depending how you think about it, and Doctor Crosstalk is in to help all you nocturnal creatures out. Need a shot of rhythm or a dose of the blues? This pharmacy is open twenty-four hours, but I'm only here 'til six and then it's early birds and worms for breakfast."

Suzanne's knuckles went white on the steering wheel.

"Doctor Crosstalk?" Fuss said with a smirk. "What the fuck?"

Suzanne had heard it before. The sort of amorphous vaudeville that could only air in the dead hours when the graveyard shift tuned in. Gil was a gifted impressionist, but she knew it was him, even though they hadn't spoken, hadn't seen each other, for five years. Doctor Crosstalk always knew what a listener needed to hear, but Suzanne wanted to stuff her fingers in her ears. Instead she watched the clock, watched the speedometer. Always trying to outrun something that was always catching up.

"We used to be best friends but now she never wants to hang out unless she can bring him along," the caller was explaining, voice thick from what was probably not her first crying jag.

"Booooo," said Fuss, blowing smoke across the console at Suzanne. She tried to blink it out of her eyes, tried to hold on to the wobbling white lines. But she didn't slow down, didn't take her foot off the gas. Pedal sinking without her permission, speedometer inching toward 90.

"How could she do a bad thing like that to a sweet thing like you?" Crosstalk crooned. Like he'd never done a thing bad as that. Like he hadn't spent the last five years fighting to keep himself out of jail, keep his name out of the news. "Well, pretty baby, listen to this twice daily for two weeks, and you'll get your groove back. Like me, it's an oldie but a goodie, from X's fourth LP, out in 1983: 'Poor Girl.'"

"He's good, actually," Fuss decided. "This guy."

Suzanne squinted through the haze into the stream of oncoming headlights and said, "Yeah." But there he was, rapping to nobody but the nighthawks and hiding behind that ridiculous cryptonym. And whose fault was that? Whatever the headlines said, he wasn't a bad man. Every terrible thing that happened happened because of Suzanne. Nobody knew, nobody but him and nobody but her, and the guilt ate away at her heart like acid until there was nothing left but a hole. X clattered and caterwauled, tore up the airwaves.

Fuss exhaled a fug of smoke and sang to Suzanne, to her poor little girl, *I try to explain why she won't say a thing, why she won't talk at all?* With the joint in her mouth and her hair in her face, she almost looked like Skelly. She reached for Suzanne's hand, but her palms were slick with sweat and the wheel slipped out of her grip. The car swerved left, she heard Fuss scream, and the guardrail slammed into the driver's side.

Nobody was hurt except Suzanne, unless you included the Vulva, which was unequivocally totaled. Suzanne felt the same, bruised and battered by the seat belt, the airbags, the bent driver's door crushing her inside the car. When Nathan arrived at the ER, she had two cracked ribs, a broken collarbone, and a bottle of Percodan she didn't think she would need—her body so numbed out on shock she hadn't yet felt a thing. Besides, she'd seen what painkillers did to people. She'd rather have pain.

"I'm fine" was all she said to Nathan, whose eyes widened at the sight of her and immediately welled up. He was getting sentimental lately, maybe because of the baby. As if Nora's raging hormones were contagious. Because she still couldn't be more than fifty feet from a bathroom in case nausea overcame her suddenly, she'd stayed home.

Outside the hospital, the sun had risen on a horrible, humid morning. Suzanne climbed into the minivan that had replaced Nathan's zippy little Mazda when the pregnancy test came back positive. Suzanne found it sinfully ugly, a great gray whale of a car with all its edges filed off. The interior still reeked of cheap air freshener and new leatherette that suctioned to her thighs the instant she sat and surrendered herself to her fate—like Jonah or Pinocchio, swallowed up by something so enormous and indifferent that there was no point fighting back.

Nathan started the car without comment. He drove with both hands on the wheel, both eyes on the road. "I think it goes without saying you're grounded," he finally said.

"Why say it, then?" She picked at a loose thread on the seam of the seat.

He told Suzanne, too often, that he considered her a daughter. He had adopted her four years ago, effectively erasing Gil from her life. But she was not a baby, not his blood, already molded and misshapen by someone else's influence. His fathering could only go so far.

"This is . . . different," he said, at a loss for a better word. How did you make a fender bender sound serious to a kid who'd seen more felonies than the district attorney before she was twelve? "You have to start thinking about your future instead of throwing it away."

"I hit a guardrail," Suzanne said. "That's what they're there for. Nobody got hurt."

"What about *you?*" Nathan exclaimed. "You have broken bones, Suzanne! And maybe it was just a guardrail, but it might not have been."

He had her there. She wasn't sure what he wanted her to say, so she didn't say anything.

"Your mother is beside herself," he said. The only thing he and Gil had in common was the way they called her that, Nora and Suzanne defined in their minds by their relationship to one another. *Your daughter, your mother.* As if men were innocent bystanders in the child-rearing process. She hoped he wouldn't talk to her half-baked half sibling that way.

"When is she not?"

"Now, that's not fair. How is she supposed to feel? You snuck out and drove three hundred miles and crashed Melissa's car trying to get home by morning. If something really bad had happened, we wouldn't even know where to look for you."

"It's not like she would have let me go if I had asked."

"Because life is not a never-ending concert tour. You don't get to go to every show you want to."

"Tell me something I don't fucking know."

Nathan sighed, frustration finally beginning to show. He wore dorky athletic sunglasses that made him look like a wannabe race car driver, but removed them for a moment to pinch the head off a migraine brewing behind the bridge of his nose. "Okay," he said, "maybe you can help me understand."

"Understand what?"

"Why it was worth risking all this, just to go see this band."

Suzanne's turn to well up. Lip trembling because that was the question Nora had never asked, the answer that never mattered. The way Nora saw it, music was the reason for all their misery, everything that

was wrong with Suzanne and society—a worldview that made her surprisingly popular with the Satanic Panic set at Suzanne's middle school
in Connecticut, where she was forbidden from ever speaking of her
father. They moved every few years to some blank place on the map for
Nathan's firm to develop, so nobody knew he wasn't Nora's first husband, Suzanne left over from a previous marriage. Nathan tried to be
the father she'd never had, indulged her obsession to the extent Nora
would allow, buying her CDs and music lessons, books and magazines,
a boombox for her bedroom. New posters to plaster on the walls every
time they moved to a new house in a new town and Suzanne lost whatever friends she'd managed to make. By sixteen she'd mostly stopped
trying.

"Music is the only thing I care about," she said, even sadder to say it
than he was to hear it. Because Nora was right, it had ruined her life,
and it didn't even love her back—the way it loved Gil, the way it loved
Skelly, the way it loved Nash and Ruby.

Nathan had no answer for that, so they drove the last two hours with
nothing to soften the distance between them but the hum of the engine
and the sizzle of Indian summer sunlight trying to fry them through
the windshield. Suzanne's broken bones finally started to ache, then
to throb, and by the time they turned into the neighborhood, her eyes
were streaming and she'd choked down two Percodan dry. She hadn't
eaten or slept for thirty-six hours, and the pills hit her empty head and
empty stomach hard. The world warped around the edges, and when
they pulled into the driveway, she thought she was seeing things.

There were hubcap-sized holes in the ugly rug of Bermuda grass
they called a lawn. The sun flashed off the dark spots in prismatic bands
of color—like puddles of gasoline making oily rainbows on the asphalt.
The door yawned open, Nora standing there in the quilted bathrobe
she'd taken to wearing since giving up the famous *Jaws* tank. Suzanne
stumbled climbing out of the passenger seat, numb and dumb from the
Percodan, half-blind from staring at the sunspots on the lawn.

"Oh, Nora . . ."

Nathan's voice gathered the world back into focus. Not sunspots.

No oil spill. Just records. All Suzanne's records. Every sliver of black wax she had collected, lovingly wiped clean and dried in the dish rack like the wedding china, fitted on the spindle with the outer edges pressed into her fingerprints. Every little world that had pulled her along in its orbit at 33⅓ revolutions until her own world and whatever in it troubled her was left behind. All ripped out of their sleeves and left to warp in the late summer heat. The needle snagged, dragged across the grooves until it got stuck in a loop. Suzanne's tapes unspooled on the carpet in Baltimore. Her crayons melting across the concrete in the blistered nowhere of Nevada. Her records going soft in a bed of hard, prickly scutch grass. It was a little overwhelming to feel so hated by the sun.

Suzanne swayed and fell sideways. She landed hard on her sling arm but, like the first few hours, didn't feel it. To her left, an original pressing of *You Really Got Me* that was one of her first big scores. Touching the toe of her sneaker, the infamous Hot Mix of *Led Zeppelin II* she'd hunted for for years. 13th Floor Elevators. *Dusty in Memphis*, Prince and the Revolution. The Clash and the Cramps and the Runaways. *Licensed to Ill* had cracked in half on impact, which didn't seem like an accident. Nora hated all of Suzanne's music but harbored a special loathing for the Beastie Boys. Maybe it was Suzanne's habit of blasting "Fight for Your Right" every time Nora tried to put her foot down about something.

But Nora had finally won. The sun beat down on Suzanne's head, searing the skin exposed by the part of her hair. She let it burn her. It felt deserved. The pain in her side, in her chest, that felt deserved, too. Her tapes, her crayons, her records. A new clip entered the rotation. The crash, or what she recalled of it, the car veering toward the guardrail. She willed it now to go another way, to go a little faster and swerve a little harder so she never had to be right here, on the lawn, with all her ruined records.

Maybe Percodan worked on that kind of pain. She took the top off and started swallowing pills, one at a time. She lost count after five but before Nathan realized what she was doing and charged across the drive to snatch the bottle out of her hands. He tried to haul her to her feet, but Suzanne was dead weight. When he realized he'd grabbed her bad shoulder, he abruptly let go, lost his balance, and fell on the grass beside her. He started to cry, in full view of the neighbors, and she wondered dimly whether he had changed his mind about wanting to be a father.

A suffocating silence descended over the house. Nathan was never home before seven, and Nora wouldn't speak to Suzanne. Though she wasn't expressly forbidden from using the phone, nobody called. Fuss would probably never talk to her again. Without her records, her CDs and her tapes, her Discman and even the old clock radio—all confiscated or destroyed, totaled like the Volvo—the bedroom that had once been her sanctuary felt more like a padded cell.

The Percodan helped. She'd called in a refill, pretending to be her mother. It worked best on an empty stomach, something she already knew and took advantage of each morning. Or washed down with a slug of scotch from the crystal decanter in Nathan's office after he and Nora went to bed. Something else she already knew. Like sucking smoke from Fuss's lips, she learned to like how hard and how softly it hit her— knocked off her feet by a huge feather pillow. She pulled oxycodone over her head and slid into a twilight zone between the waking world and a dark, dreamless limbo.

It might have gone on like that until Suzanne ran out of refills, an inflection point she preferred not to think about. The only downside was that it made school days feel much longer. By the time she walked home each afternoon—preferring the hour of solitude to the twenty-minute bus ride surrounded by her idiot classmates—she was dead on her feet and fell back into bed as quickly as possible, sometimes with her shoes on still. But one otherwise insignificant Wednesday, she came home to the sound of water running upstairs.

Sound was magnified now in the absence of music, her brain in aural withdrawal latching on to anything that could be misconstrued as rhythm or melody—the hum of the dishwasher, the rattle of the garage door, the neighbors' dog barking at the mailman as he traipsed across the lawn. The kitchen was empty; no sign of Nora except a glass of water that had been knocked over on the table and not mopped up. Unlike her, with her newfound fixations on trivets and drink rings and other things that hadn't entered her vocabulary before 1990. Suzanne left it where it was and climbed the stairs with heavy feet, camera bag swinging against her hip. There wasn't much worth documenting in walking distance, but it was better than nothing. She had a whole series now of the peculiar pinwheel shadows cast by her ceiling fan when she moved her bedroom lamps around.

Upstairs, the water was louder, the hiss of the bathroom sink embellished by an occasional splash. And another wet sound she didn't hear at all until she paused on the landing. Crying. Gagging. Maybe the morning sickness back for an encore. She knocked on the bedroom door. "Nora?" When she got no answer but the heaving continued, she broke the weeks-long silence a second time. "You need some ginger ale or something?" She knocked again, still got no answer. Decided she couldn't be in any more trouble than she already was and pushed the door open.

The room was dark, the blinds drawn, the sheets torn off the bed. The only light filtered in from the bathroom, where the waterworks echoed weirdly off the tile. "Do you want me to call Nath—" Suzanne froze in the doorway. The sink was running, overflowing, spilling pinkish water over the edge of the counter and onto the bath mat. A bloody washcloth blocked the drain, filling the basin with blooming red clouds like algae. Nora had clambered into the tub, leaving a crimson handprint on the porcelain. Suzanne couldn't remember the last time she'd seen her mother naked, probably not since Baltimore, when they lived so much closer together, shared a bathroom and everything else of necessity. Her body looked wrong—breasts striped with stretch marks, belly distended, navel puckered like the knot of a birthday balloon. She held a towel between her legs with one hand, trying to contain the spreading stain.

"Jesus—Mom!" Suzanne threw her camera bag on the floor. Nora groped at the drain, reaching senselessly for something that had already slipped away. "Mom—oh, fuck!" Suzanne tried to pull her halfway up and blood ran down her legs. Nora lunged away, scrabbling at the drain with her broken fingernails. "Mom, stop! If you want to help the baby we have to get to a doctor, okay?" Suzanne lied without caring, hoping Nora would believe it long enough to get up. "Come on!" Her body moved on instinct, the Percodan haze washed away in a flood of adrenaline. Head swimming at the smell of blood. She manhandled Nora out of the bathtub, pulled one arm around her shoulders. "Where's your purse, your purse is in the car?" An ambulance would get them there, but Suzanne could get there sooner—of that much she was certain. "Not too fast, it's not so far." They struggled down the stairs like contestants in some sort of fucked-up three-legged race. Blood on the walls, on the carpet, on their clothes, on everything everywhere every time she blinked. Nora lolled on her shoulder like a drunk until Suzanne bundled her into the passenger seat, towel tucked under her. Suzanne shrugged out of her flannel, wrapped it around Nora like a robe, then threw herself behind the wheel, started the engine, and peeled out of the garage so fast the door scraped the roof of the van. "Hold on."

She drove 90 all the way with no seat belt on. At the ER, she left the engine running and rushed inside without trying to lift Nora again. Maybe because her jeans and her tank top and even her sneakers were spattered with blood, nobody hesitated when she shouted that she needed a wheelchair and bolted back outside. Nora was shivering, forehead slick and clammy. Suzanne tried not to breathe it in, that sour iron smell. Fumbling through Nora's purse, looking for her health insurance cards, fielding questions from the orderlies. "Yes—I don't know—twenty, um, twenty-one weeks—no, I'm her daughter, other daughter—he's at work—" They wheeled Nora away without stopping, and the doors swung shut in Suzanne's face.

She approached the receptionist with questions already in her mouth, but the woman pointed with her pen to the long line of people waiting their turn, glaring at Suzanne like she'd just cut them off in traffic. "Honey? Have a seat. She's in good hands."

Suzanne walked on rubber legs to the nearest chair and sat. A valet had taken the minivan, she didn't know where. Unable to remember what he said when she gave him the keys, unable to remember anything but the blood seeping into the seams of the passenger seat. She bit her tongue, tried to breathe through her nose, tried to think about anything other than blood, but it was everywhere—on her shirt, on her shoes, on her hands. She looked down at her quivering fingers, but they didn't look like her own. Her eyes went dark, and she thought she saw black finger bones. An echo shrieked in her ear, *SOMEBODY HELP ME*—

Suzanne snapped at the waist and threw up on the floor. Orderlies descended again. They hustled her out of the waiting room, through the doors where Nora had disappeared, and into a handicapped bathroom with a set of scrubs to change into. She washed the stains from her hands and her face, rubbed until her skin was raw. When she emerged, a nurse with a very firm grip steered her back down the hall and asked, "Is there someone you can call?"

Nathan had been called already, but Suzanne nodded anyway. "Is there somewhere I can get some coffee?" It might not be good for her stomach, but it might settle her nerves.

"There's a vending machine by the phones."

Suzanne shuffled down the corridor to another waiting room where there were two phones and three vending machines—one for coffee, one for soft drinks, and one packed with uncanny, off-brand snacks. Choc-Os instead of Oreos. Fruity Chews instead of Starbursts. She dug around in Nora's purse until she found some loose change.

The coffee looked and tasted like tar. She threw it back in one gulp and reached for the handset. Was she supposed to be calling someone for Nora or calling someone for herself? The nurse hadn't specified who she should call, just "someone." Suzanne crumpled her cup in the trash and hunted around for Nora's address book. She flipped through the pages until she found the number she didn't know for sure would be there, didn't know she was looking for until she found it.

She dialed with numb, clumsy fingers. Heart lodged in her throat
like a pill swallowed wrong. The phone rang and rang and then, with a
click, someone picked up.

"Hello?"

It wasn't Gil. It was Gracie.

"Hello?"

Suzanne stared at her shoes, transfixed by the blood going brown
on her sneakers, held hostage by the recollection of the last time she
saw Gracie—at an all-night diner in Nevada, dipping her thumb in a
muddle of ketchup and smearing it down the front of her shirt.

"Hello?" Gracie said again. And then, "*¿A quién intenta llamar?*"

Suzanne hung up abruptly. She hadn't spoken to Gracie or Gil for
five years. Wasn't even sure she was allowed to—Nora never explained
what the terms of custody were, bristled and snapped on the few occasions Suzanne had brought it up. But why should anyone have custody
of her? Gil had been ruled unfit to parent, and if Suzanne's continuing
delinquency was any indication, Nathan and Nora weren't faring much
better. She'd be eighteen before long. She had a camera. She could
make change. She could make ends meet until she made something
of herself. Everything she cared about was gone or left to warp on the
sunstruck lawn, so why the hell was she still *here*?

She grabbed Nora's purse, on the hunt for her wallet again. She
couldn't go to Gil. She didn't know what flouting the custody ruling
might mean, but the guilt would kill her if she ruined his life all over
again—whatever was left of it. She called the operator, then the bus
station. She took the two twenties she found and was about to throw the
wallet back in the bag when she felt something else, stiffer and glossier
than the soft cotton texture of dollar bills after a few decades in circu-
lation. She slipped it out, surprised to find an old photo taken by the
same Instamatic that first captured Gil and Blondie: *Just Married.* This
one may as well have said *Just Born.* Suzanne had never seen it, but Gil
must have taken it—Nora, not much older than Suzanne was now, wearing a hospital gown and holding a wrinkled pink raisin with a shock of
brown hair already escaping its swaddling. Nora gazed at it with the

stupefied wonder you saw on every new mother's face. Suzanne felt hot, prickling panic creep across her chest. Groping back through the years for a moment she could remember Nora looking at her like that. She turned the photo over and stuffed her fingers in her mouth to muffle the sobs that had seized her as suddenly as her wave of nausea in the waiting room. Because there was Gil's handwriting in sticky black ball-point. *Suzanne*, it said, the letters printed so carefully, like he was trying them out for the first time. *Born July 23, 1978. (Good lungs, she's mine.)*

It was the only other thing she took with her. She left Nora's purse with a nurse, spent a quarter of her forty dollars on a taxi to the bus station, then did just what Doug had done five years ago and got on the first Greyhound to New York.

THE PASSENGER

The Lifeboat didn't get very far very fast. An old Cornershop tape
Suzanne hadn't played since high school turned somersaults through
the sweet summer air. They sat on the trailer's back bumper, sipping
a bottle of tamarind Jarritos. Phoebe passed it to Suzanne, who felt a
little guilty for doing less than her fair share of the driving. Blondie
was doing well, but hauling the Lifeboat had a learning curve. "No big
deal," Simon said when Phoebe pulled over at a rest stop to pass the
baton. "It's not that far."

Cars and trucks blew past on the narrow highway. The road looped
and twisted through the foothills of the Appalachian Mountains, where
wildflowers grew in enormous drifts along the median and kudzu swallowed telephone poles whole. The dense, vivid green of midsummer
weltered on every side. The trees were never still, never static, every
trunk a tuning fork, every leaf and branch atremble. A rare breeze
rippled across the valley and into the distance in the same iridescent eddies Suzanne remembered from her few psychedelic adventures, what
seemed like a lifetime ago.

"Where are we now?" Phoebe asked. Suzanne had the old atlas
open in her lap, tracing their trajectory with half an orange crayon
she'd found bouncing around with two dozen others in a *Jetsons* lunch
box. The label described it as not merely "orange," but "Macaroni and

Cheese." It fit in her hand like a missing piece, though she couldn't remember the last time she'd held one.

"Nearest place I've heard of is Chattanooga." Who could forget a name like that? It sounded like a passing train. They were on their way to Simon's aunt, who could—he hoped—help them rustle up some wheels of their own.

Phoebe slugged the soda, licked her lips. Suzanne could see the gears turning. Phoebe's mind was amazingly mechanical, made of interlocking cogs and wheels. Maybe that was why Simon understood her when nobody else did. *Gearhead*, they called each other, the way other people said *honey* or *sweetheart*. "Good," she said. "We're close."

Suzanne let her head hang back, sunglasses sliding up toward her forehead. They gave the whole world the warm amber fade of an old photograph.

Simon emerged from the little outbuilding with an armload of rations from the vending machines. The proverbial cupboards were bare of real food, but snacks would sustain them to their next destination. "Sweet, salty, or spicy?" he asked, his turn to play snack sommelier.

"Spicy," Phoebe said, already reaching for the packet of Hot Fries.

"Sweet," said Suzanne, taking the Skittles. An old favorite with a sharp mnemonic aftertaste. She liked to crush them between her thumb and index finger, making flat crackled starbursts when the candy shell split. Simon, always happy to eat whatever was left over, tore into a sleeve of those orange cheese and peanut butter crackers ubiquitous on grade-school field trips. A weird combination that shouldn't have worked, but somehow did. Junk food was like that.

Suzanne squished a flattened purple Skittle flatter between her back molars, elated to eat candy unselfconsciously, something she hadn't done since she moved in with Rob and her eating habits were suddenly witnessed by someone whose idea of indulgence was putting half a smear of mayo on a sandwich. Since her body had rounded and softened and everything she ate seemed to accumulate around her hips. But she'd lost her appetite and a lot of weight the last few years—the last eight months especially. A stranger in her own shrinking body. That might have been why she found the little stirrings of arousal so alarming. She'd come to dread being touched, submitted to it out of spousal obligation, and accepted the loss of her lust for anything as a necessary casualty of marriage. But the drop of sweat snaking down Phoebe's neck as she sipped her soda, the red bandana in Simon's back pocket that drew her eye like a matador's flag, the juicy burst of sugar on her tongue, woke something up in her. The whole world felt more vivid, more vibrant. A truck barreled by, emblazoned with the Bimbo bear's lobotomized smile. Next time she was in a grocery store, she'd buy a loaf of spongy white bread, smear it thick with peanut butter and strawberry jam, with a handful of greasy, golden potato chips crushed in between. Somewhere along the line her comfort foods had become guilty pleasures, and she wanted to turn the clock back to a time before guilt took her like a chronic illness. She ate five Skittles at once, helped herself to Phoebe's Jarritos.

Simon stretched, rolling his neck. "How far are we?"

Phoebe slurped, burped. "An hour, maybe two."

"Groovy," he said. "Let's move."

They exited the highway onto a narrow country road, which they followed for ten or twelve rattling miles before turning down a dirt lane, unmarked except for a sign nailed to a fence post, which read BEWARE OF DOG. Suzanne didn't see any dogs—just open fields where nothing much seemed to be growing and a distant black backdrop of pines.

"Just a little farther," Phoebe said. The daylight was dying, blue leaking out of the sky until it left a wash of ivory clouds behind. Not quite sunset yet. Humpbacked hillocks rose from the fields like burial mounds, but there was something craggy and irregular about them, sharp edges cutting through the overgrowth. Suzanne caught flashes of metal, patches of rust, the spokes of an enormous wheel casting shadows on the ground like a sundial turned sideways. What she had mistaken for mounds of earth were the oxidizing skeletons of a dozen broken-down tractors, sinking into the landscape like dinosaur bones. There were a couple of cars, too—she recognized the ocular headlights of an Oldsmobile old enough to remember Eisenhower. Weeds and lichen and a few bulbous mushrooms sprouting from the rotting up-holstery. The dirt road cut through the bizarre mechanical graveyard, which seemed entirely deserted, until a burst of movement made Su-zanne start in her seat.

"Did you see that?"

She thought it was the dog they were meant to beware of, but on second glance it was a little brown bearded goat, who had hopped up onto the hood of the sagging Oldsmobile. It paused in its perpetual chewing to watch the trailer pass before another one, calico, jumped up behind and headbutted him so hard he tumbled head over hoof into the grass. The calico goat stuck out its tongue in a triumphant, nasal bleat. A moment later there was a third, then a fourth, knocking each other around like a barnyard roller derby.

"You ain't seen nothing yet," Phoebe warned. The goats gamboled over the crumbling hulls of the tractors and trucks and cars but kept off the road. Around the next bend were a peeling red barn and a white farmhouse, lying low in the shade of two walnut trees. Suzanne won-dered who might be on the lookout besides the goats, who put their war games on hold when Simon killed the engine.

He stepped out first and Phoebe and Suzanne followed. A dog barked, if you could call it that—three booming notes in a throaty bari-tone. Another dog answered, with a volley of yaps that sounded more like laughter.

"Hello?" Simon called. "Arlette?"

"Look alive, motherfucker."

"Simon!"

Suzanne saw the gun just before the shot went off—more of a snap than a bang. He staggered back but didn't fall, and she ran like a fool right into the line of fire. That doggish laughter still rang through the rusting junkyard, but now a woman's voice joined in. Suzanne skidded in the dirt three feet from Simon when she saw the stain on his chest wasn't red but blue, He stared at the slick stuff on his fingers until one of the dogs bounded into view.

"SIMON!" she yelled again, again too late. The dog hit him with all four paws and knocked him flat on the ground.

"It's okay," he said. "I'm okay. Trouble. Trouble, get *off*." Simon threw the dog off and it circled them slowly, red tongue dangling between pointed pearl-white teeth. Suzanne had never seen a dog quite like it—with large, vulpine ears and a dense, coarse coat the color of bone. It prowled around in a low-down crouch, hackles raised, looking not quite tame.

"Can't blame her," said the woman. Big-boned, heavyset, with a graying mane of copper curls and eyes too far apart. She held an ugly black pump gun, leaning on the porch rail with one hip. "Never quite forgave you for leaving her behind."

The dog limped slightly, favoring its left foreleg.

"For your own good," Simon said, holding out one hand. The dog circled closer, nipped his fingers, then flicked her tongue across his wrist. "What about you?" He squinted up at the porch.

"Hell, I might not forgive you for coming back," Arlette said, but she was smiling—a lopsided grin with a termite hole where one canine should have been. "You always could smell dinner hitting the table from a hundred miles away." She lifted her chin, nodded past him at Phoebe. "How you doin', sugar?"

"Same as always, bitter and sweet."

"And what about you?" Arlette eyed Suzanne. "Don't think we've had the pleasure."

"Suzanne," she said.

"Well, you better come in before it gets cold." She left the gun leaning on the porch rail, left the front door open behind her.

Every corner of the house was crammed with stuff—kerosene lanterns and tentpoles and fruit crates full of rusting nails and loose door hinges. A wood-burning stove squatted like a troll in one corner of the kitchen, while coats and saddle blankets hung from horseshoe hooks driven into the walls at random. No fire in the fireplace, but a couple of casks of white lightning. Arlette clomped around in work boots, overalls, and a tatty shearling housecoat. Simon followed her into the kitchen, and before long they were working elbow to elbow, tipping potatoes out of a cast-iron skillet, turning blistered venison sausages over the fire burning in the belly of the stove. Trouble followed them in, wolfing scraps from Arlette's fingers and keeping one watchful eye on Suzanne.

She wandered into the living room, drawn by the unframed photographs tacked along the mantel. Most were of animals—a couple of horses, a miniature donkey knee-deep in snow with a scarf around its hairy neck. One of a little girl with strawberry ringlets who could have been a younger Arlette, another of a younger Simon asleep on the sofa with a bundle of fur that must have been a younger Trouble curled up on his chest.

When the food was ready, they sat at the table with mismatched flatware and paper napkins, jam jars to drink from, a pitcher of apricot brandy the color of rust. They poured gravy drippings over everything, mopped up what was left with thick slices of the spongy white bread Suzanne had just been daydreaming about that afternoon. She licked her fingers as Arlette explained her latest venture.

"Paintball," Phoebe said, smudging one thumb across the blue blotch on Simon's chest. "What gave you that idea?"

"Can't buy real guns with a record like mine," Arlette said. "But you wouldn't believe how many boys will pay good money to come play *Apocalypse Now*. Shooting at hay bales is one thing, but buy up a few old beaters and you've got yourself a bit of an obstacle course." Up close, she and Simon had the same eyes—that drooping, drowsing blue. She wiped up a smear of grease with a crust of bread and threw it under the table. Trouble snapped it out of the air before it touched the floor. The big brindle hound dog, Hank Williams, had sunk down with a geriatric groan and wasn't rising anytime soon, even for leftovers. Darkness had descended outside, pale, fluttering moths throwing themselves in vain against the windows.

"Tell me about that big yellow beauty," Arlette said, smacking her lips like she could eat Blondie for dessert. "That's a fine a set of wheels."

"Family heirloom," Suzanne said. Brandy sticky-sweet on her tongue and going straight to her head. "Broke down on me a few hours out of Miami, but Simon got her running again."

"Well, you're welcome," Arlette said. "I taught him everything he knows."

He blushed, chewed, shook his head. "You like to think so."

They ribbed each other all through dinner, trading stories from the past few months, everything that had happened since they last saw each other. When plates were licked clean and the brandy was half-drunk, Arlette disappeared into the kitchen and returned with a carton of vanilla ice cream and a jar of blackberry preserves to spoon over it. She and Phoebe got to talking shop, how many jars was she moving, out of whose general store? Suzanne carried the empty bowls to the kitchen, where Simon was up to his elbows in suds.

"Can I help?"

"Dry and stack, if you like."

For a while they worked in companionable silence, before she asked, "Arlette is your . . . ?"

"Dad's sister," he said. "Took me in for a while when I ran out on my folks. We lived in the Lifeboat about four years."

"I like her," Suzanne said. "She's colorful."

He tugged his shirt straight, raised his eyebrows. "That's one word for it."

"What's with the tattoo?" Arlette had a faded black smudge on the side of her neck that Suzanne at first mistook for soot.

"35:22–24. Book of Numbers. 'The congregation shall judge between the slayer and the blood avenger.' Something like that."

"She said she had a record." Suzanne glanced back over her shoulder. Arlette had produced a pipe from somewhere, and Phoebe was busy packing it with her favorite blend of sativa and loose-leaf to-bacco.

Simon dried his hands, folded his arms, leaned back against the counter. "Killed her husband with a kitchen knife. He was a world-class bastard. No question it was self-defense, but she did ten years anyway."

"Why?"

"Just endured it until her daughter started school so she wouldn't have to witness it," he said, and Suzanne almost dropped the jar she was drying. Chest tightening, like her lungs couldn't get enough air. "The police took that to be premeditated, since he'd been beating her half to death more or less once a week since the baby was born and she'd never defended herself like that before."

Suzanne knew she should say something, but too many memories had surged up in her at once. Long-smothered girlhood horrors and more nuanced grown-up nightmares. Everything she saw and shouldn't have, the more terrible uncertainty of what she didn't witness and could never quite be sure of. The brandy made her head swim. She poured what was left of it down the drain while Simon wasn't looking.

"What's really fucked," he went on, "is that Jennie doesn't speak to her now. Guess she forgot how Uncle Pete used to beat on her, too." A hard edge in his voice she'd never heard before. So slow to anger. Suzanne shifted beside him, thinking—again, as always—of Gil. How his voice hardened in rage and softened to soothe, how much they hadn't said to each other over the last twenty-nine years.

After dinner, Phoebe passed the pipe around the table. Fireflies appeared outside, like Christmas lights strung up six months too early. Phoebe called them lightning bugs, and when she did Simon said, "Your Mississippi is showing." The way she said it, it sounded like "light-ening bugs." They took the last of their brandy out into the yard, with Trouble close behind. Suzanne followed them to the edge of the field behind the farmhouse. The dry grass rustled and shimmered with dif-fuse phosphorescence.

"There." Simon pointed to the darker east, at something that was already gone.

"There." Phoebe pointed the other way.

That was the game, chasing the lights until there were far too many to catch, to count, and they surrendered in a fizz of dazzled laughter. There was a weird, kinesthetic music to the way the insects moved, blinking in and out of existence according to some inscrutable, macrocosmic music. Earthbound constellations, forever rearranging themselves. Suzanne watched in a pleasant, sparkling trance. Phoebe swayed side to side until she bumped one of them softly with her hip, then went the other way, rocking Newton's cradle. The breeze brushed Suzanne's hair off her forehead.

The other two must have tasted the same honeysuckle sweetness on the air. Phoebe blinked the fireflies out of her eyes and said, "I feel like a swim."

"I feel like I need to pee," Suzanne confessed.

"Meet us down by the pond?" Simon said, but with no sense of expectation—only invitation. *If you like.* When their paths forked apart, Suzanne watched their shadows melt into the pool of darkness under the heavy branches of the taller walnut tree.

She took two wrong turns on her slow stumble to the bathroom. Mirrors, she remembered, were best avoided when she was stoned stupid, but now confronting her reflection didn't frighten her, even though her hair was thick with grease, and the dust and grit of the road had made a home in every fold of her skin. She'd learned not to mind it, this far removed from beige Berber carpets and chenille upholstery, spot treatment only. She admired her rumpled reflection, preferring the version of herself who didn't care about fine lines or clean laundry or putting fucking coasters under everything. She wet her fingertips under the tap and ran them through her filthy hair, loosening the tangled roots.

It wasn't until the water ran cool that she realized how long she'd been in there. It took even longer to find her way out again, and not by the same door she'd come in through. Arlette was still up, leaning on one of the porch posts with Hank Williams at her feet, tapping her pipe into an old flowerpot. A spoon stuck out of a fresh jam jar set on the step beside her.

"Help yourself," she said. "Plenty to share." She held the jar out to Suzanne. The soft flesh of the fruit split beneath the spoon, and a burst of spice curled under her nose—cardamom, cloves, and anise. The plum went soft on her tongue, melted away in syrupy warmth.

"I could eat only this for the rest of my life and die satisfied," Suzanne decided.

"Take some for the road. It'll keep."

Phoebe's laugh drifted toward them from the dark of the yard, that fox-like yip that always meant mischief. Goose bumps prickled along Suzanne's forearms, her fingertips tingling again. "Where'd you learn to do this?" She passed the jar back, jam tacky on her lips.

"Do what?" Arlette spooned a plum into her mouth. A few fireflies had floated away from the orgy in the hayfield and blinked around her head like tiny satellites.

"Make jam. Fix trailers. Raise goats. Build a paintball course out of broken-down tractors."

"Drove a truck once, too," Arlette said. "Made furniture and license plates. Did some bookkeeping, strictly off the books."

"A real Renaissance woman."

Arlette waved her off like one of the lightning bugs. "Soon as I get good at something I get bored with it, that's all."

"I'm not good at anything," Suzanne said. Phoebe was a walking Swiss army knife. Simon could do more with eight fingers than most people could do with eight hands. And then there was Arlette, who had been beaten and battered and killed a man and came out of prison ten years later and learned to make jam.

Arlette stirred the spoon around, considered her reflection in the shallow bowl. "Simon ever tell you how he lost his fingers?"

Suzanne blinked, slow to realize. "No, he didn't." And she had never asked. There was too much blood on too many hands in her past already, and she wanted to keep Simon separate from all that. Sweet and innocent still.

"My brother Bruce," Arlette said, "his daddy"—she pointed in the direction Simon and Phoebe had disappeared—"was a world-class bastard." Same thing he had said about his uncle. "The older boys, spitting images of their old man. But not Simon. Family like ours . . ." Her drooping eyes were indigo in the dark. "It's hard to be soft." She slid one fingernail under a firefly that had landed on her shoulder, blew on it delicately—as if it were a birthday candle—and watched it fly away. "Bruce put those boys to work for the moving company soon as they could lift one end of a sofa. Trouble is, boys big enough to lift big things don't always put them down gently. Bruce Jr. and Brian dropped a baby grand piano on their baby brother's fingers. Might've saved them, sewn them back, if they had the sense to put them on ice and hightail it to a hospital. But they just let him bleed and scream and said they'd make him eat his fingers if he told Big Bruce what happened."

The jam glued Suzanne's mouth shut. She felt sick, unsure why Arlette was telling her this. She didn't want to hear it, didn't want to wonder all over again how many horrors could have been avoided if people didn't let each other bleed and scream like that. She wondered instead why some of the sufferers, like Simon, stayed soft—while others met pain like a whetstone, sharpened it and turned it on the world.

"So, he took whatever abuse Big Bruce dished out—couldn't abide his boys being careless, because carelessness cost money. Simon waited 'til they left him home alone and he left home, alone. Turned up on my doorstep a few days later. You think I had any use for a half-maimed teenager?" Arlette smiled, inexplicably. "But he needed a hand and I had two—and he's sure not good for nothing now."

Maybe that was the difference, Suzanne decided—someone to help heal the wound.

Arlette yawned, missing tooth a dark apostrophe in the corner of her mouth. "But what about you?"

"What about me?"

"Don't take a genius to see you're running from something, just like we used to be." Arlette reached for the jam jar again and caught Suzanne's hand in her callused one. She turned it under the jaundiced porchlight, traced the pale band of skin that ringed the fourth finger. "What made you leave?"

Suzanne tried to tug her hand back, but Arlette didn't let go. "I don't know," she said. "It wasn't him." She couldn't really blame Rob. He hadn't beaten or bruised her the way Arlette's husband had. Her grievances seemed so small, so slight, evidence of her own failure to be a good wife more than anything else. Another guilt that gnawed at her, an impatient scavenger trying to pull her entrails out while she was still breathing. "It was me. Trying to be something I didn't want to be. I wanted to want what he wanted but—shit, I couldn't do it. I don't know what's wrong with me." She couldn't find the right words, vocabulary rolling around her head like so many loose marbles. "I'm just not . . . *good* for people." She ruined them, without even meaning to. Eventually Rob would realize that leaving was the most loving thing she could do. She tried to smile at Arlette. Weed made her mawkish, made her say things she shouldn't. "Sorry," she said. "Don't listen to me."

"I won't," Arlette said, "because that's about the biggest bunch of bullshit I ever heard."

Suzanne blinked at her. Said, "Sorry?" again.

Arlette let go of her hand. "Would you stop apologizing? For what? For walking away from whatever made you unhappy? You don't owe anyone your misery. But you damn well owe it to yourself to quit your wallowing. Or else what the hell did you walk away for?" She glared at Suzanne with Simon's eyes. Slow to anger, but when they burned, Suzanne felt flayed alive.

"I'm—" She caught herself. Swallowed the impulse to say *sorry* again. Embarrassed by the reflex once she was aware of it—like a tic, like a tell, another bad habit she couldn't break.

Arlette's face relaxed, wide mouth going slack. Going soft. "You're nobody's wife now," she said, and though that wasn't strictly speaking true, she seemed to understand Suzanne needed permission to believe it. "You're going to live your own life just as you like. Isn't that right?" She may as well have said, *Or else.*

Suzanne's mouth was still sticky with jam, but she pried her lips apart. "Right."

"Good," Arlette said. "No more moaning and groaning about what a no-good woman you are. Just make tonight a good night." She reached for the jar, waved Suzanne off the porch. "Go on. Be young. Get naked. Don't drown in my pond."

Suzanne didn't argue. She found her feet again, watched a lonesome firefly make lazy figure eights and thought she'd take Arlette's advice—before she was too old to be mistaken for young anymore.

SUNSHINE STATE OF MIND

Rob had never been to Florida, except for the obligatory trip to Dis-
ney World when he was in elementary school. Tampa was a different
sort of playground. Some Google sleuthing from a hotel bed in South
Carolina had turned up a Louie Cafarelli who kept an office at Suzanne's cross-street coordinates, $5/23$, but what he did there was apparently a mystery even to the world's leading search engine. Rob's GPS
led him away from Ybor City's charm and kitsch, the redbrick cigar
factories repurposed as retail and restaurants. The farther east he went,
the faster the charm wore off, and soon the kitsch went with it, leaving
nothing behind but construction and destruction contractors. The in-
dustrial cycle of life.

Cafarelli's building was so like the others—flat and gray and
featureless—that Rob drove past it twice. No sign on the main road or
anywhere else. He parked the truck in a scrap of shade under a solitary
shaggy palm and went from door to door—many of them papered over,
others defaced with graffiti—until he found the one he was looking for.
He half expected it to be locked, but it swung open without comment
and left him standing in a dingy vestibule empty except for one of
those waving cats native to cheap Chinese restaurants perched on the
reception desk. There was one other door, open just a crack, at the far
end of the room. He cleared his throat. "Hello? I'm looking for Louie
Cafarelli."

"In the back," barked a voice. Rob looked sidelong at the cat, which went right on waving, unwaveringly. He glanced over his shoulder to watch the headlights on the Dodge flash to confirm it was locked, then walked past the cat and opened the door.

He saw nothing on the other side at first, but the smell hit him like a gust of wind, trying to push him back out into the lobby. It wasn't a bad smell, just a powerful one swirling claustrophobically in the close, unventilated room. An antique desk fan turned from side to side, driving the motion of the diminutive storm cell. Sunlight filtered through the smoke in stripes, the world outside trying to pry the blinds apart. A Motorola radio wedged in the windowsill blared the Rays at Diamondbacks—which wasn't going well for the local boys. Underneath, a sagging card table supported a coffeepot, hot plate, and TV set showing a dog race in black and white. Seated at a rolltop desk shoved against one wall was (he presumed) Louie Cafarelli. Muttonchops like a shag rug. Cigar the size of a bratwurst. A gold ring glinting on one pinkie and glasses with a ponderous browbar that made him look even more browbeaten than he might have otherwise. If Rob had to guess, he was probably seventy.

"Who sent you and for how much?" he said. "One month gratis, then the rate is forty-two. After that, plus seven percent per week." He peered at Rob over the browbar with a toadish smile. "Don't just stand there and sweat."

"I'm not here for money," Rob said. What did Suzanne want with this crustaceous old loan shark?

Cafarelli gargled a laugh around the back of his throat. "My mistake," he said. "Do I owe *you* money? If you think so, think again. I've settled all the debts I care to." The Rays cut away to a commercial break, fine print and side effects and limited-time offers. Cafarelli turned the volume down, eyes on the TV where eight impossibly streamlined dogs bolted after a mechanical rabbit. Rob wondered whether he had money on the race, on the game. Both at once were overwhelming in the tiny room.

"Not looking to collect, either," Rob said. Not the way he meant, anyway.

Cafarelli blew a smoke ring across the desk, something Rob had never seen anyone do in real life. Wondering what kind of hard-boiled bullshit he'd gotten himself into. "Then what *are* you looking for?"

"My wife."

Cafarelli blinked at him. "Your wife. Who's your wife? The fuck do I want with your wife?"

"I don't know. That's why I'm here. She disappeared and I found a note in her office with your name on it."

Cafarelli leaned back in the chair, arms dangling over the sides of his seat, like some knuckle-dragging great ape. Harboring a fierce and unfriendly intelligence behind the scrofulous exterior. "And you'd like to know what she might need a devil like me for."

"I would, yes."

"Can't help you. I don't ask. Never do. I've heard enough sob stories to cry myself to sleep every night I've got left in this life and the next."

"I don't think she was a . . . client," Rob said.

Cafarelli's toadish grin broadened. "I don't make a habit of other men's wives who aren't my . . . clients," he said. Toying with Rob and enjoying it.

"Then maybe you remember her," Rob insisted. Refusing to be dismissed. "Petite, curly brown hair and brown eyes, early forties. She came down to Miami to settle her late father's estate. Maybe you had business with him? Domingo or Delfuego or something." No, that was one of the CDs in the passenger seat, the Del Fuegos. Suzanne had always used her stepdad's surname, kept it even after they got married, and Rob couldn't remember her father's. Gil's. "Delgado!" That was it—he knew there was another *G* in there somewhere. "But her name is Westman, Suzanne Westman."

An alarming change came over Cafarelli. He lunged halfway across the desk, elbows landing so hard the ash broke off the end of his cigar. "I've made some bad bets in my life, but that man and his daughter have made more hell for me than any sinner deserves. I've done more right by them than *they* deserve and now, Mr. Westman, if that's who you are"—with the cigar smoldering a foot from his face, Rob did not correct him—"if you'd get the fuck out." He pointed toward the door.

But Rob stood rooted to the spot. Why did Cafarelli think he could bully him? Seventysomething and shit out of luck by the look of it. He might be the sort to keep a firearm around, and because it was Florida he could probably blow Rob's head off with impunity, but maybe it didn't need to be combative. Maybe they could commiserate instead.

"Listen," Rob said, trying a harder tone on for size. "I sympathize. I don't want to be here any more than you want me to be here, but unlike you and Gil, Suzanne and I still have some unfinished business. I'll gladly get the fuck out if you can tell me where the fuck to find her." The profanity felt good, felt justified. He rarely swore and never at his wife, but under the circumstances some swearing seemed fair. In any case, it seemed to be the language Cafarelli spoke best.

"We finally understand each other, Mr. Westman," he said, unwittingly demonstrating the limits of his understanding, "but understand this: I don't do any favors for free."

Rob felt the bulge of his wallet in his back pocket. That driving-around money might not get him as far as he'd hoped, but no matter. There was more where that came from. "No problem," Rob said. "If your information is worth something."

"She gave me an address to reach her where she'd wait for all the paperwork to process," Cafarelli said. "Someplace called the Sundew Value Inn." He pulled a drawer open and tossed a business card across the desk. One side had the contact information for a funeral services director. On the back was an address and a room number. "The first wire went through two days ago," he added, leering at Rob over the browbar. "So I'd get a move on if I were you."

Rob left Tampa in a rush, but only drove three hours back the way he came before fatigue forced him off the road. He was a younger man than Louie Cafarelli but not as young as he used to be. His back stiffened as the minutes ticked by and hurt like murder when he finally climbed out of the cab at a Travelodge that looked thoroughly deserted. He didn't plan to linger longer than it took to get some shut-eye and a shower. If Cafarelli was right, Suzanne had a head start, and once she left the Sundew Value Inn, he had no idea how he'd track her down again.

In the meantime, he decided to indulge his curiosity. He'd never pressed Suzanne about her past. Not everyone had been blessed with a home life as wholesome as his; forcing the subject seemed insensitive. But now all bets were off, except whatever bets Cafarelli had on the greyhounds and the Rays. For the first time, Rob Gabbard Googled his wife.

She wasn't the only Suzanne Westman in the world, and her website didn't come up until the third page of search results. The last batch of photos was from a wedding in Ocean City, the son of a colleague of his. She never went to weddings unless she was getting paid to be there, which was why she had insisted on eloping. At the time he thought it romantic. He scrolled past a few more Suzannes who weren't his Suzanne before he found a link to an art gallery in New York that turned out to be broken. He scrolled a little farther and found, on a site called "Wayback Machine," a few dozen photo credits for Suzanne Westman in a digitized "zine"—whatever that was—called *audionaut.* He Googled that, too, and found a Wikipedia page describing an "an underground music newsletter serving Greater New York since 1993."

He didn't find anything else. Suzanne wasn't even on Instagram—professional suicide for a photographer these days. She seemed willfully averse to her own success. *You take Polaroids!* he had pointed out. She preferred instant cameras to the DSLRs she used for events, announcements, headshots, whatever people paid her for. *They're already square. Wouldn't that be perfect for Instagram?* She had only shaken her head and said, *That's not the point of a Polaroid. It doesn't need the internet. It doesn't even need an outlet. That's what I like about it.*

She was still entrenched in last century, as if time had stopped on a dime at the end of the nineties. What was it, he wanted to know, that she couldn't get past? He closed the "Suzanne Westman" tab on his mobile browser, opened a new one, and tried "Suzanne Delgado." Nothing, but that wasn't surprising. Her stepfather adopted her when she was still a minor. Rob tried again, searching now for "Gil Delgado." Unlike his estranged offspring, his name produced a deluge of results. Rob's thumb froze, mid-scroll, over the screen. Alarmed by the number and the nature of the headlines attached to his late father-in-law. Tabloid rags and arrest reports from half a dozen states, accusing him of everything from obscenity to grand theft auto.

Christ, no wonder she didn't talk about him. Rob tapped on the Wikipedia link, but Gil's page was just a stub with a tangle of hyperlinks at the bottom. The earliest photo Rob could find was a mug shot from Miami-Dade that had been repurposed as the cover of his band's first LP, *Impersonator.* He looked about nineteen, grinning like the devil he would evidently grow up to be. More disturbing was the family resemblance. He looked just like Suzanne, or she like him. The same deep eyes, the same long lashes. Same ears, even. She was Gil reincarnated as a girl. But none of the dozen articles he read mentioned any children. The conspiracy theorists comparing notes about the catastrophic crack-up of the band either didn't know or didn't care that she existed. Most were fixated on the guitar players. There were half a dozen names in that category, but Rob couldn't tell whether it was half a dozen different lineups or if all half a dozen referred to one person. He did, however, see one familiar name again and again. DELGADO (LEFT) LEAVES THE CLARK COUNTY COURTHOUSE WITH MANAGER LOUIS CAFARELLI, read one caption under a blurry black-and-white snapshot from the *Vegas Sun.* Gil looked much older than his first mug shot, Cafarelli much younger than that afternoon when Rob had met him. Same frames, though, twenty-nine years ago, with that heavy browbar accentuating his natural scowl.

One other name caught his eye in the slurry of blog posts and message boards for die-hard fans of sordid C-list rock bands: *audionaut.*

Someone had uploaded a scan of a section called "Re-views" and a short column penned by someone called "Doug Sandusky, editor-at-large." "Ten years after the fact, it's clear that the real tragedy here is how great *Unholy Relics* really is—how many more great songs there should have been. The wasted potential makes me so angry that, great as it is, I'll never play it again. Fuck you, take your five stars." Rob squinted at the cover of the EP—how that differed from an LP, he had no idea— under re-view. On the right was Gil, older than the *Impersonator* mug shot but younger than the *Sun*. He stood beside another man with shoulder-length black hair and his own bones tattooed on the backs of his hands. The name of the EP wasn't printed anywhere. Instead, in the blank space of that bottom white border, someone had written GIL & SKELLY, APRIL 1989, the clumsy cursive clearly the work of a child. Rob glanced at the pink Post-it with Cafarelli's name and address, discarded for a coaster on the nightstand. Even as the ink bled, the *L*'s made the same dizzy loops.

Unmistakably Suzanne.

THE **A** SIDE

I AM THE D.J. AND
I'VE GOT BELIEVERS

Before long, Suzanne was just one of the road dogs. She memorized backstage floor plans in a snap and ran errands for hours without getting bored, without getting tired, without getting lost. She fetched cigarettes and hairspray and sandwiches, sniffed out the best place open late after load-out, and appointed herself the unofficial navigator, tracing possible routes to their next destination in color-coded crayon—orange was the most direct, blue likely to have the least traffic, green the scenic views.

"I thought he was crazy to bring this kid along," she heard Carney tell Doug as they unloaded boxes by the bar, sound check staggering along at the other end of the room. "But shit, she's a decent deckhand already and how old is she? Like six?"

"She's *ten*," Doug said, indignant on Suzanne's behalf, though he'd made the same mistake the day they met. "She'll be eleven before this tour is over."

"She'll be twenty-seven before this tour is over," Carney said, hacking at a stubborn strap of gaff tape with one of the utility knives hanging from his belt. He was always fidgeting with something, putting things together and pulling them apart. "The shit she's seen."

"And I'll be ready to retire," Doug said with a groan as he stretched a kink out of his back, then squatted down to heft another crate of records up onto the bar.

"Don't hold your breath for a pension," Carney said.

Suzanne wasn't sure what all of that meant, but she had seen a lot already. Gil's world was loud and chaotic and colorful. The lights and the costumes and the music itself—she went to bed every night with her head full of fireworks. She slept like the dead and often had to be carried to lobby call the next morning. She always had a sunburn, she rarely had clean clothes, she read road maps like comic books and never wanted to go home.

Not every day was a good one, though. Some felt poisoned from the start, whether they'd spent a bad night in a shitty motel or traffic made them late to sound check or the van broke down. Most dangerous of all was what they called the Black Plague, when Skelly plunged into one of his infectious *moods*. In those hazardous hours he radiated anger like a dying star, vented it at everyone in caustic asides and small acts of malice. Even Gil, whose job it was as bandleader to manage crew morale, was not immune, wrong-footed as Suzanne had never seen him when his mercurial axman made some cutting remark about the trace evidence of his accent or knocked his coffee off a table with a swift, catlike jab. One day he nearly blew them all up flicking a lit cigarette in Gil's face while he gassed up the car. But it was Nash who knocked Skelly flat and held his face against the hot asphalt, asking how he liked it and promising to rip his balls off if he didn't quit acting like a prick. Doug and Carney pulled them apart before any real damage was done and Gracie shouted, "Don't make me call Louie! Shut up and buckle up because we're getting this freak show on the road." After a few hours stewing in their own juices, they walked onstage in Columbus, Ohio, and played the best show of their lives.

The crowds could make or break an evening, too—one night they might play to five hundred eager people who bought their merch and knew their songs and clamored for an encore; the next they might find themselves in some shit-kicker bar, fighting for a sign of life from two dozen people who had wandered in for a beer and a break in the rain, dressed head to toe in camouflage like they were trying to disappear. It depended on so many unpredictable factors—the city and whether

they'd played there before, what other entertainment they had to com-
pete with, how good or bad the weather was, if the venue had done
their fair share of promotion. They never knew who they'd be playing
to until they hit the stage.

In Indiana, for instance, they played a windowless rathskeller called
Wild Bucks Tavern, where the décor consisted of water spots, cigarette
burns, and the heads of a few white-tailed bucks mounted above the bar
with tattered bits of lingerie hanging from their antlers. One still wore a
red nose left over from Christmas; the rest looked uniformly depressed.
Suzanne, usually manning the merch table with Carney, was dismissed
for lack of interest and climbed onto a barstool for a quick inventory of
the clientele—a mix of grizzled regulars with beards like steel wool and
younger men in Dickies and work boots, with bristly hair and bloodshot
eyes and a lot of notes to compare about which lounge around was best
for a lap dance these days.

"Used to be the Henhouse," one said, talking over Suzanne's head
as if she were invisible. "Had the goodest-looking girls in town, but
they're all pregnant now."

"Guess that's why it's one for the price of two anymore."

"That's it," said another. "That's why I'm here instead."

If they wanted a show, they'd come to the right place, more than
they knew. Others were more enlightened; a few knots of people, clustered as close as they could get to the tiny platform that passed for a
stage, had clearly come not for the lack of a good lap dance, but for
the band. Suzanne recognized their acolytes on sight by now—the wild
hair and wide eyes and offbeat accoutrements. Leather and lace and
enough black greasepaint slicked beneath their eyes to join the NFL. A
rainy Tuesday night at Wild Bucks made strange bedfellows.

"Here." The bartender set something red and fizzy in front of Suzanne. A cherry, shiny and red as the reindeer nose on the unfortunate
buck above her, curled its stem over the rim of the glass. "Shirley Tem-
ple," he said with great gravitas. "Tater Tots."

The man wondering aloud whether they made nursing bras for dancing girls fell silent mid-sentence, staring at Suzanne. She smiled around

the cherry stem, already working it into a knot with her tongue—a trick Gracie had shown her at some other dive in Detroit, which she'd been struggling to master ever since. He turned toward the bartender, who only shrugged, as if to say, *Your guess is good as mine.*

"Are you here alone?" somebody else asked, leaning back on his stool to get a better look at her around his drinking buddy.

"No." Pride swelled up under her ribs like a balloon about to burst. "I'm with the band."

"What b—"

But there was no need to ask, no need to answer. The lights dimmed and whistles and shouts from the greasepainted vulgarians welcomed their heroes to nowhere. Gil squinted into the gloom, looking like he'd just walked off the assembly line at General Motors in a white undershirt and canvas coveralls peeled halfway off, sleeves knotted around his waist. A lollipop stick poked out of his mouth, and a bug-eyed pair of welder's goggles held his hair at bay. Behind him, the Kills scuffled and swore and shoved each other around, fighting for a toehold between the cables and pedals crowding the diminutive stage. Nash, almost invisible in the far corner, had to hunch over the toms to keep from smacking his head on the naked pipes zigzagging across the ceiling.

"Good evening," Gil said. "To all six and a half of you."

Laughter bubbled up from the front. Everyone else looked around in consternation, like they expected to find Allen Funt lurking somewhere with a camera crew. But that was part of Gil's weird genius; he could work any room, bend every unlucky circumstance to his will.

"There's about as many of you as there are of us, and if you try to sneak out—we'll see you. Yeah, you, with the wolf tattoo." He pointed his lollipop at the offender, who stopped in his tracks. "What's your name, Wolfman?" Gil adjusted the mic stand as Ruby and Skelly futzed around with their guitars. The low, buzzing drone of too many amps too close together filled the empty spaces in the room. "Harold. Can I call you Harry?" He didn't wait for permission. "Mighty pleased to meet you, Harry Wolfman. I'm Gil, these here are the Kills." Nash was still drowning in shadows, but Ruby waved hello. Skelly did a sarcastic little curtsy and blew smoke into the front row. He would play and play damn well but, unlike Gil, he didn't care if six and a half hicks liked it or not. He'd left the dive-bar circuit behind and seemed none too happy to be back. "And if you walk out now," Gil said, "we'll just have to kill you." The crowd chuckled, warming to the joke. "You've been warned! Uh one two three four—"

Skelly wrenched the first ragged chord from the fretboard like he wanted to tear the strings off. Gil shivered and twitched and swiveled his hips fit to put the Henhouse out of business.

Honey lost her heart to a black nightbird
Who sang sweet nothings
And sour little somethings
The tremble and the twist
Oh nobody could resist
Honey woke up in the morning
Under six feet of dirt

And they were off. Gil's eclectic setlists had their own rhyme and reason, tailored to wherever in the world they found themselves. Wild Bucks hadn't had a truly wild night in years, but Gil had wildness in his blood, on his breath, in his bones. Every time he stepped onstage, opened his mouth and opened his veins, the wildness infected everyone, and they were never quite the same. The girls in their greasepaint swayed and swooned, and the boozehounds at the bar woke up for the first time in who knew how long, sat up straighter on their stools.

But wildness wasn't all he could do. Halfway through the set, when Gil had worked everyone into a lather, he said, "Rhythm section, take five," and Ruby took the Flying V with her. The Hands looked oddly empty-handed before reaching for the battle-scarred Martin acoustic propped against the wall. His inky finger bones looked incongruously delicate above the bulky dreadnought. He pinched and turned the pegs and found an empty chair between two of the greasepainted girls, who giggled and fidgeted like they might faint. Skelly ignored them— ignored everybody but Gil.

"Strings, do you know any drinking songs?"

"If I do, will you bring me a drink?"

Everyone laughed a little more easily now. A few men at the bar still squinted at Gil, mistrustful of his unabashed flamboyance, but no one seemed eager to leave. Even Harold the Wolfman had returned to his seat, watching with a guilty sort of grin.

"If I do, how will you drink it?"

"You'll just have to give me a hand."

"A hand for the Hands!" Gil demanded. "The best axman an old battle-axe could ask for." Everyone applauded as he soft-shoed between the tables. He jumped onto the empty stool beside Suzanne, helped himself to a Tater Tot with a sly sidelong wink, chased it with a sip of the Wolfman's whiskey. "I'll have whatever he's having," he said, and slipped seamlessly into a song.

You ever been to Minnie's place in Memphis?
She'd serve you red-eye gravy for a dime
I tickled the ivories there
When I was done doin' time

Skelly, thanks to his long tenure in rough joints like this one, knew not just one drinking song but dozens, not only their own but so many others. They played Willie and Johnny, George Jones and Merle Haggard, the Doors and the Replacements, *Here comes a regular,* before circling back to the next verse.

This place has changed
Since she went away
And Coyote Joe came back around
All the old lowlifes
We used to get high with
Got too damn high to come down

Gil and Skelly sang together for the first time that tour—Ruby sang backup on everything else. Skelly's voice was not so polished, not so practiced, but he sang with an unfussy thrum in his throat that reminded Suzanne of the Ranchero when the engine was just warming up. Gil, with his more elastic range, bowed around him in improbable harmony as he moved through the room, sampling drinks and cigarettes and whatever else looked tempting. He conducted the crowd through the chorus until they could sing it in rounds.

All the old lowlifes

We used to get high with

Got too damn high to come down

Gil held a glass for Skelly to sip as he played, raising it higher and higher until he was standing on a chair and the thin stream of whiskey fell like a waterfall. He threw back the last swig himself and, with his arms outstretched like a tightrope walker, bent at the waist and spit it back out into Skelly's open mouth. The audience dissolved in disgust and hilarity as they took their somber bows. Never out of sync for a second, whether they were firing on all cylinders or just fucking around. Suzanne squirmed on her stool. Suddenly jealous of Skelly, jealous of all of them, who had grown so close to Gil while he was so far from her. But she wouldn't sulk, wouldn't pout, wouldn't cry, wouldn't cause trouble. Wouldn't do anything to get herself sent packing. For the first time in her life, she was right where she belonged.

When the show was over, the band loaded out while the bar's loaded patrons downed their dregs and paid their tabs and stumbled out into the night. Suzanne—determined to prove her worth as a roadie— hauled a bag of stage clothes too rank to be worn again out to the alley where Blondie and the van were waiting. The Kills stood around smoking and sipping Schlitz while Carney and Doug tied everything down in the trailer. They had three hours left to drive before crashing for the night if they didn't want to be up at the crack of dawn tomorrow. They were nocturnal by nature and preferred staying up late to getting up early, needed time after a show to come down enough to sleep anyway. Skelly was the usual exception—for his two hours on-stage, he burned off whatever combustible substance smoldered inside him and collapsed in brooding lassitude the moment the van doors closed. Nothing excited or impressed him, so far as Suzanne could tell, but he was always annoyed about something. Tonight, the gaggle of teenagers hanging around outside the venue, trying to look older and cooler than they were—an inept imitation of his majestically bad attitude. They leaned on the wall at the corner and kept their distance until Gil emerged. Back in his street clothes, except for the goggles he'd forgotten to remove.

When they worked up the nerve to sidle over, he asked their names and if they liked the show and were they from around here? They blushed and blurted their answers until one finally asked, would he sign the new LP? Of course, he said, and asked the girl's name and how to spell it, then dashed off a note and signed it *XO*. He beckoned the rest of the band to come and add their autographs. Ruby and Nash were gracious enough; Skelly scrawled his initials with his left hand without a word, without looking anyone in the eye. He went back to lean on the side of the van, one bootheel hitched up on the hubcap. The girl scuttled off, pink-cheeked and chastised in the face of his disdain.

Ruby shook her head in Skelly's direction. "Would it actually kill you to be nice?"

"To the teenybopper brigade?" He flicked his cigarette away, ember turning end over end until it landed in a puddle and extinguished itself with a hiss. "Who cares."

Suzanne shifted her feet in Gil's shadow. Skelly had called her "ankle-biter" more than once. She didn't know where that ranked by comparison, but it certainly sounded like a nuisance.

"Since they're buying your records, you should," Doug grumbled, cinching the last cable trunk down with a grunt. It had been especially hard for him, Suzanne and only Suzanne noticed, to be the butt of Skelly's bad humors—for no other sin than the same one the girl had committed, of being too eager. That Doug thought him a god and took his abuse hadn't helped. But he was learning to fight back, however feebly, in a doomed effort to win some respect.

And tonight Gil held his ground, brushed off the Black Plague. While everyone else rolled their eyes and crossed their arms, he seized Skelly's face in his hands. "Killer, you're thinking about it all wrong. Maybe tonight wasn't your kind of crowd, but why preach to the choir? We gave these people a taste of something they desperately need, and that's not nothing. You feel me?" He pinched Skelly's cheek. "You're not Keith Richards yet. But you have fans who drove to this shithole from Kalamazoo just to see you, and *that* is not fucking nothing."

"I get it, all right? Would you get off."

"I wish you could." The Hands pushed him away, but there was a laugh on his lips. Gil caught it on his and let it out loud. "Tonight, Wild Bucks. Tomorrow, the world!"

"Fuck yeah," Nash said. "Let's get rolling."

The bad spell broken, everyone chattered and joked and threw their loose belongings wherever they would fit. The Kill Team clambered over each other and into their seats, already arguing about who drank whose beer, who had a lighter, what the hell happened to that tube of Ben-Gay? Suzanne stood there holding the laundry until she felt Gil's hand on her head.

"Ready to go, kiddo?"

Normally there was nowhere she would rather be than between him and Gracie in the Ranchero. But tonight the Kills beckoned.

"Can I ride in the van?"

Gil looked at Gracie, then through the passenger door at Doug, who shrugged. "All aboard," he said with a big silly grin. "We'll make room."

"All aboard," Gil agreed with another pointed look at Doug that Suzanne couldn't quite read. He mussed her hair. "You keep your seat belt buckled, *¿comprende?*"

"*¡Comprende!*" Her Spanish was shaky, since he'd never really tried to teach her, but she understood that much. She dropped the laundry and let Doug pull her up over the running board before anybody could change their mind.

The band didn't realize until the van was already on the road that Suzanne had landed in their midst. It was easy to disappear with the whole Kill Team in such a small space—a tempest in a teakettle. Nash and Ruby argued and elbowed each other in the front seats in an ongoing turf war over the radio. The speakers choked and wheezed like they'd been matching Skelly smoke for smoke. He'd flung himself across the backseat, leaving Carney and Doug to share the middle bench with Suzanne wedged between them. Doug was busy demolishing a jumbo bag of Funyuns, and Carney had somehow, despite the noise, fallen asleep. Arms folded, earrings jingling, a High Life in one hand and his mouth open like St. Teresa in ecstasy. Unable to resist the temptation, Suzanne wiggled the Polaroid out of her backpack and held it up to her eye.

Kssshhhhk.

"What was that?" Nash asked as the flash popped behind him.

"Sorry!" Suzanne sat on the photo since her pockets were too small to keep it dark while the image developed.

"Oh," Nash said with a backward glance. "Just point it that way, okay?"

"Okay."

Ruby peered over her shoulder. Crossed her eyes, stuck out her tongue. *Kssshhhhk.* Suzanne put the second photo with the first. Turned the camera on Doug, who hung an onion ring from his nose. *Kssshhhhk.* She pulled the third snapshot free and set the camera in her lap. She only had one picture left in the pack. Wary of squandering it, but she didn't want to miss anything, either.

Carney snorted in his sleep. Skelly, tossing Skittles over the seatback, finally hit his target, a green one landing squarely in Carney's open mouth. He woke with a start as cheers erupted around him and almost choked. Skelly kept the next handful for himself, chewed with a wolfish grin. But he saw Suzanne peering over the seat and offered the bag, shook a few into her palm. Emboldened, she raised the camera again.

"Smile," she said. But the Hands covered his face, vanishing in a thicket of black knucklebones. She was about to put the camera down, but then he spread two fingers, peeked out at her from in between, and winked. *Kssshhhhk.* She felt a little thrill of pride and pleasure. Sure she'd captured something elusive, something rare and cryptic.

"Wait, hold on— *EVERYBODY SHUT UP.*"

Ruby smacked Nash's meaty shoulder. "Christ A—"

But then she heard it. Everybody did.

"Holy shit." Carney lunged between the seats to turn the volume up. Even Skelly sat halfway up, Skittles forgotten and spilling across the seats. Static fizzed over the airwaves, but despite the weak signal, the voice was unmistakable.

Musta caught some new blues

Nothing left to lose blues

"Holy shit," Carney repeated. "What station is this?"

"Shhhh!" Ruby hissed.

I'm stalled

I'm stuck

I'm all f—d up

And I just don't know what to do

Nash laughed, slamming one enormous hand against the steering wheel. The song stuttered, snapped back just as Gil's voice dropped down deep in his chest—a slow, sultry rumble.

Musta caught the you blues

Skelly's Stratocaster went off like a rocket, every note bright and blazing.

"Oh my God," Ruby said. "Louie said we don't have the pockets for payola."

"That means they liked it enough to play it without getting paid," Skelly said, eyes a quicksilver flash in the dark.

"Gil has to hear this!" Ruby tugged her husband's arm. "Pull over."

"Pull over? It'll *be* over. Roll your window down."

"What?"

Nash floored it. The old van gave a tremendous gasp and lurched forward. Doug yanked Suzanne's seat belt tight across her lap. The gathering speed pressed her against the seat as they gained on Blondie, taillights growing in the windshield like two diabolic eyes. Suzanne's heart seemed to go through her, slamming through her rib cage and the seatback to bounce right into Skelly's lap. Her breath went with it, but what did she need air for? She had the speed and the song and the rest of the Kill Team. She could fly.

Ruby hung halfway out the window, waving and hollering as they nosed up alongside the Ranchero. "DAD! WE'RE ON THE RADIO!"

Suzanne wished she had one more photo. She wanted to remember his face like that forever, the shock of hearing his own voice boom through the night on the long, empty road to nowhere. He'd been saying it, swearing it, for as long as Suzanne could remember, but for the first time it felt possible—not just possible, but already here, already happening. Gil was becoming somebody, right before her eyes and ears.

PATIENCE

The next morning at the farm, while Phoebe and Arlette loaded crates of jam and jars of pickled vegetables into Arlette's flatbed, Suzanne decided the heat was too much and let Simon cut most of her hair off with Phoebe's fabric shears. She perched on the stool at the vanity table in one of the upstairs rooms and said, "Get rid of all this."

He eyed her reflection in the mirror, fluffed her filthy curls, untangling a few stubborn knots by unwinding each lock around his index finger. "Let's keep it soft around your face," he said. "These baby curls . . . I'm sorry, I can't. It would just be too cruel."

Happy to look however he liked, she watched the hair fall around her chair like feathers, as if she were molting. They'd brought a few cassettes up from the car and plugged in the dusty old tape deck on the dresser. It crackled and croaked through the music, but Leonard Cohen crackled and croaked anyway. *Why trade this vision for desire,* he wanted to know, *when you may have them both? You will never see a man this naked,* he promised. *I will never hold a woman this close.*

"Phoebe said she found a car," Suzanne said.

"Mm-hmm. Little Toyota pickup. Just needs a new serpentine belt." *Snip, snip.* More dark down floated to the floor, joining the ring around her stool. "We're going to take a look this afternoon, after the general store." Once they'd collected their mail and a new set of wheels, they wouldn't wait around for long. Phoebe had already booked booths at half a dozen flea markets and craft fairs strung across the southern states for the next few weeks. Suzanne envied their trajectory, their certainty. She still didn't know where she would go, had deferred the decision until it was time to part ways, a moment she knew she wouldn't be ready for when it came. She'd worried at the atlas for days, tracing the jagged routes she'd drawn so long ago on greasy bar mats and boomerang Formica tabletops. The wax zigzagged from New York to Nebraska before veering suddenly south and leaving a trail of scorched Red-Orange through the scabrous expanse of Texas. So many shows bled together, but not those.

"How soon will you leave?"

He shrugged. *Snip, snip.* "When we're ready." He set the scissors aside, then tilted her chin up. Already her head—her whole body—felt lighter. Her curls, overblown by the humidity, had started to make her look like a cocker spaniel. Now she could see her ears again, the pale stem of her neck speckled with dark flecks of split end. "What about you?"

"Not sure," she said. "But soon." As soon as she figured out what to do. Some half-buried instinct told her to go to Gracie. The tour was always supposed to end in Los Angeles, where the band could mix the next record and live like homecoming war heroes for a few weeks on the Maldonado family ranch, a couple hours up the coast. When Suzanne asked, Louie told her Gracie had gone "back home." She assumed that meant California. Suzanne left Miami with no idea why Gil had left his things to her, and she still didn't know. Gracie would if anyone did, but what right did Suzanne have, barging back into her life? Still, she didn't dare linger in one place too long, afraid of getting stuck. If Simon hadn't stumbled on her, asleep at the wheel outside the Sundew, she might have never gotten started again. Couldn't afford to lose her momentum now, even if she hadn't made up her mind.

"Where will you go?"

"Not sure," she said again. "Somewhere west." Maybe she'd kill a few weeks kicking around the ghost towns she got to know on her first fellowship, all those years ago. See if any of the specters she remembered had finally left their old haunts behind.

"Why not come with us?" Simon said, looking her reflection in the eye. "Since we're headed that way, for a while."

Suzanne almost laughed. "All three of us in the Lifeboat?"

Simon shrugged again. "Why not?"

"It's barely big enough for you two." They could make it work for a night or two, but weeks?

"It's big enough," Simon said, as if he and Phoebe had already discussed it, done the math, thought it through. "It wouldn't be the lap of luxury, but we'd make room." Phoebe's voice tickled her ear. *Love never runs out. There's enough for you, too.*

But she still said, "I couldn't," because she couldn't imagine it—intruding with all her ugly baggage in their tiny, whirligig world.

But Simon said again, "Why not?" Children asked *why*—they were full of impossible *why*s with no answers, no reasons, no certainty. One of the unnumbered horrors of parenthood. Simon, no child despite his youth, always asked *Why not?* until she ran out of answers and had to ask herself the same question.

She echoed his shrug, brown hair snowing down around her feet. "What would I *do*?"

"Whatever you like," he said, as if it were that simple. "Why not?"

"I don't know," she said, groping for a reason. This time it was Arlette, growling in her ear. *You're going to live your own life just as you like. Isn't that right?*

"Okay." He didn't argue. Didn't try to change her mind. Which made it that much harder to hold her ground when she felt his fingers in her hair again, shaking it loose and smoothing it down. He took the bandana from his back pocket and brushed her shoulders clean. "Don't move," he said, dusting the clippings from her cheeks. Questions thundered in her blood. *Why not? What the hell else did you walk away for?*

She caught his hand against her cheek, turned her face into his palm. Breathed in the smell of him clinging to the bandana—sweet and warm and mellow as apricot brandy, no less intoxicating. "Okay." She kissed the scars across his knuckles and felt him lean forward, lean in, close the small space between them. *Why not?* "Take me with you." She kissed the tender, ticklish skin just above his waistband and felt his fingers twist into her short, dirty hair.

ONE WAY OR ANOTHER

By the time Rob arrived at the Sundew Value Inn, Suzanne was al-ready gone.

"Like to help you, man," said the chubby Hispanic teenager—or was it Latino? Rob could never remember the difference but never remembered to Google it either—who seemed to be running the garage, the RV park, and the motel from the gas station cash register, which had an ungainly grandeur about it. Big and brass and completely incongruous between the racks of plastic lighters and charging cables coiled up like shiny pink earthworms. Rob noticed they stocked enough necessities that someone could post up there awhile if their tastes weren't too particular. Suzanne, for instance. There were even a few cardboard crates of citrus outside, with hand-lettered signs, $5/LB. Maybe he'd take some oranges for the road—anything with a peel was supposed to travel well. He couldn't remember where he'd learned that; it might have been an item in Casey's latest rant about vegetarians who were so concerned about the environmental impact of cattle ranching but not the environmental impact of shipping their "goddamn avocadoes all over the world." Mostly he was mad about having to grill something separate for his sister-in-law, who had recently decided she "identified as vegan." A thousand miles removed from all of them, Rob may as well have been on another planet.

"Can you tell me when she left?"

"Checked out yesterday. Like, you *just* missed them." The cashier shook his head sadly, as if he really felt the sting when what a customer needed didn't fall within his remarkably expansive purview.

"Them?" Rob said. "Who's them?"

"Them, like the two other people she was with?" Behind the boy, an enormous, ungainly crane fly threw itself against the grimy window. Nobody besides Rob had pulled up to the pumps for fifteen minutes. Who the hell was Suzanne meeting here and what the hell for?

"Describe them," he said to the boy.

"White guy, brown hair, maybe like . . . twenty-five? Three fingers on his . . . right hand, yeah." He made an *L* with his own, the pinkie and fourth finger folded down, the way Rob's nephews made finger pistols. "Black girl with braids, freckles, earrings. Tattoos, but like—little ones, all over." He gestured again, doing charades to make sure Rob understood. "Thin but like almost same height as him." He'd clearly taken an interest in the girl.

"And they left together," Rob said. If Louie knew she knew anyone else in the Sunshine State, he failed to mention it.

The cashier grinned inexplicably, clapped his hands together. He looked down to see if he'd managed to kill whatever was buzzing around him and wiped what was left of it—Rob saw some legs and a bent antenna, all too large for his liking—on his shirt. He said something in Spanish, then corrected himself. "It was crazy, man. Hauling that trailer with that car? But he worked on it—*casi*, a week?"

"Car? What car?" Suzanne had flown; he'd needed the Prius until he decided, abruptly, to take a leave from work for the first time in years.

"That car was crazy, man." Everything was crazy, apparently. "Big yellow car."

"Big yellow car." The phrase shook something loose in the back of Rob's brain. He'd missed his chance to meet Gil, at the reception for the wedding they never actually had, but he remembered the car. It made an impression.

"He said it was her car, though. The one you're looking for. They came in the Chevy."

"The Chevy."

"The Silverado." The boy pointed out the door Rob had come in through. Everyone seemed to know more about cars than he did. "He traded it to my uncle for gas, water, and beer." He ticked these off his fingers as if someone had given him a shopping list to memorize.

"Did he say where they were going?"

The boy shook his head no.

"Can I take a look at the Chevy?" Rob sensed it would be a step too far to ask to see the room. They'd probably turned it over, cleaned it up already.

"Sure." The boy shrugged. "It's unlocked."

Just to compensate him for his unquestioning cooperation, Rob bought a couple of drinks from the cooler and a bag of Golden Flake potato chips, though he'd never seen them before and rarely ate potato chips, landing somewhere between Casey and his sister-in-law on the dietary spectrum. Being away from home and his usual habits called all those habits into question.

Walking outside was like walking into a wall of hot mud, the humidity so thick it seemed solid. A wobbly heat haze rose from the hood of what he assumed was the Silverado: a dusty blue pickup with a band of lighter blue down each side. He didn't need to know much about cars to know it was old. The door groaned on its hinge and the seats were stained and balding from years of wear and tear. They—whoever "they" were—had left an intriguing collection of clutter behind. A cracked Magic 8 Ball which had lost all its fluid rolled out from under the driver's seat, dice rattling. Wedged in the door pocket with four crushed cans of orange soda, he found a foam finger from the Superdome, a couple of spent glow sticks, and a box cutter. On the dashboard was half a pack of Camels and a brass sombrero ashtray full of stickers. Each one was bright orange, shaped like a flotation ring. Around the rim, neat white stenciled text read @LIFEBOATSUPPLYCO.

Rob took one and closed the door. Nothing else to see. Walking back across the lot to his bigger, blacker pickup, he took his phone out of his pocket, but the sun was too bright to see the screen until he was back in the cab. He turned the engine on and a gust of warm air blew his hair back off his forehead. While he waited for it to cool, he tapped the Instagram icon he almost never used—sick of scrolling through countless pictures of other people's wives and children, family pets and family vacations. He typed the handle into the search bar. The profile photo showed the same orange ring, a life-sized Lifesaver hanging from the side of an aluminum trailer.

For the first time in a long time, Rob grinned. "Gotcha."

Sorely in need of a shower, Rob left the Sundew behind, drove a few more exits north, then pulled off the highway and walked into a Best Western with a mostly empty parking lot, following some primitive instinct to lie low until he landed on a plan of action. He'd been so focused on finding Suzanne he hadn't really considered what to do next, counting on the mere fact of his presence to bring her to her senses. In every version of the reunion he'd imagined—and there had been dozens, probably hundreds, by then—he'd caught her alone. The clerk at the Sundew mentioned a guy and a girl and the car and the trailer, which suggested a relationship of convenience. But hadn't their relationship begun the same way? Two strangers, stranded at the airport. He might have wondered whether their entire marriage was a relationship of convenience to her, except that she never seemed to actually need him for anything and resented his intrusion when he tried to help. *I can do it myself,* she always said. *But you don't have to,* he always replied, with diminishing returns. Another weird kink in her character he had chalked up to family dysfunction, which ran much deeper than he ever knew, according to the headlines and chat rooms devoted to the musical thugduggery orchestrated by his late father-in-law. But it was such a cliché that you couldn't just come out and say, in this day and age, that your wife had gone crazy unless you had some receipts.

By now Rob had plenty. Not just from Louie Cafarelli and the cave-dwelling corners of the internet, but from the Lifeboat Supply Co. Instagram feed. After scrolling through two years of posts, he understood the business model as well as he was ever going to: the girl bought and sold used clothes and homewares at various markets and festivals around the country. Every post included a description of the item (which might list the designer, material, condition, rarity, and year of origin), a string of numbers (which had baffled him until he learned from the cries of dismay in the comment section that these were measurements in inches), and a caption that was either willfully cryptic or simply unintelligible to anybody over thirty. *Orange Tab Tuesday*, read one below a photo of somebody's ass in skintight Levi's with an Orange Crush label stuck to the left pocket. There was a new post every other day, sometimes more often, sometimes with the next stop listed in the caption. *Fairfield Flea, be there or be square.* Three days ago, a snap of several wooden crates in the back of a truck, a woman's face reflected in the driver's-side mirror. Not the girl and not Suzanne, but a hard-looking character with graying red hair. *Bringing some goodies to Haskill's Grocery with the Lifeboat's last captain,* the caption said, which didn't make much sense to Rob. A quick Google search had taught him how to turn on post notifications, so he wouldn't miss one, just in case.

He emerged from the shower and clicked through ten different variations of ESPN before his phone chimed on the nightstand where he'd left it to charge. He lunged across the unmade bed and pulled it right out of the wall. There was a new picture, posted just a minute ago. He felt instantly lightheaded. He'd seen the girl model her own wares—hipless and titless, too slender for his taste—and occasionally a white guy who always looked half-asleep. (The eight-fingered man? Rob hadn't found a photo where he could see both hands.) Clothes clinging to them or hanging off depending on the item and how it might appear to its best advantage. *Thursday Thirst Trap* went one caption, with a little panting emoji face. Sex still sold, it seemed. But on Suzanne—who had been so averse to sex for so long, who always wore oversized T-shirts and sweatshirts like she was hiding her body from someone, who was *forty*, for fuck's sake—the coquettish angle was perverse. She wore red heart-shaped sunglasses and a black cowboy hat tipped jauntily over one eye. A grease-striped wifebeater with—obviously—no bra underneath. She pursed her lips to kiss a brown fingertip reaching into the frame from off camera. Tiny tattoo of a honeybee above the knuckle. It didn't take a genius to guess whose shades she was wearing, whose finger was in her mouth. Rob knew Suzanne was sick, maybe crazy, but this? *Sweetheart of the Rodeo* ♥ the caption said, and for one dizzy moment every hot drop of blood in his body screamed scarlet through the room. Suddenly he hated her—for every disappointment, every slight, every intimate humiliation. *Can't wait to be back in the Stockyards. Come see us in the Lone Star State!* the caption crowed. Below was a list of cities, markets, and festival dates.

"Sweetheart," Rob said, already reaching for his jeans, for his wallet, for his keys, "I just might."

THE **B** SIDE

BAD AS ME

Suzanne woke with a jolt as the Lifeboat bumped over something.
She rolled onto her hands and knees to twitch the back curtains open.
No idea how long they'd been driving or how long she'd slept, but the
road behind them hadn't seen fresh asphalt in some years. A sign for
Jackson flashed past. She closed her eyes and the atlas unfolded over
the dark, with its wax zigzags and coffee stains. Jackson meant Nashville
was behind them, Memphis up ahead. She tumbled out of bed and
hopped into a pair of cutoff Wranglers discarded on the floor. Phoebe
was at the dinette with a beggar quilt on the table and a needle in her
mouth.

"Did I wake you dragging the blanket off?" she asked.

"Might have melted if you hadn't," Suzanne said. Summer showed
no mercy in an aluminum trailer cooled only by open windows and an
AC unit older than she was.

"Sweat looks good on you."

"Liar," Suzanne said, and Phoebe blew her a kiss. "Change of the
guard?" She peered out over the window box, where Simon's crop of
hot peppers had ripened to an eye-popping red.

"He hasn't been driving that long," Phoebe said. "Probably needs
gas. She's a guzzler." Even with Gil's modifications and whatever further
surgery Simon and Arlette had performed so she could ably tow the
Lifeboat, Blondie would never be fuel-efficient.

Suzanne stretched, heard her back crack. "Shall we go soak up the scenery?"

Phoebe pinched the needle against her lips, blew invisible smoke. "I love the smell of diesel in the morning."

Each pit stop had a rhythm to it, a shopping list that never ended but only evolved. Today the necessities were toothpaste and WD-40; the sustenance powdered donuts (Phoebe), black licorice (Simon), and corn chips (Suzanne); the impulse purchases a bottle of bubbles and a bumper sticker for the International Rock-A-Billy Hall of Fame & Museum. Thus burdened with treasure, they waited for Blondie to drink her fill from the pump. Phoebe offered a donut to Trouble, panting in the passenger seat. She took it with surprisingly gentle teeth, then gobbled it down whole. She'd chased the trailer halfway to the highway when they left Arlette's, ignoring Simon's shouts to "Go home!" Finally, Suzanne said, "I think that's what she's trying to do." At first, the dog refused to let Simon out of her sight, but now she seemed comfortably certain that when he disappeared, he'd be back.

Phoebe blew a stream of bubbles at Suzanne. Such a simple indulgence. Because it served no practical purpose, in the narrow confines of their budget it felt like a luxury. Simon and Phoebe were used to hard work and a hard sort of life, but they made room for delight, however mundane. *I'd like to live while I'm alive* was something Phoebe often said. Suzanne wasn't good at enjoying things and felt guilty when she did, convinced she should be doing something else—more productive, more practical, more worth-her-time. But she was getting better. She took the bubble wand and blew them straight up into the air, watched them bob and wander, swelling with sunlight until they burst.

"Hey." Simon nodded toward the county road peeling away from the interstate. "What do you say we investigate?" Two signs were planted more or less on top of each other. One pointed to a town called, of all things, Three Way. Below that, a sandwich board for an estate sale pointed in the same direction. Phoebe let Trouble lick the powdered sugar from her fingers and wiped them on the seat of her shorts.

"I'd say how could we resist?"

They always braked for estate sales, yard sales, garage sales. Most people didn't know what they had and sold it for much more or much less than it was worth. But Phoebe was not most people. She was a born haggler and a born hustler and Most People walked away from her wrongly believing they'd gotten the better deal. Simon replaced the nozzle and the gas cap, let her take the wheel, and climbed back into the Airstream with Trouble and Suzanne. They blew bubbles out the window as they bumped along, swapping Fritos and licorice and swigs from a frothy can of Dr Pepper they found rolling around in the fridge.

"Where is this place?" Suzanne asked after the third estate sale sign floated past. They seemed to be getting farther apart, and every time she thought they'd seen the last one and they'd have to give up and go back, another popped up like a daisy.

"The best ones are a bit of a drive," Simon said. "Anyone rich enough to have a real 'estate' tends to put it far away from the riffraff." Which made sense, when she thought about it, which she'd never had a reason to do before. Life on the Lifeboat was like that.

After so many turns that she'd run out of chips and lost track of which way was north, they braked on a grassy bank behind a dozen other cars staggered along a line of loblolly pines. The air was lighter and sweeter, the unrelenting sunlight tangled in the treetops so the heat below was almost bearable. More people had followed the signs than Suzanne expected—some walking into the house empty-handed, others emerging laden with loot. Chinese lamps and silver kettles and rugs rolled up like enchiladas. The buyers were all cut from the same sort of cloth, richly but badly dressed in sport shirts and garish gold jewelry. Phoebe represented the only real melanin on the property and, together with Simon and Suzanne, brought the average age down by about fifteen years. As the Lifeboat unloaded and Blondie's purring engine curled up for a nap, they attracted more than a little attention, ranging from politely curious to appreciably hostile. Ironically not the right sort of people to be traipsing through Three Way.

Simon told Trouble to stay and made a beeline for the garage, where a couple of retirees in pleated khakis were huffing and puffing about horsepower with their hands in their pockets. Phoebe and Suzanne entered through the front door as a woman with an old-fashioned bouffant counted change out of a mahogany humidor with a tasseled brass key. A pair of French doors opened into a soaring foyer that branched into several other rooms. Shoppers and time-killers wandered through, whispering, "If it were fifty dollars *less*" or "Wouldn't your sister just love that?" In the dining room, oil paintings crowded together like a tiny museum. In the kitchen, fleets of glassware stood in regimented rows on the speckled marble countertop. Phoebe prowled around with predatory intensity, hunting for nothing more specific than a steal nobody else had spotted. She snagged a pair of copper mule mugs that clinked together festively as she proceeded through the house.

Suzanne followed her instincts into a corner office occupied only by books. They were loosely organized by subject, and, as she browsed, the shape of the family who had owned them emerged. There was a chaotic collection of hardback biographies lumped together with personal-finance manifestos with titles like *Seven Secrets of Successful Wealth Management* and *The Greatest Gamble: Mastering the Stock Market.* Surely the husband. On the other side of the room, an impressive assortment of true crime rubbed elbows with cowboy romance novels, spines cracked like half-broken horses. An unwieldy pyramid of books on ghost-hunting and paranormal encounters teetered on a side table. Suzanne recognized some of the titles. His or hers, this pile of hauntings? Probably hers. Whoever she was, she seemed to have a craving for excitement satisfied vicariously. Suzanne was three books deep in the stack when her own name flashed across a shiny black jacket. Suzanne Westman, *Dust and Bones.* Above that, the white frame of a Polaroid where two ghostly faces loomed out of a sea of sand—features scrubbed out by the sun.

"Should've known you'd be buried in the books," Phoebe said, making her jump. She'd picked up a rotary telephone to keep the mule mugs company. "What's all this hocus-pocus?" She turned over a book called *Ghosts of Gettysburg.*

"Pretty mixed bag," Suzanne said. "Lots of junk, but there are a few good histories here."

"I didn't know you were a supernaturalist."

"Well, not really. I did a series on so-called ghost towns, and some portraits of the people who still, y'know, haunt the place." She was a paranormal investigator, if anything. Trying to understand what made someone cling to someplace with nothing left to offer but the name of "home." She tried to slide *Dust and Bones* out of sight, but Phoebe had an eagle eye.

"Shit, Suze, is that you? Is that your book? Let me see!"

"No, it's nothing—"

"Are you kidding? It's so fucking cool! If I'd done this I'd talk about it all the time."

Suzanne flushed, grabbed the book away, and put it back where she'd found it.

"Oh, come on, we have to buy it!"

"Please, no—I have a hundred copies in a box somewhere I couldn't pay anybody to take off my hands," Suzanne said, which was true. She'd been too shy about showing it. Most of the photos were only of ghosts— of buildings, businesses, once-bustling downtowns—and all the flesh-and-blood subjects had consented to pose for a snapshot. But still she hesitated, wary of crossing the line dividing travelers from tourists. They weren't her stories to tell. "Let's get out of here." She retreated to the living room. "What's left to see?"

"Just the back of the house," Phoebe said, following a half step behind. "That way."

She pointed Suzanne to a sunroom where wearable treasures glittered under glass cases. It was, like the library, an eclectic collection. Ruby bracelets displayed alongside silver bolo ties, strings of pearls and velvet hatbands and spur straps studded with diamonds. Phoebe eyed a gold money clip with obsidian inlays and whispered, "In case you didn't know how rich I am, I'm the kind of man who keeps his money bound in more money." Suzanne pretended her snort was a sneeze as a woman with skin like birch bark scowled at them over a music box where a one-legged ballerina did endless pirouettes. Everything was light-years beyond their budget, so they continued into the next room, where a sign posted over the door just said GUNS.

It was a dark, sunless grotto full of oversized leather furniture: the cattle baron's version of a man cave. Guns and hunting knives were mounted on the walls like fine art, while a crowd of taxidermized animals looked on with empty glass eyes. The head of a six-point buck presided over the fireplace and Suzanne thought, unavoidably, of his ragtag brethren hanging over the bar at Wild Bucks. A sleek brown weasel had frozen in the act of climbing a branch, the sinuous twist of its body eerily still even as it gave the impression of motion. To add insult to injury, it had been repurposed as a bookend, propping up a dozen *Field & Stream* magazines. Suzanne wanted to leave immediately. Not her kind of haunted.

The critter mausoleum was connected, through a confusing series of corridors, to the largest bedroom, which opened into an equally enormous closet. "Jackpot." Phoebe set the phone and the mule mugs on a shelf and started flicking through the racks.

"What are we looking for?" Suzanne asked.

"Anything fun, funky, designer, or Pendleton," Phoebe said. She held up a faded green flannel, so long she could have belted it and worn it as a dress. "Nothing too preppy, unless it can be punked up some." Phoebe knew the value of everything, including a strong personal brand. She didn't do preppy. Didn't do formal. Didn't stock anything made after her birth, which made sense to Suzanne. Tough to think of your own youth as "vintage."

"I don't know if 'funky' does it justice," Suzanne said, holding up a red sweater that featured a dancing skeleton tangled in sequin Christmas tree lights.

"That," Phoebe said with a widening grin, "is an abomination."

"Are we buying it?"

"For"—she checked the tag—"six dollars? Obviously."

Often as not, comic relief trumped branding or taste.

"Anything else worth absconding with?"

"Hmm." Phoebe shuffled through a rack of pants and slacks. "A few too many rhinestones for me."

"This is a few too many rhinestones for Liberace." Suzanne pulled a T-shirt free, bedazzled across the bust to read I ♥ GWB. "What's GWB?"

"Suze," Phoebe said, and let the letters pour out with a thick Texas twang. "Gee-dubya-bee?"

"Oh my God." She almost dropped it. "Are they *George Bush groupies?*"

"Based on the rest of this place," Phoebe said, "what about that would surprise you?" She folded the skeleton sweater over one arm and held the door. Suzanne made a hasty exit.

"Less surprise than . . . I don't know, dismay?" She lowered her voice to a whisper as they tiptoed back through the taxidermy den. A dead beaver stared at her, looking oddly lost, frozen in the midst of gathering sticks as if it had waddled into the room and forgotten what for. "These people shouldn't have *guns*. And I definitely don't want to give them more money."

"Wait." Phoebe held her back, poked her head into the next room. They were alone with the army of uncanny stuffed animals. Phoebe's fingertips trailed along a trestle table where a collection of revolvers pointed every which way. Her hand fastened on a pearl-handled six-shooter with a long silver barrel. She twirled it once and, liking the feel, slipped it in the back of her waistband. "Two birds," she said, and tugged her shirt down to hide it—just as Suzanne had watched a hundred shoplifters do, what felt like a hundred years ago, "one stone. Let's go."

The cashier didn't look at them twice, except for a disapproving glance at Phoebe's nose ring. They walked back to the Lifeboat, cool as could be, and collapsed in a fit of laughter as soon as the door closed behind them. Suzanne had never stolen anything worth more than a cigarette and couldn't help being impressed by Phoebe's audacity. Forever mooning after people braver and bolder than she was.

"I didn't even look," she said, pushing herself up on one elbow. They'd landed in a sprawl across the cushions in the lounge. "How much were they asking?"

Phoebe lifted her hips and pulled the revolver loose. A tiny scrap of paper, dainty as a tea tag, dangled from the trigger guard.

"*Eight hundred dollars?*" Suzanne asked, gobsmacked. "For that little thing?"

"Aren't we a size queen." Phoebe snapped the cylinder out to see if it was loaded, which it wasn't. "It's more about bang for buck, pun intended. This is collectible. It would actually be worth a lot more, except it used to be part of a set and they don't seem to have the other one."

"Where'd you learn that?" Suzanne asked. "You don't seem like the gun-toting type."

"Nah." She gave Suzanne a mysterious smile, one with a history she couldn't divine. "But I've known a few." Like Simon, Phoebe was older than her years in most ways, younger in some. She could spot conmen and bullshitters ten miles away, bore the spider-bite scars of someone who'd already had and kicked a habit. She didn't talk about where she'd come from, but Suzanne didn't, either, so Suzanne didn't ask. Phoebe squinted one eye shut, pointed the revolver out the back window, and pulled the trigger. *Click.* "Bullseye," she decided, blowing imaginary smoke from the barrel.

The door banged open and Simon stuck his head inside, hair mussed from the heat so it stood out in a halo, like a young Einstein. "Hey," he said. "What's with the gun?"

"Just restoring some karmic balance to the universe," Suzanne told him.

"Never mind, I don't want to know," he said, wisely. "Do we have room in the bed for some jack stands?"

"It's a pretty tight fit for the three of us and Trouble," Phoebe said. They were learning to sleep like puzzle pieces, Simon on his back and Suzanne on her stomach, with Phoebe stretched like taffy in between. "But you're welcome to start sleeping on the couch," she told him, kicking one long leg across Suzanne's lap.

"I'm going to take that as a yes," Simon said, and pulled the door shut with a *clang*.

"Hope he hurries," Suzanne said, glancing at the Donald Duck watch she'd been wearing for a week. She vastly preferred its cartoon-ish simplicity to the smartwatch she'd worn for years and left behind like everything else. One of those gifts from Rob that felt more like an admonishment, a reminder that she could stand to exercise more, she could be in better shape, she really *could* learn to like running if only she'd stick with it long enough to see some results. "We'd better beat it before they realize that revolver is gone."

"Especially because it's not the only thing I stole."

"You should change your name to Artful Dodger Dry Goods."

"That's not bad, actually."

"Well, let's see."

"Ta-da." Phoebe handed her the book. Her book, *Dust and Bones*. Where she'd been hiding it, Suzanne was afraid to ask. "Couldn't leave it there, sue me. These old ghost towns . . . it's weird, they kinda look familiar." She flipped through the first few pages, intuiting what Suzanne had tried to capture the whole year she spent photographing them. The inexplicable feeling that you'd been there before, when no one had been there for decades. "Who knows?" Phoebe lingered on a photo of a green metal shopping cart, missing a wheel and abandoned in a wash of sand a hundred miles from any grocery store. "Maybe we'll stop through a few."

Suzanne didn't know what to say. "Yeah," she decided. "I'd like that."

"In that case"—Phoebe reached for the atlas, left in the lounge last time they found time to lounge around—"we've got a lot of ground to cover. Let's get the hell out of Dodge."

THE **A** SIDE

VOODOO IDOL

Most of the openers were local acts, and most of them were awful. The friends and family who came to hear them cheered and clapped while everyone else got louder and rowdier waiting for the main event to start. Once the final huddle formed, Suzanne was off like a shot, bobbing and weaving through the crowd with the ease of expertise. A beer hall was no different from a shopping mall when a Neiman Marcus sale was on. She squeezed through a thicket of legs to duck under the merch table and popped up on the other side like a prairie dog.

"Jesus!" Carney barked. "A hundred times I've told you not to do that!" Which was exactly why she did it, why she'd never stop. Carney was always grumbling and grouching, but he was soft and sweet as an Oatmeal Creme Pie on the inside.

"What's the sitch?" she said, a catchphrase she'd picked up from Doug.

"We need more tapes and more T-shirts, size small. And then I need change for—c'mon, man, all you got is a fifty?"

Suzanne tore into a fresh box of cassettes with the bottle opener on Carney's key ring and handed them up in stacks of five. "Tapes." She shuffled the boxes around until she found one marked with an *S*. "Tees." She counted out change for a fifty, "Minus eight for the tape and five for the poster, that's twenty, thirty, five, six, seven." The buyer stared at her, no less startled than Carney to have her spring up in the middle of his transaction. "Anything else?"

"You breakin' some kind of child labor law here?"

Suzanne smiled sweetly. "I'm a volunteer."

He flicked through the bills like he didn't believe she counted right, but couldn't find a fault and walked away shaking his head. "Weird."

Everybody else kept their comments to themselves. Carney and Suzanne were a crack team, and, so long as the line was moving faster, nobody would complain or report them to the Department of Labor. They had almost reached the end of the queue when the lights went down and a shout went up and the stragglers hurried to hand over their money in the dark. Carney clicked his flashlight on and Suzanne sat on the cash box, which was the next best line of defense after the key broke off in the lock. Small for her age, but too big to carry off without a fight.

She stayed where she was until Carney patted the top of her head. She stood up with aching knees but proud and pleased to be part of the Kill Team. Carney counted the last of the bills into the till and wedged it out of sight under some T-shirts. There wouldn't be another bum rush until the band played a ballad, which they didn't do often, because they didn't have many. Not that kind of band. They had style, they had range, they had a certain disregard for decorum. Their brand of black magic didn't work on everyone, and every night Suzanne watched a few people walk out looking spooked and scandalized. But the Kill Team relished this as much as adulation. When Suzanne asked why, Skelly broke his usual sinister silence to expound the golden rule of rock and roll: "If you don't piss people off, you're not doing it right." A peculiar guiding principle she would follow unconsciously most of the rest of her life.

No two sets were quite the same, Skelly prone to long, indulgent solos, Gil just as guilty of unwieldy improvisation and a running repartee with the right kind of audience. *They enable each other* was Ruby's diagnosis, but they challenged each other, too. A streak of sly one-up-manship drove them both to more ambitious antics, competing for the room's attention, stealing one another's thunder. But more often they met in the middle, collided like subatomic particles moving at the speed of light and set the stage on fire.

Suzanne loved watching the floor, the current of the music rippling from one person to another until they became one many-headed monster, moving almost in unison. She ached to join the congregation, but the audience was off-limits. "You stay with Gracie or Carney or Doug until you can come find me," Gil said. "If anybody gives you trouble, you're a VIP." The badge became her prized possession, hung around her neck like a medal of honor at every gig, tucked away with her Polaroids for safekeeping everyplace else. She rubbed the laminate until her thumb wore off the shine—a memento and a talisman at once.

"C'mon," Carney growled, incapable of a true whisper, but the amps were much too loud for that to matter. "Up and at 'em." Suzanne took his hands, held tight, and left gravity's grip for one glorious moment, then landed with a bump on his shoulders. He barely seemed to feel her weight and didn't mind when she grabbed the strap of his snapback to keep from falling off. Up there she could see everything, every turn of the heel and bend of the strings, every elbow thrown in anger, every sloppy, drunken kiss, every bouncer waiting by every exit door. "VIP seating," Carney told her. "Part of the package for anybody weighing less than a hundred pounds." Sometimes he left her up there all night, making change for merch buyers with arms long enough to reach. But the only moment that really mattered was "Impersonator"—Suzanne's favorite song and everyone else's.

Tonight Gil wore fishnet tights under acid-washed jeans with enormous holes in both knees. This with a black tuxedo vest and no shirt underneath. Curls combed back in a James Dean quiff, three broken watches on one wrist, a choker made of shark teeth. The band kept all their costumes in the same two ugly trunks; nobody wore the same thing twice except their shoes. Every night they walked out looking like five overgrown children playing a twisted game of dress-up. One part cowpunk and one part burlesque, all parts unpredictable.

Gil cued up the band with a flick of the wrist. He fanned himself, all hot and bothered, leaning on the mic stand like he might fall down without it. "Is it hot in here, Milwaukee?" he asked the room at large. "Or is that just me?" He cupped one hand around his ear as the crowd called out their answers. "You say it's not hot enough?" Nobody had said any such thing, but they cheered anyway. "Skelly, baby, turn it up."

Skelly gave him a lopsided leer and blew smoke across the follow spot. His middle finger flashed in a brass jacket like a shotgun shell, and when he pulled it down the fretboard, the strings squealed and screamed like the souls of the damned being dragged down to hell. Ruby's bassline butted in as Gil gossiped with the audience, pausing every now and then for a lick of his latest lollipop. He ate them onstage for a laugh, for a lark, for something to do, because they turned his tongue outrageous colors and he was too much in the habit to stop. They'd started selling them at the merch table, and Doug kept talking about an endorsement deal, but Gil and the Kills weren't exactly kid friendly, except when that kid was Suzanne. She knew every note, every word, drank it in every night like a life-saving elixir.

They say he's a skilled impersonator
Imaginary movie star
All dressed up in big ideas
Small change in his shoes
Hungry for a lick of luck
Sick and tired
Turnin', screwed

The kick drum pumped like a telltale heart. Skelly waited in the oil spill of shadows stage left, sucking his cigarette, biding his time.

Some slick equivocator
Folded fortune in the cards
You'll be shit before you shine, my son
That ugly mug won't get you far
Best get yourself a gun

BANG. The heel of Skelly's snakeskin boot cracked the stage in two. Gil howled like a man possessed as the steely Stratocaster tore through the air. The Hands flickered and flashed across the mirrored pick-guard, flinging shocks of light around the room.

They say he's some great pretender
One wild hair unto the throne

Coulda been a real contender—

CRASH. Nash smashed the cymbals. Ruby's bass fell flat against her thighs as she shadowboxed with Gil, who jerked and staggered, pretending to take her punches on the chin.

Gone to see his name in—

Knocked his lights out—

Ain't nobody home

He tilted backward, knocked right off his feet, but Skelly was there to catch him on his shoulders, still spread-eagled and shredding the strings. They fell against each other, back-to-back but toe-to-toe. "Oh, *help* me," Gil wailed. "Lord, I'm *dizzy.*" They slid across the floor, lower and lower, farther and farther, until their shoulder blades were barely touching. But the Hands moved faster and faster, teasing the Flying V into an ear-splitting frenzy. They turned at the same time—with another stupendous *CRASH* from Nash—Skelly falling forward on one knee, Gil landing flat on his back. He shivered and twitched at each fizz from the amps, Frankenstein's monster coming to life. The rhythm section gathered speed, Gil jumping and jerking until, with a gasp, he jackknifed upright—miraculously revived. "Hold on!" he hollered. Everything stopped. He rolled his eyes and flashed a smile. "Ooh, my head." Back on his feet and off to the races, with a wicked glint in his eye.

Called himself an entertainer

Of notions most notorious

Oh, ladies, don't disdain!

I was a handsome devil once

Met Old Nick at the crossroads

And fiddled to defend myself

The better devil let me go—

So sorry, sir!

Thought you was someone else

With one last percussive thunderclap, the music stopped, and the crowd went wild. That was the way it happened every night. If they got the exorcism right, then they could do no wrong. Suzanne had watched it from Carney's shoulders half a dozen times but wasn't tired of it yet. Didn't think she ever could be. She got lost in the music, seduced by the strings, mesmerized by this strange, swashbuckling side of Gil that she had never seen. It was always too soon that Carney squeezed her knee, offered his hands to help her down, and said, "Okay, Squirt. Time to earn your keep."

The merch table was slammed for half an hour after encore. Suzanne counted change and tapes and T-shirts so fast her head spun. They ran out of size medium before they ran out of patrons, and half the band was back to take the stage apart before the last stragglers had been herded outside by security. By then she was bouncing on the balls of her feet, itching to get backstage, back to the thick of things. When Carney released her, she tore across the room, dodging brooms and stanchions and wet spots on the floor. The man at the door looked at her strangely, but she flashed her backstage pass. "I'm with the band," she announced, and his eyebrows rose. "Gil Delgado is my dad." That, too, happened the same way every night. She said it so proudly—*Gil Delgado is my dad*—and they looked at her face and they couldn't deny it.

"O-kay," the man said, and stood aside to let her through.

She'd learned by then to watch for landmarks in the maze of hallways and blind alleys backstage. Left at the water fountain, right at the men's room, left again at the life-sized likeness of Joe Strummer spray-painted on the bare brick wall. Some places were so small there was only one dressing room for everyone, but Milwaukee had taken to the band and the digs were a cut above what they'd become accustomed to. The Kills shared a dressing room; Gil, for the first time, had one to himself. Suzanne basked in the glow of that name on the door—DELGADO. The sign was a good sign, evidence in fat black marker that he was somebody now. She banged on the door with one eager fist.

No matter how tired he was, Gil's arms were always open to catch her. When they all shared a dressing room, the Kills gathered to hear Suzanne's feedback. As Nash put it, "Kids don't bullshit. They don't want a buck or a favor or your name on some dotted line. They just tell it like it is." Suzanne took this duty very seriously. Already hoping that someday she might be a real documentarian, go to a show every night and take iconic pictures.

"There she is," Gil said, like she was the reason for the name on the door, not him. "Right this way and do your worst." He fell into a chair and she threw herself in his lap, not caring how sweaty he was, hot and clammy at once.

"They love the harmonica on 'Minnie's Place,' you should keep that."

"Noted. What else?"

"Ruby's mic was too hot for 'Off the Rockets.' She shouldn't be louder than you."

He curled one stray lock off her forehead. "I'll let you be the one to tell her that." Ruby's temper was like a geyser—slow to blow but when it did, *whoo! Watch out.* "What else?"

"I think you shouldn't shave," she said.

He stroked his chin. "Why's that?"

She laid her finger like a mustache on his upper lip. "You don't look like you." Before this summer she'd only ever seen him at home, off the road, where he didn't bother with razor blades. "You look like you're trying to look like you when you were Skelly's age."

"Ouch. That one went straight to the heart."

"Sorry."

"Don't be." He kissed her fingertip. "You might be right. I'll try it Sunday night and you'll tell me if you like it."

"Deal."

"How was merch?"

"Busy," she said. "We're out of medium."

"T-shirts?"

"No, underwear."

He laughed. "Now, there's an idea." She loved the sound and the feel of his laugh, how it crackled and sparked. Making him laugh felt like she could do magic. "Never change, kid," he told her. "You really are one of a kind."

"You think someday I'll be somebody like you?"

He blinked, the laugh snagged in his mouth. "Aw, honey," he said. "I sure hope not."

Her heart swerved. She'd made him laugh, then made him sad. She wanted to un-ask the question, take it back. But his answer bruised her, too—unsure why he'd renounced their precious likeness. They weren't one of a kind, or so she thought; they were two. She slid down out of his lap, kicked through pieces of his costume discarded on the floor. Little things she never noticed from a distance but the outfit wouldn't be complete without. The crucifix earring. Silver toe caps, each with two tiny spikes like a bull's horns. His style, like his stage presence, playfully promiscuous. *What do you really offer an audience?* she'd heard Louie ask on a strategy call some years ago. Gil thought about the answer for no time at all.

Something indescribable.

Thanks, Louie said dryly. *That's helpful.*

A one-of-a-kind, indescribable somebody. No sweat. But there was sweat in buckets, and blood and tears, flat tires and broken strings and late nights and early mornings with empty bellies and empty pockets in between. Music was music, inviolable in its way, but entertainment? That was a whole other animal, too big and brutish to be tamed. Even Suzanne had felt the shocks, Gil's punishing rehearsal schedules, Gracie's short temper when they ran short of time or money, Nash's frequent nausea, Skelly's evil attitude. They loved the show, loved the road, loved each other in their way, but love wasn't enough to live on.

"C'mon," Gil said, his voice too light and easy now. "Let's get outta here while the gettin' is good. Got your backpack? Got the map?" He trusted her to be his copilot, and Gracie gladly left the atlas in her custody. She'd worn her crayons down to stubs and spent every late-night diner meal making trades for better stock from whatever random selection of colors the waitress brought.

"Uh-huh." She hefted the backpack onto her shoulders but stopped with one hand on the door. Backstage brimmed with indecipherable sounds, but someone on the other side was shouting. It was a woman's voice, crazy with fear or maybe anger. "Dad?"

"Stay here." Gil nudged her behind him. As he stepped out into the hall, the hollering got louder.

"LAURIE! *LAU-RIE!* You little sh—"

"Are you looking for someone?"

Suzanne peered around the doorjamb.

"My sister disappeared back here with that *creep.*" There were two women in the hall, or rather a woman and a girl. "LAU-RIE!" The woman was the one doing the yelling, holding the girl by the wrist. She was old enough to have mastered mascara and lipstick and teasing her hair, but not too old to cry in front of strangers. Her sneakers squeaked and scuffed on the floor as the woman jerked her around.

"Let me see if I can help you find her."

"I don't need *your* help."

"You don't seem to be having much luck by yourself," Gil said politely. He turned to try the door to the Kills' dressing room, which was locked. He banged with the flat of his hand. "Strings," he said. "You in there?" Banged again, harder. "Skelly. *Eric, open the fucking door.*"

Suzanne frowned, still lurking out of sight. The knob rattled and the Hands appeared, holding another girl by the elbow. She bore a striking resemblance to the woman glaring daggers at Gil, except for her outfit, which mostly matched her friend. A poof of black skirt and a white shirt that looked like it had been run over by a lawn mower. Teased hair and too much lipstick, smeared around by now. "Sorry." Skelly leaned on the wall with one bony hip. Blew smoke in their faces and tapped the ash on the floor. "We had the music on."

"The hell you did," the woman said. Laurie changed hands like a crumpled dollar bill. Her sister snatched her from Skelly, yanked her out of the room.

"Laurie says she wants to be a musician." He shrugged, unfazed by her anger. "I said I'd show her a few licks."

"She's *fifteen.*"

A crevice of a smile around the filter. "She's good for her age."

Gil interrupted before anyone could start shouting again. "Sorry for your trouble," he said, raising his voice but not quite yelling—just filling the space, taking over the corridor. "Let me see if we can't have someone— Carney!" he called. "Would you walk these ladies out?"

They moved the way he waved them, but only after a tense little scuffle. The woman seemed to want to stay and sink her nails in someone, but the girls were grumbling mutinously, and she finally gave in to Carney's outstretched arm, sweeping them along toward the exit. Gil watched them disappear around the corner. The Hands hooked one thumb in his waistband, head thrown back like he might laugh. Still for a moment as the footsteps faded. Then Gil grabbed a fistful of his open shirt and slammed him against the wall.

"The f—"

"No, you don't talk," Gil said, one forearm pinned across Skelly's shallow chest. "I talk." Suzanne froze in her hiding place, startled by the unexpected violence, the sound of one body striking another, one body thrown against solid cinder block. Gil pressed his elbow up under Skelly's jaw until he gagged. Pulled the sign off the door with his free hand and threw the crumpled paper in his face. "This is my band. It's *Gil* and the Kills, in case you forgot." The voice that had filled the corridor a moment ago shrunk down like a secret now. "We are so close to something huge, and if you blow it for us"—Gil plucked the cigarette out of Skelly's mouth, took a long, indulgent drag, and put it right back where he'd found it—"I'll fucking kill you."

Skelly started to say something, mouth winding up like he was going to spit.

"Hey, guys?"

Gil took his arm off Skelly's neck as Doug stomped around the corner. The Hands jerked his collar straight, pulling so hard on the cigarette his cheeks made two morbid black hollows.

"We're just, uh, waiting on you two," Doug said, glancing from one to the other as if he wasn't sure what he'd just interrupted.

"On our way," Gil said, and didn't wait to see whether Skelly would follow when he started down the hall.

Suzanne stayed where she was, nailed to the floor. A panicked flutter in her chest, ears ringing with the echoes of the argument—flesh on flesh and bone on bone, that unfamiliar voice in her father's mouth, the bladed edge she'd never heard before.

THE B SIDE

NUMBER ONE WITH A BULLET

They went from Jackson to Jackson, due south on I-55. Simon had collected the urgent stuff and nonsense of life from Arlette, but Phoebe had her own administrative business to catch up on and "her people," as she called them, weren't far. They drew a wobbly line from Tennessee to Mississippi in Jungle Green and guessed they might get there by nightfall.

They arrived just as the lilac curtain of dusk was descending, a stripe of strawberry pink still smeared along the horizon. Phoebe steered the Lifeboat into a scrubby, sprawling neighborhood where houses crouched low in the switchgrass, bowlegged columns propping up porch roofs festooned with Spanish moss. They turned onto a winding street that dead-ended in a cul-de-sac littered with skateboards and soccer balls. Mismatched children stopped in their tracks to watch the Lifeboat float by. A boy in a T-shirt from the Jackson Zoo started up from a stupor on the front steps of a house that might have been his or anybody's, hollering for someone called Carla. Suzanne glanced at Simon, who shrugged and said, "The media has been alerted."

Carla, as it happened, was Phoebe's half sister and the neighborhood gossip. She had the same almond eyes and the same spray of freckles, but her hair was heavy and flat, decidedly not Black, and by the time they found a door to knock on, everybody on the block already knew they were there. She waved them inside, asking dozens of questions she left no time to answer.

"How long since we've seen you? Never stay in the same place more than five minutes, do you? Have you eaten?" She interrupted her one-sided interrogation to shout into the living room in Spanish. Half a dozen young men with beer bottles dangling from their fingers looked up from the ballgame underway on a rabbit-eared television parked on top of a plastic cat carrier. The door was open, as if the occupant had only stepped out for a stroll. Suzanne hoped Trouble, prowling around in the bushes out front, hadn't found him. "You remember Tito? Alphonse? You still drink? Eat wheat? Everybody's got allergies now. *¡Oye, Ale!*" She banged on a closed door. "*Otras personas necesitan usar el baño.* My son, seventeen, he's glued to the mirror every Friday night, you remember those years?" Suzanne had no idea it was Friday and didn't remember much of seventeen except crashing the Volvo and hauling her hemorrhaging mother out of the bathtub before she fled to New York. She elected not to answer, and Carla elected not to notice. "Have you talked to Bruno?"

"Carla," Phoebe said. "We just got here. We just walked in the door." She hadn't stopped talking long enough for them to talk to anyone else.

"Sorry we didn't bring anything," said Simon, soul of diplomacy.

The kitchen was roughly the size of a cubicle but held about a dozen people fussing over pots on the stove and casserole dishes coming out of the oven and mixed drinks in pitchers with the ice already melting. The back door was open, letting the heat out or maybe in. "Please," Carla said. "You think we need more?"

"What's the occasion?" Simon asked.

A dark-skinned woman peeling tinfoil off blistered ears of corn pinched his cheek with a lecherous wink. "Ain't you occasion enough," she said, and he blushed to the roots of his hair. *Aw, shucks.* Phoebe looked on, chewing a thumbnail, eyes alive with mischief just like the other children on the block, of the block, of this peculiar village where neighbors and families were entangled and inseparable. Content to disappear into a corner, Suzanne marinated in the harmless mayhem of too many people in too small a house, speaking three languages at once. Scraps of Spanglish tugged at her ear, but she was too shy of her gringo accent to try to make conversation. Wondering, was this what Gil's family might have felt like, if she'd ever had the chance to know them? The life he shared with Gracie had always moved to the same infectious music.

Before long the whole hoopla picked up and moved out the back door. Nobody left empty-handed, including Suzanne, who found herself holding a basket of biscuits still hot from the oven. The other houses turned out their inhabitants, too, and everyone tramped toward nothing, apparently, until a square wooden platform appeared, adrift on the sea of switchgrass. Soft, flowering spikes with tiny purple seedpods feathered the edges of everything. The sky was still light, in that manner of long Southern sundowns in summer.

As they drew closer, Suzanne saw that the platform had posts and ropes, and two three-legged stools in opposite corners. A willowy woman who could have been Phoebe's half sister on the other side leaned close and told her, "Great timing. It's Fight Night."

Suzanne traded the biscuits for a beer and a place beside Simon on an old picnic bench. Trouble flopped on his feet, ivory fur full of little black burrs, but she'd never looked more at ease. The rest of the crowd—and it was a crowd by then, ranging in age from babies on hips to elders holding elbows—settled in lawn chairs with plates from the potluck. Corn and crawdads, skewers off the barbecue, grilled pork and steak tortas, bean salad and slaw. Suzanne ate too much of everything and regretted nothing at all, scraped her plate onto the grass for Trouble to wolf down the scraps. Someone passed bug spray around, and someone else brought a boombox along. The music rollicked under the chatter and clatter of serving spoons, the heartbeat of the neighborhood.

Suzanne had only ever seen boxing on TV, never in a backyard. Two boys in their late teens ducked under the ropes to a chorus of cheers and good-natured heckling. Two middle-aged men who each bore some resemblance to their fighters climbed into the ring to rub their shoulders, offer them strike pads to punch and jab. Both wore mouthguards; one had a black tattoo crawling over one eyebrow like a caterpillar, the other a pink burn scar spilling down his stomach. Boys who knew how to take a hit. Another boy, a few years younger, walked around shaking a ballcap and taking bets in a spiral-bound notepad. Simon put ten dollars on Burn Scars, though he was smaller, younger, greener. The bookie grinned with a mouthful of fillings and moved on.

"Why him?" Suzanne asked, and Simon shrugged.

"I always bet the underdog. He always wants it more."

That hadn't occurred to her, but she sensed the truth of it. Thinking of Skelly, the scar on his neck and the scars on his hands, the way he picked fights with the world.

She reached for Simon's hand, the one not holding his beer. His scars had become familiar, comfortable, no matter how he got them. Her fingers fit perfectly in the space where his were missing. She looked around for Phoebe, the other missing piece, but she was hard to find among so many people who looked so much like her in one way or another. Suzanne finally spotted her ladling lemonade into a plastic cup while she exchanged words—and a wad of cash—with the bookie. It looked like too much for a neighborhood boxing bet, but maybe she knew something Suzanne didn't.

Phoebe made her way back and sat on Simon's other side. The fighters were on their feet, making faces and punching the air. The ring girls might have been little sisters or cousins—teeth too big for their smiles, skinny arms and legs poking out of jean shorts and tank tops probably handed down more than once. The referee had a magnificent mustache but was bald as a cue ball. He spoke in a flood of nasal Spanish too fast for Suzanne to understand. Then he stepped back to the ropes, and with the *clang* of a spoon against an old skillet, the first bout began.

The hangover showed no mercy. Suzanne lifted her head an inch off the pillow and sunlight pried her eyes open with the tenderness of a crowbar. It was early still, the temperature hovering a few degrees below one hundred, according to the ironic old Kool thermometer in the window. She rolled halfway over and found Phoebe's place empty. Flashes of last night shot through her head, made her blush at her own willful abandon. She used to be shy in bed, cripplingly self-conscious of her body and everything she didn't like about it. But two lovers at once made it pleasantly impossible to think too much about herself. Simon shifted, groaned beside her, one arm bent over his eyes to keep the brutal daylight at bay. Trouble's ears swiveled toward them, but she stayed where she was, stretched out on the floor at the foot of the bed where Simon could scratch her ears when he woke.

Curiosity bested Suzanne's headache, and she stumbled outside with a pair of heart-shaped sunglasses on. She scanned the empty street, which looked rougher and harder without the rose-tinted twilight. A collarless dog lapped at a shallow puddle in the nearest yard. The mailbox they'd blocked by accident looked like it had been run over more than once, the windows of the house behind broken and boarded up. The rusted carapace of a Chevy Impala was suspended on cinder blocks a few driveways down. She caught the heel of Phoebe's slender shadow, disappearing between two houses. Suzanne followed in her untied boots, tongues flapping at her ankles. The switchgrass waved in a barely-there breeze, and the laundry hung out to dry on a line. Old bedsheets scattered with little pink roses. She pushed them aside like a curtain and spied the posts of the boxing ring poking up out of the grass to her left. Phoebe's dark head bearing right.

The field behind the houses sloped gently downward. Just over the hill were the rest of the fence posts and moldering ropes that had—some years ago, by the look of it—been repurposed for Fight Night. A fence dividing nothing from nothing, down at the bottom of a ditch. There, too, the morning overturned the rocks and exposed the rot underneath. Beer cans and cigarette butts crushed into the clay, a few condom wrappers and other detritus discarded in a hurry. A mass grave for easy mistakes.

Phoebe wasn't there alone—the teenage bookie was back. He handed her a small box and set about balancing beer cans on each fence post still standing straight enough to hold one upright.

"Planning to kill your breakfast?" Suzanne asked. "I think there are plenty of leftovers."

Phoebe smirked as she flipped the cylinder of the revolver back into place. Slid the box of bullets into her back pocket. "Figured I'd see if I can still shoot," she said, "since I'm all asquint this morning anyway."

"Is he still taking bets?" Feeling braver, Suzanne turned to the bookie. "*Diez dólares, ella no golpea nada.*"

He laughed, silver teeth flashing, but she wasn't sure whether he was laughing at her joke or her Spanish.

"*Diez dólares,*" Phoebe repeated, shaking her head. "*Vete, Martín.*" She turned her cat eyes on Suzanne. "*Y tú, págame.*"

Suzanne was pleased to understand, even if it cost her ten bucks. She picked a fence post to lean on while Phoebe squared up and Martín made himself scarce.

"Where'd you learn Spanish?"

"My dad and his girlfriend," Suzanne said. "Sort of."

"That's funny. Me too." Phoebe nodded vaguely toward the cul-de-sac. "My dad and his kids from the first marriage. My mom and the kids from her first marriage, they speak French. Sort of."

"Did they have any other kids together?"

"Nope." Phoebe closed one eye, the revolver poised in her outstretched hands, like a bird about to take flight. "I'm obviously an accident; they were both too old for babies by then."

"Funny," Suzanne said, too—though it wasn't, not really. "Mine were too young."

The first shot went wide, but not by much. Nothing stirred in the switchgrass, the houses still sleeping, the report lost in the long fissure in the earth where the fence had fallen down.

"That why you never wanted kids of your own?"

"Partly, maybe." She kicked at a jelly sandal half sunk in the mud. "Just can't relate to kids. Never really got to be one."

The second shot hit home. The can spiraled off its post with a bright, shiny *ping* that made Suzanne shiver, not unpleasantly. Phoebe grinned. "Pony up."

Suzanne didn't regret her bad bet. She liked watching Phoebe shoot, without asking why she was such a good shot. She dug around in the pockets of yesterday's shorts, unsure where she'd left her wallet, her phone, her last wad of cash, things that seemed so important to keep track of a few short weeks ago.

"Might have to wait 'til we're back in the Lifeboat," she said. "Got nothing on me."

"I could give you a chance to win your money back."

"How's that?"

"*Diez dólares,*" Phoebe said. "*Puedes pegar una lata con estas cinco balas.*"

"You bet I can?" Suzanne asked, not sure she'd heard right. "You're as bad a bettor as Simon." He'd lost his money last night but didn't seem to mind. Phoebe was more mercenary.

"Nuh-uh." She shook her head. "You think you're no good at anything, but you're always proving yourself wrong."

The old Suzanne would have argued and demurred, defaulted to self-deprecation. But she didn't miss the old Suzanne, so she said, "Okay. Show me."

The gun was surprisingly light. The sun flashed off the barrel, filled every fine scratch in the steel with liquid gold. "That's a good grip," Phoebe said, long arms reaching around her, guiding her into position. "Helps control the recoil." Straightening one elbow, bending the other. "This foot forward. Lean in with that shoulder." Phoebe's body moved hers easily. Hips shifting behind her, heartbeat steady against her back. "Level the sights, front sight centered in the rear notch. Cover your target. Eye on the prize."

Her hold almost slipped. The pendant she hadn't removed since Phoebe hung it around her neck back at the Sundew dragging her down like a sinker on a fisherman's line. She'd heard that before. *Shoot to kill or play to win, never take your eye off the prize.* Suzanne blinked the memory out of her eyes, held the revolver steady. Phoebe's slow pulse like a pace car, keeping her anchored in time.

"Finger on the trigger, but be gentle. She needs a soft touch."

Suzanne thought, then, of what Arlette had said. *It's hard to be soft.* She relaxed her grip.

Phoebe licked her earlobe, tongue tart and pink as powdered lemonade. "Good," she breathed. "Don't pull. Just squeeze."

The shot snapped the lazy morning in half. Suzanne thought she'd missed, before she opened her eyes wider, watched the can spin on its post, then topple and fall to the ground.

THE **B** SIDE

I HATE MYSELF FOR LOVING YOU

Rob parked the pickup on a side street where the pavement had cracked and split along miniature fault lines and tiny stubborn weeds pushed their shoots up toward the sun. He'd left his sunglasses on a hotel nightstand somewhere in Alabama and narrowed his eyes against the glare.

A white vinyl banner hung motionless in the dead air between two steel barricades that blocked off the parking lot, welcoming shoppers to the market. On the other side, a sea of pop-up tents hung out their own banners, with folksy appellations like "Vagabond Vintage" and "Deer Tick Dry Goods." The whole thing felt vaguely medieval—the gathering of guilds, the dust of commerce underfoot. Appropriately arcadian music from banjos and harmonicas and what sounded like an accordion underscored the aromas of burnt sugar and baking spices, the sharp, charred smell of coffee roasting somewhere.

Rob followed the flow of the crowd, took things up at random and set them down again. He exchanged a few damp dollars for a bag of almonds and a tube of sunscreen made from goat's milk, bought a pair of cheap shades from a white woman with dreadlocks selling dream catchers and wind chimes made from sea glass and frayed shoelaces. "Many blessings," she said with a kind of stoned serenity as she pressed his change into his palm. He put the sunglasses on and the world turned Coke-bottle brown. A man with gauges hole-punched through each ear sold him a cup of coffee he described as "fair trade, single origin" with "a nose of roasted pecan" and "molasses undertones." Rob just tasted coffee. He ignored the ludicrous array of liquids masquerading as milk, squeezed from seeds and nuts and even, somehow, hemp. What the hell happened to half-and-half? He passed a stall scooping whimsically alien mushrooms into paper bags, another hawking artisanal honey infused with everything from rosemary to habanero. Unbelievable the lengths some people would go to to avoid an honest job.

He assumed, rightly, that the girl's booth would be easy to find. A battered orange throw ring hung from a bar overhead, with LIFEBOAT SUPPLY CO. stenciled on the plastic with white paint. He drifted around the periphery, enjoying the little thrill of espionage. She took no more notice of him than she did of anyone else. He watched her count change and collate crumpled tens and twenties with a blackjack dealer's dexterity. Rings glinted on her fingers, minuscule tattoos inked on every joint between. She was densely freckled, brown pinpricks dusted across the bridge of her nose as if she'd been seasoned with pepper. She flashed a gap-toothed smile once in a while, congratulating customers on an impeccable pick, a flattering fit, a terrific find.

Rob moved closer, hands in his pockets, bag of nuts and sunscreen swinging from one wrist. She sold a little of everything, more than he'd seen on the Instagram feed; besides the racks of clothes, there were trays of jewelry, mismatched teacups and coffee mugs, books and magazines, some old electronics with the rust scraped off and the chrome buffed up. A transistor radio had been cracked open like a crab, innards on display, tiny pliers and screwdrivers piled in a cigar box beside it. The familiar Silvertone decal caught his eye. He picked up the speaker cone and turned it over, looking for he didn't know quite what.

"You interested in that radio, man?"

The girl's voice sharpened—had a snap now like a rubber band pulled taut. He looked up, alarmed to find her looking back at him. She was prettier than he'd given her credit for. Full mouth and a supple sort of luster to her skin. He believed the word was "dewy." But her eyes were hard as two steelie marbles. She had a handful of those, too, mingling with their brightly colored brethren in a penny-candy jar.

"Sorry." He set the speaker down. "I had one like it as a kid."

"How old are you?"

He chuckled at the quickness of the question. "My grandad's," he said. "Not much value but the sentimental."

"Not a watcher of *Antiques Roadshow,* I guess."

"What?"

"You'd be surprised" was all she said.

"You fix all this yourself?" He gestured at the rest of her merchandise.

"Find, fix, unfuck . . . whatever it needs."

A girl who'd been sifting through a basket of iron-on patches finally settled on three she liked and stacked them on the table with a pack of pornographic playing cards. "I *love* your shirt," she told Freckles. It was (surely) vintage Hawaiian—tropical blue with huge yellow hibiscuses blooming all over it. Threadbare and breezy, three sizes too big.

"How much do you love it?" The tattoos flickered into motion as Freckles tallied price tags and banged the numbers out on a ten-key adding machine as old as anything else under the tent.

"Is it for sale?"

Freckles looked down, considering. "Thirty bucks."

"Sold!" the girl exclaimed, round cheeks flushed like she couldn't believe her luck.

"Groovy." Freckles crossed her arms and grabbed the hem and swept the shirt off over her head. She was wearing a bra or a bathing suit top underneath, so loosely crocheted that one dark nipple poked through. Another band of freckles unfurled across her collarbone—the Milky Way in negative.

Rob caught himself staring and turned abruptly, pawing at random through bundles of coasters tied together with twine. Painfully aware of her wrapping everything up in the shirt still warm from her skin and damp from her sweat. Women had never made him nervous, certainly not this side of thirty, not since he was married and settled and beauty became an abstraction—something he admired from a distance but no longer pursued, like an athlete in early retirement. His wife was beautiful, and so were other women, but their beauty hadn't mattered before the ugly revelation that she found them beautiful, too. He was reasonably confident in his looks when measured against other men, but women? That felt unfair, unnerving. Ironically, emasculating. He couldn't stop stealing glances at the girl who had bewitched Suzanne away from him, wondering why, *why* was he so transfixed by her casual indecency? Maybe it had something to do with how long it had been since he'd seen anyone's tits, which he realized before he realized why he realized it, which was that he was holding Suzanne's two perfect tits in his hands.

He didn't recognize her at first. Hair lopped off in a shaggy little pixie, half-hidden under that same black cowboy hat with concho studs around the brim. She was naked to the waist besides the hat, those heart-shaped sunglasses, a coat of lipstick, and a long, dangling necklace, the pendant pointing into the V of her cleavage. She held a pearl-handled revolver, aimed at the photographer. In the time between, someone had drawn a curling black bandit's mustache on her upper lip and glued a pair of star-shaped sequins over her nipples like pasties. Rob untied the stack of coasters without asking. They were all made from snapshots with similar arts-and-crafts embellishments, sandwiched between a felt backing and a square of acrylic. Not all of Suzanne.

He looked up, trying not to stare at Freckles or the Polaroid cameras for sale among the other electronics. The girl who'd bought the shirt off her back had gone.

"How much for these coasters?" Rob asked.

NEW BLUES

Suzanne had learned to live in sweat and salt and not much else, the Lifeboat warming in one sunny corner of the RV park while Phoebe was off at the market. Three people and a fifty-pound dog in the Airstream made privacy impossible, modesty absurd. They shared their clothes like everything else, and every now and then Phoebe stripped them down and dressed them up like dolls again in something old but new. She would sell anything if the offer was right, and Suzanne learned to like discarding all her old disguises, being somebody new every week.

This week she was lazy. This week she was sunburned. This week she had painted her toenails banana yellow and worn the same frayed chambray for four days. They were short on menswear, though they used the term loosely, so Simon was reduced to swim trunks and a gingham bib apron with a white ricrac trim. Unlike Suzanne, he hadn't cut his hair for weeks and it flopped in his eyes every time he bent over the stove. His solution to this problem was a backward cap from Crater Lake, forelock spilling over the strap in a tangle of prodigal curls. He whistled along to whatever came on the radio—jingles hawking car insurance and fabric softener, gonzo country and organs grinding away at every baseball game. They assiduously avoided the news, turned it off automatically when it intruded in the odd, sweatbox oasis of the Lifeboat. At first, guilt gnawed around the edges of Suzanne's subconscious; it felt irresponsible to ignore the way the world was going to hell in a handbasket, but then again, what could they do? Three shiftless, thriftless people with no more money or power than would fit in their pockets.

"Can I help?" Suzanne asked, nursing a cold drink and idly flipping through an issue of *Creem* from the year before she was born. Springsteen on the cover, stranded halfway between Elvis Presley and Catholic schoolboy with his long black sideburns and tight white polo.

"Mm." Simon sucked a smear of butter from his thumb. "You could crack this, and crank that." He pointed overhead with a bottle of beer clutched in his three-fingered hand. A small Sony radio hung from one of the cabinet knobs.

Suzanne unstuck her thighs from the vinyl booth with a sound like Velcro tearing loose. "You've got one open already," she said. "Don't you?" He could have misplaced it; the Lifeboat was crammed so full of stuff it wasn't uncommon to set down a drink or a book or a half-eaten sandwich and find it days later under a lampshade or a hubcap Phoebe had picked up somewhere and thrown down somewhere else.

"This one's for the bread," he said after a glug from the Dos Equis taking up valuable counter space between the sink and the stovetop.

"For the bread?" Suzanne stood on her tiptoes to turn the music up. Bob Seger, paying tribute to the queen of Motor City radio.

"*She knows music,*" Simon sang, and slung one arm around Suzanne. He two-stepped her in a tight little circle in the tiny kitchenette. "Rosalie! *Ros-a-leeee!*" Trouble's ears swiveled toward them where she lay on the shag rug in the lounge, forever envious of Simon's other lovers. "Great song," he said. "I dunno why Seger hates his early stuff so much."

"Sometimes the shine wears off," Suzanne said. Impossible not to think of her own early missteps, the half-baked creative projects she'd been so sure of at the time but decades later only wanted to forget. "Tell me about this bread that needs a beer."

"You've pretty much got the gist of it. Bread needs a leavening agent, and beer's got one—ha-ha—baked in. The yeast in the beer reacts with the starch in the flour"—he whisked their single all-purpose spatula around their single all-purpose mixing bowl—"and behold! She is Risen. Or she will be. Pop that open for me?"

Suzanne wedged the bottle cap against the edge of the counter and gave it a whack with the heel of her palm. It popped off and *ping*ed against a cabinet door before rolling out of sight. Phoebe would probably find it in six weeks and glue it to a picture frame in need of a little pizzazz. Simon emptied the bottle into the bowl, bubbling and frothing until the flour soaked it up. "Will it taste like beer?" Suzanne asked.

"That and whatever else we put in it. What are you hankering for?"

"What have we got?" It was a game they played every day, every night. What did they have, and what could they make of it? Most of their meals were more a smorgasbord of mismatched snacks, but when they spent a few days in one place and Simon had time between jobs, he threw things together to keep them full. Trail mix concocted from M&M's and breakfast cereal, cookies crammed with oats and jam and bits of broken pretzel. And now, beer bread. Economically, it made sense. Flour was cheaper than store-bought loaves, and beer was one thing they never ran out of. Suzanne opened the fridge to find a jar of pickles and a cheap block of cheddar. "Cheese?"

"That'll go nicely with these." He'd uprooted a clump of chives from one of the window boxes. She rinsed the bulbs and dug up the one paring knife they hadn't misplaced while Simon grated and stirred, grated and stirred. "Girl, you're making that harder than it needs to be," he said when he looked up and found her performing surgery on the chives' long, tubular leaves. He took the knife away and reached for the scissors instead. He gathered the chives in one hand and snip-snipped, like trimming split ends. "First lesson in cooking on wheels," Simon said. "Never use a knife when scissors will do, unless you want to end up like me."

I could do worse, she was thinking when they heard a scrape and a shout and Phoebe stuck her head in through the open door.

"Gimme a hand," she said, already hefting a battered black footlocker up the steps. Suzanne grabbed the other handle and hauled it over the threshold.

"What's this?"

"Some guy traded it for a Harley jacket and a bunch of old Hot

Wheels nobody was buying. You're going to flip for this shit." She sniffed the air. "We brewing beer in here?"

"Baking bread," Suzanne said. "Let's see if Simon can spare me."

"You're spared," he said. "Too many cooks for this kitchen anyway."

Phoebe threw the latch on the footlocker before Suzanne had set her end down and it spilled its guts all over the floor, startling Trouble out of her stupor. Dozens of tapes and records thrown together with most of a Moog theremin that must have met a violent end. Phoebe righted the trunk and sat on top of it. There was nowhere else to sit with Trouble on the rug and the rest of the lounge crowded with merchandise doubling as décor until it was stickered and sold—throw pillows and board games and a rolling globe bar cart some enterprising soul had converted into a turntable. It was woefully unstable when the Lifeboat was in motion, but Suzanne had done her best to balance the tonearm, and it played all right if they sat still long enough.

"Motels, Gun Club, Godfathers, Hüsker Dü . . ." Suzanne still loved the feel of vinyl in her hands—loved the liner notes and the mysterious etchings in the runouts, even cherished the ringwear and notched edges and crushed corners. Old records felt lived in, like old books. "Whoever this belonged to had great taste."

Phoebe whistled. "I'll say." She held up a little baggie of snow-white something that had tumbled out of the sleeve of a Richard Hell LP. She dipped one fingertip and ran it around her gums with a quick, business-like flick. Blinked her eyes open a little wider. "Why, yes, that's vintage Bolivian marching powder." She peered into a Stranglers sleeve. "And there's more where that came from."

Simon looked up from the beer bread. "Didn't think it was that sort of score."

"Neither did I. Poor moron, he really had *no* idea." Phoebe considered the baggie, looked up and found the two of them staring at her. "Calm down, I know I can't afford a coke habit." Mind like an abacus. She set the baggie aside and resumed her dig. "Speaking of marching powder, fuck me, Tommy Bolin. That goes in the spin pile."

The "spin pile" was a rattan magazine rack where they kept the few records they played in frequent rotation, never more than would fit in the mud-brown Coleman cooler disguised as a coffee table when it got hot enough to warp the wax. Everything else was up for auction.

"Put it on," Simon said, reaching for the radio dial. "I can turn this off."

"No!" Phoebe exclaimed. "Put *this* on." She flipped the next record around. Nothing got her blood going like a good find, especially if it was a musical one, but Suzanne's whole body went cold. Despite the suffocating heat, despite the sweat creeping down the back of her neck. "Oh man," Phoebe said. "I hope that guy is very happy with his Hot Wheels, because I've never even seen this in the flesh."

Suzanne had. Suzanne had seen it a thousand times, had pushed a thousand copies on a thousand puzzled concertgoers wondering why there was a fourth grader manning the merch table. That legendary LP, that flash of alchemical fire between a pyrophoric frontman and a volatile guitarist. On the sleeve, an unmistakable skeletal hand—black ink on white skin, long fingers curled around a soft yellow peach, something dark and viscous dripping from a split in the peel. *Don't Stop the Rot.* Whether that was a curse or a prophecy, she could never decide.

Phoebe was already lifting the Northern Hemisphere off the platter when Suzanne grabbed her arm. "Please—don't play that." She couldn't explain the swoop of panic that had pulled the world out from under her. How many nights she'd fallen asleep wearing a tour tee as a nightdress, with the same words splashed across her back, noxious black juice dribbling down her chest.

"Why?" Phoebe wasn't looking at her. "I thought you liked Gil and the Kills. This is peak Delgado; he's a total maniac."

"Phoebe, I know who he is!" She didn't mean to yell. Trouble raised her head, ears standing at attention.

"Okay," Phoebe said with a frown. "So, what's the objection?"

"My dad." Suzanne let go, gestured limply at the record. Witchcraft stamped in wax. She hadn't heard those songs in years. As much as she had loved them once, she couldn't listen to them anymore. The music

wound around her heart and squeezed until it bled—just like that oozing piece of fruit.

Phoebe stared at her. "I— Holy shit, Suzanne . . . Gil Delgado is
your dad?"

Suzanne folded her arms. "Was," she reminded her. "Was my dad."

"God, I'm sorry." Phoebe set the record down as if it were made of
glass. Peering at Suzanne more closely. "Jesus, you *look*—" She stopped
herself. "I should've realized, but I didn't know he died."

"Neither did I," Suzanne said. "Not until—he left me Blondie."

A streak of disbelief crossed Phoebe's face. Still connecting all the
dots. She almost laughed. "Holy shit," she said again. "I'm sorry, I know
it's not funny, but— We've been driving around all this time in *Gil Delgado's car?*"

"Mine now." Suzanne clenched her fists to keep her hands from
shaking. "But his, yeah." She didn't know why she couldn't say "ours."
They'd been "we" so briefly.

Simon's sad, drooping eyes were sadder than usual. Hurt she hadn't
told them sooner.

"Sorry for yelling," Suzanne said. It seemed insane to mourn this
way for a man she'd barely seen since she was eleven, but there was so
much she never got to say. Some things she would take to her grave.
Grief, though—grief could be grasped. "Just haven't heard his voice
since . . . oh, I don't know." Since that tape in the glove box she'd told
nobody about.

But she was tired of flinching away from everything that scared her.
Fear hadn't just stolen her father, but the kind of life she might have
lived if she hadn't been afraid to seize it sooner.

She reached for the record, coaxed it out of the sleeve. She paused,
turned it over. She'd always liked the first track on the B-side, where
the noise died down enough to hear Gil's breath around the microphone. She blew the dust from the grooves and set the platter spinning. The needle descended and the speakers crackled. She knew why
audiophiles rhapsodized about *warmth*. That crackle warmed her cold
blood like tinder catching a spark. She steeled herself as best she could

for what was coming, but it still hit her like a haymaker. She might have fallen without Phoebe and Simon there to hold her up.

Lost sight of the county line
Uh-hum drum light-years ago
While this bad year goes rollin' on I'm
Waiting for Godot

It was almost a lullaby, tender and brooding.

Give it one more day
Give it one more week
I got nothing else to do
And I'd hate to break my streak—
Give me one more day
I'll be on my way

The rhythm section kept their distance as the Hands did invisible conjuring tricks in twelve bars.

Doc, you got to help me
Doc, I'm suffering
I don't feel sad
I don't feel bad
Don't feel a goddamn thing

Suzanne swayed, pulled by the song like the tug of the tide, holding fast to other hands she knew by their rings and their scars and their missing pieces, the way they fit in hers. They kept their silence as the uncanny cradlesong grew teeth.

Musta caught some new blues
Nothing left to lose blues
I'm stalled
I'm stuck
I'm all fucked up
And I don't know what to do—

The strings ran her through. She'd squeezed Simon so hard she broke the skin and blood seeped under her fingernails.

Baby, got the you blues
Won't pick up the phone

I'm best left alone
Lyin' here bruised and abused
The music unwound, unspooled, melted into orgiastic misery.
Musta caught some bad blues
Best you ever had blues
Can't come to the door
I'm too sick
I'm too sore
I'm too ill
I'm still
Licking my wounds
Babe, I'll be fine
Don't mind losing my mind
Just musta had too much of you

But it wasn't enough. Gil was gone again, just like he always was—a ghost in the groove and the static in the room.

PART 3

HARD CANDY

Snapshot: NYC, 2001

Suzanne spent every day shooting fake food for restaurant menus.
She spent every evening at the *audionaut* office and every night in a bar
or a club where every band on the bill was still struggling to become
somebody. She spent as little time as possible in the one-bedroom apartment she shared with two roommates and a cockroach infestation of
biblical proportions. Poison only seemed to make them more aggres-
sive, and every time she called to complain to the Russian landlord, he
conveniently forgot he spoke English—an ability he conveniently recov-
ered the minute rent was due. She'd slept on the sagging sofa in Doug's
office more than once, even after she found a job and a place she could
(almost) afford to live. He wasn't faring much better financially, but
when she turned up at *audionaut*, he didn't hesitate. Didn't even ask
questions. Just opened the door and offered her half of whatever action
he had, just like the old days at Most Wanted. The rest of the staff made
fun of her for fucking him, which was weird and wrong but easier to go
along with than explaining the real reason he mothered and brothered
her by turns. An intimacy with a long, unspoken history that the boys in
the ranks who probably would have liked to fuck her themselves readily
misinterpreted. Sometimes she played along and told wild stories about
how good Doug was in bed, just to do them both a favor. The writers

grudgingly respected Doug; they grudgingly left Suzanne alone. If she couldn't be fucked, why befriend her at all?

She wasn't in the market for friends anyway. The shine of New York had worn off; when you were broke and lacked any real job skills, the city was less exciting than it was impossible. But to say so to die-hard "New Yorkers"—most of whom were really recent transplants, performing their devotion with the delusional zeal of the newly converted—was tantamount to sacrilege. So Suzanne was excommunicated from the social life of the office and everywhere else. Fine by her. It was exhausting talking to so many worldly people for whom the world beyond the Five Boroughs simply did not exist. She was sick of the subway, sick of the traffic, sick of the tourists. She wanted wheels, wanted them badly, wanted to get the hell out.

But wheels cost money, and of that there was none. Her day job barely paid the bills; *audionaut* was a labor of love. Doug paid them what he could, but it wasn't much. "The world didn't end on Y2K, but I think print culture might've," he admitted to Suzanne the last time they both stayed late, passing a bottle of cheap red back and forth. He was the only person she found easy to be with. She didn't have to explain anything. He didn't ask about Gil. Nobody else at the rag even knew her name used to be Delgado.

But she couldn't always keep him contained. One of the hazards of the zine was being surrounded by the increasingly rare breed of people who still preferred vinyl, who wore the obscurity of their musical taste like a medal of honor. Gil and the Kills, however short-lived their glory, however degrading their downfall, had since been cited as an influence by so many other, more important somebodies that their name was bound to come up.

For instance, when someone went digging for something to liven up the mood. Suzanne was still staring at her monitor, flipping back and forth between two shots of last night's gig, comparing them detail by detail, like a game of "spot the difference." Everyone else was killing time, the rubbery hours between the shop closing up and all the clubs opening. Before long the boys—and they were all boys—would fan out in different directions to cover as much musical ground as possible, and as many bars in between. Doug had tried to hire more women, but they never stuck around long, leaving Suzanne to wonder whether she was weaker or tougher than they were. Was she holding her ground against the vainglorious masculine bullshit, or was she just taking it all lying down? Did she really give a shit either way?

Not today, she decided, taking a slug of lukewarm Miller Lite and choosing one of the photos at random. The band wasn't going to make it big, their readers would glance at it once and never think of it again. She checked her watch. She still had some business in the darkroom, but she wanted quiet and wouldn't get that until the writers cleared out. Most of them were on their second beers already, arguing over whose turn it was to DJ.

"Radio Birdman, Biz Markie . . ." She heard the CDs *clack* together, the telltale *swish* of someone thumbing through the LPs. "Dirtbombs, Dead Kennedys . . . oh shit? Who was listening to this?"

"Oh *shit*!" someone else echoed. "I haven't thought about them in forever."

"Is this Doug's? The vinyl's, like, wicked hard to find."

"*Don't Stop the Rot*," said someone else. Suzanne stiffened in her seat. "What even is this?"

"Never heard of Gil and the Kills? They made all kinds of headlines when you were, like, nine."

"One of them OD'd or something."

"Late eighties? Shit, who didn't."

Everyone laughed. Suzanne hoped that would be enough to change the subject, redirect the conversation. There were so many other examples of wasted life and talent to choose from. *Don't put it on*, she pleaded with the universe. *Don't put it on.*

"Weren't they pals with Babel Mouth? The DeWitts did everybody in."

"Yeah, Delgado wrote 'Bad Business' with Vince. That's a great track—put that on."

"No!" Suzanne yelped before she could stop herself. Then, to cover her outburst when they looked her way, added, "*Don't Stop* was already out when they toured with Babel Mouth. They were on the road for *Barbarella*." Like that was the reason she remembered. It was why most people remembered the record, if they remembered it at all. Most people her age were too young. She felt a shameful flicker of relief to be called Westman now, even if she still sometimes started her surname with a strange hybrid letter halfway between *D* and *W*. It looked a little like a treble clef, her own hand mercilessly mocking her. Because as much as she loved music, she could never play it. She was—the great tragedy of her life, bar one—completely lacking any natural talent.

"Shit, she's right?" somebody said, as if that were a surprise. Suzanne, in the absence of talent, had simply become a fanatic. Her encyclopedic knowledge of music history was a source of endless wonderment to men, even the ones she worked with. Someone dropped the needle on an opening riff she knew better than her own name. She clenched her fists as Gil's voice echoed down the years, like a sorceror summoning demons. *Strings!*

"Yeah, that was the tour." The writers resumed ignoring Suzanne, turned back toward one other. "Start-to-finish carnage, like Nicky fucking shot somebody."

"I think he only *thought* he shot somebody."

"What?"

"Nicky DeWitt was drunk half his life and dumber than a bag of hammers when he wasn't," said someone else. "I bet Skillman set him up."

Suzanne's heart seized at the jagged snarl of the Flying V. In those infamous Hands it wrought havoc, but it stopped on a dime with a screech. For an instant, no instruments—just Gil's fanged, ferocious vocal in total isolation.

Baby's not a joybanger, baby needs a fix
Baby ain't no daytripper, baby gets her kicks
YEOW!
It's a pretty slick business

The guitar came through the wall like a wrecking ball, knocked Suzanne twelve years back in time. She'd be eleven forever.

"You know what? I'll say it," someone said. "They were actually better than Babel Mouth."

Baby's not a joybanger, baby's in a pinch

Baby ain't no ingenue, baby's got the itch

OW!

It's a pretty sick business

"That's why I thought it was Skillman he shot," someone else answered, still thinking of Nicky DeWitt. They had it all wrong, but Suzanne wasn't going to correct them. "Because he was replacing him in the lineup? Or he was fucking his sister or something."

"Could you blame him if he did?"

"Replace Nicky or fuck his sister?"

"Same thing."

Everyone laughed again. Suzanne hated them, she realized with sudden and startling clarity.

Little Miss Adventure

Didn't need no convincing

He said, Girl, you've gone straight to my head

She said, Shut up and kiss me

But it's, uh . . . strictly business

The song fishtailed into another bloodcurdling chorus—Gil and the Flying V fighting for dominance, until Gil gasped for breath and Skelly sliced into a solo.

"By all accounts a total skid mark, but *shit* could Skillman play."

"And the pipes on this guy, are you kidding?"

An answering snort. "Delgado? Never did anything half this good before or since."

Unlike Skelly, whose legend could only rise, Gil had committed the cardinal sin of lingering on the scene too long. He lost his cult-hero cool, his infamy by association, and became, somehow, *embarrassing*.

"Maybe he wasn't worth much on his own, but with Skillman he was brilliant."

"They hated each other. It was all for show, the way they played live."

Suzanne felt the words coming up like vomit. Because that wasn't right, wasn't the case, and even if Skelly was a skid mark and Gil was embarrassing, she couldn't suppress the impulse to set the twisted record straight. "It wasn't that simple," she said. "Gil wanted to be David Bowie and Skelly wanted to be Jimmy Page. Too much weird ego to share one stage." In retrospect she understood it better than she could have at eleven, how the same rivalrous flirtation that fired them in the studio and the spotlight was no less incendiary in the wings and on the road. Throwing them together with the DeWitts was like throwing gasoline on a flame. Louie knew that and he did it anyway.

The boys finally shut up to listen as the song barreled toward the breaking point. Skelly throttling the strings while Gil bawled his guts out. Nash waled on the kit and Ruby's bass juddered like a jackhammer.

But baby ain't no joy now
She left him strung up
Shit outta dumb luck
Don't talk, dumb fuck
Good goddamn! It's a risky business

The music came apart at the seams, high-hat going over backward, feedback screeching through the speakers, all four voices joining the fray as they thrashed through the last verse.

And it's he said, she said
This shit'll never end
Made a little mess
When he made her little Missus

Suzanne abruptly stood up from the computer, the Flying V chasing her through the office. Her stomach was churning again, but this time she thought more than words might come up. She made a beeline for the darkroom.

She's all hands off, back talk
Backbite, walk it off
Boy, whatcha gonna do
WHAT DID I TELL YOU?
This bitch'll be bad for business

She pulled the door shut behind her and threw her back against it.

Music still thundering through the wall. She hung her head between her knees and waited for the dizziness to pass, counting the steady *drip, drip, drip* of a leaky film tank dribbling developer on the floor. She needed new equipment. She needed a new job, a new city, a new self, a new everything. She'd settle for new nightmares, even. The old ones were beginning to bore her.

She raised her head when someone knocked. "What?"

"It's me."

She sighed, opened the door. Doug closed it again behind him, shutting out the noise of the perpetual pregame. "Hey, kid," he said, the only person who still called her that. "You okay?"

"I'm fine."

He knew her too well to believe her. "How about I fire all of them?"

"That would be nice." She'd often wondered whether the two of them could run the whole operation themselves. He could do all the writing and she could take all the pictures—if they could both learn to be in ten places at once. The only place Suzanne really wanted to be anymore was anyplace else, but she didn't want to be ungrateful, which was why she'd been stalling, losing her nerve every time she started to tell him about the fellowship application.

But maybe because her guard was down, when he looked up at what she was drying on the line and asked, "What's all this?" it didn't occur to her to lie.

"Oh. Um. I've been putting a portfolio together." In the dim crimson light of the darkroom, Doug's red beard was unremarkable. He squinted at the nearest 8x10, saw it wasn't of a concert, wasn't of a show. She still took photos of things besides performers and plastic food but kept them mostly to herself, uncertain of her skill in every other realm.

"Cool," Doug said. "I like this one. Reminds me of—well, you remember."

She did, much as she didn't want to. What happened in Vegas did not, as it happened, always stay in Vegas. The photo Doug picked out was actually taken in Atlantic City, on their last drive down to interview some has-been hair band playing one of the small rooms at Harrah's. She'd captured the moment the old woman beside her won a modest jackpot, her wide eyes magnified by enormous glasses that reflected the neon whirl of the slot machine. They both got lucky. Suzanne was hoping she might get lucky again.

"What's the portfolio for?" Doug asked—no expectation in the question.

Now that he'd opened the door, she had no real choice but to go through it. "Listen, Doug." She felt the word vomit coming up again. No matter how many times she rehearsed these kinds of conversations, she wound up blurting and babbling anyway. "I applied for some fellowships. I probably won't get any of them, but . . . if I do, y'know, I'd like to go."

"Oh. Yeah, of course. You absolutely should." He was almost too insistent, overcompensating for the split-second hesitation, evidence of nothing but surprise. "If that's what you want, I mean. If there's anything I can do to make it easier here—"

"No, it's not that," she said. Both of them glancing toward the door that separated them from the rest of the staff, the bone-rattling riffs of *Don't Stop the Rot*. She hated to let Doug down—he'd been so good to her for no good reason. They were more than even. "It's just . . . I dunno, my whole life has been kinda fucked up." She hadn't even realized how much until she heard other people talk about their parents, their childhoods. Their stories didn't end in bloodshed or jail time or scandalized headlines. "It's nobody's fault," she said. "Or everyone's. It doesn't matter." Holding her elbows, hugging herself. "But I don't want to stay stuck in it forever. And it's hard not to be when I'm here."

"Yeah, of course," Doug said again. "I understand." But he didn't, not really. He understood better than most, and she'd let him believe they remembered the same things. Let him go on thinking they were both just innocent bystanders, because she wished she could believe that, too. "Gotta go your own way. Wouldn't expect anything less." She was still Gil's daughter, for better or worse. "But I'll be here," he said.

"I'll always be here. And you better stay in touch. Don't think I won't come after you."

Doug could always make her smile, no matter how dire the circumstances. "We are panopticon," she said, glancing up at her photos, drying in the red light.

"Damn right," Doug said. "Panopticon sees all."

"Thank you," she said.

"For what?"

"For everything." For taking her under his wing and never asking whether she was acting too rashly, if she should call her mother, if she had any regrets. For seeing her when she was invisible to everyone else.

"Anytime, Pint Size," he said. "I should be the one thanking you."

He opened his arms, wrapped her up in a trademark Doug Bear Hug. She'd miss that about New York, if she missed nothing else. She squeezed him hard and made a note to tell all the boys he'd broken her heart before she left for good.

THE **A** SIDE

IF YOU WANT BLOOD

After Milwaukee, the band played a string of sold-out shows in the Upper Midwest and were riding high when they touched down in the Twin Cities. The whole entourage took a field trip to Electric Fetus for an interview with a couple of rock jocks from WLZR, because "Bad Business" had generated just enough airplay to elbow its way onto the charts. They woke up in Minnesota to the news that *Impersonator* had been pulled along in the wake of *Don't Stop the Rot*, and both records were selling faster than stores could restock them. Merch sales had doubled in tandem, and if they didn't find a way to crash out more tapes and more T-shirts, they'd have nothing left to sell. Gil was taking calls from Louie nightly now. Gracie, too, was glued to the telephone, multitasking so ferociously that Doug and Carney learned to anticipate her orders and be halfway done with everything by the time she told them to do it.

The goal, she explained to Suzanne one morning while Gil was in the shower, was to keep the band focused on the music, focused on the fans. "They don't need to see how the sausage gets made," she said. "They need to feel like rock stars so they can act like rock stars so everyone will start to believe that's what they are." Gracie didn't want or need any glory for herself. She worked tirelessly but invisibly, always out of sight behind the curtain. Without the crew there would be no band, and they all seemed to be there for the love of the music—like

Suzanne, true fans. And while self-mythologizing came naturally to Gil, who'd been acting like a rock star since he was a teenage grease monkey, it was his brainchild, his baby. He wasn't about to relinquish the reins, even to Gracie. They kept their heads bent together when they weren't on separate calls, whispering in Spanish. Suzanne could tell it wasn't just sweet nothings from the way Gil's brow furrowed, the way Gracie cracked her gum and cracked her knuckles.

The rest of the Kills, however, surrendered whatever responsibilities weren't laid directly at their feet with palpable relief. Nash seemed to be training for some kind of prize fight, waking up early each morning to put his boxing gloves on and beat the stuffing out of whatever pillows and couch cushions could be rustled up in his room. He ate whopping meals and drank Gatorade by the gallon, so he could walk onstage every night and pummel the kit with such muscle and lust that he snapped sticks like pretzels and ripped right through drumheads as if they were onion skin. Ruby said she sweated enough onstage and what she really needed was beauty sleep. "Not as young as I used to be," she confessed to Suzanne with a wistful, faraway look. "You're still baby-faced, but just wait. The years will catch up to you, too." She stayed in bed until the last possible minute and spent the rest of the day massaging, plucking, painting, and teasing until she landed somewhere between the Rockettes and the Bride of Frankenstein.

Skelly maintained his cold-blooded indolence. Unlike Nash, who had bulked up so much he was starting to look like the Minotaur, he stayed lean and rangy as a wolfhound. He ate one enormous meal at breakfast, then had cigarettes for lunch and Jack Daniel's for dinner. After every show he collapsed in the back of the van, muscles jumping and twitching under his skin while he swallowed fistfuls of candy to replenish the stores of energy he burned through like phosphorus onstage. For hours afterward, his mean streak simmered close to the surface. Suzanne knew not to approach him like that unless he summoned her for something. Once, to untangle a chain that was hopelessly knotted in his hair. She had good eyes, small fingers, and the sense not to talk too much. She worked with her tongue between her teeth and her pulse fluttering in her ears, nervous about hurting him, making it worse, upsetting the delicate balance of his temper. Everything was going so well that he and Gil were the best of friends again.

"You keep that one," he told her when she finally got the clasp undone.

"What is it?" she asked, afraid that if she asked why, he might take it back. He was capricious like that, and though she had never wanted it before—had never even noticed it in the jumble of metal hanging off him all the time—she was instantly consumed with greed. She wanted it for whatever small part of his power it had absorbed from his skin, from his sweat, from the strands of broken black hair still threaded through the chain. As if his ability to bend music to his will might be transferred to her through osmosis. He held up the pendant—a ridged metal tube with a steel-tipped point at one end, the other edged with black fletching. Everything he wore seemed to double as a weapon. She couldn't tell whether surrounding himself with sharp objects was a weird attempt at self-defense—like a hedgehog showing its spines—or reckless disregard for his own bodily harm. Maybe both.

"That's the last dart I threw at the bar where I was gigging until Gil walked in with Louie," he told her. "They used to be made from crossbow bolts. Shoot to kill or play to win, it's all the same game." He dropped the arrow in her hand and it pricked her palm, drawing one bead of blood, like a suicide pact. "That's why," he said, "you never take your eye off the prize."

She understood that already, in her own way. She had an eye, even if she didn't have the touch for a guitar. The Polaroid didn't shoot well at night, from the dark of the house into the blare of the stage lights. She'd need a different camera for that. But it hung around her neck everywhere else, and she had taken it upon herself to document the tour, sensing she was part of something undeniably historic, which was just wishful thinking just a few weeks ago. Somebody ought to make some kind of record that wasn't pressed on vinyl, because *Don't Stop the Rot* was unstoppable now.

Or so they thought. In Nebraska, Suzanne learned firsthand what a "clusterfuck" was. There was a slight distinction to be made between a clusterfuck and a shitshow, according to Carney, the undisputed authority on such minor vulgarities: a clusterfuck was the direct result of poor planning and bad decisions; the indiscriminate chaos of a shitshow could and would follow.

The venue wasn't really in Lincoln, like they'd been told. It wasn't even really a venue, but rather an old airplane hangar marooned in a cornfield miles outside the city. A rusting crop duster had been repurposed as a lighting rig, spotlights mounted under the wings like aerial rocket artillery. The sound booth stood twelve feet off the ground on a tower of unfinished scaffolding. There were no windows and no stage to speak of—just a few threadbare Persian rugs thrown down on the concrete. The audience surrounded the performers on all sides, face to face and eye to eye. It looked too close for comfort to Suzanne, especially after the last few promoters rolled out the red carpet—food and drinks and whatever else they asked for, a separate dressing room for Gil. But the band laughed it off; they'd played in worse places.

The music started two hours late due to a snarl of unfortunate but completely foreseeable circumstances. The show was oversold, too many people packed into a building that wasn't and probably never had been up to fire code. "For a bunch of hicks, they sure look mean," Ruby said, peeking through a slit in the so-called safety curtain that sectioned off one end of the hangar. Soaking wet and roaring drunk after waiting around for ninety minutes in the rain, the crowd—mostly boys, riding the line between adolescence and adulthood, beards bristling through their baby fat—had worked up a collective temper. The first opener was a trio from Omaha viciously bullied out of the ring after only fifteen minutes. The second act was made of sterner stuff, wielding the same three crunching power chords in predictable configurations. They were mean, ugly, and loud, and held their ground with a naked derision the audience could at least respect. Performance as blood sport.

Suzanne watched the first two acts crouched under the crop duster, keeping close to Carney while Gracie argued with the promoter, who kept shaking his head, jowls aquiver, a bulldog ridding itself of a bothersome fly. Suzanne didn't catch the particulars over the noise from the floor, but she heard enough familiar metonyms—like "gate," and "take," and "door"—to know the problem was the money. It usually was. "Well?" Gracie demanded when the mayhem subsided long enough for the frontman of Mean, Ugly, and Loud to announce their imminent departure to a mixed chorus of jeers and applause. "You want to pay up or you want get on the mic and tell these people the show's already over?"

Suzanne couldn't hear the answer, but she saw a grin flash across Gracie's face, and a moment later Carney gave her a nudge and said, "Ten minutes to showtime. Run!"

She skirted the edge of the room, kept her distance from the mass of bodies eddying around the rugs. When she ducked through the safety curtain, the opening vocalist was vomiting into a mop bucket in one corner, and in the other Gil and the Kills trawled through the costume trunks for finishing touches or watched the clock, waiting for their marching orders. Suzanne zigzagged past the smell and splash of bile and yanked on Gil's elbow. "Ten minutes," she told him. "You're going on in that?" He'd unearthed a pair of leather pants, laced halfway up over a mesh catsuit. Dog collar, fingerless gloves, eyelashes drawn on like Raggedy Ann.

"I am if we've only got ten minutes," he said, smudging the pencil under each eye with one fingertip. Less girlish that way, but not much. "How's the weather out there?"

"It's a clusterfuck," she said. Skelly was the only one to smile—a feline twitch of his long upper lip.

"It sounds like a riot," Ruby said, shifting foot to foot. Nash kneaded her shoulders with his big, callused paws. Mean, Ugly, and Loud were winding up their set with a flood of scum-sucking sludge—the mash of sound grinding through the hangar not appreciably different from a mudslide coming down a mountain. The audience answered in kind, laughing and spitting and cussing and hissing and spilling their drinks on the floor.

When the Kills huddled up, Suzanne stayed close. She didn't want to leave them, didn't want them to leave the comparatively safe port of "backstage." A chill crept up her legs, wrapped its clammy fingers around her spine. Fear tasted like metal in the back of her mouth. But Gil was easy, Gil was fine, Gil was unflappable. "Sure, it sounds bad, but listen to the shit these guys are playing. I'd be pissed if I paid for this, too."

Nash grunted agreement.

"Problem is," Gil continued, "they've made up their minds to hate us already." Pressed against his hip, Suzanne could feel him thinking, scanning the airwaves in the room, calculating at lightning speed how best to send a signal through the noise. He clocked Ruby's buzz of anxiety, Nash already sinking into a defensive crouch. Only Skelly mirrored his cool. When Gil caught his eye, he smirked around his cigarette. Then something odd happened, and Suzanne was certain that only she saw it, tucked tight between them. Gil tugged his ear, and Skelly lifted one of his necklaces to kiss the pendant—a tarnished silver cross, the bigger twin of Gil's left earring.

"Here's what we're going to do," Gil said with a smirk of his own. "We're going to *love* how much they hate us."

Ruby and Nash looked at each other, then back at him.

"We've been hated before," he reminded them. "We've been hated by everyone! Promoters and reviewers and record execs—who in this business hasn't told us to go fuck ourselves? Hasn't told us that nobody would ever buy tickets to whatever this shit is that we're selling?" He glared around the circle, daring them to contradict him. "Nobody. We've had to ram it down their throats every step of the way because those corporate pricks don't know shit about music. So, neither do these corn-husking ratfuckers. Let's teach them a lesson. Suzanne!"

She started, stood at attention. "Yes?"

"What's the first rule of rock and roll?"

"If you don't piss people off, you're not doing it right?" She looked up at Skelly, who gave her a wink, as if they were both in on some secret. He tapped the cross on his chest again—she looked down, touched the sharp point of the dart that he'd given her. Eye on the prize. His hard nerve reassured her more than Gil's smooth talking; it was Gil's job to put the others at ease. But Skelly winked just at her, with one elbow on Gil's shoulder. She didn't understand the magnetic push and pull between them—a love affair and a power struggle transmuted through some esoteric magic into music. Yin and yang, light and shade, the needle and the counterweight.

"Good." Gil rolled his eyes, ran one hand through his hair. "I just love being loathed! It confirms my suspicion that I'm doing everything right."

"Two minutes, Gil," Nash said, eyes on the clock shifting closer and closer to doomsday.

"Go now," Gil said to Suzanne. "I want you to watch the show with Doug tonight. No buts. Kiss for luck." He bent his head, offered his cheek. She kissed him, careful not to smudge his makeup. "All right!" She heard his hands meet with a *smack* as she scurried toward the ladder. "What are we here to do?"

This time, Skelly interrupted the ritual. "Enough dicking around," he said. "Are we gonna stand here and talk or are we going to go and piss these people off?"

Up in the sound booth—like the lighting rig, less a real booth than a plywood crow's-nest—was not a bad vantage point. Suzanne hunkered under Doug's elbow while he worked the board, adjusting dials and sliders, crunching sunflower seeds and muttering to himself. "Some concert," he remarked. "How's morale holding up?"

"They're ready for a fight," she said, watching the hangar floor, unsurprised to see they'd closed the big bay doors. Too many people trying to push inside without tickets. Gracie had gotten her way, but the Bulldog did not look happy, lurking at the back of the room with half a dozen pugnacious policemen.

"They'd better be," Doug said, peering over the board with a queasy expression. "These assholes haven't stopped fighting since the show started." Suzanne fingered the dart around her neck like a protective amulet. Hoping they could work their magic, work the room, crank the music up and blow everybody down.

Sweat prickled across her forehead. So many bodies crushed together after such a biblical downpour blurred the whole evening like
steam on a mirror. Even Skelly's sunglasses fogged up when he emerged
from behind the safety curtain. He took them off for once, and the
motion rippled through the room. Gil always entered first. But Skelly
was on the warpath tonight, pale face and dark hair and eyes smudged
with oily black liner, crowned with a halo of smoke like the queen of
the damned. He flexed his fingers, spread those inky finger bones like
he was just itching to use them. All the sound and fury subsided at the
sight of him, and the band cut through the crowd like royalty moving
through a mass of peasants come to market—chins up, axes on their
shoulders if they had them. Ruby's nerves had settled or she'd had
time to hide them, walking the concrete like a runway. Nash was so
big and bearlike that nobody who valued their life was going to look
at him funny. Gil gave them more trouble, prowling through the audience with camp, vampish menace. A few people catcalled, some slurred
indecent proposals. When they did he paused with one hand cupped
around his ear to better hear. Playing along, playing it up, playing the
hand they dealt him and raising the stakes with each wisecrack, each
insult, each "Play some fucking songs already!"

"Can't rush genius, darling," Gil answered. "Cozy up while we get
comfortable." The usual foreplay, but this time they took his come-
hithers literally. The crowd closed in, toes at the edge of the rug. A couple of wolf whistles, a few curses flung at the police, the promoter, the
first two acts, the act of God that left them all out in the rain. Gil made
a sad pouting face, exaggerated by his rag-doll makeup. "Did you get a
little wet out there? Well, never mind—welcome to the late show!" He
threw his arms open wide, and Nash gave him a drumroll. "It might get
a little wet in here anyway." Raucous laughter at that, enough to drown
out the dissenting opinions, the people who grimaced and gagged. *Get
a load of this guy.* "We're Gil and the Kills and I believe 'barnstorming'
is the word for what we're about to do. Strings!" he shouted, and Skelly
ripped into his opening riff with malevolent relish. Suzanne understood now that look that passed between them, how the battle plan

clicked into place. Skelly craved a hostile audience. Wowing a crowd that was already on your side proved nothing, but making a tough one eat their words was delicious.

For a while, it seemed the night might go their way. However weird their outfits were, Gil and the Kills played a killer live show, and that was all anybody wanted in the first place. People slam-danced in a wild fit of violence through "Off the Rockets" and "Bad Business." Some performers might not have known where to turn, but Gil was born for theater in the round. He never stopped moving, never stood still, pulled the mic from its bracket and twirled the wire like a showgirl's feather boa, wound it around his neck like a noose, ran it between his legs and let Ruby yank the other end to flip him over for a perfect somersault. "Impersonator's" defibrillations left him convulsing on the rug while the crowd battered the floor with their fists, adding their own chaotic percussion.

Suzanne watched for the signals Gil had devised to cue up different sets and different songs. What, she wondered, was the run of show for such a clusterfuck? They could play it safe, but no, they wouldn't—Gil and Skelly both had an appetite for self-destruction. They locked eyes across the stage, Gil tugged his ear again, and Skelly crossed himself. He handed the Flying V off to Carney and slung the silver Stratocaster over his shoulder, loosening the strap so it hung low on his hips, long torso bending back over his heels. Every time the mirrored pickguard caught the lights, it refracted neon rainbows around the room.

"What's with Disco Dick?" Doug said. His lionization of Skelly had gradually given way to dejection. Everyone else had embraced Doug as part of the Kill Team, but—no matter how hard he tried, because trying too hard was part of the problem—to the Hands he remained an object of disdain. Not the kind of fan he cared about. "No way," Doug said. "They're not going to—"

"Looks like they are," said Suzanne. Skelly only used the Strat on a couple of songs, and he only wore it like that when he needed more room to maneuver.

"Here?" Doug hissed. "Do they have a death wish?" But he was already mucking around with the sliders to find something that sounded more like an abattoir and less like a bucket of chum.

"I guess that's why they're called 'the Kills,'" Suzanne said, but still felt a splinter of dread. "Papal Bullshit" was the reason Nora banned the album in the house and a calculated risk they'd taken only once or twice on tour. In Buffalo half the audience walked out. (*Just too fucking Irish* was Gil's terminal diagnosis.) But this crowd had not shown much interest in that kind of passive protest.

She shivered as Skelly's fingers slithered down the fretboard. The Strat whimpered and whined, then released a piercing shriek tangled and entwined with Gil's. Shriek was all he did for a while, yelps of pain or pleasure in reply to every bend of the strings—each note a shiny silver pin stuck in him like a voodoo doll. Suzanne fingered the dart around her neck. The song sounded like voodoo, sounded like sorcery, sounded like something obscene and unholy, the Tower of Babel tumbling down.

No accident, of course, and when words at last took shape, they were perversely familiar.

Thou shalt not worship strange gods (except me)
Thou shalt not take the name of your strange god in vain (only vanity)
Thou shalt not kill (until strange gods demand)

On the list went, with increasingly questionable emendations. Gil gathered speed, leading or following Skelly's frenetic arpeggios, voice and guitar weaving around each other in sinuous symbiosis. They reached a fever pitch in the same instant, the Hands moving so fast the inky bones blurred, while Gil ranted and raved without stopping for breath.

Thou shalt not (except)
Thou shalt not (unless)
Thou shalt not (only)
Thou shalt not (until)
Thou shalt not
Kill
Kill

KILL

Suddenly, drums. The silver Strat blazed like lightning.

Those who live fast shall die slow

A devil like you oughta know

Good-lookin' stiffs don't get much love

Unless the undertaker's getting lonesome

A gasp and a filthy laugh. Gil turned his palms up like a preacher.

Well, what's hell to a heathen?

Be wiser what you believe in

Sin's a fiction for children and fools

He slid down the mic stand, the post protruding between his legs. The audience a restless hush.

Get down on your knees—

God's easy to please!

Oh you sinners, you know what to do

A roar from the crowd, delight and outrage intertwined. The band crashed back in, Nash pummeling the drums like they'd done him some terrible wrong, Ruby grunting in time. But nobody watched the rhythm section when the Hands had a solo. Gil ceded the spotlight and stayed on his knees, begging for mercy at the altar of the screaming Stratocaster. Skelly flipped it over, played upside down, offered it like a holy relic to kiss. A sickly *squelch* as Gil's tongue ran down the neck, head disappearing for one hazardous moment into Skelly's groin. The audience recoiled en masse, then lunged in closer. Some laughing, some swearing, one red-faced hellion screaming, "*FAGGOTS!*" Another word Suzanne had learned only recently.

Blithely unbothered, Gil blew a kiss and leapt to his feet and grabbed the guitar cord, reeling Skelly in like a fish on a line. The Hands never stopped moving, but the music pitched and rolled and swerved as they circled each other. Skelly stomped on the cord and spun Gil like a top. In one fluid motion the Hands unhooked the strap, swung the Strat around Gil, and bent him right over it—bucking and yowling like a cat in heat while the infamous Strings went right on singing.

"Jesus Christ," Doug said, though Christ had clearly left the building.

People pushed and shoved and screamed their heads off. The loudest of all still calling, "*FAGGOTS! FUCKING FAGGOTS!*" Suzanne saw the Bulldog bare his teeth, the policemen beating their batons in their palms. The circle was closing, the space around the rugs shrunk to a margin of inches.

A squawk of feedback pulled them apart. Gil went bowlegged back to the microphone, looking dazed and confused and turned inside out, Skelly grinning fit to kill, one string snapped like the tail of a kite caught in a maelstrom. The guitar made sickly spirals toward the depths. Gil's breath rushed in the rafters, but the crowd was still rowdy, more than one person hurling invectives now.

A devil like you oughta pray
Or there'll be hell to pay
But the Book of the Law is forbidden to read
No one tells you until—
"COCK-SUCKING FAG!"

Something hard and bright arced through the light, and Gil dropped like a dead man. Some people thought it was part of the act, but not Suzanne. Her heart ruptured and burst and flooded her body with acid. "Dad!" She leapt toward him on instinct.

"NO!" Doug shouted. "*Suzanne!*" But she was already falling, head-first through a gap in the rails. As the floor rushed up at her, time stretched and slackened, and she watched it all in murky slow motion. The high-hat toppled over as Nash snatched Ruby out of danger. The brute who'd thrown the bottle lunged onto the rug, looming over the unmoving lump that was Gil. Carney threw fists and elbows without caring where they landed, lifting people off their feet and flinging them out of his way. Suzanne twisted in the air, saw the welter of bodies beneath her and Skelly's white face turned up—transfixed, watching her fall. She hit someone's shoulder so hard it knocked the air right out of her. She tumbled sideways and crashed into the concrete, unable to scream when something slammed down on the back of her leg. Carney had hauled the red-faced thug off Gil, but he came right at Suzanne—stomping with his huge feet as if she were a cockroach he could crush underfoot. A thump to the ribs and the world flickered around her. She gulped silently as the foot came down again, but Skelly got there first. He swung the guitar like a sledgehammer, knocked the guy flat in a spray of broken glass, head snapped so far back it hit the floor before the rest of him. Hands tangled in the bloody strings but not taking any chances, Skelly smashed one hard bootheel in his face. Teeth exploded out of his mouth and skittered across the concrete. Suzanne fell backward into blackness.

She jerked back to life with a gasp as air rushed into her lungs. Her body still limp and boneless, buffeted by bodies bigger than hers. She couldn't see, face crushed against something slick and hot that was dragging her along. No, dragging something else and holding her in a hard, one-armed grip. "Carney," Skelly called hoarsely. She felt more than heard it, a wheeze and a rattle just under her ear. "Nash! Gracie! Shit, *fuck*—someone fucking help me!" She'd never heard his voice break like that. She could smell the adrenaline coming off him like steam, that sharp metallic tang of fear. "Jesus *Christ*—"

Not just adrenaline. Blood, all over both of them. Skelly fell against the wall, the shattered Strat still hanging from his left arm, pulling him down toward the floor. Suzanne a dead weight slipping from his grip. She struggled to lift her head, the dart spinning crazily at the end of its chain. Shards of mirror radiated around them. The Hands shook and trembled, knuckles lacerated by the broken glass that used to be his pickguard, a gash in the heel of his palm so deep it touched bone. Blood streaming down his wrists. They'd escaped into some sort of auxiliary hallway with sallow fluorescent lights that turned the smears and splatters purple on the concrete. "*Fuck.*" Skelly sucked the stale air through his teeth—thinking her unconscious or too much in pain to care if he cried. Arm still bent at that horrible angle, bound to the broken guitar. "*Please,*" he begged the empty hallway. Then mustered what was left of his voice again to scream, "*SOMEBODY HELP ME!*"

No answer. They hung suspended there, slumped halfway down the wall.

When the door banged open at the end of the hall, a dozen people barged in at once. Gracie and Carney and Nash and the dog-faced promoter, Ruby and Doug and the gang of policemen who'd stood in the back of the room and done nothing while the audience tried to eat the band alive. Everyone ran at them, cops pushing Gracie and Ruby aside in a clamor of curses and cries of "*What the hell are you doing? He needs a doctor!*"

They didn't even help Skelly to his feet. They wrenched Suzanne away, rolled him over, and cuffed him right there on the floor. The Hands bent and quivering behind his back, tattoos torn to ribbons. They cut the Stratocaster off and left him lying facedown in a puddle of his own blood until a squad car came to take him away.

Gil, Doug told her, was already gone.

THE **B** SIDE

STILL GOT THIS THING FOR YOU

When Rob arrived at Cowtown Coliseum, he realized at once that he didn't blend in. He scuffed his toes in the dust while he waited in line for an iced tea so sweet it tasted like a punch in the teeth. He dropped the full cup in a trash bin and wiped his hand on his shirt, knocking a couple of buttons loose while he was at it. Less middle manager, more (he hoped) Marlboro Man.

Single seats were easy to find, and nobody looked twice at a fellow alone at the rodeo. Maybe he was a horseman, a gambler, an oil baron out for a little amusement—what did they know? The crowd had the loose, rowdy mood of the back bleachers at a baseball game. People watched but not closely, not without talking, not without chomping on sunflower seeds. A thin crust of masticated shells covered the walkways like mulch. Some cognitive dissonance between the hayseed way of things and the superscreens showing replays of riders getting knocked down, bucked off, fucked up. One hit the dirt headfirst, resulting in a tense intermission while medics bundled him onto a stretcher. Hard to say who had the rawer deal, the cowboys or the bulls. Rob eyed the nearest animal, the foam of sweat on its twitching flanks. He pictured that slab of muscle ground up and served on a bun with pickles and onions and thought, suddenly, that he might start identifying as vegan, too.

But he wasn't there to soul-search. Freckles had posted another Western collection that morning. Rob had just woken up, thinking he had a day to catch up to them in Marfa. Much smaller town, they'd be easier to track down. He refreshed his feed as soon as his gummy eyelids opened, as had become his habit, and was greeted with another lewd photo of his runaway wife. This time Eight Fingers was in the picture, too, with no shirt on and Suzanne on his back. Ankles hooked around his waist, arms around his neck. The photo cut her off below the eyes, but Rob knew every freckle and mark on her body. *These cowgirls are off to the rodeo,* the caption said. And Rob decided, why wait for Marfa? Fucking hippie town was full of trailers anyway—he'd be looking for a Lifeboat in a haystack.

So he came to the Stockyards instead. He shifted his feet on the sunflower shells and scanned the stands for familiar faces, like a live game of *Where's Waldo?* But Suzanne, unlike Waldo, had changed. He was too far to see her freckles and scars and didn't quite recognize her even when he looked right at her. She'd gained back some of the weight she'd lost, pink-cheeked and plump, hair unkempt and curling around her ears like a little boy's. She wore clothes he'd never seen before—patched and faded Levi's, a too-big hockey jersey from a team she didn't follow. Hiding in plain sight. On her left, Freckles sat with her arms folded, a can of beer cradled in the crook of one elbow. On the other side sat Eight Fingers, watching the show with his basset-hound eyes.

Rob picked himself up, elbowed his way back down to concessions. He stood in line for too long and bought two beers so he wouldn't have to go back. He sucked down the stale, sour foam with stale, sour disdain. Asking himself, as he did a hundred times a day since he bought the Dodge, what the hell he was doing, what the hell *she* was doing, and how the hell they wound up where they were. Sickness and health, richer or poorer, to have and to hold. He'd made all those promises and meant them, but there was nothing in the vows about what to do when your wife of six peaceful years went plumb fucking crazy. Suzanne had always had a screw or two loose, but that was part of her charm, something that set her apart from the wives of the other men he worked with, who all seemed vaguely interchangeable.

He slugged the beer and let his eyes wander, finding other couples scattered through the stands and guessing from their body language how long they'd been together, how happy they were, if there was trouble in paradise. The standard deviation of a woman was decidedly different this far south and west of where he'd lived all his life: the hair, the hips, and the breasts were bigger, the smiles wider, the laughter louder. Not trying not to take up space.

After an hour or so the lights dimmed and the music changed. A follow spot fastened on a trick roper mounted on a palomino mare who stood so still Rob guessed she was heavily tranquilized. The lasso whirled and bloomed and spun overhead, each flick of the wrist weaving figure eights through the air. It responded to the rider's touch like a live thing, sinuous and reptilian. Snake-charmed in spite of himself, Rob watched the loop grow larger, larger, until it was large enough to swallow horse and rider at once. It whirled in a circle, dropping to the dust and rising up again until it spun, like pizza dough or a flying saucer, ten feet above the roper's head. The horse came to life at last as the lasso turned sideways, tipped over, and transformed from a ring to a wheel, a turning, churning O. They took off at a gallop as the music swelled. The rope wheeled all the while, opening wider and wider until they leapt right through it, moving like one animal, some strange two-headed centaur.

Abruptly it was over, people stomping and whistling and battering their seats. The music dropped away and left the mare motionless, carved from marble again. The roper stood in the saddle with one arm outstretched, hat in hand, rope coiled around him like a pageant girl's sash. Ladies and gents, presenting Miss Texas. He bowed and Rob sat back in his seat, surprised to find his shirt wet with sweat, as was the beer can he'd forgotten between his legs. A dark patch of denim inside each thigh made it look like he'd pissed himself. His annoyance crept back, spread from the damp fabric to his damp skin like prickly heat. He drank the rest of the beer in three cumbersome swallows, crushed the can, and threw it on top of the sunflower seeds in a fit of petty revenge.

The rodeo, like the Super Bowl, sprawled across three or four hours,

alternating between bursts of action and stretches of boredom kept at
bay by a barrage of advertisements blaring from the jumbotrons. Rob's
eyes flicked from the opposite stands where he'd spotted Suzanne to
the screen hanging over her head. After a reel of rodeo sponsors, they
turned to, of all the stupid things ever conceived by event promoters,
a Kiss Cam. Syrupy synth pop stirred the air as couples or unlucky rel-
atives seated side by side saw themselves onscreen and laughed and
blushed and kissed or didn't. Were they sloppily eager to show off their
love, too shy to use tongue, mortified to have their intimacies magnified? Teens with the acne-scar stigmata of their tender age, whose
friends would make fun of them no matter what they did; middle-aged
marriages drunk already on their one weekly outing; one leathery old
gentleman who tipped his hat back and let his wife take him by the
bolo tie and pull him close. And then, when he wasn't looking for her
for the first time all day all night all week all month all his miserable
life—Suzanne. Everywhere he looked, Suzanne.

Eight Fingers looked up first, filling one half of the heart-shaped
frame. She followed his gaze and made a too-familiar face, that
scrunched-up smile she smiled in spite of herself. Rob hated when she
smiled at him that way, the way she smiled at noisy neighbors and boor-
ish clients and ugly babies. But this time she closed her eyes for a kiss,
and Eight Fingers caught her lips on his like he'd done it a hundred
times before. The sickness twisted in Rob's guts, a poison or a parasite
winding his insides up in knots. Then she turned, let Eight Fingers go,
turned toward Freckles, and kissed her, too. The camera swung away
amid squawks of surprise. But Rob hadn't lost her, knew just where she
sat, how many rows down and how many seats deep. Not just smiling,
but laughing now. She laughed until she buckled, gasped. Rob lurched
to his feet and slipped on the sunflower shells, woozy from the beer or
the heat or driving for days without any sleep. Everywhere he looked
but always out of reach, Suzanne.

THE **B** SIDE

POOL HALL RICHARD

It was, in fact, Suzanne's first rodeo. She had no idea it would be so
loud. The Easterner in her had pictured something quaint and rus-
tic, a relic of the cowpoke days—not the wrecking-ball riffs of AC/DC,
interrupted by the announcer's booming baritone as he rattled off
the names of horses and riders. When a bull first slammed his hooves
against the bucking chute, she jumped and dumped popcorn all over
her lap. Broncos hurled cowboys like rag dolls, ropers yanked steers
clean off their feet, and barrel racers boomeranged around the ring so
fast and so low that their spurs skimmed the dirt. Her heart slammed at
the exhilaration of it, the steaming musk of hair and hide.

By the time it was over, the big blue sky had faded away and left
behind thick slabs of pink marbled with white veins of cloud, like a
steak done rare. The Stockyards were still crowded, threesomes and
foursomes and moresomes lured by lighted windows and neon signs
advertising the "world's largest honky-tonk" or the "world's best barbecue," candy stores and historic hotels that boasted hosting everyone
from Garth Brooks to Bonnie and Clyde.

"What now?" Simon asked.

"We should eat a real meal, probably," Suzanne said, recalling that
morning's breakfast of crushed Frosted Flakes and dried cranberries.

"What are you in the mood for?"

"Something cheap and greasy."

"Darlin', you came to the right place," he said, imitating Phoebe's drawl. That might have been what made her turn and look, and find they were alone.

"Wait, where'd Phoebe go?"

"Don't worry, she'll turn up tomorrow." Simon's slow grin under Simon's slow eyes. "Phoebe loves a barrel racer."

Suzanne might have guessed as much from the way she watched them from the edge of her seat. It reminded her more than she liked of Skelly, watching Vince DeWitt like a hawk on the hunt from the VIP balcony in Kansas City. But they didn't begrudge Phoebe her appetite, the occasional vanishing act, knowing that she, like Trouble, would find her way back before long. "I guess we'll just have to entertain each other," she said to Simon.

"I know just the place."

He led her away from the wholesome racket of families with children straggling back to their cars, winding down for the day. They elbowed their way into a crowded saloon with a longhorn's head mounted over the brass rail bar. It had been there, according to a cockeyed plaque on the wall, for more than a hundred years. Some of the patrons looked like they'd been there longer. Bikers and cowboys and thoroughbred women clustered around two battle-scarred pool tables and a fleet of smaller two-tops with mismatched chairs. ZZ Top blasted through the room. Simon spied a booth about to empty and let Suzanne swoop in while he went to the bar.

"Beer?"

"Bourbon."

"Food?"

"Fried."

"Right back."

Suzanne settled against the wall under a flaming neon skull advertising ghost pepper tequila, thinking she might try that if she got drunk enough to throw caution to the wind. The heat of the day and the frenzy of the rodeo had thickened her blood to slow-moving molasses. She kicked her feet up, knowing no one would care—the floor was a pulp of sawdust and peanut shells, the walls finished in graffiti. The booth itself was a pair of old church pews blackened by cigarette burns or perhaps the wrath of God. The *bump* and *clack* of billiard balls ricocheted off Billy Gibbons's big, bad guitar.

Simon returned with two doubles stacked in one hand and two plastic baskets balanced in the other. "The lady asked for grease." He slid the fried pickles toward her. "The lady asked for whiskey." He set her glass beside them.

"The lady loves a man who comes bearing corn bread," she said, peering into the second basket as Simon sat down.

"The man aims to please," he said with a wink—which happened in slow motion, like everything else.

"I'll keep that in mind." Her lazy blood stirred. She tore a corner off the corn bread and her taste buds sang. She licked her fingers. Who needed napkins? She'd lick the crumbs right off his face if he leaned across the table.

He bit the end off a golden spear and steam curled around his chin. He breathed out in a round-mouthed O. "Hot."

"Just how some like it." It was so nice to *want* things. She swirled her whiskey around, watching the ice tumble and roll. The taste lingered on her lips, sweet and smoky.

"When these gentlemen are through," Simon said, nodding toward the nearest stretch of felt, "how'd you like to lose a game of pool to a guy with eight fingers?"

"Might need a few more drinks in me before I can take the humiliation." She wondered how hard she could hustle him. She'd played more pool with Doug in five years in New York than most people played in a lifetime. She downed her bourbon, daring him to take the bait.

"That can be arranged." He knocked back his own and slid out of the pew. "Don't go anywhere."

"Wild horses couldn't drag me," she promised, reaching for a pickle. She leaned back against the wall in the white-hot, stone-cold glow of the grinning skull. Closed her eyes and felt the whole building thrum as the subwoofer thumped and boots hit the floor. She could live the rest of her life in that booth and not miss much, she thought. She was still daydreaming in that direction when the sudden *thud* of something hard hitting the table made her eyes snap open.

He'd lost weight and hadn't shaved for days. Dressed like he was on his way to audition for *Walker, Texas Ranger*, but still unmistakably Rob. Ice lanced through her veins.

"You should use a coaster," he said, "if you don't want to leave a ring."

She looked down, found what had made the *thud*. One of Phoebe's coasters, with Suzanne in front of the camera instead of behind it, for once. She looked up again and saw he expected her to be ashamed. She ignored the coaster. Set her drink on the table. "What the hell are you doing here?"

"What the hell are *you* doing here?" he said, because that was the way their arguments always went, repeating each other and reversing the blame and going in circles like that until the sun went down or came up again.

"Having a drink," she said, fighting to keep her voice calm while every alarm bell in her body went off at once. Rob never wanted to be the only one yelling—he just wanted to be able to say, *You yelled at me first.* She'd fallen for it too many times not to know better by now. "And you're not invited," she said instead. "How did you find me?" He'd insisted they enable location sharing for their devices, *just in case something happens.* So she'd snapped her SIM card in half after leaving him that last voicemail and hadn't turned her phone on since. What for? When she needed one she borrowed Phoebe's.

Rob ignored the question just as she'd ignored the coaster. Nostrils flared like he'd smelled something rank. "Could you set aside whatever midlife crisis you're clearly having for five minutes so we can talk?"

"About what? I have nothing else to say to you."

"This is not how grown-ups solve problems, Suzanne." She hated that voice—the snide, scolding tone and the sigh that went with it, as if he were terribly weary of explaining the ways of the world to her. Never mind that she'd seen more of the world and its terrible ways before she was twelve than he'd ever seen in his life. "It's time you came home."

She thought of Trouble, chasing after the Lifeboat. "I am home," she said.

"What's that supposed to mean?" Rob asked, without giving her time to answer. "You can't just run away from me."

"That's weird," Suzanne said, anger muscling through the shock of suddenly seeing him there. "Because I'm pretty sure I just did."

His hand shot across the table, caught her by the wrist. She tried to pull free but he tightened his grip, squeezed so hard her fist went slack. "We're still married," he said. "A marriage isn't over just because you say it is."

She yelped at the pinch as he jammed her wedding ring back on her finger. Instantly flung back through the days and weeks to that last disastrous anniversary, the hard bump of her hips against the cold bathroom counter as he tried to get his pants unzipped and get his arms around her. "Stop! You're hurting me—"

"You're hurting me, Suzanne!" he said, raising his voice over hers, over the noise of the tables around them. In the dozy, drunken bedlam of the bar, she knew she was invisible. She eyed along the wall, looking for an opening, looking for an exit. "I love you, goddamn it, and when I said forever, I meant it."

"This is how you love somebody?" She pulled against his grip. "Let go!" But he didn't, and he wouldn't. He'd make her chew herself loose.

"Oh, you don't know shit about love," he snapped. "Your parents didn't love each other and they never loved you the way they needed to. You wouldn't know love if it *bit* you." She winced as a spray of spit hit her face. "It doesn't make any sense, Suzanne—throwing everything away because you're afraid of being a real family? What happened to you? Tell me that."

"Get your hands off me," she said. "Or I'll scream." He hesitated. She started to draw a breath in, and he finally relented, released her. She worked the ring off her finger again, looked him dead in the eye and threw it across the bar. It fell like a stone and disappeared underfoot, in a slurry of peanut shells and cigarette butts. Rob lurched halfway out of the pew but caught himself. Torn between chasing after the ring and keeping her there in the booth. "I want a divorce," she said, savoring the way his face blanched, then went red as a beet. She was so tired of trying not to make him angry, when he made it so laughably easy. "But I'll get a restraining order first, if you can't restrain yourself."

"You want to talk about *restraint*?" Rob said. Warming to his anger now. Talking low and slow, eyes crawling all over her, taking his time taking her in. "You, with him, with her, with your tits out like some truck-stop whore." The words sounded wrong in his mouth—too coarse, too vulgar, trying too hard to sound like a tough guy. But the edge of loathing, that was real. She'd felt the pressure of his desire before, but not quite like this, not with this shade of revulsion. "Christ. Look at yourself."

She considered the coaster. He wanted her to be ashamed, and for the first time since they said *I do*, she simply refused. "I've never looked better," she said. Seeing the ease of her vulnerability, the way her face had softened. Worry lines ironed out. Laugh lines deeper.

Rob eyed her haircut. "Forgive me if I disagree."

She laughed—a sharp yelp that caught her by surprise as much as him. "Oh, sweetie," she said, because she knew how much he hated it, because only his mother called him that and only when she wasn't listening. Wanting to wound him now. Two could play that game, and she was better at it, always had been but had always tried to show *restraint*. "Let's not pretend you ever had taste." She reached for another fried pickle and felt it snap between her teeth.

A white flash of rage drained his face again, even in the moody blue light. "Excuse me?"

"Rob, your favorite band is Dave Matthews." She crunched through the pickle, wiped her fingers on her jeans. Hoping he might be disgusted enough to just get up and leave.

"What the fuck does that have to do with anything?" Insulted, but unsure why.

"Everything, actually." Not that she could explain it in a way that he would understand. "It doesn't matter. Do us both a favor and go home."

She expected him to keep fighting. Was prepared to fight back. But instead of scolding or shouting, Rob folded his hands. Shook his head and said, "To what? To an empty house and a hundred thousand questions about where you are and what you're doing? My wife is sitting right here, and I'm supposed to go home and start my whole life over alone?" He spoke so quietly it was hard to hear him. Suzanne shifted on the hard wooden pew, feeling penitent for the first time all night. It would be harder for him—the child of a happy marriage and a mostly happy family for whom that pattern provided the only possible blueprint for a life.

"Rob, I am sorry," she said. Not for leaving, but for fooling him and herself into thinking it would ever end any other way. "But if what you want is a family, you can have that. There are plenty of women out there who would gladly give their firstborn to a nice guy with a savings account and a steady job."

"But not you," he inferred. Finally getting the gist.

"Not me," she said. Tired of saying it, tired of the assumption that she would change her mind when she was older, when her friends started having babies, when she met the right man. What if she wasn't the right woman? No one ever asked that question.

Rob was no exception. "Not you," he repeated, brow furrowed. "Help me understand, how did we get here? Was I so cruel to you that just asking—"

"It wasn't just the asking," she said. "It was everything that happened after. It was everything that happened before. We weren't *happy.*"

"I was." He said it so readily, he either had no doubts or had never really stopped to think about it.

"Well, I wasn't," she said. "I wanted to be and I thought I could be and I tried to be and I wasn't."

He ran one hand over his jaw, the salt-and-pepper stubble that some younger woman would swoon for, that would make his teenage daughters' friends giggle and call him a silver fox, that would make his teenage sons look longingly in the mirror, willing their own beards to grow in. She could see it for him but couldn't make him see it for himself.

"And this," he said, looking around the tumbledown bar. Eyes lingering where her wedding ring had vanished into the crowd. He tapped one finger on the table, making crumbs skitter and jump in the corn bread basket. "*This* makes you happy."

She could see it the way he saw it—the balding bikers and cheap drinks and loud music. Time flattened so the hour of the day and the day of the week didn't matter. Nothing certain, nothing urgent, no higher power to answer to than hunger, of body or soul. "Yes," she said, as sure of herself as he had been a moment ago.

Rob stared at her. "I refuse to accept that."

She laughed again. "You know, for a minute there I almost felt bad for you." That was how it always went; when they disagreed, his will won out. About work, about money, about getting married in the first place. He wore her down, refused to give ground. But not now. "You don't get to refuse. When you have irreconcilable differences, you get divorced. That's what grown-ups do. Ask Brad, I'm sure he's got a few good lawyers he can recommend for you. You can have the house, you can have the car, you can have whatever you want, I don't care."

"I want you to come home."

"And if I don't, do you plan to drag me by the hair?"

"I might if there was any of it left."

She clutched her empty glass a little tighter. Ready to make a hell of a scene if he touched her again. She'd let him talk her into getting hitched because she didn't know what else to do with herself, but Gil's money—that was something. An answer and a question at once, but enough for her to live on, so long as she lived like this. Better than living like that, like she owed him happiness even if it destroyed her own. Like she owed him her misery, as Arlette had put it. "Christ," she said, feeling the emptiness of the name as they sat there, pew to pew, some crumbling sacrament determined to make them suffer for their sins. "Listen to yourself. Quite the family man you'll make."

"That's not fair."

"I don't care."

"You'll regret this."

"Tell yourself that, if it helps you sleep at night."

"No, I mean to make sure of it."

"Are you threatening me?" She didn't think him capable. But he'd done a lot of things in the last half hour that the Rob she thought she knew never would have done.

"Call it a guarantee."

"Rob," she said, "you need to leave."

He settled back in the booth, made a show of making himself comfortable. Reached for the corn bread and tore it in half. Answered with his mouth full, which seemed more grotesquely unlike him than anything else. "And if I don't, do you—"

"Am I interrupting?"

Simon stood there with a drink in each hand. Drowsy blue eyes sizing up the situation more quickly than it seemed. Rob turned toward him, body coiling and tightening, a snake winding itself into a knot. "You know, buddy, you are," he said. "In kind of a big way."

Simon was still watching Rob as he asked, "Suze, everything okay?"

"It has nothing to do with them, Rob," she said. They were all talking across each other—looking at one person while they spoke to the other, having three separate, intersecting conversations at the same time. "It had nothing to do with him or her, just you and me."

"Well, that was what it was supposed to be, to have and to hold, just you and me—not you and me and he and she."

"Our tab is paid," Simon said. Sip of whiskey. "If you'd like to go."

With a chuckle, "*Still* interrupting."

"Rob, it was already over."

"We are still married."

"*We* are nothing." Suzanne snatched the second glass from Simon and swallowed it down, grabbed his hand when it was empty. "*We* are leaving." Simon started toward the door with Suzanne close behind, but Rob caught her elbow and yanked her back.

"Not again, you're not." He was out of the booth, on his feet, fingers dug so deep in the soft hollow of her arm that her wrist spasmed, grip broken again, and she lost hold of Simon.

"LET GO!" She was so tired of telling him that, she made sure he heard her this time. She shouted as loud as she could, loud enough that the nearest tables finally twisted on their stools and the pool game ground to a halt.

"NOT AGAIN, I SAID—"

Simon put one hand on Rob's chest and pushed him backward. Not hard, but his heel hit the pew and he lost his balance and let go of Suzanne to catch himself.

"Sorry to interrupt again," Simon said, polite as he could be about it, "but she said let go. She said we're going. Suzanne?"

Fury at her own smallness, her softness, burned so hot in her stomach she thought she might spit fire if she opened her mouth. She swept her hair out of her eyes just in time to watch Rob throw an unwieldy punch. The forward lurch of his body knocked her against the table, and everyone who had stopped to watch jumped up at once. But Simon didn't even duck. All he did was move. A half step to one side, leading with his head. He never took his eyes off Rob, following his clumsy swing, his unchecked momentum, following as he found nothing to hit, then hit the back of the pew with a muffled *crack*, like a billiard ball had bounced off the table and onto the floor.

Rob crumpled, knuckles split like they'd been unzipped but no blood yet—his body in shock, not quite caught up. A few beer drinkers and hell-raisers laughed; one slapped Simon on the back. "Some ice over here, please?" he said to the bartender who had barreled over to break up the ruckus. "Sorry about that." He fished a couple of twenties out of his pocket and dropped them on the table in front of Rob, still hunched and gulping, choking on his own tongue. Simon took the coaster and pulled Suzanne out of the bar before anyone could ask questions.

They walked without stopping, without speaking. She lost count of how many blocks, propelled by some violent adrenal velocity impossible to burn off except with forward motion. Before long she was leading Simon, his weight behind her bringing her down gently, like a drag chute. She slowed until she stopped and exhaustion flooded from her face to the soles of her feet, a bucket of cold water dumped over her head. She pitched against him, tears jumping into her eyes. "I'm sorry," she said.

"Why?"

"I don't know."

"Then don't be."

That irrefutable logic. He looped his arms around her and rested his chin on top of her head. Held her like that until she stopped shaking, oblivious to passersby, the Stockyards still flush with life. Animal smells thick in the air, tender flesh hanging off the bone or dripping juice on hissing coals. When she lifted her head he hooked his elbow around her neck. Started down the street, back toward the Coliseum, where they'd parked the car. "Come on," he said with keener instincts than any doctor for how to cure what ailed her. "Why don't we go for a drive?"

THE A SIDE

NO MORE NO MORE

Gil and Skelly spent the night behind bars, Gracie spent the night trying to bail them out, and everyone else spent the night having their injuries examined—under strict orders, long distance from Louie, to *document everything,* including Suzanne. Her small body had already turned black and blue, which might be their best chance to get Skelly's assault charges dropped. Her turn to save him. She would have done anything. She would have eaten every piece of broken glass that broke his skin. She would have kissed the foot that kicked that bastard's red face in. The tender violence of the thought surprised her. She'd never wanted to hurt anyone before but understood it, all at once. The need to sink her teeth in something.

"You poor thing," cooed the nurse reading her chart, unaware of the visions of bloody retribution dancing through Suzanne's head. "All banged up on your birthday."

Suzanne blinked at her stupidly. How long had she been in that room? Her brain felt as tender and bruised as the rest of her. "What day is it?" she asked, but she couldn't remember what day yesterday was, or the day before that. Time was a Ferris wheel on tour, turning and whirling and spinning in circles, but also standing still. Every motel room and every backstage and every gas station in between had started to look the same. If her birthday had come and gone while no one was looking, they'd been on the road for a month.

Before the nurse could answer, Gracie burst through the door. "Suzanne!" she gasped, clutching her side. "Can you stand?"

"Wait, now, she's in no condition—"

But Suzanne was already out of bed. "Where's Dad?"

"He's okay, c'mon—"

"Excuse me, you can't just—"

"Excuse *me*," Gracie said. "Are you this girl's mother?"

The nurse bristled. "Are *you*?"

"Not yet," Gracie said, leaving both of them to wonder what that meant. "But I do have her mom on the phone." Which was apparently enough to grant Suzanne permission to go. Gracie led her down the hall and around the corner. "It's okay," she said, to herself or Suzanne, "we're just in time."

"For what?"

Gracie pulled a handset off somebody's desk and crouched down to look at Suzanne. "I'm sorry, baby," she said, dark eyes wet, red lip trembling. She brushed the hard lump under Suzanne's jaw. She didn't even know what hit her there. "We promised we'd call on your birthday. You ready?"

Suzanne was not ready at all. Not ready to be another year older. Not ready to talk to her mother and Nathan. She wanted to say, the same way Gracie said it, like it hurt to admit it, *Not yet*. But she didn't want Gracie to cry. Everybody hurt too much already. She held her hand out for the phone.

"Mom?"

"Hi, sweetheart!" Nora's voice was shrill and distant, the line crackling like Rice Krispies. "Oh, I miss you so much! I can't believe you're eleven already."

"Me neither," said Suzanne. Did a birthday count if you missed it?

"Did you take any good pictures?" Nathan and Nora had given her her gift before the wedding. Since they'd miss her birthday, why not have it early? They'd bought her a few packs of film for the Polaroid, a hobby Nora had gradually warmed to, unlike Suzanne's obsession with the stereo. She'd even dusted off an old camera of her own, for the first time that Suzanne could recall. She'd never been to Europe before. Every week when Gracie flipped through her notebook to find which country, which town, which hotel they were in, Nora rhapsodized about the museums they'd been to and the food that they'd eaten and all the adventures they'd had. Europe sounded like Neverland.

"Uh-huh," Suzanne said, which wasn't untrue. Nora did not ask for specifics. They could never afford more than a few minutes; all Suzanne had to do was ask one or two questions and Nora would fill the time describing wherever they'd landed. This week, some island in Greece.

"This morning we went to a dig site where they're excavating this gorgeous tile floor from thousands of years ago. It just took my breath away."

"Wow," said Suzanne, who had only recently become acquainted with that feeling and didn't understand how it could be a good thing.

"I told Nathan we might have to retile the bathroom to match," Nora went on. "I don't think I can live without it." But she seemed to be doing just fine without Suzanne, which was probably why Suzanne didn't feel worse for not telling more of the truth. She glanced up at Gracie—her eyes puffy and purple with exhaustion, chewing absently at a hangnail. She must have run out of gum. When she saw Suzanne looking, she stopped. Worry creasing her forehead. *Okay?* she mouthed. She and Gil had never asked her to lie to Nora, but Suzanne knew not to say anything that might disrupt the honeymoon euphoria. Because, before yesterday, she'd never been happier, either.

Sadness ran her through so suddenly she swayed on her feet, reaching blindly toward Gracie, who caught her and rocked her and whispered in one ear, "It's okay, baby, I got you" while Nora chattered on in the other.

"Maybe for your next birthday we'll bring you. The pastries here! You'll never want to eat cake again. When we get home you won't even recognize me, because I'll have gained twenty pounds . . ."

"Okay, Mom," Suzanne said, fighting to keep her voice steady for Gracie. Who stroked her hair and hummed in her ear and promised, again and again, "It's okay, baby, I got you."

*   *   *

Nora was right about one thing. Suzanne did not want cake. Not even rainbow cake from the bakery counter at a twenty-four-hour diner called Zora's where Gil insisted on celebrating as soon as he was out on bail. It wasn't much of a party, and Suzanne was embarrassed more than anything until she realized it seemed to come as a relief to the rest of them. Something to talk about other than the huge pile of shit they'd stepped in. Everyone ate dessert for dinner. Doug told tales of Suzanne's best busts at the record store, with mythic exaggerations. Ruby shuffled and cut a tarot deck on the table and read Suzanne's cards. "Eleven is a powerful number—the first master number," she said, slyly smiling. "It'll be a big year for you."

It had been a big year already. She wasn't sure how much bigger it could get. As Ruby shuffled and bridged, shuffled and bridged, Gil kept one hand on Suzanne, mussing her hair absentmindedly, cutting everything with the side of his fork rather than letting go to reach for a knife. She didn't mind; it saved her the embarrassment of clinging to him like a much younger child, dismayed by their brief separation. She wanted to cry at his scabbed and bruised and swollen face, the shiny black welt curled like a leech around his left eye.

The rest of them didn't look much better. Besides the lump on her jaw, Suzanne's face had escaped serious damage, but everywhere else was mottled with soft spots like a bad banana. Ruby's lack of beauty sleep had taken a toll, her cheeks sunken, mouth drawn, all but two of her fingernails broken. Nash had an ugly scratch across his cheek, which he owed—he admitted sheepishly—to the studded epaulettes Ruby had been wearing when he threw her over his shoulder like King Kong. Carney was the worst off besides Gil, with a busted lip and one earring ripped out, leaving a long, stretched slot behind, crusted brown with blood. Even Doug hadn't escaped the wrath of Nebraska. His headlong rush down the ladder when Suzanne went over the railing had dropped him right in the thick of things, where he soon lost sight of her but took an elbow to the nose for his trouble. It, like Carney's lip, had doubled in size and deepened in color until, with his frazzled red hair, he strongly resembled the Muppet Animal. (He did a surprisingly good impression of his doppelganger, which Suzanne suspected was also an impression of Nash.) Gracie's injuries seemed more psychological. The last forty-eight hours running damage control single-handedly had left her with an ashen, vacant look. Every now and then her eyes would flicker back on and she'd summon a smile for Gil or Suzanne—palpably relieved to see them both in one piece. She had to be the TM first and the girlfriend second, and that meant shoving her own feelings aside when the Kills were in peril.

She might have been the only person who felt Skelly's absence more acutely than Suzanne. He'd been sent to the hospital straight from the jailhouse in a hail of prayers and diabolical bargains struck on behalf of the sorcerous Hands. Without them, there was no band. Every time Suzanne closed her eyes she saw his trembling fingers, heard his ragged scream for help, and every hair on her head stood on end. When everyone sang "Happy Birthday" in their hoarse, croaking voices, she wished as hard as she had ever wished for anything that all the king's horses and men could put Gil and the Kills back together again.

She blew the candles out and Gil said, "We thought we'd get you something to match that cake," even though she'd barely touched it—too sickly, too thickly frosted. But the gift came wrapped up in the funny pages, Hägar the Horrible leading his army of misfits on another half-cocked crusade. Doug pulled a face at her across the table as she tore the paper off.

"Crayons." Not just any crayons, but Crayola No. 64. Four rows of sixteen pristine points, with a sharpener built in. She'd never had a box that big before. She hugged it to her chest and finally, belatedly, started to cry.

"Shit, she must be beat," Nash said as Gil folded her under his arm. "She's just a kid." He said it in a voice of faint wonderment, as if he'd forgotten that along the way. Maybe they all had. They lapsed into a gloomy silence, underscored by some lugubrious power ballad on the radio. Cinderella with the warning that you don't know what you got until it's gone. Suzanne extracted herself from Gil's armpit and had hiccupped half a "thank you" before she realized nobody was looking at her anymore. Their heads had all turned toward the door.

"*Mi amor*," Gil said, and Gracie sat up straighter. "*Llévalos al motel. Necesito tener una audiencia sola con el Rey.*"

Gracie glanced at Suzanne. "*Pienso que ella no te va dejar, después de ayer.*"

Suzanne knew some of the words, but they spoke too fast for her to remember what they meant. She wasn't really listening, watching the man who had just walked in and drawn their eyes like a magnet. His arms looked too long for his body, swinging below his belt as he walked. Dark hair sprouting from each knuckle and the V of his collared shirt. He wasn't wearing a tie, but a heavy gold chain like a collar around his thick neck. It was difficult to say where his beard stopped and his sideburns began, but his comb-over was fighting a losing battle against male pattern baldness. Suzanne's first impression was of a large, lumbering monkey—which should have been funny, but was instead inexplicably menacing. This must be King Louie.

"*¿Tiene el mapa?*" Gil muttered, shifting his legs under Suzanne.

Gracie's eyebrows rose. "*Está más pegada a ese mapa que a ti.*"

"*Bien—ella puede dibujar.*"

"Well, well," said the monkey man, sidling up to their table. "Aren't we having ourselves a nice little party."

"Good to see you, Lou," Gil said. "There's cake if you're hungry."

"Not much appetite, don't mean to be rude." He looked down at them with a grin that was more of a grimace. The long nose and beady eyes made her think of a mandrill, with their blazing faces and yellow saber teeth. "Had a pick-me-up on the plane."

"We were just looking for the waitress anyway," Gracie lied, with a warning look at the rest of them that precluded argument.

"I'll take care of the waitress," Louie said. "You all go on and sleep it off."

They rose en masse, as if it were choreographed, said their goodnights, and followed Gracie out. The windows reflected the customers inside, the world beyond a wall of dark. Gil lifted Suzanne off his lap and nudged her toward a nearby booth. "I need a minute with Lou, eh? Take your crayons and order whatever you want." He wiped the trace of a tear off her cheek with his cuff. "Think about your next wish. The birthday's not over yet."

She still didn't want cake. When the waitress came back, she asked for french fries. "With maple syrup," she said.

"On the fries." The waitress peered over her glasses at Suzanne like she might not be quite right in the head.

"On the side," she said. It was something she'd learned from Skelly, who liked french fries but hated ketchup and helped himself to pancake syrup off anybody's unwatched plate when he needed a fix. The crispy, salty fries and the sweet, sticky syrup made a glorious mess, and as soon as she tried it once she knew she'd never reach for the ketchup again.

"Whatever you say." The waitress walked away shaking her head.

Suzanne spread the atlas—*el mapa*—on the table and gingerly opened the Crayola 64. So many colors to choose from she didn't know where to start. Their next destination was California, where they would have two weeks to regroup and recover before the next leg. She chose Raw Sienna for the easy path, due west. But if they dipped south—she chose another crayon, Spring Green, for the scenic route—maybe they could go see a ghost town. She'd seen photos of an old mining camp in a brochure at one of the motel reception desks and asked Doug what a ghost town was.

That's what it is, it's like a ghost of a town, he said. *That used to be there and isn't anymore.*

Why?

Dunno, he said. *All kinds of reasons. Probably none of them good.*

But things that weren't good sometimes made great photos. She'd learned that snapping Polaroids of every shambling dinosaur and sun-bleached alien they met along the highway. Most were prefab and none were convincing—just cartoonish science fiction monsters, as if a toddler's drawing of E.T. or a T. rex had come to life. But through the lens of a camera they looked different, assumed a kind of tragic dignity. She thought the ghost of an old cowboy town must be even better.

The tip of her crayon hit a fault line in the map and left a streak of green south of Aspen. The hot prickle of tears in her eyes again. They might not even get to California.

"Fries, syrup on the side." The dish clattered onto the table, and Suzanne pushed the crayons a safe distance away, determined to keep them like new as long as she could. The first fry was too hot to touch and too hot to taste but she gobbled it down anyway, salt and syrup sticking on her lips. She looked sideways, not trying *not* to eavesdrop.

"Babel Mouth," Gil was saying, leaning low over the table on his elbows. "You're fucking with me." Suzanne stopped chewing. That was a name she knew. She remembered their album *Hard Candy* from that first day at Most Wanted.

"I ran into their rep at Mutt's last little gathering. They're short of support for their next leg—Texas, mostly. Vince took exception to something somebody did or said, who knows. Who cares. But now nobody else will do. It's all you."

"Vince DeWitt," Gil said. "Wants us to open."

"You've already accepted, by the way. We'll catch them Tuesday night in Kansas City, so you have some idea what you're in for, because you only get two rehearsals before Dallas."

"Louie," Gil said, "we can't play two weeks of gigs that aren't even ours between now and Denver. This is our only break, and everybody is *broken*."

"I'm not finished," Louie said, and Gil fell silent. Fingering the cup of coffee that had been going cold in front of him since El Rey sat down. "You only get two rehearsals before Dallas, but then you get to split the bill at Wrecking Ball. You're coheadlining the festival, mostly on the strength of your bad reputation. Congratulations," he added. "You can't buy this kind of publicity. Trust me, I've tried."

Gil stared at him. *Glared* at him. "What are you talking about?"

"I understand," Louie said, "you've been a little preoccupied. But since you haven't had time to pick up the paper, I may as well tell you you're all over it. Both of you. Nancy Reagan is already calling for your heads, and I'm going to see if I can't get you condemned by the pope. That song's been banned on stations that had never even heard of you before yesterday and never would have played it anyway. The promoter was salivating over the phone—he wants you all onstage together. That's Vegas for you. Go big or go home."

"That's great, Lou," Gil said darkly, "but didn't you just come from the hospital? You saw Skelly's hands. He can't play. *We* can't play. It's not like he has an understudy."

"I'll get him a doctor."

"A doctor? Be serious—"

"I already talked to him."

"You what?"

"Gil, don't get pissy with me," Louie said, tipping his chair back on two legs, hands laced over his gut. "I've been doing my best to keep this shitshow afloat for nine years, because I'm a sentimental old fool and I think you could really make something of yourself. But not if you keep making stupid mistakes. Eric's the one with ten bloody fingers and twenty-two frets to play, but he's game. Now, are you going to get on board, or are you going to blow your big break just because you *need a break?*"

Suzanne's latest french fry hovered an inch from her mouth. The phrase shook another black memory loose in the back of her brain. Gil at Skelly's throat, promising, *If you blow it for us—*

"All done?"

She jumped in her seat, dropped the fry in her lap. "No," she said before the waitress could whisk the dish away again. Suzanne picked the fry from between her knees, where it left a tacky brown streak. When she looked up, Gil was sliding into her booth, and Louie was gone.

"Can't take us anywhere, huh?" Gil said.

"Sounds like Louie wants to take us to Texas." She dunked a fresh fry and smacked her lips. Gil's mouth and eyebrows made the same straight line.

"That innocent exterior," he said, "it's very deceptive. Or is eleven the year you turn cunning?"

"Ask me next week," she decided. Everyone seemed to see her future so clearly, could imagine her eleven or twenty-seven. But they all saw something different, and they couldn't all be right. Suzanne didn't know who to believe, wasn't sure if growing up was something you did or something that just happened to you.

"Deal." Gil filched a few of her fries, forwent the syrup. "Now. How about those wishes?"

"I already made my wish," she said, glancing at the other table. The rainbow cake had been cleared. The waitress seemed keen to get rid of them, and who could blame her? Seven people in leather and chains, faces disfigured by two-day-old makeup, either victims or perpetrators of some kind of violence. Suzanne wondered whether she'd seen the headlines Louie mentioned.

"Aha. But since you're so cunning, you might have suspected your old man is a genie." He folded his arms and bobbed his head like Barbara Eden so a couple of curls fell in his eyes. Hiding the shiner for a moment. "Instead of one wish, you get three."

She knew he was trying to make it up to her—the forgotten birthday, the chaos and confusion, the danger he hadn't been the one to save her from. The longer she spent around Gil and the band, the less he seemed infallible or invulnerable. Which didn't make her love him less, but more. She could see now how he needed her, too—someone to believe he could be somebody long before he was. Nora had lost that faith a long time ago, and with it any faith in him. But Suzanne kept the fire burning, even on the coldest days. Sensing her advantage and deciding to take it—she could be cunning, perhaps, with a little more practice—she said, "I want to see Babel Mouth in Kansas City."

His mouth and eyebrows made that disapproving equals sign again, but he only sighed. "Sounds like you'll get to see them sooner or later," he said. "All right. It's a date. You can tell me if you think they're worth the hype." Because Babel Mouth was already where Gil wanted to be. They'd graduated from clubs to theaters, hundreds of tickets to thousands. "Hard Candy" and "Barbarella" snarled across the airwaves every few hours. "What else?" Gil said, squinting at her with one swollen eye. "One wish left."

Under any other circumstances, she might have been afraid to ask. But if not now, maybe never. Suzanne took a deep breath. "I want to learn to drive."

They drove half an hour into falling night. Suzanne slid across the seat to stay close to Gil. She loved Gracie and the Kill Team, but she never had him to herself. He hummed along to the radio, lollipop tucked in his cheek. She didn't know where they were going, and it didn't matter— so long as he was warm and breathing, humming, driving.

After another ten minutes, he said, "This'll do," and turned into a parking lot with one streetlamp that still worked, yellow light pooling on the cracked asphalt like sour milk. The building the lot belonged to looked abandoned. The windows had been papered over, the sign rusted beyond legibility. It might have been the ghost of a grocery store; the letters remaining above the doors spelled P P S G O C RY. But Suzanne had never felt less like crying. She sat up straighter, wishing she had her camera, but it was too dark for a good picture anyway. Gil climbed out and beckoned her into the driver's seat. While he rattled around at the tailgate, unhitching the trailer, she grasped the wheel tightly. The leather was still warm from Gil's palms, and she placed her smaller hands where his had been. The engine's eager vibration plugged right into her nervous system. She tasted it again—that animal musk of adrenaline. Her own this time. Hot and salty and sweet, like syrup on french fries.

"Now, your legs aren't long enough for the pedals yet," Gil said. "We'll learn that part in a few more birthdays." He lifted her up and set her down again in his lap—much more gently than usual, as if she were made of glass. Her bruises throbbed and smarted, but she barely felt them. "That's good." He adjusted her hands. "Hold on up top—no matter how cool it looks to drive around with one elbow out the window."

"You drive like that."

"Well, when you've been driving for twenty years you can drive like that, too. Baby steps, baby girl."

"I'm not a baby," she said. She'd never been babied, really—but least of all today.

"You're still my baby," he said. "And growing up too fast for my liking." Eleven today, twenty-seven by the end of the tour, or so Carney had said. "I'm going to let go and we're going to go slow, eh? Get a feel for the wheels."

Suzanne's heart beat a hundred miles a minute. She felt Gil's legs shift and the car rolled forward. The steering wheel wanted to turn in her hands, but she held it steady.

"Good," Gil said. "When you turn, slow down at first, then speed up again as you straighten." She guided Blondie to the left, then the right, drawing an enormous *S* across the lot. She did a few more like that, and Gil let her go a little faster. The ease of each turn like a sidewinder snake, twisting across the sand. Gil stopped the car and said, "Let's try it in reverse." They tilted the mirrors this way and that until they found an angle Suzanne could work with—too short for the driver's seat, even in Gil's lap. "Backwards is trickier," he warned. "Pull the wheel the same way you want the *back* end of the car to go."

She fudged it the first time. Not so intuitive, but Gil talked her through it, describing the way the wheels on the ground worked with the wheel in her hands until she could see it, understood the geometry. After that it was easy. She reversed in a perfect circle around the streetlamp in the middle of the lot.

"You're a fast learner, that's for sure," Gil said, more to himself than to her. "Okay, let's try a figure eight. Another circle around this pole, then that one over there." That tripped her up, since the second lamp was out and she had only the ruby-red glow of the taillights to guide her. "Again," Gil said when she finally managed an ungainly infinity. "Practice makes perfect." She did two more, then three, going steadily faster until she was dizzy and giggling and Gil stopped the car.

"What's so funny?"

"Backwards figure eights," she said. "When do you drive in backwards figure eights?"

"You never know. Someday you might have to back out of a tight spot in a hurry, and you'll be glad if those figure eights are second nature." He ruffled her hair, grown much too long. "Any last birthday wishes?"

"I like being on the road with you," she said, head pillowed on his shoulder, his strawberry breath a sweet heat on the back of her ear. "Can I come on the next tour, too?" It wasn't a wish; he wasn't a genie, whatever he said. She heard him sigh and knew the magic of the night was running out.

He looped his arms around her like a seat belt, like he could keep her safe from whatever might come swerving across her path. "Honey, we have to talk," he said. "I know you lied to your mom, about being all right." Nathan and Nora were hours ahead and blissfully unaware of everything afoot on the other side of the world. But Suzanne didn't even have to lie about being all right, because Nora didn't ask.

"I didn't lie," she said. Heart still beating hard, but hurting now. Voice already wavering at the recollection of how her last denial landed. *I didn't steal anything.* She hadn't stolen, and she hadn't lied, because that was the rule: no outright untruths to Nora. "I am all right."

"You have no idea—" And Gil's voice broke, too. He cleared his throat as if it were a temporary glitch in the mix, nothing more. "We're lucky the Hands has such fast reflexes," he said, and she heard it again, that sour note—shame or jealousy or something sickly in between. "Gracie agreed it would be better for you to go on ahead to California. Stay with her sisters on the ranch an extra week or so."

"No!" Suzanne pushed herself up and away from him, trying to turn around in his arms and look him in the eye. "Don't make me go!"

"Suzanne." He held her tighter. "Try to understand, if something happened to you—this is getting too crazy. If Louie has his way—and Louie always does—this thing, I don't know, babe, it's bigger than me. It's bigger than me now." His voice faded out. Like he had never considered that possibility, because it was his name on the marquee. But it wasn't his name on the label. Wasn't his name listed first now. He was just a name on a list that started with Babel Mouth.

"I'll be good," she said. "I promise. I know it's my fault, but I didn't mean to!"

"What's your fault?"

"Skelly got hurt helping me." She couldn't seem to stop doing that. Messing everything up without meaning to. Gil and Nora, Gil and Skelly. Every time she tried to get close to someone she drove someone else away. Of course she couldn't stay.

"Oh, honey, no," Gil said, stumbling over his words, without a ready answer. "He needs a doctor now, that's all. He's just glad you're okay."

That was the first time she knew for certain that he'd lied to her. She squirmed out of his arms, retreated to the passenger seat with her knees folded up under her chin. Battered ribs aching. "I don't want to go," she said. "I'll be good. Please, don't make me go." Because without him and the road and the music, what would be left of her? Whatever Carney said, she wasn't twenty-seven yet, she was barely eleven, she didn't know how to be somebody of her own. She was crying again, so tired and sore and confused she didn't even know why, wiping the tears away with small angry swipes at her face. And Gil was crying, too, holding his arms out again, catching both her hands in one of his before she hurt herself, swearing up and down that it wasn't her fault, nothing was her fault.

"Don't cry, baby, okay?" he said. "Shh. I'll talk to Louie. We'll work something out. Don't cry."

FUCKING INSTAGRAM

Rob was a problem. His sudden appearance at the Stockyards had forced Suzanne to lay it all on the table in the diminutive dinette. She'd already given up Gil, let the bare fact of him out to Simon and Phoebe, who understood on some level what it meant to be his kin. But Rob was different. Rob was her own doing, and he was clearly coming undone.

"I don't understand," she kept saying. "I don't understand how he found me."

"What I don't understand is why you ever married this guy," Phoebe said.

"Nobody else asked," she said, and didn't explain, because that much they couldn't understand—how lonely it looked on the wrong side of thirty when everyone else was already married and starting a family. One by one you lost your friends to spouses and children. They forgot how to talk to you, invitations got lost in the mail, before long you realized you were just an odd number screwing up the seating arrangement. Staying single past a certain age was a social extinction event. "It doesn't matter. What do we do?"

Her instinct was to split up, but Simon and Phoebe shot this down at once, uniformly offended by the suggestion that they'd abandon her to the machinations of her crazy ex—"Well, not yet," she reminded them—husband. But doing things in threes meant majority rule.

Suzanne argued fruitlessly for a minute or two and was forced to give in when Simon pointed out that she was the wheels.

"Going nowhere fast without you and Blondie," he said. "So, where to?"

She hadn't planned to take them there, but when had her plans ever gone accordingly anyway? "I think I need to talk to Gracie." She still had so many questions, and Louie had only given her more. He was just the executor, he insisted. He and Gil didn't talk much toward the end, too many hatchets to bury by then. But they'd been yoked together for so many years, the knot was tough to untangle. Another bad marriage. *I only know what he wanted*, Louie growled down the phone when he first summoned her to Florida. *Don't fucking ask me why.* She didn't know when Gil left California, but she knew Gracie didn't go with him. Suzanne needed to understand that, as much as anything else. All that time she'd spent telling herself he was fine, that Gracie was taking good care of him. She had no idea what she would say to her, but she had a few days to figure it out. There was a lot of the Southwest left to drive through.

"Longer we stay in one place, the more time we give Rob to regroup," Phoebe said. "No sense sitting around." That fit into her plans nicely. "Western wear is all anyone wants anymore," she explained. "Best to go to the source. We'll have to move some merchandise if we want to keep moving." Simon couldn't work until they stayed still long enough for him to rustle up some clients. Suzanne wouldn't get another cash infusion for a while and didn't dare swipe a card anywhere until she knew how Rob was tracking her. So they packed up camp and started west. Simon took the first shift driving, with Trouble on the passenger side.

West of Fort Worth the hours crawled by, sticky and slow as tar on the asphalt, Blondie dragging the Lifeboat through barely there towns and thirsty oilfields where skeletal steel derricks pecked at the parched earth like starving birds. Suzanne sat at the table with Rand McNally and a jar of iced tea sweating in her hand. Déjà vu prickled under her skin. Not just the lurking recollection of two weeks on the road with Babel Mouth's pillaging army, but also the nomadic months of her first fellowship, collecting ghost stories from cities and towns and mining camps left to the callous indifference of time. She'd taken to leafing through *Dust and Bones* when it was too hot to sleep. Some of the photos she didn't remember taking; the ruins bled together in her memory, boarded windows and rusting trailers that barely changed from site to site. But the names she recalled, each one penned on a Polaroid frame. Gilliland, Barstow, Toyah, Glenrio. If they passed through again, she wondered whether a smell on the breeze or a shadow in the dust would remind her when she last set foot there, who she was back then. Her younger selves grew more distant over the years, receded until they might as well have been casual acquaintances—people she recognized but barely knew. Probably better that way.

"Suze." Phoebe's voice wafted in from the bedroom. "Come model something for me." The digital storefront kept the cash flowing between flea markets and fairs. They stopped at a post office every few days to pack and ship items all over the country, each envelope stamped with her trademark ring buoy.

Suzanne traded her tank for an olive drab field shirt with U.S. ARMY stitched above the left breast and both sleeves torn off at the shoulder. Something Skelly would have worn. "Buttoned or tied?" she asked, poking her arms through the holes where the sleeves used to be.

"Tied," Phoebe said. "Somebody'll buy it hoping it makes their cleavage look like yours." They had such different bodies, they ogled and envied and flattered each other in turn. Suzanne had always wanted long limbs like Phoebe, the nimble ease that made her look good in anything. But Phoebe was curveless and angular, obsessed with Suzanne's softer hourglass. She cinched the shirttails tight around Suzanne's waist. "Right there, you're a smokeshow, don't move." She took ten photos from ten different angles, squatting and standing and bouncing around on the bed until she got what she called "the money shot." "That's the one. Thanks."

"Want it back?"

Phoebe shrugged, tapping away at her phone, adding filters and captions and hashtags cleverly orchestrated to maximize engagement. She knew more about marketing in the digital age than she ever could have learned in school. "Wear it 'til it sells," she said. A bump in the road pitched Suzanne onto the bed. She fell flat on top of Phoebe, who grunted and laughed and rolled her off to go hunting around for the phone that went flying out of her hand.

"Hey," she said. "Suzanne."

"What?" Suzanne struggled to get halfway upright with the Lifeboat lurching along.

"I don't know," Phoebe said, peering out the back window. "There's this black pickup I keep seeing—like it's tailing us."

"Black pickup?" Suzanne followed her eyes. One of those hulking trucks with wheels big as hay bales hung back about two hundred feet. Weird, for that testosterone fever dream of a vehicle. Usually, they loved the passing lane or tailgated obnoxiously until they bullied everyone out of their way. But this one cruised patiently in the Airstream's wake.

"Maybe I'm paranoid," Phoebe said.

Suzanne squinted against the glare on the windshield. They passed under a cloud, and in the brief pool of shadow she saw a swoop of sandy hair. One hand on the wheel, wrapped in a wad of gauze. "Jesus," she said. "It's Rob."

"*Rob?*" Phoebe looked up from the phone she'd unearthed in the bedclothes. She'd never seen him, hadn't met him, was busy entertaining a pair of barrel racers when he found Simon and Suzanne at the bar.

"Must be a new car; I've never seen it before."

"Shit," Phoebe said. "What do we do?"

"How the hell does he keep finding me? I don't—" Except she did, suddenly. She grabbed Phoebe's phone and scrolled through the Lifeboat Supply Co. feed. Clothes, homewares, Simon, Suzanne. Every square tagged when and where, so Phoebe's customers could find her when she passed through town. Everywhere they'd stopped since leaving the Sundew Value Inn five lifetimes ago. "Instagram," Suzanne said. "He's following us on fucking *Instagram.*" It must have been so easy.

"Fuck," Phoebe said. "I'm so sorry, I didn't think—"

"I should be sorry—neither did I." She never thought he'd chase her like this. Never meant to bring him down on their heads.

"We'll go dark," Phoebe said. "Get off the grid."

"We'd have to lose him first."

"Not likely," Phoebe said. "Not dragging this boat behind us."

"We'll just have to outsmart him, then." Suzanne didn't feel particularly smart. She felt dangerously stupid, staring through the tiny back window at the Rorschach blots behind the wheel. The dark smudges of his mouth, nose, eyes. Hiding in plain sight in that ugly black truck. Outrage sharpened her mind to a needle point and slipped it into a groove. The belt moved, the record turned, the speakers popped and sparked to life. She didn't need to outsmart him. Rob had gone crazy, but she could go crazier. For once, she had the advantage. Crazy ran right through her veins.

She grabbed her book out of the windowsill and bolted off the bed, moving too fast, catching her hips and shoulders on the protruding shelves and corners that made the Lifeboat an obstacle course even when it wasn't moving. She crash-landed at the dinette, where the atlas was still spread on the table. Her fingertip zigzagged across the Southwest. The names came thick and fast. All the old ghosts peering over her shoulder, waking up to take a walk with her again. The dead left their impressions, the nation's lust for blood and money scrawled across the map of history. Lobo and Rhyolite, Goldfield and Tombstone and Death Valley Junction.

She reached for the nearest crayon and dragged a jagged line across the desert. The point snapped off and left a scabrous streak of wax in the wastelands of New Mexico. Phoebe, who had sensed the need for silence, broke it now to ask, "Where are we going?"

It wasn't on the map, but Suzanne knew how to find it. She thrust the map aside, flipping through the book, not looking for names but for photographs now, one she would know when she saw it.

"Sanctuary."

THE **B** SIDE

COLOR ME ONCE

Rob was not a violent man. Except for childhood dustups with his brothers, he'd never been in a fight. Suzanne had brought something evil out in him that was not so easily subdued again, but flying off the handle at the bar had not gone his way. Eight Fingers outmaneuvered him by keeping calm—probably easier when you had that stupid, half-sedated bearing all the time. Rob let his evil feelings get the better of him and it had cost him dearly.

He didn't go to the hospital, though he probably should have. Instead, he drove one-handed to a liquor store and bought a bottle of vodka. He took a swig, tore one of his undershirts in half, stuffed it in his mouth, and doused the open gash across the back of his hand. For half a minute the wound was on fire, a laser carving into his skin all over again. He choked down a handful of Aleve with another gulp of vodka, which tasted like rubbing alcohol, which hopefully meant the wound was clean. He could have picked up a first aid kit but didn't want to leave a trail of memorable interactions.

He'd spent the rest of the night in the Dodge, mapping every RV park within a reasonable distance of both the market and the Stockyards. As soon as the sun rose, he rolled through a drive-through, wolfed down three McMuffins in quick succession, chased that mass of salt and grease with a large black coffee and another nip of vodka, just to dull the pain, then started crossing parks, resorts, and campgrounds off the list.

Most were gated, but most of the bleary-eyed attendants hadn't seen anybody matching his descriptions. If they wanted to know why he was asking, he told them he was trying to collect a debt, which tended to divert suspicion off himself. Every attendant more invested in protecting their own interests than a deadbeat guest. Other RV parks were left open to interlopers, and he drove aimless loops through half a dozen tawdry little tin-can villages. You could tell who was only passing through and who had been there longer by the pathetic attempts to personalize each plot. Fake flowers and cheap fluttering signs that said HOME SWEET HOME. Airstreams were easy to spot, baking under the sun like potatoes wrapped in tinfoil. But none of them were the Lifeboat. He'd clocked so many hours staring at it on Instagram that he would have recognized it instantly—by the weathervane on the roof or the orange Lifesaver hanging on the side like a spare tire.

When he finally found it, he wasn't sure it wasn't a mirage, not quite trusting his eyes after however many hours he'd gone without sleep, losing blood and letting Svedka make up the difference. He idled outside, waiting for a sign of life, but all he saw was a dog that looked half-wild, more like a coyote than a house pet. Big, wide mouth and pale, sandy fur, with a bottle-brush tail that swept its paw prints out of the dirt behind it. It lay at the steps of the Lifeboat with a dead woodchuck between its paws. Bringing home breakfast, apparently, while Suzanne and Freckles and Eight Fingers slept off whatever perversity they got up to last night. Watching them on the jumbotron had thrown gasoline on the embers of his imagination.

He had combed through every photo on the feed for evidence of Suzanne, evidence of what it was about Freckles and Eight Fingers that appealed to her. They were young, yes, but Suzanne had never been particularly interested in people younger than herself. If anything, the opposite. She'd grown up too fast in most ways—he understood that now, thanks to his equally rigorous research into his late father-in-law—but in so many others she was still a child. Just like Freckles and Eight Fingers, opting out of responsibility, refusing to grow up. And Suzanne's attraction to them—it must be young lust, nothing more.

That should have made it easier to swallow, but it didn't. After all the rebuffs and excuses and not-in-the-moods, the idea of her naked body tangled with their naked bodies made his palms sweat. Yes, he was ready to collect a debt.

He'd never been in a fight, and he'd never been on a long road trip, either. Didn't see the appeal. Maybe because his father had always driven sensible sedans, rather than roaring around in a pony car in that brazen shade of lemonade—like a peacock showing its plumes. All flash and no substance. But Rob had learned to like the brute power of the Dodge. The bellowing engine, the searing headlights. Smaller cars got out of his way automatically. He owned the road.

He'd sifted through the CDs Suzanne left behind, to take his mind off the dull pain in his hand that had sharpened, slowly but surely, as the hours dragged on. Springsteen was a name he recognized at least, but *The River* was more film noir than he expected, a bitter waltz across the octaves that proved a fitting soundtrack for the desolate ribbon of highway between Fort Worth and Phoenix. "Point Blank" caught him right between the eyes. "Fade Away" and "Stolen Car" cut him to the quick with their terrible relevance.

"Get a grip, Gabbard," he said to himself, but his grip had never been shakier. Knuckles split and swollen and purple as overripe plums. The whole thing was so lurid he couldn't quite believe it, but Bruce's rugged crooning made it all feel justified somehow.

He started the album over again when it ended. Why not? They'd been driving for hours and would drive hours more. If he was quick he could stop for gas and a leak and a cup of coffee and catch up to them again in a few minutes—the Dodge had more horsepower than the Kentucky Derby, and when it was hauling the trailer, the Ranchero was mercifully slow. Still, they had the advantage of driving in shifts. Going it alone, Rob was doomed to semipermanent delirium, subsisting on short snatches of sleep and fast food he never would have touched under normal circumstances. His sweat stank of onions and peanut oil. He hadn't had a shower for days. He caught his own eye in the rearview mirror. Dark circles, deep lines. He hadn't shaved even longer than he hadn't showered, and his beard, which had always grown in darker than his hair, had started to grow in gray.

She's taken a decade off your life, old man, his reflection seemed to say. He shook his head, tried to blink the sinking sun out of his eyes. Too dark for sunglasses now, but when the light slanted through the windshield just right it was blinding.

"So it would be crazy to give up now," he reasoned. After everything he'd done already. He could not—*would* not—go back without her.

Maybe there's no going back, the man in the rearview mirror said.

He considered that as the eldritch silhouettes of wind turbines drifted past. He'd only seen them in pictures before and had no idea they were so enormous. Their size and their stubborn silence unnerved him. Skeletal shadows against the striated sky. Stars tumbling down from the big, deep blue to stick like pins in the warmer band of orange burning low to the ground.

"Not to the way things were," he decided. "Something better." Brad was right. He'd smother her with love. Forgive her for everything—even Eight Fingers—and give her whatever she wanted so long as she didn't break his heart again. Casey was right, too. She'd come around. They all did, eventually.

Except the secret dykes, the mirror reminded him.

It wasn't exactly a secret. She told him before they were married that she'd been with women, but it never seemed like a serious threat. Just an adolescent indiscretion, something to fire his fantasies every now and then. But he could make that bargain—if she would come home and recommit to the vows she made, they could talk about another woman in the bedroom. It was supposed to be a collaboration, marriage. A compromise. He could let her have that if she could let him have a family.

Is that a good idea? his reflection asked. *What kind of mother would she make?* Clearly, she wasn't stable. But motherhood would mellow her, like Dana and Claudia. She just needed more purpose in life, something to give her direction, a reason to get up in the morning. Children could only change her for the better, surely.

Are you sure?

He glanced up with a twinge of annoyance that felt a lot like a budding migraine. A vicious little pinch right behind his right eye. "Shut *up*," he said.

It was dark enough for headlights now, a burnt fringe of vermillion clinging to the earth at the edge of his eyesight. But he didn't reach for the switch, wary of spooking the Airstream. A light burned inside, but someone had yanked the curtains shut while he was talking to his other self. He tried to rub the migraine out of his eye with one clumsy finger. Insomnia did not agree with him.

"Shit!"

The Boss hiccupped in the disc tray. Rob's bad hand screamed as he grabbed the wheel, swerved on instinct. He hadn't seen their turn signal, but they were veering off the highway. He missed the back bumper by the skin of his teeth, and without their headlights or taillights to guide him, plunged into unbroken darkness ahead.

"Shit shit shit shit shit—"

He flipped the headlights on and they flooded the road. He looked back over his shoulder just long enough to watch the big silver bullet of the trailer disappear.

"Mother*fucker*!" He couldn't lose them like this, not now, not here in the middle of nowhere. He glared into the dark until he realized how empty the darkness was. Nothing oncoming, and nobody behind him except—he glanced up at the man in the mirror. "No going back, my ass."

He pumped the brakes and yanked the wheel. The tires screeched, the back end of the truck fishtailing across both lanes. He kicked the gas pedal down and the engine howled. The speedometer leapt past 80, 90, 95 before a sign flashed out of the dark. He made a hard right and found himself at the intersection of nothing and nothing. There was a gas station with one light stuttering over the pumps. He killed his headlights and drove around the other side. No car, no trailer, not even a cashier inside. Nowhere else to go, either. Nothing but desert in every direction. One dusty road snaking away to the south. Another winding away north. But not a sliver of silver, not even the red eye of a shrinking taillight.

He revved the engine and went south at random. Drove at a break-neck speed, spurred by blind rage and blind panic. Five minutes at most he'd lost sight of them, and they were gone without a tire track. The shadows had swallowed them whole. He made another hairpin turn and sped the other way. The north was just as empty, just as desolate—a sea of scrubland between him and the distant humpbacked hills. He drove back and forth, north and south, faster and farther each time.

The empty light came on just before sunrise. He skidded onto the shoulder and let go of the wheel. Knuckles bleeding afresh. Dawn brought the world out of hiding again, but not the trailer. Not the car. Nowhere to go from there, but somehow Suzanne was gone.

THE **A** SIDE

NICE BOYS DON'T PLAY
ROCK AND ROLL

Tuesday night in Kansas City, and the marquee that welcomed BABEL MOUTH also said SOLD OUT. A barrier that apparently did not apply to their incumbent opening act. Louie led the band and Suzanne up several flights of stairs with crimson carpets so scuffed and slashed they were barely hanging on to the floorboards. The wallpaper, too—a fussy, floral Victorian—looked like it had seen the wrong end of a saber-toothed tiger. The veneer of vice and sleaze didn't distract from the fact that this was a different kind of gig and a different kind of venue. Mirror balls instead of bare lightbulbs, hardwood and carpet instead of concrete, merch and admissions running like a well-oiled machine.

Gil and the Kills came armed to the teeth in their most fiendish accoutrements. Ruby showed more skin than she usually did, in a sleeveless corset that cinched her waist impossibly small. Nash, who didn't have to drum for once, showed off his collection of heavy tarnished rings. Wary of looking like he was trying too hard, Gil had nevertheless tried three different jackets before landing on the one Gracie picked out in the first place, black denim spattered with bleach stains, all the original hardware replaced with razor blades. Nobody was looking at any of them, though, with Skelly at the head of the column, Louie holding one long arm behind him, keeping a very necessary distance between him and everyone else. *Make way, don't touch,* whether because he was dangerous or vulnerable thrillingly ambiguous. Ticket holders

moved out of their way automatically, unsure if Louie was protecting
Skelly from them or the other way around. He alone had arrived in
his street clothes, his only unusual accessory the bandages hiding the
famous Hands. He was already bleeding through the gauze, red spots
blooming like rosebuds across his knuckles. Nobody but Louie had
seen him since Lincoln. He still looked like hell but wore it undeniably well—exuding gruesome black glamor with his hollow eyes glaring
through a slick of dark liner he never really washed off but only reap-
plied. As soon as they passed, whispers and rumors and giddy specula-
tions flew in their wake.

Louie played the parts of compère and enforcer at once, shepherd-
ing his head-turning charges up the stairs and into the rarefied air of
the VIP balcony, where they had an unobstructed view of the stage and
standing room below. Gil kept one arm around Suzanne the same way
Louie kept the Hands tucked under his wing—holding her back from
the railing as if he'd developed a fear of heights. She kept close to
him instinctively. Gracie, Doug, and Carney weren't on the guest list,
but their table was quickly surrounded by new people, most of whom
wrung Louie's hand, talked to Gil, and tried to talk to Skelly if they
were feeling brave. Suzanne lost track of who was who after the first
round of introductions and lighting cigarettes and ordering drinks,
but one was a label rep, one was from radio, one had a camera. All
men, each with a disinterested young woman dripping from one arm,
if not both. The girlfriends, if that's what they were, all wore the same
vacant, lobotomized look, like they'd been to the same show and heard
the same conversation a thousand times already. Suzanne didn't understand how they could possibly be so bored.

"They're going on cold," she heard someone say. "No opener after
the NOLA fiasco. A fit was pitched."

"Gird your loins," someone else said with a nasty grin angled at Gil.

"Vince DeWitt sounds like quite the little fascist," Ruby said, apparently checking her reflection at the bottom of her glass. Apart from Gil,
she seemed the least enthusiastic about jumping into bed with Babel
Mouth.

"Maybe," Louie conceded. "But if Il Duce had half the brains of this organization, he might still be in power instead of strung up by the ankles."

Suzanne understood why he'd brought them all, with the decision already made. He had grander ambitions for Gil and the Kills than they even had for themselves. Peering over the railing, she was stunned by the size of the room, the number of people. For one vertiginous instant, the floor rushed up at her, but she blinked the illusion away. This was no airplane hangar, no bare-knuckled free-for-all, even if Babel Mouth's acolytes were even wilder to look at than four hundred half-drowned corn-huskers mad enough to tear some out-of-towners limb from limb.

No opener meant there was nothing to distract from how long everyone had been standing around, pushing and shoving to get to the bar while canned music blared through the house. Tension spiked at random around the room—a fist would be thrown or a girl would scream and security would wait and watch and let it play out for a while. Their passive presence only stirred the pot, driving people in unwitting eddies toward the middle of the room. Here was what had happened in Lincoln by accident recreated on purpose, but kept just under control. It would feel like chaos might erupt at any moment on the floor, but with a bird's-eye view, Suzanne could see the intelligent design.

Babel Mouth walked right up to the line. Waited for everyone to get a little pissed off before they took the lights halfway down. Then left them down while nothing else happened. The Kills glanced at each other in the woozy shadows of the mezzanine. Just when everyone was starting to mutter and cuss, four people skulked on from the wings in platform combat boots, long leather dusters flapping behind them like bat wings.

"Hey, Nick-ay!" someone screamed, but nobody in the band seemed to notice. They reminded Suzanne of the Lost Boys—especially Nicky, with his shock of white-blond hair spiked like a shark fin before it fell down the back of his neck in a ratty little fringe. Even in the dim light, a webwork of blue veins made crazy crosslines up and down his arms.

He walked on wielding a sunburst Telecaster so disfigured by burns and gouges and other bodily harm it barely looked like an instrument. Instead of a capo, a set of dentures—in the same rough condition as the guitar—clamped like a piranha to the splintered headstock. The other three musicians faded upstage. For a while Nicky did nothing but turn the pegs and test the strings, filling the room with a low, fizzing drone. Was he just tuning, or had the show started? Nobody seemed to know. The uncertainty had almost grown unbearable when Nicky was abruptly satisfied, and the endless drone buckled under a steamrolling wall of guitar. The amps were so loud they threw Suzanne back in her seat. General admission was all in an uproar, leaping and hollering and throwing themselves at the stage in a demented danse macabre.

"Holy shit," Ruby said, grimace gone slack. Nicky played guitar like he was chewing gristle, with a steady, grinding violence. Throwing his body forward on one foot and back on the other, he slammed on the strings with every vein bulging like it might burst. But where, everyone wondered as that locomotive riff drove on and on, was Vince? The house lights were still at half, Nicky and his minions thrashing away in the shadows until the sound and the lights snapped off at once and a voice in the darkness incanted,

I wanna be evil, I wanna be mad
I wanna be nasty, I wanna be bad
I wanna be evil, I wanna be mean
I don't wannna get better, I just wanna
SCREEEEEEEEEEEEEEEEEEEEEEEEEEEAM

The auditorium howled and the music came back like a thunderclap, lights blazing so hot they struck everyone blind. When they blinked the ash out of their eyes, there was Vince in a column of boiling white smoke, both hands lashed to the microphone. She had a boy's name and she had a boy's voice—a hoarse, soaring holler that cut through her brother's saw-toothed guitar—but there was nothing else boyish about her. She had a holstered six-shooter tattooed on one thigh, her feline physique wrapped in the same black electrical tape binding her hands to the mic stand. She wore nothing else except for a studded collar with a heart-shaped red tag and a steel cage muzzle strapped over her face. She didn't even have shoes on.

Another blinkered "Holy shit," from Gil this time. For her diminutive size, Vince DeWitt was alarmingly *loud*. She thrashed through her mask until, with a guttural shriek, she tossed her head hard enough to fling it off. Everything stopped, everyone shocked for a moment by her beautiful face, blue eyes peering out from a frame of dark ringlets, red lips drawn back from her pearly white teeth, just like the back of *Hard Candy*. Her breath thumped in the microphone, panting from the effort of tearing the mask off.

I wanna be evil, I wanna be wrong—

Nicky deadmelted into a grim, grisly slide Suzanne dimly recognized.

I wanna be beaten, I wanna . . . be your dog

Vince took the mic stand down with her and dragged it around on her hands and knees while Nicky and his hoodlums resurrected the Stooges. Vince hissed and crawled, belted and caterwauled, held every eye in the room with tyrannous magnetism. Suzanne looked away only to look at the others, to watch them watching her. Louie with a smug sort of sneer, Ruby and Nash both grudgingly awed. Gil followed every move with fanatic precision, measuring her performance against the ripple effect it had on the audience. On the far side of the table, Skelly as she'd never seen him, pitched forward in his seat like he was about to leap out of it, dull eyes darkly alive.

Suzanne had learned to sleep through whatever went on in the room next door, and sometimes in the next bed. Gil and Gracie usually behaved themselves when Suzanne was in the room, but once or twice they'd mistaken her for sound asleep when she wasn't. She didn't understand what they said—it was all in Spanish, but not the same dialect. Gil's deep and throaty, *R*'s rolling in like the tide. Gracie's vowels long and elastic, stretching like the bubble gum she wrapped around her tongue. It was a strange education in intimacy, overheard in the dark from the other side of the room. But Suzanne didn't mind; it was better than what Gil and Nora had always done when they thought she was sleeping, which was bicker and argue and snap at each other in a shared language of spite and resentment she understood all too well.

Now that they were card-carrying members of the Babel Mouth outfit, the hotels were bigger and nicer, but the nights were much messier. The DeWitts kicked the door down of every town they played and dragged bedlam behind them wherever they went. While their roadies and flunkies were scarcely better behaved than the band, management moved with the ruthless efficiency of a wartime privy council. Nicky's guitar tech acted more like an elder brother, bullying or babying him as the occasion required, but Vince needed no looking after. She was five feet three inches of venom and vinegar and she had the whole operation wrapped around her little finger.

She watched Gil and the Kills' first opening set from the wings in Dallas, wearing the silk robe she slithered around in backstage. It was a tight forty-five minutes, no showboating or bullshitting, which was just as well since the Hands had barely begun to heal. They had half the crowd in their pocket and the other half rolling their eyes until Skelly, in a fit of bitter frustration at his own limitations, ripped most of his stitches out ripping into the fretboard and smeared fresh blood all over his fresh new SG—the body a yellow so noxious and toxic Suzanne didn't know what to call it. Even Crayola 64 failed her; there was nothing to match that sulfurous sheen. The label had sent it with Gibson's compliments as a replacement for the shattered Strat and incentive to get well soon. It had a caustic, stinging tone—like the strings were peeling apart and splintering off into six other time zones. A nod to his shredded tattoos, black jackal jawbones yawned around the bridge like a pair of forceps, about to take a bite out of his fingers. From then on, whatever he played grew a mouthful of fangs.

Suzanne was growing a pair of sharp canines herself, or that's what she was dreaming three nights later when a trickle down the back of her throat made her cough and roll over. She didn't remember where she was at first, waking up into the harum-scarum airplane hangar, screams and feedback shivering through her bones. The bitter taste of blood or adrenaline burning the back of her tongue. She couldn't tell them apart anymore. No one told her rock and roll was such a gory business. She fumbled across the bed until she found the edge of the nightstand and turned the bedside lamp on. Half past three in the morning. The ferocious noise soaking through the wall was only the ongoing after-party, that was all.

Suzanne wobbled into the bathroom to squint at herself in the mirror. Her nose had started to bleed in her sleep—not the first time it had happened that summer. Heat, sun, and forced air had baked them all dry. Even the grown-ups couldn't stop sniffling.

The nosebleed wouldn't stop. She'd used all the tissues but didn't want to touch the towels. Everything was nicer now, which meant more expensive. She didn't know who paid the bill if she damaged something and couldn't risk getting herself shipped off to California, so she did what Gil said every night when he put her to bed: "You come find me or Gracie if anything happens." He swore he wouldn't leave their floor. Still—thinking of Vince, barefoot, half-naked, lashed to the microphone, an image she couldn't scrub out of her mind—she thought she should at least put some shoes on.

The party wasn't hard to find. Vince would be holding court in a suite at the end of the hall if tonight was anything like the last two. The novelty had worn off for some; the Kill Team were already sick of being bossed around by Babel Mouth's crew and opted instead for the bar—any bar—after load-out. Suzanne weaved between roadies and groupies and the occasional journo just like she'd once dodged shoppers at the mall. Nobody paid her any attention—a kid with a nosebleed in a too-big Sun Records T-shirt was only one of two dozen weird things they'd seen since stepping off the elevator.

Inside Vince's suite, so thick with smoke and choked with cologne it was like wandering into the Great Bazaar, she followed the sound of Nicky's braying laughter. He was easiest to find by ear; Doug had no doubts he'd blown his eardrums out and couldn't modulate his own volume anymore. Despite his ragged genius with a guitar, offstage he was always too loud, always off tempo, always harshing the vibe—a walking fuzzbox that distorted every room he walked into.

Suzanne found him with his boots on the coffee table and Skelly at his elbow. They both had the same glazed expression, Skelly's thousand-yard stare burning through his sunglasses while Nicky looked slack-jawed and stupid—a glass of red wine sloshing in one hand, arm around one of his half dozen harridan girlfriends, who had nodded out against the wall behind her. But slow he was not. He'd produced a Colt .45 from somewhere and spun it around his trigger finger like an Old West gunslinger. He wasn't, like Skelly, truly ambidextrous, but with that pistol he could have fooled most people.

"'S how we got started," he was explaining. "Dad was a trick shooter, Mom was an escape artist." It sounded like horseshit until you saw him spin that pistol, watched Vince chew herself loose every night. Her repertoire was not limited to muzzles and electrical tape. She had handcuffs, straitjackets, and—if rumor could be believed—an iron maiden torture cabinet.

"Funny," Skelly said. "My mom was a seamstress and my dad was a sadist."

Nicky guffawed like that was hilarious. The girlfriend lifted her head long enough to ask, "What's so funny?" and dropped back against the wall without waiting for an answer.

Skelly shrugged and said, "Well, he's dead now, isn't he?" which brought Nicky to the brink of hysterics again.

"Have you seen *my* dad?" Suzanne asked, interrupting because there was no other way to be heard, her small voice trampled underfoot by a gaggle of press people helping themselves to the liquor cabinet over Skelly's left shoulder. They hung around Babel Mouth like a flock of vultures, chummy and friendly on the surface of things but just waiting—Suzanne could see it in their hungry eyes—for something to go deliciously sideways.

"Ankle-biter!" Nicky crowed, as he always did on the rare occasions he realized Suzanne was there. A pet name he'd picked up from Skelly, but she hated the way he said it. She knew without asking that he didn't remember her actual name, thought that probably wasn't personal. He couldn't even remember which girlfriend was which, most days. "What's awry with your face?"

"Nothing." Suzanne wiped her nose on the back of her wrist, trying not to stare at Skelly's hands. After splitting and scabbing and splitting open again, his knuckles were puckered and purple, the bristly black sutures sticking up out of his skin like spines. A nosebleed was nothing to bitch about. "Bitch" in its verb form was another recent entry in Suzanne's subconscious dictionary.

"She's metal," Nicky decided. "I like her."

"Yeah, she's a real rock and roller," Skelly said, eyes like subway tunnels but fixed on Suzanne. His pupils were always too big now, or too small, but it was the first time since returning from the hospital that he looked at her and seemed to see her. And didn't seem, as she had suspected, to hate her. Maybe that was just the wine and whatever else was circulating in his system. Louie had, as promised, brought along a doctor. "Dad's that way," he added, head tipping toward the opposite corner where the blue haze of Louie's cigar turned circles around the light fixture.

She swam upstream, bumping into people who were all busy bumping into other people and rarely looked down to see what they'd tripped over. The easiest way to move was to keep to the edges of the room, but the perimeter presented other obstacles. Sprawled on a divan with her bare feet still filthy and a cigarette wand in one hand, Vince was half listening to one of her handlers say something about a couple of gate-crashing groupies who were stuck in the elevator. That wasn't her problem, but it did mean the next infusion of refreshments would have to find another way up.

"What-fucking-ever." She waved him off. Still wearing that baby-pink robe, with a fire-breathing black dragon embroidered on the back. The revolver inked on her thigh peeked out from under the hem. "Give me an hour and if all these people aren't out of my room, I start biting heads off." He scuttled away, probably to relay that whim down the chain of command. Guests would be persuasively bundled up and hustled out and helped down the stairs, or out the window if they really outstayed their welcome. But with Nicky waving a gun around, nobody was likely to try anything funny. "Ooh," Vince cooed, spying Suzanne. She'd taken a liking to her after she shyly asked to take her picture in the limo after their first night out with the Kills. Sometimes she seemed to want to play big sister, but more often she was more like a big cat playing with its food. "Poor baby, what happened to you?"

"Nothing," Suzanne said again. "Just my nose."

"Well, you won't be the only one," Vince remarked, to a chorus of laughter from her vampire brides. "Wait, tell me." She leaned closer, catching Suzanne's hand fast between both of hers. Black hair and blue eyes and soft, milky skin like Snow White. But the ring in each eyebrow, the stud in her lip and each side of her nose, gave her a devilish symmetry. She always wore dark lip liner, but painted her plump little pout eye-popping red or electric pink. Against her white skin and white teeth the effect was hypnotic; everybody—man, woman, and other—watched her mouth when she was talking and sometimes when she wasn't. "Have you tasted blood before?"

Suzanne was no more immune to Vince's perverse allure than anyone else, which confused and frightened her enough that she tried to keep her distance. "At the dentist," she said, because she couldn't talk about Nebraska, couldn't talk about the blood on Skelly's hands and the blood in her throat and how she couldn't quite tell which was which anymore. A whole mouthful of teeth tumbling like loose dice across the floor. That was what made her think of the dentist. She had nightmares now where she couldn't open her mouth without all her teeth falling out. "I have to find my dad." She slipped away while the Vincelings cackled and spilled their drinks on the carpet and looked around for someone to refill them.

Gil was over by the windows with Louie, who was doing most of the talking to a clutch of men in collared shirts with mustaches like *Magnum, P.I.* Holding Gil at his side like a piece of arm candy. The members of the band had become props as much as much as product, summoned to stand beside Louie and look the part while he sang their praises and made extravagant promises of their continued success and earning potential. Because he—like Nora's old manager at Macy's—thought the intrusion of a child might dim the shine of his prize jewels, Suzanne was even warier of approaching him than Skelly or Vince. She was considering filching a few napkins from the bar and going back to bed when Gil spotted her, standing right behind Louie, which had proven to be the best place to escape his notice.

"Lou," he said, smothering a smirk at her cunning and a frown at her face, "I'll be right back." Louie nodded as Gil slid past him and conjured up Nash to take his place. Of the four of them, Nash fared the worst at parties, and more than once had tried to follow Doug and Carney to the bar instead of back to the hotel. Ruby could be diplomatic, could be charming, usually enough for the both of them, but Nash's job, as Louie made plain after his first escape attempt, was to look big and mean and sound even bigger and meaner. Two things that came naturally to him when he was so much out of his element. He stood there, miserably tethered to Louie, like a dancing bear on a chain.

Suzanne grabbed the back of Gil's belt and rode in his slipstream toward the door. The party showed no signs of slowing down; if Vince wanted everyone out within the hour, heads would have to be cracked. But that was a normal day for the Babel Mouth brigade. *Wanna make an omelet, gotta break some eggs*, she'd heard their TM say to a hysterical concierge after one of his goons threw a paparazzo into the pool from a third-floor fire escape. *By the way, we're still waiting on room service.*

Even without Louie, shaking hands and making introductions like he was on some kind of campaign trail, Gil's progress through the room was slow and circuitous, frequently derailed by people who wanted a piece of his time or attention or had just mistaken him for a member of Babel Mouth, which happened as often as anything. He was somebody now, but there would always be somebody bigger.

This time, though, he was just as fed up with the hubbub as Vince. Suzanne could see the impatience, the exhaustion, deepening the lines around his mouth and eyes so that he almost looked his age, for once.

They passed the same screwball scenery she'd seen on her way in—Vince and her murder of crows, Skelly and Nicky plus a couple more girlfriends, taking turns with harebrained pistol tricks. The cluster of press growing bored with the lack of fiasco. For a bunch of people who never seemed to need to be anywhere urgently, they were always hunched over their watches and patting their pockets for their keys.

"Almost there, kid," Gil muttered. Her nose still hadn't stopped bleeding, leaving spots on her shirt in Violet-Red. She'd started to see the world in shades of Crayola 64.

They were in spitting distance of the door when a short, loud blast flattened the drunken rumpus of the party. Several people screamed, others gasped, a few just laughed. Gil had, in one reflexive motion, snatched Suzanne off the floor and crushed her to his chest. Nicky had finally let his girlfriend fall when the gun went off and he dropped it in surprise. Skelly pitched sideways over the arm of the sofa, laughing his head off even as a spray of red wine dripped down the side of his face. Suzanne had never seen him laugh like that, helplessly shaking, eyes watering behind his shades. Nicky left his girlfriend where she landed and scrabbled after the gun, but Louie got there first. He swept the smoking pistol off the floor and held it aloft with one long orangutan arm.

"C'mon, Lou," Nicky whined. "Give it back."

Louie glared down at him with the withering derision of a man who'd been babysitting beastly little hellions with guitars for so long that even the DeWitts didn't faze him. "Jump," he said, still holding the gun out of reach.

Nicky looked around and even in his stuporous haze realized he couldn't do that without doing some violence to his execrable *image*. A moment too late he reverted to scabrous belligerence, throwing himself back down beside Skelly. "What the fuck are you laughing at?" he demanded, and everyone else wisely averted their eyes. Suzanne glanced at Vince, who had already summoned Nicky's guitar tech, was probably issuing orders to have him tied down for the night. It wasn't uncommon for him to be thrown into bed with his boots on, bound to the headboard with extension cords or Vince's spare stage restraints, just to keep the chaos contained. In the morning they'd send one of the girlfriends, if they could find one who was lucid enough, to stand in the doorway and throw things from a safe distance until he woke up.

Gil said nothing, but left the suite without a backward glance. He carried Suzanne into their shared room, into the bathroom, plopped her on the counter. "Everybody's getting their warpaint this week," he said, bending down for a better look. She tilted her head back. Sniffed. Nothing happened. "Probably just dry." He soaked a washcloth in cold water and mopped her face clean. Evidently it didn't matter who paid for the linens. "When was the last time you washed your hair, kid? Starting to look like Sk—" He stopped, not liking where the thought was headed. "Tomorrow morning," he said instead. "Squeaky clean before lobby call, all right?"

"I'll be the only one," she said.

"Well, hopefully you'll start a trend. Let's see, still bleeding?"

"Little bit." She dabbed at her upper lip with her fingertips.

"Since you're a road warrior now, you won't mind a little field medicine," he said, and she shook her head no. She could handle it. Nothing much surprised her anymore, not even Gil sticking his finger in his mouth, then sticking it right in her nose. She squirmed but didn't squirm away. Didn't know whether to laugh and finally gave in to the impulse. "Hold still," he told her, laughing a little bit, too.

"Dad, what are you *doing*?"

"Saliva," he said, "helps blood clot. Learned that from an old bass player from Colorado. Asked him why he was always picking his nose at high altitudes. Turned out he had a reason."

She'd learned to trust Gil's "field medicine" over the years. Even if it didn't work, the weirdness distracted her long enough that she forgot what hurt in the first place. Every time he started to feel too far away—his time and high moods increasingly precious commodities—something pulled him back. Did she really need him to stem a nosebleed, at eleven? Guilt rose in her chest like nausea, a feeling so familiar now it never really went away, just subsided temporarily. She checked

her reflection. Her hair was a tangled mess, greasy and stringy and starting to fall in her eyes. But her nose had stopped bleeding. Just needed a
dab of Gil. "Your old man's not crazy yet," he said, and looked less than
his age again, all the hard lines going soft. He started to say something
else, but a sharp knock on the door made him look over his shoulder.

"I'm okay," she said, embarrassed by her clinginess already.

"You sure you want to put yourself back to bed?"

"Yeah. Go be somebody," she said.

"All right." He gave her his cheek. "Kiss good night."

He slid back out into the hall, pulled the door shut behind him.
But Suzanne wasn't sleepy, wasn't ready to lie back down and stare at
the ceiling, listen to the party breaking up. And since they hitched
their wagon to Babel Mouth, all the most interesting things seemed to
happen without her. She tiptoed across the room and didn't exactly put
her ear to the door because she didn't exactly have to. Gil's voice always
carried—wouldn't be much of a frontman if it didn't. Louie, too, had a
timbre that bored right through drywall, though his was flat and nasal.
She missed the opening remarks but could guess well enough.

"What did you think they were, a gospel group? For a guy, you look
all right in pearls, but clutching them doesn't become you."

"I guess you'd rather have me too drunk to stand up, shooting the
light fixtures down."

Suzanne heard the telltale *tick* of Louie's heels clicking together.
The posture he always adopted when something that shouldn't have
needed an explanation needed one. Hands in his pockets, chin pinned
to his chest so his underbite was slightly more pronounced. "Gil, here's
how I see this," he said, when what he meant was *Here's how you see this, if
you know what's good for you.* "It's a demand for rebranding. The lovable
circus freak thing, I don't love it. You have a chance now to get out of
the freak tent, but you're going to have to act like you belong in the
big top."

"You want to rough us up a little, fine," Gil conceded, though Suzanne heard the anger simmering in him, too. "Wrap Skelly in tinsel,
stick an apple in his mouth, and chain him to his amp if that's what gets

the label off, but I'm here about the *music*. We're not Mötley fucking Crüe. That's not what we do. We're three professional musicians and one walking liability who now, thanks to Nicky DimWitt, is up to his eyeballs in benzos and blow. That's not my show!"

"You're right," Louie said with a bit of a growl. "It's *not* your show. You're the warm-up act. You're just happy to be here. Your ego needs to take a backseat before they change their mind about letting you guest-star at Wrecking Ball."

"My *ego*?" Gil said. "For Chrissake, Louie, I've got my kid with me!"

"You wanted to bring her along," Louie said. "Not me."

"The schedule you've got us on, how else will I ever see her? I only have her now because Nora's on a never-ending honeymoon and I *swore* things wouldn't be like this. Don't make a liar of me, Louie."

"Gil. You know I love you. You're a once-in-a-generation bandleader, which is why I've been sticking my neck out for you since you weren't much brighter than DimWitt. But I don't give a shit about your personal problems. I need a rock star, not a family man. Understand?" Suzanne heard the cold *smack* of his hand on the back of Gil's jacket. "I can't believe I'm saying this," he said, as if he truly regretted it, "but right now I need you to be more like *Eric*."

That was enough to keep her up all night. Gil never came to bed.

PART 4

IDOLS IN THE FIRE

Snapshot: Staunton, 2013

Rob's aunt Emily owned five acres, five horses, and an eighteenth-century Quaker meetinghouse that Suzanne mistook for a barn. She had, for some unfathomable reason, volunteered it as a venue for the belated reception of the wedding that never happened. Rob called it a "barbecue," lip service to Suzanne's pleas to keep it low-key, but the resemblance to a barbecue began and ended with the menu. Everyone came dressed for a wedding except the bride.

Profoundly out of place at her own party, Suzanne kept her mouth too full to talk much. Distrusting everything with "salad" in the name after finding Jell-O in one and whipped cream in another, she had surrendered to the familiar and the fattening: pimento cheese, deviled eggs, hush puppies dripping with honey butter. There were three options to wash it all down: lemonade, bourbon, and applejack brandy. Between the sugar and the booze, she was woozy by noon. The humidity did not help. It was only May and vaguely overcast, but the ground was wet from last night's thunderstorm, the sunbeams that broke through curdling in the grass. The only person suffering more than Suzanne was Dana, seven months pregnant with Rob's next nephew. Technically Suzanne's nephews now, too. It was her first time meeting her in-laws. Casey worked for the Department of Defense and answered every question about his job with such exaggerated secrecy that Suzanne was certain his security clearance went no further than the parking lot. He still wore a class ring and a haircut that probably would have described itself as "fiscally conservative." Brad, the middle brother, was an insurance claims investigator, disastrously drunk, "between marriages." Not "divorced" or "unattached" but "between marriages," as if the next wife were inevitable. No children—that he knew of.

"Will you move right away or live like lovebirds for a while?" Dana asked, fanning herself with a paper plate. She wore simple but expensive jewelry, waving off compliments with oblique remarks about sensitive skin and "cheap metal." "Rob's got that second bedroom but no idea how to use it."

"Oh. I don't know." Already she resented the blanket assumption that she'd just pack up and move into Rob's house. "I like my apartment, having my own workspace." She'd turned her closet into a darkroom but admittedly had not used it for months. Not wanting to waste film shooting the sort of shit she was shooting. She was so tired of weddings she put her foot down when Rob asked if she had a photographer friend they could hire. Instead, she left a jumble of instant and disposable cameras out on one table, trusting the guests to pick them up and photograph their friends and put them down again, which would make more honest memories anyway.

She squinted, searching a little desperately for her husband of six short weeks. There were a lot of things they hadn't talked about, and Suzanne only began to realize how many once they got back to Dulles, back to Earth, as husband and wife. That he even wanted to have a reception had come as a surprise. In his native element he barely resembled the bumbling vagabond she'd fallen for in airports and rental cars. Strange turn of phrase, as if love were an elaborate ruse.

Dana smiled, half-delighted and half-scandalized. "Keeping your name, too?"

Another conversation the newly minted newlyweds hadn't yet had. "I work under my name," she said, and was saved from having to say anything else when one of Casey and Dana's boys—she couldn't tell

them apart—appeared out of nowhere and leapt at his mother, yanked
her arm so hard she threw her drink at Suzanne's crotch.

"Noah! Look what you've done! Apologize, please."

"No!"

"It's fine," Suzanne said, to the toddler's shrieks of *No! No! No!*
"Would you excuse me?" With no real destination in mind except "else-
where," she started across the . . . yard? Meadow? Pasture? She wasn't
sure what to call it and Aunt Emily was too busy playing hostess to
inform her. She grabbed a napkin off the nearest table and dabbed
half-heartedly at the lemonade stain on her white pants. Everyone had
already sweated through their suits and sundresses, most of the children wearing their ice cream by now, so why not look like she'd wet
herself? She retreated to the bar.

The man serving drinks looked desperately in need of reinforce-
ments. He asked, "Are you the barback?"

"I'm the bride."

Big laugh. "Many happy returns."

"Make it a double, why don't you."

He tipped an invisible hat and handed it over. Suzanne lingered at
the bar, which was not really a bar but several whiskey barrels lashed
together with a braid of eyelet lace and horsehair—a well-intentioned
stab at shabby chic that came off as bizarrely incongruous. The whole
day was bizarrely incongruous. She and her whiskey and her wet crotch
were still waiting for nothing in the shade of the dogwoods when the
incongruities multiplied.

A familiar incidental music had crept up on the unfamiliar scenery.
The crunch of tires on gravel. The muffled roar of a 428 Cobra Jet engine. The Modern Lovers crackling through the breezeless afternoon.
Blondie, rims dimmed by the dust of country roads but still a standout
among the mild-mannered Camrys and Corollas and occasional F-150.
There was nowhere left to park in the loosely defined "lot" on the near
side of the paddock where Aunt Emily's horses ambled around, lashing
at flies with their willowy tails. Suzanne wondered suddenly where the
horsehair holding the bar together had come from.

"There you are." Rob's voice shocked her out of her trance, and she nearly dropped her drink. He beamed at her—really beamed. He had the straightest teeth she'd ever seen, and no poker face whatsoever. The smile gave way to concern. "What's wrong?"

"Nothing, I just—" She tried to summon a smile of her own, without success, and settled for a shrug. "Didn't think they'd show."

"Who?" He followed her gaze across the grass. Blondie's doors opened, disgorging the only two people besides Suzanne who seemed to have missed the memo about the dress code. Gil was unmistakably himself in black Levi's and patent creepers, but the years since she'd seen him last had somehow blurred the border of his person. Maybe he'd gained weight, or lost hair. It might have been merely mirage. Gracie was aging gracefully, but with a characteristic refusal to kowtow to decorum. Lipstick too dark for the season, hair still cut in a curly boyish bob. Strangers in a strange land.

"Gil and Gracie." She was so sure they wouldn't come that she hadn't really considered what might happen if they did. The many calamitous possibilities erupted in her imagination at once. "Oh God." She grabbed for Rob's hands, feeling dizzy.

"How can I help?"

"Keep them far away from Nora. Preferably in the next county."

"You got it." He swooped in for a kiss, and she forced herself to relax her grip and let his fingers slip through hers. She watched him go with an inopportune lurch of desire. She'd never had a partner or even a person she could really rely on besides Doug, but Rob's devotion never swerved, never wavered—even when she was fickle and mistrustful, shrinking from affection like a feral cat.

"Dad." She turned back around and there he was. Same aftershave. The whisper of bay rum went right to her head, or maybe that was the whiskey. She didn't know what to do. Kiss his cheek, shake his hand? How did you greet your father after twenty years apart?

Gracie saved them both the trouble. "¡Dulce! Come here." She pulled Suzanne close and squeezed her tight, as if no time had passed at all.

Gil cleared his throat, eyes hidden behind his shades. Hair still mostly dark, but sideburns trimmed too short, to hide the gray. "This is a barbecue? Feels like a funeral."

She hadn't realized until he killed the engine and the Modern Lovers went with it that there was no other music. The silence had probably been sawing on her nerves all morning. "It's a reception," she said.

"Don't you usually have the wedding first?" He ran one hand over his hair like a metal detector, not close enough to actually touch it, just to catch any curl out of place.

"We did," she said after another desperate gulp of whiskey.

He seemed to be looking right at her, or possibly through her. His glasses were too dark to tell. She thought, inconveniently, of Eric Skillman. "Guess our invitation got lost in the mail."

"There were no invitations. We sort of eloped."

"You ashamed of him or something?" Gil looked around the . . . field? Range? Farmyard? Who gave a shit. He turned back to her with a twitch of surprise. "You're not pregnant, are you?"

"Do I look it?" she asked. Of course, the damp crotch of her linen pants did give the impression her water just broke.

"You look perfect," said Gracie, flashing a warning glance at Gil. Neither of them wore wedding bands, despite Gil's fixation on the proper matrimonial order of things. "He's a lucky man."

Funny, I was just thinking the opposite, seemed the wrong thing to say. Instead, she said, "Are you hungry? There's plenty of food." Deferring to Aunt Emily's good taste, they'd forgone the ritual of smearing frosting on each other's faces in favor of lemon bars and tiny peach tarts.

"I wish we could stay," Gracie said. "Gil's back's been bothering him, and it'll only get worse until he can get off his feet. But we wanted to drop by and bring you this." She held out a white gift bag stuffed with gold tissue, a price tag still clinging to one handle.

"Oh. You shouldn't have— We said no gifts." Now she sounded like she was scolding them. Suzanne had no idea how to interact with parents as an adult, Rob's or her own or anyone else's. Maybe because she'd never been parented much, in the usual sense of the word. "I mean—thank you, really. It's so thoughtful." Was it? She couldn't guess what was in the bag, what they would buy for a wedding no one was invited to. Aunt Emily Post, she was sure, would know the protocol—or did they gloss over such fractured families in finishing school?

"Least we could do, since we're only passing through. I'll just put it over here." Gracie backed away, toward the tables where Suzanne had scattered her cameras. Pops and flashes and bursts of laughter punctuated the drone of conversation and insects in the grass. "But you two should have coffee tomorrow," she called. "We don't check out until eleven."

"I—that would be nice," Suzanne said, suddenly alone with Gil. Maybe it would be better, easier, to talk to him without all the Gabbards gadding about. "Where are you staying?"

"Nowhere fancy," Gil said. "Holiday Inn."

"There's a diner off the highway," Suzanne said, because she'd spent every morning there for the last few days, under the guise of getting away to get some work done but craving a cheaper slice of life than the in-laws were accustomed to. Nobody seemed to miss her. She glanced back at Gil, feeling ten and shy again. "Nothing special, but the specials are good."

"Sure," he said, and looked away, looking for Gracie, or the source of the flash and the *kssshhhhk* of a Polaroid camera that had once been so familiar. Something streaked across his face—maybe a grin finally getting the better of him. Or maybe he really was in pain. "Nine o'clock?" he said as Gracie sidled up beside him again.

"Sure," Suzanne said. "Nine o'clock."

Before Rob returned, eager to shake hands with his father-in-law, they were gone.

Suzanne arrived early on purpose. The sign said PLEASE WAIT TO BE SEATED, but "being seated" simply meant a nod and a wave from the waitress, clicking her nails on the counter until "Steak and eggs, over easy!" appeared. She'd waited on Suzanne three days in a row.

"You look like you had a wild Friday night," she remarked, flipping to a fresh page in her notepad. Suzanne had only slept a few hours and hadn't had time to shower, still wearing last night's mascara, last night's sex hair. "What can I get for you, doll?"

"Coffee, please," she croaked.

The diner was mostly empty—too far from town to attract the church crowd. Or maybe it was the smoke. Suzanne pulled a cig out of the pack she kept in her handbag, kept secret from Rob. Emergency rations for mornings like this one. She half hoped Gil wouldn't show. But when the waitress returned with a menu, Suzanne said, "Make that two," because the bell had just clattered against the door, and she heard the squeak of patent creepers on the hard tile floor.

"Denver omelet, hold the onions!"

The diner always played Motown. It was too early for the squawking rock jocks of Top 40, but Smokey Robinson went well with countless refills of blistered black coffee turning to tar after fifty years at the bottom of the urn. It was still Suzanne's favorite brew—that charred aftertaste of burnt popcorn.

Gil dropped into the booth across from her. He was twenty-five years older but didn't quite look it. With a stab of sadness she realized nobody would spy them through the window now and know without asking, father and daughter. Her reflection sagged against the glass, prematurely aged by hard luck and bad habits.

"Hi, honey," said the waitress, sliding a menu in front of Gil as she filled Suzanne's mug. "Something to drink?"

He summoned a smile. Never could resist flirting with a waitress, no matter how frumpy or unfriendly. This one was a midrange model: fortysomething, full lips and a spray of sunspots, the telltale scar of a melanoma removal making a dent in her chin. "I'll have what she's having."

The waitress filled his mug, too, and left them the pot. "You got it."

When Gil looked back at Suzanne, the smile was gone. He could turn the charm off as quickly as he turned it on. He removed the sunglasses with apparently great reluctance and set them on the windowsill beside the squeeze bottles, nozzles crusted over with condiment snot. "Chicken and waffles, biscuits and gravy!" called the cook.

Gil nudged the ashtray toward her. Yellowing ceramic with a questionable likeness of Dolly Parton peeling off the bottom. "Can't believe you can smoke indoors anywhere anymore."

"Precisely why I like this place," she said, glad to have found some common ground. "Want a light?"

He squinted out the window like the smoke hurt his eyes. "I quit."

She snorted before she could stop herself. "Bullshit." But she blew her smoke the other way. "Um. Sorry. That's great. What's the secret? You've been trying to quit since I was nine."

"Doctor's orders," he said, and didn't elaborate. "When did you start?"

"Oh. I don't know. New York." Did he even know she'd lived there, run away from Nathan and Nora at seventeen, went looking for Doug instead of looking for him? The same dilemma tormented her even after she turned eighteen and took custody of herself. The whole year she spent shooting the Southwest for her photo book, she wrestled with whether to send him a copy before realizing she wouldn't even know where to send it. Maybe just as well; with *Dust and Bones* she buried her butchered childhood, out there in the desert with everything else she would have given anything to forget.

The waitress reappeared just as the silence was starting to sour, and Suzanne made a note to leave an extravagant tip. "What'll it be?"

Gil's order seemed to be the doctor's orders, too—egg whites with spinach and mushrooms, toast instead of pancakes, a side of fruit instead of bacon.

"And for you?" Suzanne's stomach still hadn't settled from yesterday, and while the smoke helped her nerves, it was not helping her nausea. She asked for a side of fries, topped up her coffee from the pot on the table.

"Not hungry?" Gil asked. "Not like you."

"Just a little queasy."

"Sure you're not pregnant?"

"Why do you keep asking that?" Sure, she gained weight as soon as she cut back on smoking, but she didn't look *expectant*. How would he even know what to expect? They hadn't been in the same room since she was just a kid. She'd lived a whole life without him since then.

"This whole thing," he said. "Married in Mexico, no one invited . . . Just seems sudden."

"You and Nora knew each other for about five minutes before you were married with me," she said.

"And look how that turned out. I didn't mean you!" he added—fast but not fast enough. He gestured out the window at the parking lot. "It turned out like I don't set foot inside the building at your wedding reception because your mother's in there and we both know how that would go."

"And you think that's just because you rushed into it?" He'd vanished from her life for twenty years, been ruled unfit even for visitation, but now he wanted to sit down and start dispensing fatherly advice? She stabbed her cigarette out on Dolly's forehead. "I'm hungover, not knocked up, all right? Christ."

"I see," he said, eyes darkening as he looked her up and down, more slowly now. He picked up a spoon, stirred nothing into his coffee. In the yellow light of the diner, he looked smaller than yesterday. "I'm sorry we couldn't stay." Why did he come? For the same reason she invited him, probably. They had ruined each other, in some unspeakable way, and no matter how many years they spent apart they were still shackled together by everything they couldn't change. Clinging to the foolish hope that they could leave the past behind them. Suzanne had nearly shaken it, but Gil never would. It followed him too doggedly, too close. If she let him back into her life, what else would he bring through the door? "Seemed like quite the party," he said lightly. "You've got some pretty important friends now, I guess."

Strange word to choose, "important." Whom did he even talk to, on the short walk from the parking paddock and back?

"Rob's friends, mostly." Her friends were fewer and more diffuse, spread out around the country, while he'd lived in driving distance of the house he grew up in all his life. Opposites attracted, supposedly, while two people too much alike pushed each other away, magnets with the same polarity. Pretending to steal glances out of the window, she studied their faces in profile. Would she turn into Gil as the years went by and age made her androgynous?

"Tell me about him." Gil opened his hands, a curious gesture halfway between invitation and surrender. "Rob."

"What do you want to know?"

"What does he do? What does he like? I know nothing about him."

She had no idea how to explain Rob to Gil, or vice versa, had breathed a sigh of relief to see Blondie disappear before Rob returned from running interference with Nora, who adored him. With his good job and good manners and "good family," he was the inverse of Gil—a wayward, walking catastrophe. That the rest of the world had come around to her way of thinking only vindicated Nora's conviction that he was the reason for all her misfortunes. She hadn't seen him, either, since the custody hearings, but never quite forgave Suzanne for being "just like your father." As she tried to explain Rob to Gil, Suzanne couldn't help wondering when or how she'd turned into her mother.

"He's at Chemonics, but not a consultant." She heard herself saying this whenever anyone asked what he did, ashamed to be so ashamed of it. Consultancy was the thirtysomething version of joining a fraternity, and her zinester, scenester streak died hard. "He's a pitch man, more or less," she said, because that was something Gil could understand. "Sells potential clients on their services."

"Sounds important," Gil said again, even as his eyes glazed over. "Where'd you find a guy like that anyway?"

"The American Airlines desk at National." Hard to imagine a less romantic venue. They were on the same flight canceled for inclement weather. No other flights that night. "Then again at Enterprise." There was only one car left and Rob got there first. *Well*, he said. *I'd be willing*

to share. To which she replied, *I'm so tired I don't even care if you murder me. Let's go.* Which was the blueprint for their whole relationship,
really. "No rental cars left, so we shared one." Suzanne was already
past thirty, the watermark after which everyone sane and attractive
was already taken and you started to wonder why you weren't. "He's
a good guy," she said, sensing Gil's uncertainty, realizing now maybe
his rudeness was an inept attempt at paternal protection, something
she'd never experienced the way most teenage girls did. Fortunate, in
retrospect.

"Well, I'm glad to hear that," he said, and they lapsed back into
silence when the waitress reappeared with their plates. He peppered
his egg whites liberally. No salt, she noticed. "And what about you?" he
asked. "You stopped updating your website."

She didn't know he knew she had a website. Which meant he also
knew she'd published a book but didn't send him one. "I'm sort of in
limbo," she said. Not eager to admit how long she'd been flounder-
ing. She'd lost her love of photography after memorializing one too
many trite domestic milestones—things that happened every day, were
entirely unremarkable except to the subjects, aglow with the delusion
of their own significance. Which was surely why she never felt that way
about her own wedding. Marriage was a symbiotic arrangement, or supposed to be. It gave her someone to lean on, but ironically hitching
her wagon to Rob had only increased the pressure she felt to find her
footing before she became a "dependent" in more than the legal sense.
Wary of disappearing into the ranks of married women who ceased to
be anything else. "Sorting through my portfolio, thinking about the
next creative project," she said, the first outright lie. She hadn't been
able to summon any enthusiasm for an original series. She drizzled
syrup over her fries.

"I see," Gil said. Watching the syrup puddle on her plate. Squinting
at Suzanne like he wasn't quite sure what he saw in her. Following in
Nora's backward steps, married off to a corporate drone with no real
prospects of her own. But she'd forgone the respectability that should
have come with it, the decency that Nora craved so desperately after

a decade with Gil. Suzanne couldn't outgrow or outrun her origins so easily. Still cheap despite her decent husband, reeking of booze and cigarettes and yesterday's sunscreen and sweat. She remembered, with a painful jolt, like the seat belt that snapped across her chest when she hit the brakes too hard, where she'd seen that scrunched-up look before. In a motel corridor somewhere in Ohio, banging on the door of Skelly's room at two o'clock when they should have left by noon. Her foot twitched under the table, trying to slam on the brakes and swerve out of a head-on collision. But it happened too fast, just like a crash—the inescapable revelation that maybe she'd been molded more by Eric Skillman than Nora or Nathan or Gil or Gracie, was more his piece of work than theirs, more his miscreation. Self-obsessed and self-destructive, not who she was meant to be or even who she thought she was. Nobody's daughter after all.

It wasn't until a week later, when she and Rob finally got around to opening all the gifts they said not to bring, that she remembered the little white bag with its crumpled tissue paper. Inside was a small square frame holding a photo she never knew existed. Gracie must have taken it with the Sun 640, sometime that summer. Gil, with a lollipop stick poking out of his mouth and one elbow out the window. Half a smile on his lips and the other arm looped around Suzanne, sound asleep with her head in his lap, one dirty bare foot clutched in his hand. As if it were a rabbit's foot that could bring him sterling luck, so long as he held on tight enough. She'd forgotten how to cry by then, but a hot, horrible feeling came over her so fast she nearly blacked out. All the anger and anguish at how wrong they both were. Because he wasn't really the reason the whole thing went to pieces. Everything might have worked out all right, if not for her.

THE **A** SIDE

SLIP OF THE TONGUE

When Gil and Skelly next walked onstage together, the energy be-tween them was no longer electric but radioactive. Gil's good sense of humor had given way to a nasty one, apparently overnight. Whether that was his way of refusing—or following—Louie's orders to act more like a rock star ought to, Suzanne wasn't sure. The Hands had given all of them hell in one way or another since Nebraska—not just a Black Plague when he was in pain, which was always, but more like a black hole, a walking void that ate away at everyone around him. But the pills were almost worse, making him "slow, sluggish, and stupid" or "bitchy, twitchy, and paranoid," depending what he mixed them with. "Just what the world needs," Doug said, stabbing at the sliders during sound check in Houston, "another strung-out, smacked-out waste of talent like Nicky DeWitt. This rate, that guy'll be dead long before twenty-seven." Skelly was mistaken for a member of Babel Mouth even more often than Gil, but unlike Gil he'd stopped correcting people, which might have been why they suddenly seemed to be playing in two different bands even though they were on the same stage.

Opening for Babel Mouth was never easy. The audience was hostile by default. Gil suffered most, unfavorably compared to the headlining vixen before he even opened his mouth. A crowd accustomed to Vince's death-defying, naked mayhem was not easily impressed by Gil's punkabilly pedigree. They'd cut the campier numbers from the set, drawing instead on their hardest, loudest, most ferocious material. Gil's exorcism looked more like an electrocution, especially with the Hands swinging that flashy new ax over him.

Sowing chaos in one way or another with one DeWitt or the other was all Skelly seemed to live for anymore, except that yellowjacket SG—baptized in blood and brimfire and known now by its own name, the Jawbreaker. He was conspicuously bored by the rest of the music, but the jawbones could hook him right out of the haze and his eyes would burn back to life, like the lights going on in an abandoned house as you walked by. The guitar was two deadly curves, two devilish horns, and a slender neck that begged his tricky fingers to run all over the fretboard. It made Suzanne uneasy, how much it looked like Vince. Even when she was nowhere to be seen, she was right in the middle of things.

Skelly and Gil spat sparks at each other through their whole set in San Antonio. Skelly kept his distance, forcing Gil to chase him around the stage for the first four songs. He ran himself ragged, clothes soaked through, face and chest a deep angry red. Too canny not to notice how crowds crescendoed the closer they came to each other, their choreography—half memory and half improvisation—had always been a game of cat and mouse, Gil darting between the other musicians, ducking out of sight behind the drum kit only to sneak up behind Skelly again and purr right in his ear. Not too shy to fetishize themselves. But now Skelly was changing the game, breaking the rules. Wouldn't let Gil get anywhere near him, but circled around him in a widening spiral, like a predator stalking its prey. By the end of "Off the Rockets" Gil's feet were so tangled in wires and cords that he was, like Vince, more or less bound to the mic stand.

And when Gil couldn't move, he couldn't keep his hold on the crowd—couldn't find the weak points, the bubbles of disinterest that needed a taste of the spotlight, needed the show to come their way. All he had left was his voice, and he'd already pushed it past its limits. No time to recover between one leg and the next, no room for vocal rest when Louie was dragging him off to an interview every minute he wasn't being paraded around smoke-choked hotel suites where everyone had to shout. The pure, smooth tone of his high notes now had a shiver, a rift down the middle. He stretched himself even further in the fight to be heard over the Jawbreaker, snarling through gruesome, two-handed solos. But in a set that was less than an hour, Gil rapidly ran out of patience.

He didn't even finish the second verse of "Bad Business" before the strings interrupted. Skelly's knuckles were still bruised and bloody and swollen, but between the so-called "doctor" and reckless self-medication, he could play through the pain. And it *sounded* like pain, like torture, the SG screaming and babbling on the rack of the merciless Hands. He shimmered with sweat, oily rivulets running down his neck and chest, wet hair clinging to his hollow cheeks. He might have been in a trance, or the throes of demonic possession—fingers moving like quicksilver while his eyes shuttered and rolled and his feet weaved beneath him in a strange unstoppable dance. But Gil put a stop to it abruptly, lifting one tangled foot and stomping on the Jawbreaker's cable hard enough to yank it out. The game turned on its head, Gil racing around with the wire in his teeth while Skelly hurled curses at him and the roadie who couldn't get another one plugged in fast enough.

The audience loved it. Gobbled it up and goaded them on. Suzanne watched from the wings, with a pinch of anxiety squeezing the air out of her. How many antics were part of the act? She looked sideways at Louie, a looming bulk in the shadows, beady eyes following the boys' every move. The Jawbreaker was finally reunited with the amplifiers, returned with a rabid, deafening vengeance, and tore the finale to ribbons. They left the stage a wreck behind them, the aftermath of some unnatural disaster.

But for once, Babel Mouth fared even worse. Nicky blundered through the first five songs in spineless disarray, chords so sloppy they were barely recognizable, pumping and wagging his headstock at the crowd like he was armed with a machine gun and he meant to mow them down. The rest of the entourage looked on from the wings but made no move to intervene. Nobody moved without orders from Vince.

Halfway through "Barbarella," Nicky lost his balance or simply gave up and fell flat on his back. He landed too close to his amp and feedback screeched through the theater. The crowd clapped their hands over their ears until the plug was pulled for the second time that evening. Nicky was still as the dead, but the rest of the band kept chugging along like nothing had happened. Maybe nothing had. Nicky falling down drunk, drugged, or both in the middle of a show surely wasn't an isolated incident, but Suzanne still found it unnerving—the way he just lay there, the way they just left him. She'd heard the saying *The show must go on*, but who wanted to watch this kind of show?

Vince must have been thinking the same thing but thinking much faster. Suzanne didn't hear what was said or see who signaled. The music never stopped, but Vince turned to the audience with a coy little "Oops!" Her red lips split into a smile. "My big brother can't hold his liquor. What's a poor girl to do?" She shielded her eyes from the glare of the stage lights. "This looks like no kinda place for a lady to go walking alone." She murmured the first sulking verse of "Hard Candy" over the slow, steady *boom* of the bass drum.

Wrong side of my bed of nails
Still tangled in his shirt
Must be I've got a grudge
My love just won't budge
When my lover, he treats me like dirt

Skelly walked back into the light. He stepped right over Nicky to a chorus of whistles and shouts, the Jawbreaker hung low on his hips. When he struck the strings, Vince shivered in the invisible grip of delight. But Skelly was patient, Skelly was cool, feeling his way into the song.

Beat me and cheat me
Love me and leave me
Bad man, madman, do your worst

Vince rocked on her small sticky feet. Skelly and the rest of Babel Mouth pointing their instruments toward her like compass needles finding north. The music reeked of sex and sleaze, her breath hot and wet in the microphone. Arousal oozed through the room.

Bruise me, abuse me

Just don't refuse me

I kinda like it when it hurts

A shattering frenzy of strings and percussion. The crowd weltered and roiled and roared from their guts, seething like magma squeezed up through the Earth's crust. Suzanne was paralyzed, brimming with an unfamiliar thrill. It was coming off everyone now, that pheromonic haze of bodies grown hot to the touch. Girls on the floor squealed like piglets, grown men in the wings shifted and flexed and sniffed the air.

With Nicky a dead weight and Gil on the sidelines, there was nothing to keep Skelly and Vince apart. They flew together but stopped short of touching, orbiting in such intricate elliptical figures it was impossible to know who was following whom. Vince echoed every lick of the strings with a cry, with a wail, voice bending around him as he teased screams of pleasure from the SG—urging her higher, pushing her further, until they broke out into the stratosphere in weird unholy harmony.

When she was finally out of breath, Skelly lunged into a solo while the drummer and rhythm guitarist battered away at the bridge. He played with his whole body, writhing and twisting, the muscles of his abdomen ridged and hard as the frets of his guitar. But slamming on the strings like that came at a cost, and the sutures on his right hand burst open. He wrung the Jawbreaker's neck with a snarl, then flipped it over, one hand to the other. *Bloody knuckles, bloody knuckles, bloody knuckles,* the audience chanted as his fingers slipped and skidded on the strings. He looked up and froze, watching the whole room watching Vince watching him. He ran his tongue over the back of each hand, licking his paws after the kill. Too much for a sick little kitten like Vince to resist.

She hit him with her whole body, screaming right into his teeth.

I LIKE IT WHEN IT HURTS

The audience roared the words for her; she couldn't sing with her tongue in his mouth, and he couldn't rip another note from the Jawbreaker with his bloody hands all over her. Pandemonium in the wings and on the floor, everyone losing their heads at once.

Even Skelly was thrown—Vince had him by the hair and made him buckle his knees, her pretty face masked in sweat and blood and slicks of lipstick.

I'm your misery queen
Got me down on my knees
And I'm begging you please—

She flung him to the floor, put one filthy foot under his chin.

Sink your love teeth in me

Vince licked her lips in the microphone, Skelly's narrow chest heaving underneath her. He took his red hands off her thighs and bucked the Jawbreaker up to meet them.

DO YOU LIKE IT WHEN IT HURTS?

Crashing, thrashing bodies overturned the auditorium. Two or three dozen people tried to climb over the railing to get a piece of Skelly or Vince. But abruptly she broke away—eyes blazing, teeth bared, a slaughterous pink foam on her lips. "*CAMERA!*" she bellowed, but she didn't wait for security. Before the kid with the camcorder even knew he'd been spotted, Vince was on top of him. She moved more like an animal than Suzanne had ever seen, leapt right off the stage from all fours and went headfirst into the crowd.

Skelly found his way back to his feet and looked down on the brawl with a barely-there grin. Suzanne thought of Gil's word, *warpaint.* Scarlet backspatter all over his face. The Jawbreaker gnashed on as Vince savaged the boy with the camera until her own handlers had to pull her off. The Hands wrenched one last shriek from the strings. Then wiped his mouth and left the stage, to ravishing applause.

Babel Mouth left Texas in shambles and drove west like so many bats out of hell.

"How we got out of there without every Texas fucking Ranger on our tails, I don't even want to know," said Doug.

Carney laughed. "Why do you think we're not going through El Paso?"

Suzanne gloomily traced the highway on the map. She no longer had the privilege of plotting the route, only recording it after the fact. If they didn't deviate from their trajectory, they'd pass through Roswell. "Sure," Doug said, peering over her shoulder, chewing beef jerky right in her ear, "why get busted for drugs when you can just get abducted by aliens?"

To Suzanne's disappointment, they drove through Roswell by night, and she didn't see any aliens—not even the still, silly gas station kind. No time to waste, Gracie explained. No rest for the weary. There were only a few days left before Wrecking Ball. But Louie and the invisible, ominous presence of "the label" had taken the liberty of booking a recording studio in Phoenix with the humble request that Gil and the Kills produce some kind of hit to keep them in rotation until they could get the next album together. Morale didn't matter so long as the sales numbers kept climbing. That their turn playing handmaidens to Babel Mouth might move the needle seemed more than likely; they'd made headlines again, or at least Skelly had.

Papers and magazines littered the studio, picked up and discarded by any of the half dozen people crowded around the mixing desk. There were always more people now, and while some of them were there for a reason—the engineer, for instance, ensconced in his headset and doing his best to ignore everything happening over his shoulder—others hung around just to hang around. Suzanne, whose reason to be there was to fetch lunch, had found a corner for herself between the couch and the wastebasket, where she sat glumly picking at a greasy quesadilla. She was so excited to see the inside of the studio, hear the band work through some new tunes. If they could just get some time to play together without Louie and the label breathing down their necks, everything might not feel so rotten.

But it was never just the band anymore, and even when it was, it wasn't. Skelly had unceremoniously moved his things out of the van and onto the Babel Mouth tour bus. "We're never getting him back," Ruby said. She and Nash remained in the van with the crew, who no longer had much to do since Babel Mouth's team took over all the AV. "That's the way it always happens," Nash said with a shrug when they were left out of the interview lineup for the umpteenth time. "Nobody gives a shit about the rhythm section."

Nobody except Gil. On the other side of the glass, he and Nash had been pushing the drum kit around for twenty minutes, trying to get the biggest possible *boom* out of that peculiar trapezoidal room. He wanted to do it all the old-fashioned way, stay true to the sound of four people and their instruments tearing up the stage. No small feat to bottle lightning like that—especially when your star guitar player had better things to do. Skelly was already in the studio with Louie and Vince when the rest of the band arrived. They'd done a rough cut of something called "Handful" and played it back a few times to the general fawning of all assembled. It had a good hook, Vince and the Jawbreaker entwined in sneering, waspish duet.

Has anyone ever told ya
You're kind of a handful
Always coming down like an anvil
When a softball would strike me just fine

"Are you two planning to record together?" asked a slender blonde Suzanne hadn't seen before. She stood out, ironically, because she was the only person in the room who didn't look like the morning after a Halloween party gone horribly wrong. Blue jeans and a breezy white button-down. Normal amount of makeup.

Skelly ignored the tacos, chips, and guacamole, taking long pulls from a bottle of Jack while Vince picked at a scab on her knee, feet thrown across his lap. No shoes as usual. They exchanged a conspiratorial glance. "Just fucking around," Skelly decided.

Anyone ever told ya
You're sort of a horror
How many more of your tricks can I fall for
By accident or design

"At least, we are if anybody from the labels asks," Vince added, twisting one eyebrow ring. Her pretty face was mottled with bruises from her flying leap into the audience in San Antonio two nights ago. Suzanne wanted to hate her but couldn't help admiring her audacity. She was barely twenty and not much bigger than Suzanne, but that didn't stop her going toe-to-toe and head-to-head with all the men around her and always coming out on top. The way she handled reporters was less antagonistic but a master class in misdirection; everyone walked away thinking they had a scoop before realizing they had nothing concrete to hang it on. She kept contradictory rumors circulating constantly, so nobody could pin down the truth and conversation would, perforce, continue. From her corner, Suzanne watched Skelly's reaction—unsure how invested he really was, if he was in on the gambit, whether they were just using each other.

"You certainly made an impression onstage," said the blonde, scanning a paper on the table with a headline that hollered MOVE OVER, OZZY: SKILLMAN AND DEWITT ARE A MATCH MADE IN HELL. Suzanne had already read the column at a newsstand while she was waiting for tacos. It didn't mention anybody else by name. "Is that something we can expect more of?"

"I don't make decisions," Skelly said archly. "I'm just a guitar."

"Just?" Vince reached for the newspaper, crossed her ankles, left that little provocation lying on the table. It was strange to see her in street clothes instead of electrical tape. She wore a white babydoll nightgown under a leather vest encrusted with studs and pins and her hair tied up on top of her head with a string of red rosary beads.

The blonde glanced through the glass, where Gil and Ruby and Nash had arrived at a configuration they were happy with and stood looking expectantly toward the booth. "Guitar is a big part of the sound, isn't it?" said the blonde with a strained sort of smile. Suzanne could tell she did not care for Vince. Women who weren't the Vincelings seemed to dislike her instinctively, which surely had everything to do with how she had all the men eating out of her hand. Whether it was envy of her appeal or her power was more difficult to say.

Skelly swigged the whiskey like it was orange juice, angled a look up at Louie. "Lou, you're fired. She's our manager now." Louie chuckled, chewing another cigar, keeping one eye on Skelly and one eye on the rest of the band.

"Fuck it," Suzanne heard Gil say faintly. "I can do the rhythm. Let's just get started."

The blonde chuckled, too, a small, unfunny laugh she kept pinned behind her lips. With the unspoken challenge of Vince basking between them, she held Skelly's steely gaze longer than most people did. "I'm flattered," she said. She wasn't. Like Louie, she'd probably endured too many dirtbags who thought they were God's gift to music to take him too seriously. "But you seem like you'd have a hard time taking orders from a woman."

"What gave you that impression?" Vince said with a snort, turning the paper around. It was, Suzanne noticed, a pretty good photo. In black and white, Skelly and Vince jumped out of the background, where everything blurred into shadow. Skelly on his back with the Jawbreaker, Vince looming over him with her bloody mouth wide open.

The blonde only smiled. Skelly did not. "My mom and my big sister raised me," he said, and Suzanne heard the ice in his voice before anyone else did—hair standing up on the back of her neck. The dart hanging more heavily on her chest. "I've been taking orders from women all my life, so you can take your shallow assumptions and shove them up your tight little ass."

The blonde blushed vermillion. Vince giggled, curling her toes. Skelly's blue and swollen knuckles dangling between her knees. He stared at the blonde with that soul-sucking sangfroid. Eyes going empty, the Void looking out.

"Eric," Louie said, only because she was the media, and even that with an indulgent overtone. "Retract the claws."

Hearing his given name pulled Skelly back into his body. He relaxed against the cushions, and everyone else in the room relaxed, too. Most of them probably didn't even realize the way they seized up at the first flick of his snakewhip temper, but Suzanne felt it immediately, that whiff of danger.

Gil couldn't have picked a better time to interrupt but couldn't have picked a worse opening line. He walked in, ignored everyone except Skelly, and said, "We're on the clock. No girls in the booth."

"She's press," Louie said, pointing at the blonde.

"Then you can stay," Gil said. "Tell the world the ugly truth."

"Actually," she said, already rising to her feet, "I think I've got more than enough."

"Glad to hear it," Gil said, and lost interest in her the instant she left his peripheral vision. His gaze settled, instead, on Vince.

"I'm in a band," she said.

"Not this band," Gil said. "So could I have my guitar player back?"

"*Your* guitar player," Skelly repeated.

"Last time I checked your name was still on my payroll, Killer," Gil said coolly.

"And if you'd like to keep it there, you'll reconsider being such a cunt." Skelly looked up at him impassively. Screwed the top off a small white bottle and popped a pill in his mouth, washed it down with another slug of whiskey. Everyone else in the booth had faded into the wallpaper except the engineer, who either couldn't hear them through the headset or was just pretending not to.

"How many of those have you had today?" Gil asked, letting the profanity fly right past him. Nash and Ruby looked on blankly from the other side of the glass.

"I don't know, *Dad*, how many have I had?"

Suzanne felt the sting of that word as much as Gil did. Vince bit her lip, eyes flashing from one of them to the other with undisguised glee, as if they were a tennis match and she had no skin in the game. Because she didn't, Suzanne thought—with a sharp stab of loathing. She squeezed the tip of the dart without thinking, let it prick her fingertip.

"Louie," Gil said, still looking at Skelly—not with bitterness, but a drawn and pained expression. Sick at heart, Suzanne thought the saying was. "Get him off this shit. Or the label won't get their album, if that's all you care about." He left the booth and had his own headset back on before anyone could catch up to him. "Rube, let's run through the vocals on that second verse again," Suzanne heard him say. He'd been scratching out lyrics on the backs of napkins during microscopic breaks in the action.

"Strings," Louie said, in the dour tone he deployed when Skelly finally crossed a line that warranted a scolding. "Can we get something down on tape? I'll make sure you have the night off."

"Do you see my hands?" He raised them helplessly. They'd given up trying to put the stitches back in. The wounds would scar badly, that much was certain, but it hadn't stopped him noodling around with Vince. On the other side of the window, Nash had the brushes out, coaxing little whispers from the cymbals. A slow, downtempo shuffle. Ruby and Gil braiding melodies together, Gil's voice still shivered and raw. But it worked for the song, what they had of it so far.

Woke up feeling down today
Went for a walk in what's left of the rain
And all that's left of loving you
Came crawling back again

"I know," Louie said to Skelly. "Let's get through the afternoon and I'll send the doctor to your room."

Ruby and Gil made interesting harmonies together; he sang the high parts and she sang the low ones—throaty and soulful. Not many of their songs were what you could call "pretty," but this one was. It didn't feel right in that room, where things could turn so ugly in an instant.

So I sit under the Midas tree
Where my friends used to sit with me
Before you and me and everything
All turned to gold

"Fine," Skelly said. "But tomorrow we're going to talk about my contract."

"Sure," Louie said with an unctuous grimace. "We'll do that."

Don't fill your pockets up, cuz you might sink
At least, that's what I used to think
Now maybe I don't know

Skelly disentangled himself from Vince, who blew Louie a kiss and took the rest of the hangers-on with her. "Attaboy," Louie said, arm around Skelly's bony shoulders. "If I know you, soon as you're in there you'll take all this tension and turn it into something *really* explosive . . ."

Hadn't they had enough explosions? Enough blowups and break-downs, dustups and wipeouts. They'd been zigzagging across the continent at a breakneck pace with all the dash lights on, and Suzanne couldn't shake the feeling that if they didn't take their foot off the gas, they were headed for a crash.

Who pulls the weeds in Eden?
Who trims the trees?
Must be God's the gardener
But he's not minding me

When the door closed behind Louie and Skelly, she found herself alone with the engineer, who had yet to react to anything not happening between his earphones. Nobody—not even Gil—had noticed she was still there. She stood in the corner, not knowing what to do with herself. Then she slowly sat back down, to listen to the music.

Troubled times in paradise
I must be on my way
I feel it in my bones, my love
Here comes the rain

ASK THE ANGELS

The Lifeboat's door cracked open in the morning and let a splinter of sunlight in. Nothing on the other side, so far as they could tell.

"Better let Trouble out first," Simon advised, and Suzanne stood aside to let the dog pass. Hackles raised, shoulders shifting under her fur. She tiptoed down the steps and landed with a soft *whump* in the sand. Raised her head to sniff the still air, then ventured farther from the trailer, tail whispering behind her. Coast evidently clear. Suzanne followed her and Simon followed her and Phoebe followed him. They stayed close together without saying why. The emptiness of the outside world echoed. Trouble vanished into the landscape, a shaggy white something slinking between the rocks and weird alien fingers of ocotillo reaching for the sky. The road was only a rut in the sand, camouflaged among the rattler tracks and ghostly impressions of last week's flash flood. Sanctuary might protect them from one kind of menace, but there were so many others. Suzanne's nerves crackled in the heat.

"It's even spookier in the daylight," Phoebe said. Eyes darting behind her sunglasses. They'd killed the headlights and driven by moonlight until they'd gone around a bend and the more immediate danger lay ahead. Suzanne couldn't quite believe they'd made it in one piece—it was a rough road even without a trailer to haul. She'd driven it before.

"What happened here?" Phoebe asked. Buildings still stood, some older than others. The assay office and a general store had been there over a hundred years, the saloon even longer. Paint peeling off the false front advertised cold drinks and a card room. An empty bridle hung from the hitching post outside, swinging eerily in the dead air.

"Hell." Suzanne shrugged. "Hell happened here." She walked a slow zigzag through the center of town. The post office had buckled into a heap of timber and adobe, undoubtedly harboring snakes and scorpions in its puddles of shade. On the other side of Main Street, a lonely barbershop still stood. The pioneer village rubbed elbows with more recent derelicts. A high school and a fire station, with their windows shattered and roofs caving in. Behind the garage, a few cars were rusted beyond recognition, and half a dozen trailers had been halfway reclaimed by the elements. Some of the inhabitants' belongings still lay around—dog bowls and trash barrels and a bike with a bell on the handlebars. A yellow sign bleached white by the sun said SLOW, CHILDREN AT PLAY. It was hard to believe there had ever been children, ever been play, ever been people at all. Most of her old photos of Sanctuary were of ordinary objects, melting into the landscape like time on a Dalí canvas.

At the end of the gravelly wash of Main Street rose the modest towers of the Mission San Juan de Ortega. Two crosses still pointed skyward, but the largest had broken off the campanario and landed upside down in the sand. Bad omen.

"This was a Spanish church," Suzanne said. "Overrun or abandoned sometime in the 1700s. Prospectors looking for the mouth of the spring that fed the cistern a hundred years later found silver instead. They called the mine Agua Bendita—holy water—but by the time the town grew up around it that sounded too Catholic, too superstitious. So they changed the name to Sanctuary." She led them into a small square courtyard meant to offer shelter from the elements or the Apaches, or whatever else came along. The spring remained, reduced to a trickle snaking down the rock face into a basin of stone. White alkali left an ominous ring at the high-water line. "People drank from the spring to cure all their ills, to get a little taste of benediction. But when the mine modernized, it poisoned the groundwater."

They gave the basin a wide berth. No less superstitious than their ill-fated forebears. Decades ago, Suzanne felt a deathly calm come over her there but didn't resist it. She'd only ever felt at home in places that didn't exist, with people who weren't there, either. She led Simon and Phoebe past the dark mouth of the chapel. The cruciform shadows of the bell towers stretched across the dry, pebbled yard beyond the outer wall. A more solid cross stood crookedly at the center. Smaller ones marked smaller plots, ringed with rocks.

"There weren't a lot of children, but children died first." Some were marked only with planks or furniture posts. Most of the names had been weathered away, but a few clumsy epitaphs remained. The dead identified by family ties. BELOVED HUSBAND. MOTHER AND WIFE. OUR DAUGHTER. STILLBORN. "Boom to bust, ashes to ashes, dust to dust."

"I'm surprised this isn't a state park or something," Simon said.

"Some ghost towns are." Those weren't the ones she remembered. She remembered the ones that went on not existing, whether anybody else remembered them or not. "Some are privately owned. Most aren't worth the investment. Tough sell for a tourist, trekking all the way out here when there's only this to see." Which was exactly what they needed—just like she had when she last set foot there. Somewhere to hide, where no one would ever go in their right mind.

"You'd just about have to be crazy," Simon said, looking over his shoulder. From the cemetery they could see the whole sprawl of the town. No signs of life but Trouble, sniffing around under the creosote.

Suzanne shaded her eyes and looked the other direction, back toward the distant highway. "I'm counting on it."

Maybe Rob was some kind of crazy. But even if he followed them into the desert, he had no way to find them. No road signs pointed the way to Sanctuary; it wasn't on any maps anymore. Suzanne had hunted it down in archives, in old yellow newspapers, on internet forums and microfilm. The photos she'd taken of it were all washed out, except one. She picked her way across the cemetery, wondering if her silent subject was still there.

A crude statue of an angel stooped under the weight of a horseshoe hooked around her neck like a noose. Men were quick to hang their angels once the luck ran out.

THE **A** SIDE

HOT HOT HOT!!!

The Wrecking Ball rehearsal stage was two hours outside Las Vegas, where the performers and their necessary personnel spent two brutal, blistering days in a kind of temporary shantytown. Though it was technically still inhabited by sixty-three stubborn or lunatic people, Suzanne heard La Caldera described as a "ghost town." She was ecstatic to finally see one, but the reality was, like so many other things, a quietly crushing disappointment. Instead of hitching posts and saloons with swinging doors falling off their hinges, they found a dust-choked cluster of squat, square buildings bleached a dirty white like half-buried bones. There was only one false-front building in town, with a peeling sign that simply said DRUGS. All the doors and windows were boarded over and slapped with NO TRESPASSING signs, so no one could even see what was inside.

The ghostliest part of the town, Suzanne decided, was down at the south end of the road, where four rows of identical gray trailers were beached on a bare patch of gravel. These were the best accommodations La Caldera had to offer. Most of the performers were being shuttled to and from a nearby motel each morning and recovering in whichever tin can their act had been assigned between bouts of punishment in the unforgiving heat. Apart from the narrow dirt road they'd come in on, there was nothing to see in any direction but rock and sand. Suzanne had never in her wildest Crayola daydreams imagined there could be so many shades of brown.

"Really thought we'd be closer to the Strip," Doug said, squinting into the blank far distance in the direction of Las Vegas. Suzanne turned an aluminum can over in the dust. Soda or beer? She could usually guess by the colors. She'd learned from the bus driver that La Caldera had been an informal staging area for tours and festivals for fifteen years or so. Anything they found was probably left behind by last year's lineup. She saw another glint of metal, which turned out to be an old tin of chewing tobacco. Everything coming up fool's gold. The cemetery was the only place she left the stones unturned. So many of the deaths were surprisingly recent, the graves heartbreakingly bare. When did a town die off? she wanted to know. Who decided it couldn't be saved?

"This sucks," Suzanne said. She'd never said it out loud, but she'd felt the urge for days.

"What sucks?" Doug said with a sigh that said enough. Everything sucked. Everyone hated each other unless they were fucking, and sometimes even that didn't help. The band was selling more tickets and selling more albums than they ever had before, but all that seemed to matter was making sure they sold more.

"This *sucks*," Suzanne said again, louder, so it rang off the bare, solemn stones.

"Welcome to the dark side of corporate." The one good thing in a few bad weeks was that she got to hang out with Doug again. Babel Mouth had gobbled up his responsibilities until the festival, where he had been entrusted with pushing exactly one button. He sat down on a burned-out old tire so large it might have dropped off a passing airplane. "Promise me something, Pint Size?" he said, squinting at her from under the brim of the old Coors cap he still wore.

"Shoot," she said.

"Look, I know everything's gone fucking sideways," he said. "But promise me you won't blame the music, okay? However this goes or whatever happens when we get back to Baltimore . . . the music was good, y'know?" He shook his head with a sniff of a laugh, like he still couldn't believe where he was. "The music is *great*. That's why the rest

of it feels like shit. Makes the songs seem, I don't know, endangered."
He mopped his brow, looked around. "Like this whole haunted horror
town." If she wasn't imagining it, his voice was beginning to split, just
like Gil's. "Anyway. Hold on to that part, okay? Don't let anything tar-
nish it. That part stays gold."

"Okay," she said. "Hey, Doug?"

"Shoot," he said.

"I have one picture left. Can I take one of us?"

He blinked at her. "Don't you want to save that for the show?"

She shook her head no. She had pictures of all of them. Of Gil
and the Kills, of Gracie and Carney, even of Nicky and Vince. But she
wasn't in any of them. And if she didn't take one now, it would be like
back in the studio, when she disappeared before their eyes. It would
be like none of it ever happened to her, like she'd never been there
at all.

"Sure, if you're sure."

"Sure, I'm sure."

Doug climbed to his feet, brushed off the seat of his jeans. "Where
do you want to be?"

"Mm . . . here." She moved him, crab-walking sideways, to a dip in
the earth where the light was good, not so harsh, filtered through a
slow-scudding raft of cloud. "Good."

"Mm, here." He pulled the Coors cap off and fitted it over her unruly curls instead. "*Now* you look like a roadie."

Doug held the camera out where it could capture both of them.
Suzanne had never taken a photo of herself before and felt exposed on
the other side of the viewfinder, the curious black eye of the lens looking right at her in a way no one had for a while. No choice but to trust
it, with no way of knowing how the photo would turn out. She steadied
Doug's hands and said, "Ready?"

"Ready."

"One . . . two . . ." *Kssshhhhk.* The camera spat the photo right in
their faces, like it was sticking its tongue out at them. Suzanne slipped
it into her pocket before the sun could wipe the image away, the way

it had wiped all color and life from the landscape. "Thanks," she said from under the brim of the baseball cap.

"Anytime, Pint Size."

They stood side by side until a small, mean breeze rose up and swept a fine spray of sand and grit against their shins. The walkie-talkie on Doug's belt bleeped. One of Gil's better inventions. They could talk to Blondie right over the airwaves.

"Doug?" Gracie's voice, thinned by the distance and the stress of the last few weeks. Even her Spanish had flattened, came in a rapid-fire stream of elisions Suzanne couldn't pick words out of anymore. "We're ready to test the Toaster."

"Okay," he said. "On our way."

Suzanne didn't want to go back. A new and dismal feeling. With Gil and the band and the music was the only place she'd ever wanted to be—until, well, *recently*. Time had warped along some invisible axis, and she was losing something she never really had the chance to grasp. She followed, slow and silent, behind Doug, still scanning the ground for a flash of gold or silver, as if there were some buried treasure that she might have missed.

The rehearsal stage loomed like a mirage on the horizon, the heat making it wobble and quiver as if tectonic plates were shifting directly beneath it. There were no wings to speak of, everything behind the scenes exposed by the skeletal scaffolding. A thin, white tarpaulin flapped against its cables, trying to take flight. The shade it provided covered most of the makeshift stage, despite its being significantly larger than any stage they'd worked on before. A big blank canvas to start over on, or so Suzanne was hoping.

The tarp blocked the sun but didn't do much for the heat. Everyone looked like they'd been hosed down head to toe—even the people standing on the sidelines, including Louie and Gil. While Doug was dragged away to learn how to operate the mysterious Toaster, Suzanne slipped into Louie's shadow, picking up the thread of the argument that never seemed to end right where it left off.

"It's bad enough we have to share the bill with them still, but—"

"They want all of you together. That was the deal."

"Does it have to be at the same *time*?"

"You're not hearing me. Without Babel Mouth, there's no room for you in this lineup. It's you with them or it's just them. There's no just you. After San Antonio, the promoter is insisting. The press will be huge."

"Lou, I'm sorry, I have my limits." Suzanne followed Gil's eyes to the opposite wing, where Vince was talking to the choreographer—a peculiar figure who had arrived on the scene sometime yesterday and started bossing everyone around, swathed in feathers and animal print like some kind of androgynous pimp. "I can't sing with her."

"Why? Because she'll blow you off the stage like she's been doing the last two weeks? Since you don't seem to know what's good for you, I'll spell it out. We're talking about tens of thousands of people. If you can play nice with Vince for one hour—that's all I'm asking—it might change your miserable life. But never mind the fame and the fans, if that means nothing to you. Let's be practical. If you walk out now, let me remind you just how much *money* you stand to lose." He laughed, one long arm snaking around Gil's neck. "Think about it. Aren't you sick of being broke and in debt and doing things for money that you'd *really* rather not . . . ?"

Gil's lip twisted. He'd never had enough money, and Nora never let him forget it. "But Lou . . ." he started to say, but Louie had his limits, too.

"*No* 'but Lou,'" he said, and did something Suzanne hadn't seen before in all their bickering. He grabbed Gil by the back of the collar, even catching a fistful of hair so he grunted, head bent back. "You shut up and listen to me for the next thirty seconds and then you don't say anything." The words echoed around Suzanne's memory. Gil, with Skelly pinned against the wall, saying, *You don't talk. I talk.* "I don't man-age people who make themselves unmanageable. So you're going to get with the program and go out there and act like Babel Mouth is the best thing that ever happened to you because besides Eric fucking Skillman, they are. Otherwise, I'll keep Eric, and tomorrow you start looking for new management. He's young, he's hungry, he'll play with all his fucking fingers falling off. He'll get another shot. But you? You've had your chances. It's now or never." Louie released him, thrust him away toward the stage. Gil stumbled, looked back at him with fury for a moment before he saw Suzanne. Standing there where she wouldn't be seen. And that heartsick look choked off whatever he had been about to say, leaving Louie the final word. "When you're as big as Vince you can be a diva," he said. "But we've gotta get there first."

The choreographer clapped his hands with a sharp *snap* that echoed in the dead air like a rifle report. Louie waved Gil toward him with a limp twist of the wrist. *Run along.*

Suzanne found a cable trunk to sit on and watch as the festival engineer walked everyone through what was going to happen. The Toaster, it transpired, was a hydraulic lift that worked like a springboard at Sin City scale. Something they used for magic and acrobats and other dazzling, high-flying acts.

"Okay! Here's how it works," the engineer said, stroking the sweat from his handlebar mustache. "We set the lift and lock it. You two climb into the basket. You, what's your name?"

"Doug," Doug said, lumped on a stool with his arms crossed beside the fantastical black contraption, its legs folded up underneath it like the rungs of Jacob's Ladder.

"Doug!" the engineer hollered. "When Doug gets his cue, he'll push that button, and up you pop, just like toast." He grinned through the mustache. "Any questions?"

Doug pointed. "What's with the mannequins?"

The choreographer's lackeys had hauled two statues onstage and were marking their feet with bright green spike tape.

"Allow me to introduce Nicky Monroe and Skelvis Presley." On the right was a rough likeness of Marilyn Monroe. White dress, blond wig, and a large, unflattering photo of Nicky taped over her face. On the left was an even rougher likeness of the King, with Skelly's face taped over his trademark sneer. "They'll stand in for your guitars until we're ready to run this through for real. Don't want anyone losing their heads just yet." Because the grand plan, as the choreographer interrupted to explain, was not just to throw Vince and Gil ten feet in the air for their entrance, but to throw them clean over their respective axmen. "It's a real showstopper. Or starter, in this case," the engineer said with another loony grin. "Break a leg!" They had the next two hours to learn to stick the landing.

The first few times they tried it, nothing went right. Gil kicked the King's head off and Vince went rolling across the crash mats so fast she almost tumbled into the pit. The choreographer had insisted that she "Put some fucking shoes on, are you mental?" and laced her so tightly into a pair of black boxing boots that she couldn't, she complained, bend her ankles if she tried. It was the first time she seemed uncertain and out of her element, but that brought out a new ferocity in her. She gritted her teeth and got back on her feet and climbed back into the basket and said, "Again. Again. Again."

After the first few pop flies, the excitement and silliness wore off for the spectators, and the heat and the boredom set back in. To the sound of the hydraulic lift hissing its way down and rushing back up again, boots and knees and elbows hitting the mats, grunts and yelps and curses from all involved, Suzanne wandered the weird exoskeleton of the rehearsal stage until she'd circled all the way around and was eclipsed by Louie again.

"Fireworks, I don't like fireworks," he was telling the engineer. "Too . . . I don't know. Patriotic."

"The fireworks are pretty standard. It's Vegas, you know? People want pizzazz."

"Look, this isn't a baseball game." Louie squinted around at the sea of sand stretching in every direction. "They tested nuclear weapons out here. Go bigger."

A cry of laughter made everyone look toward the stage space. At first Suzanne couldn't tell what had happened. Vince had Gil by the hand—she looked oddly childlike beside him, in her tiny black leotard, T-shirt flapping around her like the tarpaulin—and kept jumping up and down on the crash mat, not according to the choreography but in agitated little bunny hops. Gil stood there looking bemused as she yanked his arm around, beet red in the heat.

"Well, holy shit," the engineer said. "I think they did it."

So they did it again and again. They didn't nail it every time but started to nail it more often than they didn't. Once they knew they could, it wasn't daunting but exhilarating. They'd land side by side, pitched forward on their toes, grabbing for each other's slippery fingers to keep from falling over. The choreographer ran around in circles, shouting encouragement. "Beautiful! Gorgeous! Fantastic!" The only problem was that Gil kept knocking Skelly's head off. He was bigger and heavier than Vince, and Skelly had about as many inches on Nicky as Elvis had on Marilyn. "Again!" the choreographer cried every time it happened. *"Again!"*

"Where'd you get the dummies?" Louie asked. Suzanne could tell from the way he chewed the end of his cigar that the gears were turning.

"We found a whole dumpster back behind Sands," the engineer said. "One man's trash."

"So nobody would miss them."

"Why?"

Louie gnawed on the cigar. "Why not burn the old idols?"

The engineer watched as Skelvis's head went rolling by like a tumbleweed. "Now, there's an idea." He looked back toward the trailers. "Where are Sid and Nancy, anyway?"

"Wait!" Vince's voice rang out from the basket. Every other conversation stopped, every head turning toward her. "This isn't working. We should switch."

"What?" the choreographer said.

"He's taller, I'm smaller. I'll jump Skelly and Gil can jump Nicky. Besides"—she peered over the railing, seeing the arc of her leap in the air, Nicky's face under Marilyn's hair—"if somebody's going to be down there staring straight up my snatch, I'd rather it wasn't my brother."

The choreographer, nonplussed, pointed to the headless Elvis. "But it's all right for him."

"Hasn't killed him yet," she said. "Okay?"

Nobody would touch that one. Scandalizing people, Suzanne had come to understand, wasn't just something Vince did for fun—it was a way of keeping everyone else off-balance, so she could take over the room. "O-kay," the choreographer said. "Fire away."

They put Skelvis's head back on, did it again, and stuck the landing. Vince didn't wait, but kept hold of Gil's hand and pulled him right back into the basket again. And again. And again. When they'd done it five times flawlessly, Gil was laughing, too, racing her back to the basket as soon as he touched down on the mat. Even sliding around in their sweat, losing their grip on the rails or each other, they could do it. They could do it every time. The tenth time they landed, their knees buckled under them and they collapsed in a heap.

"Not bad for an old dog," Vince said, knocking her shoulder against Gil's. But now there was no malice in it.

"Not bad for a young runt," he said, and seemed to mean it. She laughed at that as much as anything. Suzanne looked on, unsure how they could forget it all so quickly, put it aside for the sake of the spotlight. But Gil smiling after everything—she felt short of breath. While she was still watching them, Louie turned and looked right at her, held her gaze until she understood that he'd always known she was there. Right behind him. Watching and listening. "So. You see why I push them," he said in reply to a question she hadn't asked out loud. Then he turned back around and didn't speak to her again for twenty-nine years.

"All right," the engineer decided. "Let's try it with live guitars."

While the choreographer fluttered around Vince and Gil, making them drink water, breathe deeply, work out the kinks, Nicky and Skelly were summoned from wherever they'd been lurking. Two gangly black buzzards skulking through the dead landscape, shrinking under the sun like they hadn't seen it for weeks. They climbed the stairs to the stage with dubious expressions, eyes sliding toward the battered mannequins. Marilyn had lost an arm, and Elvis's hair was melting down the side of his head. "Better if they don't know that used to be them," the engineer said.

The choreographer bullied them into their places while Vince and Gil climbed back into the basket. Nicky, utterly brain-dead, held his guitar so loosely it would have fallen right out of his hands if it wasn't strapped on. Skelly had a firmer grip on the Jawbreaker, fingers moving restlessly over the frets as he looked up at the blinding white sky.

"And now, for all the marbles!" the choreographer announced when he was satisfied Nicky wouldn't keel over and fall off his target. The lift hissed down. Nicky and Skelly stood rigidly still. Gil took one deep breath, then nodded to Doug.

"Viva Las Vegas," Doug said. "Here goes nothing." He slammed his hand down on the button.

They didn't even need pyrotechnics. They were pyrotechnics per-sonified, the shear of the music scorching the earth, singeing the air, smoking in their sweat and blood like brimstone. Skelly and Nicky shredded the strings, egging each other on to more and more daring musical feats. A thundering fusillade of percussion as Nash and the Babel Mouth drummer smashed at their kits, fighting to overpower each other. The two bass guitars, throbbing like the heartbeat of the Earth itself, drove the music on. Suzanne vibrated in the wings, every cell alive and sparkling with light. This was what they were missing, what they had lost, the blaze of faith and fury that made their music a force of nature, an act of God, dawn and Judgment Day at once. She bounced on her toes, longing to run out and meet them, be swept up in the savage glory of it all.

She lost herself in the sound until someone muttered into their headset, "It's time. Let's make some toast." Unlike the rehearsal stage, everything was smoke and mirrors now. Suzanne couldn't see the lift, couldn't see the basket, didn't even know where to look. She shivered as something cool and silky brushed her arm, surprised when she turned to find Vince's catlike face an inch from hers. It was the pink robe she felt, that shimmer of silk on her skin.

"Here." Vince pressed something hard and heavy into Suzanne's hands. "Take this."

"What is it?" she asked, not trusting her an inch.

"For posterity," said Vince, the black fan of her eyelashes closing in one slow, deliberate wink. "Our little secret." And then she was gone, just a whip of pink silk across Suzanne's cheek. She fumbled to turn the thing over.

"Vince incoming," the headset said. "Cue Toaster in ten, nine, eight—"

It was the camcorder. Battered and scratched from when Vince had wrestled it out of the bootlegger's hands. The green light was already on. Suzanne didn't have time to think. She hit record and raised the viewfinder to her eye.

"—three, two, one. Breakfast is served."

Gil and Vince arced through a darkening sky like shooting stars. People gasped and screamed and pointed up for one weightless moment before they came back to earth, tumbled right over the twin pillars of lightning that were Skelly and Nicky, and landed—*SLAM*—at the same instant. A roar moved through the crowd like a wave, gathering power and speed until it crested and crashed against the stage.

"Cue mannequins." There were ten of them now, frozen in their vogue poses like a line of chorus girls on each side of the stage. "Three, two, one. Fire in the hole."

Marilyn's head exploded in a shower of sparks and confetti. Then Elvis. And on down the line, heads bursting like balloons. Even Ruby was laughing now, and Nash, flinging burning blond hair off the snare drum. Who cared about the old heroes? Gil and Vince were Adam and Eve and the world was being reborn. They hit the stage and dove headfirst into "Bad Business," moving so fast nobody knew where to look. Suzanne's head spun trying to follow them with the small, sharp eye of the camera. Gil's voice soaring over Vince's harder, harsher one. They danced around each other, colliding and dividing, flashing by at the speed of light. He let her have the last line and she took it with relish.

This bitch'll be bad for business!

The crowd howled with laughter. "Bad Business" screeched right into "Barbarella." Gil and Vince were pure fire together and blowing the roof off the world. Thirty thousand people swept up in their momentum, shell-shocked and spellbound.

Everyone, *except* one. When Suzanne tore her eye away from the camcorder, she saw what she hadn't through the viewfinder. Nothing in the rhythm changed, nothing in the music. Everything in sync, in step. The Hands flashed as fast as they always had—a blur of black magic, blood and bones. But when Suzanne looked up at Skelly's face, it wasn't his. Instead, the Void stared back.

THE **B** SIDE

ONCE UPON A TIME IN THE WEST

They learned to be ghosts. They parked the Ranchero in the empty garage and anchored the Lifeboat among the other trailers, where the solar panels could charge in the morning but the walls of the mission would cast it in shade for the brutal afternoon. It quickly gathered dust and sand—silver siding hidden from the naked eye, like any other lump of precious metal.

The days were long and deadly hot. "But if pioneers could hack it in the 1850s, why not us?" Phoebe asked. They learned from the lizards to conserve their energy, dozing in the shade when the sun made the sand shimmer like water. They ate sparingly, supplementing what provisions they had with the pink fruit of prickly pears growing in clumps downslope from Main Street. Trouble was no trouble; she killed cottontails with ease and soon graduated to jackrabbits. Phoebe shot a quail and Simon cooked it on a coat hanger over a fire built from broken fence posts.

"Quail, stale beer bread, and cactus fruit," Phoebe said. "Most of the major food groups."

"At least nobody's going to die of scurvy," Simon said cheerfully.

"I'd worry more about dysentery," said Suzanne. "Did you ever play *Oregon Trail*?"

"I'd rather be here than trying to cross the Rockies," Phoebe decided.

"I'll remind you you said that," Simon said, "when the temperature hits a hundred and ten again."

"The nights are something, though."

The sun took a long time to set, and it was a spectacular show—the desert lit up from below, molten gold rolling down the hills like lava. Suzanne dreamed up a new box of crayons dedicated to the desert sky, because even the most vivid colors in the most robust collections couldn't do it justice. She needed Prickly Pear instead of Wild Strawberry, Sunburn instead of Sunglow, Velvet Midnight instead of Indigo. The temperature dropped precipitously after dark. They rooted through Phoebe's backstock to find sweatshirts and socks and wrapped themselves up tight beside the fire. When the flames died down to embers, they watched the stars instead. So far from the glaring electric lights of civilization, the band of the Milky Way sparkled like sugar. Clouds of cosmic dust traversed by shooting stars and satellites. Suzanne had never been good at wishing, but she wished on every one—for what? For sanctuary, for an angel, for deliverance from the mess she'd made of everything. She walked around with the unshakable feeling that had followed her out of the graveyard. Treading on borrowed time.

One morning, which might have been the fifth or sixth, nobody could remember which, Simon said, "I'm going to take Blondie into town."

The nearest town was barely a town, more of an outpost on the side of the highway. A gas station, a motel, a nondescript café serving the worst version of all the usual fare. Almost as much a ghost town as Sanctuary, but not quite.

"What for?" Phoebe asked. "We've got plenty of food." They'd stumbled on a treasure trove of jarred and canned goods on one of their exploratory expeditions. Pinto beans and green chiles and tomatoes and cornmeal. It all tasted the same after a few decades, but they had plenty of condiments rattling around in the trailer.

"But it hasn't rained." He glanced back toward the mission, toward the poisoned spring. "We're out of water."

Suzanne knew it was coming and wished for a storm every night.

Summer was the wet season, but the skies were not on their side. She didn't think Rob was nuts enough to wait around that long in the middle of nowhere, but still she said, "You shouldn't go alone." There was no cell reception and the walkie-talkies couldn't reach over the hills; they'd tried.

Simon shook his head. "Better if I do. He's probably moved on, but if he hasn't"—he gave her a slow, subtle smile—"not my first rodeo."

Phoebe, busy cleaning her gun for the fat little quail pecking at the dirt behind an upturned patio table, answered before Suzanne had the chance. "Better take Trouble with you."

WILD DOGS

Rob nodded on his stool at the counter. There was no back, which was a good thing—when he started to slip, the sudden tug of gravity rudely woke him up again.

"More coffee, sugar?"

He wasn't sure whether the waitress was calling him sugar or asking if he wanted it.

"Please," he said. Still remembering his manners. She was probably his age but looked older. Sun-spotted and leathery after years in the desert. Eyes like a raccoon and neck like a turkey. No wedding band, but he'd heard her mention a son and daughter to the cook flipping eggs on the grill. He wondered what happened, whether their father had left her, or she left him, or he was never really in the picture to begin with.

"That sandwich'll be right up," she said.

"Thank you." Maybe she wondered the same things about him. Why he had eaten there three meals a day for the last five days. Wedding band still on his finger but no wife in sight. Then again, most of the diners at Pete's Café were single men. He'd chosen it not for the menu (uninspired), the portions (enormous), or the prices (laughably low), but because there was nowhere else to eat except the Valero and nowhere else with an unobstructed view of the intersection. If they came out of hiding from either direction, he'd see them.

He slurped his coffee and scrolled through Freckles' Instagram feed. Nothing since Fort Worth, when she'd posted a selfie outside a record store in the Six Points neighborhood. *Great cratedig, Born Late,* the caption read, which was Greek to him. Rob tried to curl his fingers into a fist, but pain slashed across his knuckles and blood squeezed through the scab that had finally crusted over in a hideous mass of gray and yellow, like curdled buttermilk. He hadn't yet worked out what to say when people asked what happened. "Gentlemen's disagreement," he'd told the waitress, and let her draw her own conclusions about how the other guy had fared.

The other guy. Rob sat up straighter on the stool, phone clattering down on the counter. Turned toward the dirty windows that spied on the gas station across the street. He didn't see the car. Didn't see Freckles or Eight Fingers. No sign of Suzanne. But he did see a dog. A dog he'd seen before and remembered because he'd never seen a dog quite like it—that long, lean body and the coarse white hair. Wolfish tail sweeping the ground. It sniffed around a trash bin at the end of the parking lot, opened its mouth to show gleaming white teeth and a long red tongue.

Rob slid off the stool and crossed the café to a booth by the windows. Watched the dog with narrow, burning eyes. He'd been seeing things he knew weren't there. A common side effect of sleep deprivation, or so Google had told him. Maybe a desert mirage. He didn't know why the dog unnerved him. It just looked wrong—too big, too white, too wild. Some skinwalker slinking out of the badlands in broad daylight. He caught his own reflection, realized he'd been slipping in and out of his skin just as easily.

Tick tock, the backward Rob in the window said. *Going to let them get away again?*

Rob waved him off. Ignored his smarting knuckles. Then froze in place, hand still raised. The dog had lifted its head, closed its mouth, looked right at him.

"Gave me a turn, disappearing like that."

He had a sudden, startling impulse to strangle the waitress. In the instant she'd distracted him, the dog disappeared.

"If you want, I can move your things over here," she offered, peering past him at the nothing out the window. "Brew with a view."

"I need to go," he said. And, to make up for his strangulation fantasy, however short-lived, added, "Excuse me," and dropped a twenty on the table. He was out the door before she could ask where the fire was.

The heat hit him like a battering ram after a few hours under the rattling swamp cooler, but he didn't have time to be bowled over. Nor could he afford to be seen. Fortunately, five days driving aimlessly around the same patch of sand had given him a pretty good lay of the land. The pickup was parked on the other side of the café, invisible from the filling station. He left it there and went around the back of the building, where the dumpsters were hidden behind a row of wooden slats with plenty of cracks to peer through. The stench was so intense his stomach somersaulted. Ripe garbage fermenting under the desert sun. He pulled his collar up over his nose, but that wasn't much better—his body reeked of sweat and the stale cigarette odor of the motor lodge. He spent most nights driving around, reasoning that if they made a move they'd do it after dark, stealing an hour of sleep and a shower in the hottest part of the afternoon. He'd fed the desk clerk some line about being a PI, forked over a couple of twenties to buy his vigilance, and promised there'd be more where that came from if he saw anything. Every time he passed the desk he asked, and every time the clerk shook his head gloomily. But finally—*finally*—here was a stroke of luck.

He'd lost track of the dog, but he found the car. Hard to miss. No amount of dust could camouflage that shade of yellow, hide those four-eyed headlights. It was parked at one of the pumps, nozzle fitted snugly in the fuel pipe. So, they were ready to make a run for it. Eight Fingers emerged from the station alone, bags in each hand that looked heavy.

"Where are you hiding out, you little shit?"

Eight Fingers set the bags on the passenger seat, replaced the nozzle, looked around. Gave a short, sharp whistle and waited. The dog emerged from a cluster of bushes growing around the Valero sign. Rob held his breath, though there was no way the dog could hear him from that distance. Or could it? The dog's ears swiveled like satellite dishes, eerily independent of each other. At another word from Eight Fingers, it leapt into the bed and sat, tongue dripping on the back bumper.

Rob kept both eyes on the taillights as the car swung out of the lot and barreled down the road south. Rob knew better than to jump in the pickup and follow. Instead, he jumped in the pickup and drove back to the motel.

When he walked in, the bell clattered against the door and the clerk looked up from the pages of an old porno mag, pages riffled by the oscillating fan. "Haven't seen anything, man," he said preemptively.

"No problem," Rob told him. "Got another question if you've got the time."

"Do I look busy?"

Rob leaned on the counter. "The county road, running south."

"What about it?"

"What's out there? Looks like a whole lot of nothing."

"You about guessed it," the clerk said. "Probably somebody cooking meth out there somewhere. Not a lot else."

"Ranchers?" Rob asked. "Little farm towns? Any reason at all to drive out that way?"

The clerk chewed on the question. "Dinosaur bones, I guess. We get them, what're they called, proctologists? Going out there to dig stuff up." Rob decided not to correct him. "People come in here with metal detectors sometimes. I think maybe there's an old mining town, but nobody lives out that way now."

"Mining town." The phrase stuck in his brain like a burr.

"Lotta those around here, or used to be. See?" The clerk handed Rob a brochure, but he didn't even need it. Didn't need to see the photos, read the names, learn the story. Because he'd already seen them, already heard them, forgotten all about them until this very moment. The boxes and binders and folders of photos. The stacks of bound books in the attic that Suzanne knew she'd never sell but didn't know what else to do with. Ghost towns, mining towns, all the lands of the lost she'd wandered before finding her way to him.

"Thank you," he said. "May I take this?"

"'Course," said the clerk. "But be careful. No service. Don't want to get lost out there."

"Thank you," Rob said again. He peeled the last twenty off his wallet and slipped it between the pages of the magazine. In no hurry now. He'd waited a long time; he could wait a while longer. He stretched his bad hand. Knuckles weeping. He'd watch and wait until Eight Fingers was out of the way. How much trouble could two unarmed women give him? He smiled at the clerk. "This has been very helpful."

PART 5

DUST AND BONES

Snapshot: Alexandria, 2018

Rob was waiting for Suzanne at a table for two marooned between the bathrooms and the bar. The jazzy schmaltz of Dexter Gordon escorted her across the dining room. She sat down, aware that she did not look remotely worth the wait. He leaned across the table to pluck a pencil from her hair, which fell down around her ears in a limp, wilted twist. The waiter materialized immediately and she ordered "the salmon" at random. He nodded and asked whether she wanted anything to drink besides water.

As he swanned away, Suzanne surveyed the other diners. They ranged from middle-aged to one foot in the grave, and she wondered where she and Rob fit in—what threshold of senescence they had crossed to look like they almost belonged there. A quartet drunk on a girls' night out bitched about their husbands and their babysitters while savagely excavating a tureen of spinach dip. Balding lotharios at the bar flirted with the redhead mixing drinks, who laughed at their jokes and smiled for their tips but rolled her eyes every time she turned her back.

When the wine appeared, Suzanne sucked down half the glass without coming up for air, still hot and cotton-mouthed from the walk from the Metro station, dress sticking to her thighs like flypaper.

"Maybe we should have ordered a bottle," Rob said.

"Maybe I will when the waiter comes back."

He pursed his lips before wrangling them into a permissive smile that made her want to throw the rest of her Chablis at him. "It's an occasion."

It didn't feel like one, despite the white tablecloths and unspoken dress code and entrées so high class that the only price listed was "market." Like their wedding reception and so many other "occasions" in between, she was an unwelcome guest at her own party. Rob tried, in his way, but everything he said seemed insipid, even when she was only half listening, attention torn between the mundane things left undone in her haste to get to the restaurant and the marvelous things she imagined she'd be doing on this so-called occasion five years ago. She had pictured trips around the world, adventure whenever they could get it between his job and hers, honeymooning someplace new every year.

Instead, they went to dinner. This year he talked about an upcoming department meeting until the entrées were cleared, then ordered chocolate cake to share and asked if she'd changed her mind about having children.

Suzanne watched herself reach for her wineglass as if she were a stranger two tables away, heard herself say, "Have I *what*?"

He repeated the question like he thought she hadn't heard him. "I asked if you'd maybe reconsidered starting a family."

"Absolutely not."

"You haven't even thought about it?"

"Would I keep it to myself all this time?"

"I did. Not the whole time," he added, as if that made it better, softened the shock, "but—recently, yes. I've thought about it a lot."

She set her wine down slowly. She'd only had two glasses, actually, but the world seemed unfirm, unfixed, about to crack open beneath her. "Rob, we talked about this." It was one of the only things they *had* talked about before they signed the marriage license. "We agreed." That they had their careers to consider. Their finances. Their responsibilities and ambitions. Everything they shouldn't pass on to the next generation.

But all of that had changed, or so he was telling her five minutes later when the server returned with a wedge of cake so thickly ganached she thought the table tilted underneath it. A rum-soaked cherry perched on top with juicy indecency. Suzanne grabbed it, unsure whether the waiter had heard her fingernails tapping her glass and deciphered the Morse code for SEND REFILL URGENTLY. She put the cherry in her mouth, squeezed it between her molars until it burst like a blister.

"—as good as promised me a promotion next year," Rob was saying, "but we could live on my salary now and maybe even buy a bigger house."

She chewed and swallowed in silence, pushed her tongue around.

"Sweetheart?"

She picked the cherry stem from between her teeth and set it in the center of her plate. A perfect little knot, shiny and warm from her tongue. "What about my job?"

"You hate your job."

"That doesn't mean I'd rather have kids." She'd wondered since her salmon disappeared whether she might be the victim of a wildly misguided practical joke. Rob had missed the mark before. But now he wore the sour, wounded pout he put on whenever he felt himself wronged. He stabbed at the cake, tines cracking against the plate. "This is not what we talked about," she reminded him. She wasn't the one going back on a bargain. "Not what we planned for."

"Like everything else has gone according to plan?" he asked, with stinging sarcasm that didn't suit him, didn't come naturally. It sounded like he was doing a bit. "Things change, Suzanne."

"Sure do." She matched his sarcasm with much greater natural aptitude. "We're not thirtysomething anymore. It's too late."

"There are so many ways now," he said, as if that were a relief. "It's not too late. But it might be if we wait." He gave her one of his gooey little grins, reached out with one hand open. "We can't just work until we die. Don't you want more than that?"

Her hands lay limp and dead in her lap, tongue glued to the roof of her mouth by the inability to articulate just how much more than that she'd wanted and given up on already.

The grin faltered. The hand withdrew. "It's not so crazy, is it? I want to be a dad!"

"Then you never should have married me."

A pop like a gunshot made her jump in her seat.

"Happy anniversary!" Champagne frothed from the bottle in the server's hand, leaving a spray of yellow puddles on the tablecloth, like dog piss in the snow.

They drove home without speaking. Suzanne shucked her shoes off, insteps aching after three hours in heels, and was bowled over by the thought of how your insteps would ache after nine months carrying a baby, never mind the next five or six years of picking up children and putting them down, the ten years after that picking them up and dropping them off and driving them around.

"Listen," Rob said, sinking down on the couch. "I'm sorry. I shouldn't have sprung that on you."

Suzanne stayed an arm's length away. The rules of coupledom dictated she should exchange an apology for his, but she didn't feel sorry for anything. "Let's just stop talking about it," she said. "Please."

"Yes, okay," he said, hands landing flat in the air in front of him, playing an invisible keyboard. His unconscious sign language for *That's settled.* Which it wasn't. "I have something for you."

"We said no gifts." An agreement he tended to ignore, which he tended to do when it suited him. It was hard to be angry at someone for giving you a gift without feeling like an asshole, but Suzanne was used to feeling like an asshole and it didn't bother her much anymore.

"Christ, you make this hard. I didn't spend anything. I just . . . thought you would like it. *Sorry.*" He had a particular talent for what she thought of as the "backhanded apology," which wasn't really an apology but exaggerated self-flagellation designed to make her feel even more like an asshole than she already did.

"Well, I don't have anything for you." She never knew what to buy for him anyway. He didn't really have interests. He barely had hobbies.

He played pickup basketball with some guys from work and could argue about bad calls for hours with Casey and Brad. For someone who didn't have much of a sense of humor, he was inexplicably fond of stand-up comedy. Suzanne had sat through more than a few terrible sets as his date, wondering what he would even laugh at, unsure what to make of it when he just laughed at everything.

"Oh, I don't care," he said. "But I found this the other day when I was looking for—just open it." He handed her something inexpertly wrapped in jaunty polka-dot paper left over from somebody's birthday. She thought she recognized the bow from a deplorable bottle of Irish cream her mother sent last Christmas. It had eventually gone bad in the back of the pantry, making the kitchen stink of sour milk until they realized where the smell was coming from.

Suzanne slid one fingernail under the Scotch tape and tore the paper off. It was a photo frame, holding a Polaroid she'd never seen before but intuited at once was the work of the Sun 640. It had the faint blur of motion common with candid snapshots. People who didn't know they were being photographed didn't know to stand still. She'd never seen a picture of herself, grown up, next to Gil. The resemblance was even more forceful than it had been in her youth. They even mirrored each other's posture, fingertips dipped in their front pockets, shoulders back as if they were each pulling an invisible drag chute behind them.

Her breath got stuck in her throat. Beside her, Rob was yelling the way he did when something startled him, like getting mad would scare it off. "Don't cry! Why are you crying?"

"Where did you get this?"

"It's from our wedding! Our wedding *reception*," he corrected himself, as he'd been doing with increasing bitterness over the years. "It was in a box with our passports and some other stuff, and I thought you might like to have it."

"Yeah," she said. "You thought that because you didn't grow up in my fucking family."

"Jesus," he said, but she was already standing up, already walking away from his predictable "I'm *sorry*."

She didn't care whether he was or not. Rob, with his two brothers and two parents and completely two-dimensional understanding of how human beings could make and break each other. In the bathroom, she threw her dress on the floor, not caring whether it wrinkled. She bent over the sink and splashed her face, trying to rinse that photograph out of her eyes before it was all she could see.

"Suzanne, sweetheart? I can tell I touched a nerve." She didn't hear Rob come in, and when he tried to slide his arms around her she leapt away from the stiff insistence of his erection. Alarmed that he could even be aroused under the circumstances. "I didn't mean to upset you." Their sex life had been lukewarm for a while—a casualty of marriage, she assumed, the natural maturation of a relationship that had never been passionate, exactly—and while his cock had occasionally irked her with its incongruous timing, she had never found it threatening. Its independent will seemed malevolent now, like it was puppeteering him. Determined to see the anniversary through to the logical conclusion, no matter how disastrous the opening maneuvers, he kissed her with her face still dripping wet—his tongue a small, intrusive extension of the erection, trying to pry her lips apart.

"Rob." The word was lost in the mash of his mouth. "Rob! Stop—" She hit him in the chest with the heel of her palm, like a running back blocking a tackle. But she was five two and he was six one and she only knocked him backward half a step. "Please, don't," she said. "I'm . . . not in the mood."

"It's our anniversary," he said slowly, sounding out every word like English was her second language and she might not understand.

"I know that. But I need you not to touch me, because it's freaking me out right now." More honest than she wanted to be, with every nerve squirming under her skin. She couldn't be there in that room, with Gil still in her mind, with him.

"Is this about what I said at dinner, now? For Chrissake!" His voice echoed in the cold tile enclosure of the bathroom "Forget it, all right? Just forget it."

"How could I possibly forget that?"

"You act like I confessed to murder—it's a normal thing to want, Suzanne!"

"Maybe for somebody *normal*," she said, goose bumps rising on her arms. When had she ever given the impression of normalcy? She had never tried, never pretended, and he claimed to love her strangeness, how interesting she was. A woman with a history and a mind of her own. A conversation piece at office parties.

"Let's just drop it, all right? Try to have a nice night, or what's left of it."

He reached for her again, and again she recoiled, jerking away harder than she needed to, harder than he was holding her. Her elbow cracked against the corner of a cabinet, and she yelped at the sudden blaze of pain. "Fuck!" She squeezed her arm, felt blood between her fingers, a flap of skin curling away from the wound.

"Would you hold still? I'm trying to help!"

She twisted out of his grip, clutching her elbow, smearing blood down her bare, soft stomach. "Rob, I'm sorry, I can't." She bolted out of the room and through the first open door she saw, pulled it shut behind her. Soft, muted darkness, the pale scent of laundry soap. She groped along the nearest shelf and found a washcloth to hold against the wound. Not caring that it was white before, not caring that it was red when she mopped away the water and mascara smeared across her face.

THE **A** SIDE

GIMME DANGER

The Wrecking Ball after-party went all night, and everyone was wrecked by morning. Nicky had to be carried back to the bus while the first stirrings of dawn crept shyly up the sky toward the neon overstory. Everyone else clambered aboard the bus or the van of their own volition. They were halfway back to the motel before Suzanne realized the Ranchero hadn't followed them out of the lot. Gil, Gracie told her, had stayed behind to shower and shave and do a twenty-four-hour publicity blitz with Louie and Vince. Louie hadn't stopped grinning like a cat full of canary all night, growling in Gil's ear between handshakes like a cornerman between bouts, "*That's* what I'm talking about, *that's* the stuff I knew you were made of, *that's* what's going to make you a star." Because he was one hell of a somebody—no denying that now.

Two hours north and east, the sign outside the Desert Iguana Motor Lodge advertised not air-conditioning but REFRIGERATED AIR. The lot was mostly empty now, the other performers already packed up and gone to the next destination. Gil and the Kills wouldn't be far behind. Suzanne, still blinking Las Vegas out of her eyes, fell asleep on top of the bedspread and did not wake again until Gracie shook her gently.

"Don't get up." Suzanne mumbled something senseless, one foot still in dreamland. Gracie lifted that unruly curl off her forehead. "I gotta pick some things up from the cleaners, but you know where to find everybody."

Suzanne snuffled into the pillow a little while longer, but it was too hot by then to go back to sleep. In daylight the room felt smaller and shabbier. Curtains the color of creamed spinach, carpet the color of bile. Beyond the sandblasted window glass, the sun had just begun its slow descent, a swollen orange egg yolk sliding down a white-hot wall of sky. She stood on her tiptoes to peer down at the pool. In the stifling room the Technicolor blue looked deliciously clean and cool. She wriggled out of the *Don't Stop the Rot* tour T-shirt she'd been wearing for three days and dug through her backpack until she found her swimsuit balled up at the bottom.

Outside, the breeze blew dust in her eyes as she went barefoot along the second-floor walkway, past a dozen identical doors, all painted the same imprecise color. She thought through her Crayola No. 64, wondering which one she would use—Blue-Green, or Green-Blue? The trim was decidedly Apricot, the railings Raw Umber. She forgot her imaginative paint-by-numbers when the poolside concrete scorched her feet, forcing her to hop across the patio until she reached the patch of shade cast by the motel sign. An enormous horny lizard curled its tail around the post and stared into the distance with one unblinking yellow eye.

She lay on her stomach with a flyer for Dinoland Miniature Golf she'd picked up in the lobby when they arrived, eager to color in the cartoonish theropods. But coloring alone was too simple, did not hold her attention. She glanced up at the gargantuan iguana and decided to turn Dinoland Miniature Golf into the Dinoland Miniature Motor Lodge. She started with the foreground, planting a signpost below the toothy grin of the largest T. rex. Instinct told her he should be green but, thinking of the iguana again, she reached for a sandy brown instead. By the time she'd filled him in, sweat was dripping from her forehead onto the paper. She left her masterpiece unfinished and slipped into the water.

She'd learned to float a few years ago from a boy whose name she didn't remember, in the shallow end at the YMCA. *You have to lie still,* he said. *Like you're dead.* He held her up with two fingertips until she could do it, loosen her muscles and fan out her limbs like she was making a snow angel. At the Iguana watering hole, she pretended to be dead, like the dinosaurs, frozen forever in mud. The sun tried to slide between her eyelids but she kept them shut tight, suspended on the slippery surface between the blistering heat of the day and the venomous blue sting of chlorine.

She lay there so long her fingertips turned to raisins, and only opened her eyes when the heat behind them receded, when darkness came over her like a thunderhead. She squinted up at the sky, where the sun had sunk lower, turned redder. Less Orange-Yellow, more Yellow-Orange. The sign cast a timekeeping shadow over the pool, like the gnomon on some enormous sundial. Suzanne blinked in the unexpected square of shade. She couldn't remember whether she'd put sunscreen on, or when. Like Gil, she browned more than burned, but the desert was different—no moisture in the earth to soak up the glare.

She dog-paddled to the edge of the pool. After however many weightless minutes, her body felt so heavy that her arms wobbled as she lifted herself out, one knee scraping the concrete. She sucked her teeth, but the pavement was too hot to sit still, too hot to walk on, and she ran on tiptoes to the safety of her towel. She stood dripping on one end, frozen for a moment by the unexpected transformation. The sun had moved and dragged the shade away with it. The crayons she left on top of her drawing to keep it from blowing away had melted, bleeding out across the page. A tiny crime scene, a minor extinction. She stooped to gather everything, hoping feebly that she could salvage a couple of crayons if she left them on top of the air conditioner, ready to cry at her own carelessness. When she bent, her skinned knee stretched and burned. Blood thinned by the chlorine had run down her shin, trickled between her toes. She rolled everything up in her towel and limped up the stairs.

She dropped the towel on the bilious carpet and dripped all the way to the bathroom, the raw skin of her knee squeezing blood to the surface like a sponge on rewind. The cheap toilet tissue went to pieces that stuck in the wound. In the spotted mirror she looked feral, hair a sweaty tangle, cheeks and collarbones flushed, lips cracked and dry as the asphalt outside. In the high afternoon everything in the desert died for a few hours more than slept, rousing again when the sun had set and the temperature eased by a couple degrees. She gulped at the tap, but the water tasted metallic and mineral and made her even thirstier than she'd been before.

She turned on the tub and poked her knee under the stream, which loosened the toilet paper but stung so badly she nearly screamed. The water swirled away down the drain with a yellowish stain. Fresh blood still seeped to the surface. It wasn't much but wouldn't stop; she felt it thumping in her temples like there was too much for her veins to hold.

She thought for a moment, what to do. Skelly's room was next door. If anybody had Band-Aids to hand, it would be the Hands. Normally she never would have disturbed him on an off day, when he slept through the afternoon and snarled like a wildcat if you woke him. But with Gil and Louie and Vince all tied up downtown, she wondered whether anyone had done a welfare check. After last night, she had a funny feeling someone should—but nobody else had been looking at him, for once. Maybe they didn't see what she did. She left the room, pulling the door shut behind her.

The next door was locked. She knocked gently. "Skelly?" she called as loudly as she dared. "It's Suz—"

The door opened, and standing there was a man she'd never met. He looked like a lamppost—impossibly tall and impossibly thin, his head too big for his body. His eyes were thin, watery blue and one pointed the wrong way. "There's a kid out here," he said, looking down at Suzanne with the other eye.

"She's one of ours," Skelly said from somewhere inside. *Ours.* That sounded all right.

The lamppost gave her a grandiose bow and held the door open. The room looked like a dust devil had come through—dirty clothes everywhere, some hung up on the backs of chairs or thrown over lampshades to dry. The curtains were drawn but the sun still forced its way in, illuminating every fingerprint on the TV screen and the bottles on the coffee table, some still cold and frosty. A few waxy coffee cups glistened with condensation, standing in their own little puddles of sweat. Skelly stretched across the sofa with no shirt on and his jeans half-buttoned, dark, curling down creeping up toward his navel. Cigarette clinging to his bottom lip, full ashtray at his elbow, smoke hanging around his head in a hazy gray halo. He strummed the unplugged Jawbreaker, and her ears strained automatically toward the soft twang of the strings.

"Meet Elko," Skelly said. "He's a friend."

"Hi."

Elko squinted down at her like Popeye. "Howdy-do," he said. Over his shoulder, in an armchair in the darkest corner, Nicky had nodded out against the wall. He looked dead again—still dead drunk from last night, maybe.

"What's new, Susie Q?" Skelly sucked the cigarette, eyes boring a hole right through her from behind the veil of smoke. A song she didn't know groaned on the radio—a Hammond organ playing just enough notes in a strange minor key that the room sounded rancid.

"Do you have a Band-Aid?" She stood on one foot like a stork to keep from bleeding on the carpet, not that it would make much difference. "I scraped my knee." She tried to swallow the sand on her tongue. All she could think of was something cold to drink. She blurted out, "Can I have some Coke?"

Skelly considered the question. Looked at Elko, then back at Suzanne, with a sideways grin she didn't understand. "Knock yourself out." He propped the guitar on the cushions beside him and handed her one of the coffee cups—still half-full, still half-cold. "Grab me that bag," he said to Elko, nodding toward the carryall on the floor. She thought it belonged to the doctor. "Let's see this knee."

Elko dropped the bag on the couch, wiped his nose. Sniffling like he had a cold. Suzanne gulped greedily at the Coke, drank without stopping until it was gone and left a wrong, bitter taste on her tongue. Her mouth was still dry, but her suit was still wet and goose bumps climbed her spine despite the stifling heat. Skelly sat halfway up, stubbed his cigarette out, and lifted her under both arms. She was used to being lifted and carried and swung up on shoulders by Gil and Carney and even Doug, but not Skelly. She landed in his lap with an uncomfortable bump, both feet dangling between his knees. His skin felt sticky, her arm pinned against his chest as he straightened her leg, one heel cupped in his ragged hand. She could have been in the hallway in Lincoln again, crushed against his ribs. But he didn't have that warm animal smell now—he smelled like smoke and something else, something sharp and sour.

"Whose is she?" Elko asked, chewing one filthy fingernail.

"Gil," said Skelly. "Who else?"

"Little thing. Like a doll."

"I'm eleven," Suzanne said nonsensically.

"And you only weigh about eleven pounds," said Skelly. "Hold still, little thing. Little sting." He reached for one of the liquor bottles. She knew most of the whiskey labels by now, but this was different, something in Spanish. Thin amber liquid dribbled onto a bandana he'd pulled from the bag, and she gasped and grabbed his wrist when he pressed it to her knee. "Just to keep it clean." It burned even after he took it away, wiped up the smear of blood zigzagging down her shin. He peeled a Band-Aid apart, then a second, pasted them in a crisscross over the scrape. "X marks the spot."

Elko giggled like a girl. She felt dizzy. "Can I have some more Coke?"

"Sure," Skelly said, with that same sideways grin. In a strangely playful mood. "There's plenty." Elko giggled again. She finished the second cup in five long swallows, but the bad aftertaste stuck around. Skelly shifted, one arm looped loosely around her. A slick of sweat forming where their skin touched. Nicky grunted, mumbled something, then lapsed back into oblivion.

"Susie Q, you're a cool kid," Elko said. Giggle and sniff. She didn't like him and didn't want him to like her, but flushed when Skelly said, "Must be my influence." His swollen knucklebones drummed a beat above the Band-Aids on her knee. After last night the scabs had formed fresh, clotted seams of burgundy. "If it were up to her old man we'd be Gil and the Killjoys." Elko giggled, fit to burst. Skelly rolled his eyes at Suzanne. "Cut us another one, will you?"

She didn't know what that meant, but he wasn't talking to her. The arm around her tightened as he leaned forward, reaching for, of all things, the Gideon Bible balanced on the arm of the couch. Dusted with white, like plaster had crumbled and snowed down from the ceiling. Skelly licked one fingertip and dabbed it up. Moved to put his finger back in his mouth but paused with that rawboned hand in Suzanne's face. "Want to have some real fun, ankle-biter? Open up."

Maybe it was sugar; he had such a sweet tooth but so little appetite. Her mouth was already open, still dry as chalk from the heat and the dust and the wrong-tasting Coke. Her head felt like a fishbowl that might, at any moment, topple off her shoulders and shatter on the floor. All eleven pounds of her slumped against his chest. She could feel his heartbeat against her back and was overcome by a heady, carnivorous hunger to take his fingertip between her teeth and taste his skin. Then it was there, in her mouth, on her tongue, the gamy, salty smell of him sliding around her gums. Electricity crackled down her spine, made every wet hair on her head stand on end. But then the taste went bad, the acrid burn of battery acid buzzing between her teeth as his fingertip withdrew.

"Where's that good book at?" Elko asked.

"Here."

Skelly's arm tightened around her again. As he stretched toward Elko, Bible in hand, Suzanne grasped clumsily for another cup. It still tasted bad, but better than whatever the Hands had put in her mouth. Her gums tingled, saliva pooling under her tongue. Her head getting heavier, heart beating too hard. Or maybe it was his heart, knocking against hers, their bodies so entangled she couldn't tell the difference.

"Where's that card?"

"Can't find your bare ass with both hands, can you?"

"Not in here. Not in this mess."

The Hands laughed. Hands everywhere. His palm was hot on her thigh, powdered-sugar fingertips splayed on the back of her neck. She swallowed again and again but her gums wouldn't stop buzzing. Mouth full of bees. She wanted to spit, wanted to cry, wanted to wriggle out of Skelly's grip and wanted him to hold her tighter, afraid of the way her heart was pounding, the way the room was shifting and sliding and wouldn't stay still. A bloody sunbeam broke through the curtains, flashed off the yellow SG.

"Feeling better, baby girl?"

The skeleton hand on the back of her neck turned her head for her. One bruised knuckle slipped under her bathing suit strap. His face so close to hers she could taste the last cigarette on his breath.

The door opened with an ugly scrape. Elko swore and dropped the Bible he was holding, like a maître d' with a dinner tray. Gil froze in the doorway, staring at Skelly and Suzanne. "What the hell's going on here?"

Skelly sat halfway up, Suzanne drooping over his arm like a ventriloquist's dummy. Her body moved too slow, her eyes too fast, jumping back and forth from Gil to Elko to Nicky in the corner to the Hands still holding her.

"What's it look like?" Skelly said, but he didn't sound so sure of himself. Elko had finally stopped giggling, left eye rolling loosely in the socket like it wasn't screwed in right. "We're just fucking around."

"Not with my fucking kid you're fucking not." Gil's voice was a razor wire. She shivered in her wet swimsuit, every muscle twitching and trembling. "Suzanne, go back to our room and don't open the door."

She fell more than slid out of Skelly's lap. She stumbled away, holding on to the furniture until the daylight widened enough between Gil and the doorjamb for her to slip though. One hand brushed the top of her head, and for a few steps she felt almost steady. Then the door slammed behind her and the heat crashed down like a wave. She staggered the wrong way, hit the railing with her chin and crumpled. The iguana stared through the bars at her with its beady yellow eye. She smelled, for an instant, the wheyish putty of her perfect crayons puddling in the sun. Her stomach heaved again and this time everything came up. Most of it went over the bottommost rail, splattered on the pool deck below. When her guts unclenched she wiped her mouth and dragged herself off the concrete. The Band-Aids flapped against her knee, hanging on by one corner, already soaked through.

The first door she tried didn't open, and neither did the second. She couldn't remember which room was theirs, her head still heavy and swollen. Finally, a knob turned in her grip and she recognized the room on the other side. The hideous carpet and hideous curtains, Gil's suitcase overflowing on the floor. She jumped when something heavy hit the other side of the wall. Voices climbing over each other. Too muffled to make out the words, who said what, who was who. The gristly music still grinding away underneath. Gil always argued with Skelly, the same way he'd argued with Nora—the familiar back-and-forth of two people handcuffed together and blaming each other for however they got there. But this was different, like Gil and Nora's last smashup, the brawl there was no coming back from. She didn't need to hear the words to know that much—their voices sawed off and raw, tearing into each other without caring how hoarse they'd be tomorrow. Suzanne's skin crawled with invisible ants. She scratched herself red, raking her fingernails up and down her arms as if that might make the itching or the sickness or the snarling from the next room stop.

She blundered into the bathroom, where the sallow white light sucked the life out of everything. The vomit stink followed her in and clung to her even when she peeled her swimsuit off. She turned in tight circles on the crusty bath mat, wanting to vomit again and disgorge whatever had made her so ill. The Coke or the sun or the dusty Bible, Skelly's fingers in her mouth. The ruckus ongoing on the other side of the wall. It was all her fault, she felt that instinctively, the terrible reiteration of her place in the middle of whatever went wrong between Nora and Gil, between him and everyone else. Unsure what she'd done but sure of the wrongness all the same.

The shouting reached a fever pitch, hurtled to a place beyond the human. Words forgotten, language stripped of logic, every utterance a howl from the guts. Suzanne slammed the bathroom door but couldn't shut them out. She shrank into a ball, hands over her ears, squeezing her head so hard she thought her skull would crack.

Everything stopped with a dull sort of crash, as if a piece of furniture had toppled over. She stayed where she was, wound up tight, eyes squeezed shut but rolling restlessly behind their lids. Heart still beating like a hummingbird's wings. Breath racing in and out, hot and cold on her upper lip. She sat impossibly still long after her backside started to ache. Afraid to make another wrong move.

THE **B** SIDE

GIMME SHELTER

Sanctuary had given them time and a place to hide. But now they needed to move. More urgently than ever, after days and days out there in the desert, Suzanne needed to see Gracie. Louie's voice, or an echo of it, whispered in her ear, *Now or never.* The course was plotted, the tank was full. All they needed were provisions for the journey west.

Simon left on another supply run with Trouble in tow. "He's such a provider," Phoebe joked, throwing the Lifeboat's doors and windows wide open at the first hopeful whisper of a breeze. It was after five, the temperature beginning its slow decline. They sat on the floor in front of the fridge, sipping from the same bottle of water. Phoebe had found Suzanne's photos in there, the envelope she didn't dare pull out of the cold. But what had felt like such a desperate secret back at the Sundew Value Inn was easier to talk about now—now that they knew about Gil, knew about Gracie.

"They grow olives and almonds and wine grapes," Suzanne explained, about the Maldonado sisters. "Family operation, but it's a big family."

"That's her?" Phoebe asked when Suzanne handed her a snapshot. Gracie blowing a big pink bubble, head cocked as she poked one earring into place.

"Yeah." There were so many things she still had to ask, had to know. Gracie was the only place to go.

"She's pretty."

"You remind me of her," she told Phoebe. Another bare honesty. Sanctuary drew it out of her like a dowsing rod.

"Flattery," Phoebe said, "will get you everywhere with me."

"How about Paso Robles?" Suzanne took a crayon from the mug between them, dragged it across the atlas. "It's about twelve hundred miles, but we should stay off the interstate."

"And go through the Mojave," Phoebe observed. "Haven't had enough desert yet?"

"No way around it, this part of the world," Suzanne said. "We go south, we're in Joshua Tree. North, Death Valley."

"I hear it's lovely there this time of year."

Suzanne's turn to smile. Take a sweet slug of water. Wherever they went, the first thing she wanted was a shower. She could live in her sweat and the sand for some time, but her knees and elbows were beginning to grow scales. Before long she'd be more lizard than anything else.

"Whoa." Phoebe had flipped to the next Polaroid in the stack. "Is that Vince DeWitt?" With her electric blue eyes and her shocking red mouth, the rings in her eyebrows and studs in her nose.

"Yeah," Suzanne said. "I took that the first night the Kills opened, in the back of the limo. The writing was on the wall, even then." Over Vince's left shoulder, that slope of pink silk, loomed a too-familiar shadow she still thought she saw out of the corner of her eye sometimes.

"And this?"

"Ruby and Nash." Goofing off on a rare day off, faces poked through a carnival cutout of the Flintstones they'd spied at some lonely roadside farmstand. Ruby was Fred, Nash was Wilma.

"Where are they now, anyway?"

"I don't know," she said. "Doug would, though. That's him, there." Funyun hung on his nose in the back of the van, when a crowd of a six and a half was the worst problem they had. "And there we are again." The next photo Phoebe had already seen, on the cover of *Dust and Bones*. The snap they took together, which never stood a chance against the heat. Even when the image first developed, it had been gray and pale as a ghost. The faint outline of a man and a child under the sun. They could have been anyone. But she knew it was her and she knew it was Doug and that was all the proof she needed that she hadn't imagined it all.

"I wish it had turned out better," Phoebe said. "I'd like to see a photo of you at that age—when I can see your face."

"There might be one—there," Suzanne said. She found the photo Gracie had given her. Asleep on the seats, her bare foot in Gil's hand.

Phoebe grinned, showing the gap between her teeth. "Oh, that's so sweet." She ran one finger around the frame. "I don't know how I didn't guess . . . you look so much like him."

"Yeah," Suzanne said again, and the old refrain shot through her head. *Gil Delgado is my dad.* Something she'd been so proud of, and then so ashamed. But she had no more use for shame these days.

Phoebe flipped to the next snapshot and stopped. "This must be Skillman."

Suzanne had buried that photo in the back of her mind with other memories best kept in the dark. But no denying it—the ink on his fingers gave him away. Before the blood, before the Void, when he was still just Skelly. "Must be," she said. One gunmetal eye peered out at her, frozen in time.

"These are . . . I don't know, important." Phoebe frowned, fanned the photos in her slender fingers like a hand of cards. "Besides, you had a good eye, even at—what were you, eleven?"

"Ten, when I took that one."

"Wow," Phoebe said. She'd found a photo of Gil, one Suzanne took across the table in Houston, when the bruises on his face were still blue. "Suze, people should see these."

She'd kept them to herself for years because they were all she had left of that summer—the only summer before or since that mattered, until this one. "Someday," she said. "Maybe."

Phoebe lingered over Gil, over Skelly. "Do you . . ." she said, starting to ask the unaskable question.

Suzanne shook her head. "I don't know anything. Not for certain." That was the hardest part. The unspeakable uncertainty she'd never spoken of out loud.

"I'm sorry," Phoebe said. "I can't imagine."

"I can," Suzanne said. Because she had, every sleepless night for twenty-nine years. She'd imagined every way it might have happened. Every way it might have been avoided, every way it was inevitable. She lifted the dart still dangling down her chest. Metal warm from her skin. That strand of dark hair tangled in the chain could have been her own, but no way to know. "This was his," she said, watching the arrow spin, light catching the grooves. She didn't know why she'd kept it. Why she hadn't taken it off since the Sundew but wore it around her neck like a bad luck charm. Every time she tried to get rid of it she lost her nerve—like every evil thing she'd ever said or done or thought or seen might be unleashed on the world as soon as she let go. So she held it tight and kept it close and did not struggle even when it strangled her.

Phoebe stared, transfixed by each flash of light on the bristly black fletching still clinging to the barrel. Her hand twitched toward it, but Suzanne closed her fingers again. Her burden to bear, whether or not that was fair. "Suz—" Phoebe started to say, but broke off, ear turned toward the open window. "Simon's back," she said, and Suzanne heard it, too—the crunch of a car approaching over the gravel. She stashed the photos back in their packet, back in the fridge, with her last and most precious cassette. She trusted no one with that. Not yet.

"That was fast."

She realized too late that something was wrong. The engine noise was a flat, angry gargle—nothing like Blondie's sonorous purr. She'd stood halfway up when the door banged open. Rob was in the trailer.

"Hi, honey," he said. Face sunken and haggard, right hand so swollen it looked more like a club. "Hope you're packed."

He didn't wait for an answer, didn't give her time to think. He lunged and the room collapsed around them, the whole little world of the Lifeboat folding in. Suzanne crashed against the counter, Rob's good arm snaked around her waist. She shouted and kicked and scrabbled to get ahold of anything solid, fingers raking across the range, still tangled up in the chain. Phoebe snatched a flashlight off the window ledge and swung at his head. He caught it on his forearm, caught Phoebe by the hair and threw her into the lounge. She hit the cooler and toppled over, bringing an avalanche of junk down on top of her. Suzanne elbowed and stomped at his feet, but he lifted her right off the floor and dragged her toward the door.

A shot rang through the trailer, crushingly loud as it ricocheted off the aluminum siding. Rob's grip slackened, eyes wide and glaring into the wreckage of the lounge. Phoebe was still on the floor, but she'd found the revolver. Rob ducked wildly as her second shot hit the wall. Pinned against his side, Suzanne remembered the dart, the small sharp thing biting into her palm. *Somebody help*— She gripped it tight and sank the point between his ribs. Rob cried out and swatted at whatever had stung him. Suzanne broke free of his arms, lost her balance, and went headfirst out the door. She rolled down the steps and landed hard on all fours. Pain like shockwaves up her arms and legs, every drop of blood in her body on fire. No thought in her head but to draw him away from the Airstream, away from Phoebe.

"ROB!" She flung a rock at the side of the Lifeboat. "COME AND GET ME, YOU SON OF A BITCH!" She knew he'd follow—he'd chased her this far. If she slipped out of his reach again, he'd jump in that big, black truck and run her down like a dog.

Unless.

The pickup. He'd left the engine running. Almost like he'd planned a kidnapping before. She didn't waste time weighing her options. She sprinted to the truck and clambered inside.

A third shot. She stared out the window at the Lifeboat, no longer rocking on its wheels but terribly still and silent. The door gaped open until a body filled the empty space.

Rob's club hand dribbled fresh black blood. The other clutched his side. Eyes sweeping the barren landscape in the thin, fading light. He hadn't seen her, the truck's windows tinted dark enough to hide behind. She slid down in the driver's seat, too low to be seen through the windshield.

She heard his feet in the dirt. His long, careful stride. "Come out, Suzanne!" he called. "I'm not angry, I just want to take you home." Venom swelled in her veins. Too cold to be called fury now. The necklace still tangled around her wrist, that poison dart dripping beads of blood onto her bare thigh as it swung like a pendulum. *Shoot to kill or play to win.* "Suzanne!" She wrapped her fingers around the wheel. Found the pedals under her feet. This time Gil's voice kissed her ear, and a spellbound calm came over her. *Someday you might have to back out of a tight spot in a hurry.* She grabbed the gearshift.

Rob stopped in the swath of rocky no-man's-land between the pickup and the trailer. "SUZANNE!" He filled his lungs and shouted her name. It struck the stone and the sound rebounded ten times louder, a thousand voices howling all around, *SUZANNE.*

She put the truck in reverse, slammed the gas pedal down. Rob's head whipped toward her. He stumbled and started to run but slipped in the sand and the bounding echo pulled his feet out from under him. Suzanne's hands had never been so steady. She spun the wheel and gunned the engine and rode the swerve hard home. Not even the shock of impact could make her flinch, not even as the tires bucked and bumped and skidded onto flat ground again. The pickup stopped with a lurch. Dust filled the windshield, swirling across the lilac sky like smoke. Rob was a crumpled, formless mass, ten yards in front of the car.

She stared straight ahead until a flicker of movement made her look up. A flash across the mirror. Phoebe, stumbling out of the Lifeboat. The future in the rearview. Suzanne let go of the wheel with numb, white-knuckled fingers. Put the truck in park, dropped down out of the driver's seat. Phoebe staggered to meet her.

"What happened?" Her lip had split and her nose was already swelling. "I thought I got him but he just kept coming and— Where the hell did he go?" She followed Suzanne's eyes past the pickup. *"Oh."*

He hadn't moved. Limbs twisted and crushed, neck bent at a weird, wrong angle. Blood smeared halfway down his body from the hole in his shoulder. Phoebe was frozen for a moment, then sidled past Suzanne. She nudged his limp left foot with her toe, glanced back at the pickup. "Dodge Ram," she remarked. "Ironic."

Suzanne wanted to laugh. Nostrils flaring at the old familiar stink of adrenaline. Hands shaking with the aftershocks. But the cortisol receded so fast, abandoning her to the blank, white violence of what she'd just done. The dart still hung from her wrist, still dripped in the dirt. All her bloody sins lashed to her arm and dragging her down like Skelly's broken guitar. But Phoebe and Simon, they didn't need any more scars. "When Simon gets back," she said in a voice that was hollow and flat and not her own, "you should take Blondie and go."

"And leave you alone?" Phoebe said. "Are you crazy?"

"Are you?" Suzanne said. And then she did laugh—that scream of a laugh she'd heard her mother make in dire straits. She laughed and gasped and gagged on the dust still choking the air. "Phoebe, what the fuck! What the fuck did I just do?" She shoved her away when she reached for her hand. "No, you have to leave, you have to go." Her disbelief had jagged teeth—it pounced and shook her like a rag doll until all her bones came loose. "I killed my husband!" she shouted. "I fucking ran him over!"

"Sure did," Phoebe said. "But I shot him."

"So *what*?" Suzanne shoved her toward the Lifeboat. "You have to get out of here!"

"No!" Phoebe yelled back. "I won't leave you here with him—would you leave me? We're in this shit together, whether you like it or not." Suzanne tried again to argue, tried to push her away, but Phoebe was stronger. She caught her in her arms and did not let go. "Would you just shut up and let me hold you? Jesus." The fight went out of her then. With her face pressed against Phoebe's neck she started to cry, to sob and shake, too tired to keep it all walled up anymore. "Hey," Phoebe said. "I've got you." Just like Gracie told her once, *I got you.* "Safe now, okay? It's over."

It wasn't true then and it wasn't true now, but Suzanne let herself believe it, just for a minute. A thin, furtive wind swept her hair out of her eyes, dried the tracks of tears that cut through the grime on her cheeks. They stood with their backs to the bones of the town as each stratum of cloud blazed with the wild light of sundown. Shocking Pink, Blue-Violet, Bittersweet.

They stood like that a long time, silent as the darkness thickened, threatening rain. The earth cooled under their feet. A chill had wormed under Suzanne's damp clothes by the time the approach of an engine made them turn toward the ghost town road. Only Blondie, only Simon. Bringing Trouble back from town to find more trouble than he'd left.

THE **A** SIDE

HOLD MY LIFE

Suzanne might have passed out, or fallen asleep, or slipped into the twilight crevice in between. When she woke, it was as if the past few hours never happened. She thought she was still in the pool, still floating. But the shadow that came over her this time was not the watchful iguana. She blinked her tired eyes open to find Gracie's wide ones staring back. Her lipstick was smudged outside the lines on one side, sweat beading on her brow.

"Hey, baby," she said, whispering like it was a game of sardines. "How're you feeling?"

"Mm." Suzanne squirmed, and every joint in her body burned. How long had she been crumpled on the hard bathroom floor? She was still naked. "Thirsty."

"Let's get you dressed, okay? We'll get you something—well, something else to drink."

Suzanne didn't understand but didn't ask questions. Gracie gave her a T-shirt of Gil's that hung halfway to her knees. She pulled on a clean pair of underwear, shorts, and some flip-flops. Gracie helped her stand, ignoring the blood on her shin.

"You remember how to get to the restaurant?" she asked, shuffling through the stuff on the nightstand before she found a roll of cash bound with a rubber band, the take from the merch table over the last few days. There was a diner across the road, with a peeling mural in the parking lot that welcomed you to the MILKY WAY CAFÉ, where the burgers and shakes were OUT OF THIS WORLD.

"Mm-hm." The curtains had been drawn, so Suzanne couldn't tell what time it was. Her mouth tasted like she'd been licking the carpet, but at least her gums weren't full of pins and needles anymore.

"Take this." Gracie pressed a couple of tens into her hand. Her fingers refused to close tightly, numb from however long she'd been curled up in the corner. Gracie crouched down, still with that wide-eyed look. "I want you to cross the road *very carefully*. Get something to eat, and wait for me there, okay? I have to help Gil with something."

"Okay," Suzanne said, too confused to argue. Head still thick with fog.

Gracie gave her a brittle smile. "Good girl," she said. "I'll be there quick as I can."

Suzanne found herself out on the walkway alone. The sky was almost dark, sunset oozing along the horizon behind the black buildings. A few precocious stars piercing through the higher blue. The temperature had cooled but barely, the night still dry as fire until a breeze brushed the heat off her skin. She flip-flopped down the walkway, down the stairs, and waited by the side of the road. Over her shoulder, the enormous iguana looked on.

The highway was an inky black ribbon twisting through the sand. The Milky Way Café might have just touched down for the night across its narrow lanes. The OPEN sign must have burned out, but below it, the word LATE fizzed in and out of existence—a cryptic message from the great beyond. It's late, you're late, it's too late or it never is, better late than dead on time. Traffic was sparse, the approach of each car merely the whine of a mosquito until it grew to a roar, headlights blooming around the bend of the last hill like the eyes of some nocturnal animal. A semitruck whooshed past, and Suzanne scrambled across the road, shoes flapping at her heels.

The same waitress who'd served them last time asked, "Three again?" She wore her bleached-blond hair teased into almost a beehive, but her eyebrows were a rusty shade of red, penciled on in an expression of arch surprise.

"I think so," Suzanne said, unsure if Gil was coming. "They're on their way."

"You got money?" the waitress asked, and when Suzanne nodded yes, she grunted as if she didn't approve of children dining alone but consented to seat her in an empty booth by the windows. "You need a menu?"

She shook her head. "Grilled cheese, please." She felt queasy, but Gracie told her to eat.

"Bacon and tomato?"

"Okay."

"Fries with that or applesauce?"

"Applesauce." It would go down easier. "With cinnamon."

The waitress softened slightly. "You got it." Her eyes lingered on Suzanne's face, the new bruise already tender on her chin, where the last bruise hadn't yet healed. "Something to drink? Glass of milk?"

"Water, please," she said. "And coffee."

The eyebrows conveyed her astonishment. "You sure about that?"

"Sure, I'm sure," she said, which was what Gil always said when someone asked that. She still didn't feel fully awake.

"If you say so." The waitress clicked her pen on the back of her notepad and bustled off. She returned a moment later with two mugs, one full of coffee, the other of crayons. Suzanne felt tears in her eyes. "Thank you," she said, and the waitress patted her shoulder before departing with the coffeepot to top up other diners—mostly single men, probably truck drivers, hunched over plates of steak and eggs, biscuits and gravy, chile rellenos. Across the street, the sun had set on the Desert Iguana. A few lights were on, but not many. The lizard illuminated weakly from below, claws wrapped around the narrow strip of fluorescent white that said, as always, VACANCY.

Suzanne stirred sugar into her coffee and dumped the crayons out on the table. Her eyes welled up again watching the naked nubs, points worn flat or snapped in half, roll across the children's menu that doubled as a place mat. Thinking of her Crayola No. 64, reduced to a smear of wax. She picked up a crayon—no wrapper left, but Cobalt if she had to guess—and idly shaded in the faces of the aliens peering around the extensive list of milkshakes. Not just vanilla, chocolate, and strawberry, but mint chocolate chip and butter pecan and blueberry cheesecake.

"There you are." The waitress slid a plate in front of her. Two triangles of grilled cheese, still shiny with butter from the griddle. "Let's not get grease on your drawing." She swapped Suzanne's half-colored place mat for the blank one across from her. "Don't they look a little blue," she said of Suzanne's aliens. "They must be from Neptune."

"They don't have mouths," Suzanne said.

"That's true. I suppose that'd make me sad, too. But you've got a mouth, so best get to eating before it gets cold. You could use a pound or two."

"Can I have another cup of coffee? Please?" Already she felt more alive, more herself.

"I guess that's up to you, with your mom and dad not here to tell me otherwise. Serve them right."

"They don't mind," Suzanne said in a smaller voice. Not bothering to explain that Gracie wasn't her mom—not yet, anyway—and Gil had been giving her coffee since she stopped bottle-feeding. *Stay sweet, mi cafecita.*

"You're a sweet kid," the waitress said, an unwitting echo of him. "I'm sure they don't get much trouble from you."

Suzanne wanted to tell her she had it all wrong, that all their trouble started with her. But she didn't know how to say it, so she stuffed the grilled cheese in her mouth before the waitress could see her lip tremble.

But the waitress wasn't paying attention. She stood with both hands on her hips, staring past Suzanne, across the highway to where the Iguana languished in the sand. At first Suzanne thought the OPEN sign had come back on, the way the blue and red lights flashed across the glass. But peering past her own dumbstruck reflection she realized they were lightbars, police cars, maybe an ambulance. All converging on the motel parking lot.

"Lord Jesus," the waitress said, eyebrows hitched up an inch higher than usual. "That place. If there isn't always somebody up to no good over there."

Suzanne stopped chewing, grilled cheese gone to paste in her mouth. Under the iguana, the lights whirled in silence. No sirens. She didn't know what that meant.

The waitress shook her head and, eyeing the one bite of sandwich Suzanne had taken, said, "Eat up, but don't rush. You stay right where you are until someone comes to collect you."

No hiding her trembling lip now. Suzanne choked the sandwich down, tucked her lip behind her teeth, and bit it hard. The waitress looked at her and the sandwich and back out the window again.

"Where is your daddy, anyhow?"

Suzanne didn't know, didn't answer.

"Well, never mind," the waitress said, false nonchalance belied by her floating eyebrows. "Just another night at the Iguana, probably some junkie took too much." She patted Suzanne's shoulder again. "You stay as long as you like."

Suzanne watched out the window until the last streaks of sunset faded away and only the garish carnival lights of the squad cars remained. A few shadows passed between them and her. Probably people, but in the formless dark they could have been anything.

Suzanne doggedly choked down tiny bites of grilled cheese, chasing the slippery tomato with slurps of applesauce. Gracie and the waitress had both told her to eat, so she ate, wary of doing wrong without knowing and bringing hell down on their heads again. An hour's torturous effort and her plate was clean. The waitress whisked it away and came back with a chewy black brownie the size of a brick, "on the house." Again, Suzanne wanted to cry. She loved chocolate, loved brownies, normally would have gorged herself without hesitation. On the jukebox or the radio, Chris Isaak crooned "Lie to Me."

Eventually, all the lights across the street went off, or the cars drove away. The night too deep to see by then. She glanced at the Coca-Cola clock above the door. Half past eleven when the bell rattled and Gracie walked in. Her eyes flashed around the diner until she spied Suzanne.

When she sat down, she was out of breath. A nervous twitch at the corner of her mouth. Before she could say anything, the waitress appeared with a menu. "Something for you?" she said in a tone of sour disapproval. What kind of woman, she may as well have asked, leaves a child alone so long at this time of night?

"A cheeseburger, hold the onions."

"Something to drink?"

"I'll have what she's having."

The waitress clicked her pen a little harder than necessary, then left them alone. Gracie shook a cigarette out of the pack and lit up. Hands barely trembling.

"We saw the lights," Suzanne said.

"I'll bet you did." Gracie looked around for an ashtray and, realizing there wasn't one, flicked her cigarette into Suzanne's empty applesauce dish. "I'll bet everyone from here to Sacramento did."

"What happened?"

Gracie gave her a wobbly smile. "I should ask you." Up close, she looked like she'd been in a fight. Lipstick smeared, curls disheveled, one earring missing. A small, dark stain on her shirt. She saw Suzanne staring, folded her arms. "Nobody . . . hurt you?" She didn't seem able to ask what she wanted to ask. "You're okay?"

Suzanne didn't answer that. Didn't know yet. "Where's Dad?"

"Gil—" Gracie cleared her throat. Took her time taking a drag. When she spoke again her voice was almost steady. "Gil had to go with the police. He's banged up some but he'll be all right."

"Can I see him?" She needed to see him, needed to tell him how sorry, how sorry she was for everything.

Gracie shook her head. "Not tonight, baby."

"Tomorrow?"

"Oh, honey. I don't know."

"You can't smoke that in here."

Gracie started, looked up at the waitress with loathing. "Sorry." She stabbed her cigarette out in the puddle of applesauce.

The waitress set her cheeseburger down with a scowl. "This isn't a roadhouse," she said, eyeing Gracie's mussed hair, her missing earring. "Or whatever it is you're used to."

"I'll keep that in mind." Gracie glared daggers at her back. "Cow," she muttered, and took a huge bite, condiments dripping over her fingers. A few nails broken. Instead of reaching for a napkin, she wiped her hand on her shirt, smearing ketchup and mustard over the stain that was already there. She set the burger down again and seemed to lose interest in it altogether. It sat there going cold, keeping Suzanne's abandoned brownie company.

"Did Skelly beat him up?" Suzanne asked. "I heard them fighting."

Gracie reached across the table and seized Suzanne's hands, eyes deadly dark. "No, baby," she said, low and slow. "You weren't feeling well. You fell asleep. It was just a bad dream." Gracie squeezed her so hard it hurt. "You understand? You didn't hear anything."

She didn't see Gil the next day, or the day after that. On the third day, word got around that Eric Skillman was dead. Dead already when the cops arrived at a cheap motel with a bad reputation on the outskirts of Las Vegas. Gil Delgado was only half-dead and ambulanced to North Vista. Nicky DeWitt was still in the room and not making much sense but surrendered himself as if it were a relief to let someone else take the reins. Without his sister he looked lost and small and overwhelmed by the world.

The outlets that reported it all reported something different. Some said it was murder, some said it was theft or a drug deal gone wrong. The only thing rumor agreed on was that Skelly had had his skull smashed in with his own guitar, and that guitar was gone. Five days before his birthday, forever twenty-six. The Kills died like they lived, a stone's throw from greatness.

Suzanne heard it on local radio, waiting for Gracie in the passenger seat at a filling station in a suburb of the city improbably called Paradise. She'd never been in the car without Gil before. That, like everything else, felt irreparably wrong.

"Brief update on the late unpleasantness at the Iguana," the jock rattled off. "Police have an APB out on cocaine cowboy Peter Elko, who's got a record longer than my high school transcript and was seen leaving the scene in a black Pontiac. Nicky DeWitt and Gil Delgado are both still in custody. This is only the latest and greatest of bad turns for Gil and the Kills, which started with a stageside brawl in Nebr—"

Gracie leaned through the window to shut the radio off. Suzanne didn't look at her. She looked out the other window at the glitter and gloss of Las Vegas, turning to grit and grime in the daylight. "Hey," Gracie said. "You know not to believe everything you hear."

Suzanne picked at Blondie's upholstery. WHAT HAPPENS HERE, STAYS HERE, a faded billboard promised. "I didn't hear anything," she said. They drove the rest of the way to McCarran in silence.

The airport induced the same unpleasant vertigo Suzanne had felt for the first time a few short weeks ago. Everything glowing neon green, or plated with chrome, or carpeted in undulating waves. Palm trees made of metal sprouted right out of the floor. A video-game version of the real desert outside: McCarran 2000. Under any other circumstances, Nathan would have had a lot to say about the project.

"They beat us here," Gracie said, to herself more than Suzanne. Nora and Nathan were woefully out of place even with their fresh Mediterranean tans, but the woman standing off to their left was an even more obvious outlier. Shapeless black dress and flat saddle shoes much too young for her age, streaky gray hair frizzing out of its braid. Suzanne knew at once that she was Skelly's mother. She had none of his unflappable indifference, starting at every sound, but she had his mouth—or he'd had hers. She winced away from everyone who brushed her in passing, like it hurt to be touched at all.

Gracie chewed her lip, unsure who to go to first. Before she could make up her mind, Nora saw them. She left Nathan holding the bags and came at them head-on. Suzanne heard Gracie mutter, "*Mierda.*"

"Suzanne, take your things," Nora said sharply. "Where the hell is your other shoe?" She'd slipped out of one flip-flop on their rush from the parking lot. "You look like a beggar."

"Hey," Gracie said. "You've got every right to be angry, but don't take it out on her."

It was exactly the wrong thing to say. Nora wheeled toward Gracie, the whites of her eyes livid green in the weird neon maze of the airport. "Don't you *ever* tell me how to handle my daughter," she said. "When I need mothering advice from a glorified groupie, I know who to call. Suzanne! Take your things."

Suzanne shouldered her backpack; Gracie didn't seem to feel it leave her fingers. "Gil should be out of the hospital in a few days," she said. "If you care."

Nora let out a laugh that was almost a shriek. "Care? I hope he rots there." She grabbed Suzanne by the wrist, like she might try to make a run for it. "If not, I'll see him at the custody hearing."

Gracie's eyes slid past Nora, back to Suzanne. "Fly safe."

"Go to hell."

Suzanne stumbled on her mismatched feet, the remaining flip-flop still trying to fall off as Nora dragged her back to where Nathan was waiting, looking around and up at the ceiling, unsure where he fit into the filial negotiations. Mrs. Skillman had not moved. She watched Suzanne change hands with watery incomprehension, as one woman let go with great reluctance, and the other seized and clutched the child she did not seem to want.

THE **B** SIDE

BABY DID A BAD BAD THING

They found a few shovels in a tumbledown shed behind the general store. Suzanne had chosen a plot in the cemetery, not far from the hangman's angel. All night they dug in the hard, brittle earth. Thunderheads rolled across the sky, but rain never came. They worked by the light of Blondie's low beams, which threw long shadows behind every marker, every makeshift headstone.

When morning broke, they had a hole seven feet long and five feet deep. Suzanne sat down with blistered hands and a few loose boards. She took a stick from the cold fire and looked at the memorials left behind by a town exhausted with mortality. The dead identified by who they'd left behind, who would miss them now that they were gone. HUSBAND AND FATHER, DARLING DAUGHTER, PRECIOUS INFANT. FAMILY MAN, Suzanne wrote with her crude bit of charcoal. Maybe he'd rest easier that way. It felt right in its wrongness, a fitting monument to their marriage. Another tender lie.

Simon and Phoebe returned, dragging the body behind them, wrapped in an old saddle blanket. Not so different from the countless cowboys and bandits and prospectors who had gone west for fortune and glory and found a grisly end instead. "Better luck in the next life, Rob," Suzanne said. They lowered him slowly, took up their shovels, and filled the grave in.

They lit the fire one last time and burned everything with a name on it. His driver's license and his credit cards, the papers they found in the truck. They packed up the Lifeboat and hitched it to Blondie. They were about to start their engines when Suzanne abruptly turned back. She retraced her steps through the graveyard, returned to the unlucky angel. Rob wasn't the only one who had to stay buried there, in that place that didn't exist. Still, her fingers were clumsy as she lifted the chain from around her neck, a dark crust clinging to the arrow. She'd carried it this far, but it had served its purpose, done its bloody work, and she was too tired to carry it further. She hung it around the angel's neck instead and it looked like it belonged there—another golden, gleaming thing already gone to rust. "I wish I could have saved myself," she said. "Saved us all the trouble." But she was learning how. Better late than never. She watched the dart swing in silence for a moment, then started back the way she came. Nothing left to say, one killer to another.

Suzanne climbed into the pickup alone. She started the engine and held the wheel hard. Simon and Phoebe followed in the Ranchero, and they left Sanctuary behind. When they'd gone a safe distance, Suzanne shut the engine off again and climbed down out of the cab. She took her CDs from the glove box and she and Simon wiped everything down while Phoebe disappeared into the Airstream. She came back with the stash of vintage cocaine she bought by accident. Careful not to touch anything, she scattered it over the seats and the mats, like ashes, like voodoo, like *agua bendita.* "Just to confuse the matter," she said. "If anyone ever finds it."

It was a terrible *if.* But the desert was home to so many ghosts, and kept so many secrets.

They didn't linger. Suzanne left the doors and windows open. Inviting the elements in to do their worst. She went back to Blondie, slid into the driver's seat. The leather embraced her with the faint scents of bay rum, black coffee, hard candy. She turned the key, glanced in the rearview to watch Simon and Phoebe climb aboard the Lifeboat, with Trouble close behind. She reached for the sunglasses still hanging from the visor. The stereo sizzled and the engine hummed. Atlas spread on the seat beside her. She lit a cigarette. Fastened her seat belt. Pointed her wheels toward the west.

THE **A** SIDE

WHERE DO WE GO NOW
BUT NOWHERE?

The apartment looked even smaller, even shabbier, once it was
emptied out. In the weeks before the move, Nora was in a merciless,
unsentimental mood—so eager to pack up and leave Baltimore for
greener pastures that anything that threatened to delay their exodus
was unceremoniously dumped in the trash or left out on the curb
for the city to retake. Strangely it was Nathan who gently checked
her impulse to purge all evidence of her former life. "I know you
don't want to remember it now," he said when she seemed in danger
of discarding something too hastily, "but someday you might." She
answered, again and again, that she didn't think *that* was likely, and
again and again he reminded her that where they were going there
would be room for a few extra boxes, so why not take a few keepsakes?
Just in case.

The last years they'd spent there hadn't been good ones. But Suzanne had never lived anywhere else, except for a string of hotels and
motels and the webwork of highways between them. It looked like a
ghost town with the furniture gone, all the walls bare except for the
faded outlines where pictures used to hang. The mulchy old rug in
the living room had been rolled up and heaved in a dumpster, the sofa
she'd slept on since she outgrew her crib left on the curb with the rest
of the garbage, where the wino who still haunted the bus stop soon
claimed it for his own. She watched him from the window with a stab

of proprietary jealousy—scratching himself and shouting at passersby and spilling his liquor on the cushions where she'd eaten her lunches, done her homework, dreamed her silly girlish dreams.

She'd have a real bed all her own once they got to Connecticut, but what for? She never slept through the night anymore, but bolted up in fits and starts with sweat going cold on her forehead. She was too old for nightmares now. When Nora and the custody evaluators asked, she lied and said she didn't remember them. Adults had been telling her what to do and what to say, what she'd heard and what she'd seen and what was just a bad dream, for so long that she didn't trust her own eyes and ears. She kept waiting to wake up on the sofa again and hear Nora crashing through the kitchen, Gil's muffled voice on the phone. She didn't know whether she'd ever hear his voice again unless she heard it on the radio. She hadn't turned it on since Gracie shut it off while Blondie idled at the pumps in Paradise. She knew the songs so well by then—every word, every lick, every click in the mix—that they looped through her head all day and all night until she cried her eyes raw and begged and prayed to whoever was listening to please, just make the music stop.

She tried to remember what Doug had told her, *That part stays gold.* But she would have given all the gold in the world to bring Skelly back to life, to bring Gil back to her.

"Suzanne?" Nora's voice, calling her from the hall. Not screaming like she used to do, but the downstairs neighbors probably still wouldn't be sorry to see them go. "Honey?" She leaned in through the front door. Coat on, purse under one arm, like she was just popping in for a visit. "Everything okay?" She'd been asking that a lot lately. She'd taken a few days to cool off after Las Vegas, but then the fight went out of her, and she treated Suzanne like a breakable thing all through the custody hearings. Tender and weepy and prone to petting and cuddling her in a way she never had before. At first Suzanne suspected it was for show, an act she put on to persuade the evaluators that all she wanted was to keep Suzanne safe from her mad, bad, and dangerous father. But she was the same way when they were alone—as if she'd forgotten, somewhere in the whirlwind of Nathan and Europe and moving to Connecticut, how much she really loved her, and was trying now to make up for the lapse. Suzanne knew it couldn't last. Too much bad blood between them already, and blood was all they seemed to have in common.

"Yeah," Suzanne said anyway. Lying again, trying to sound like everything was actually okay. Like they did this every day. Talked across the empty apartment that had always been too full before. "I just—I think I left my toothbrush in the bathroom."

"Can't forget that," Nora said. Suspecting nothing, or deciding not to. They were "starting over," or so she kept saying, and that meant they'd have to learn to trust each other again. "Come on down when you're ready," she said, sensing at least that Suzanne might want a minute to say goodbye to the only home she'd ever known. That she needed to do that alone. "We'll be in the car." She walked out, and she didn't look back—leaving Suzanne wishing she could turn the page and start a new life, just like that.

When Nora's footsteps faded away, she tiptoed down the hallway, into the back bedroom she'd always avoided, the room where Gil and Nora tried and failed to keep their misery walled up. The bed was gone, and the dresser, the closet door hanging halfway open, naked hangers askew. They'd left one last wastebasket for the cleaners to use and take out to the curb when they were through. She got down on her knees and pushed the wads of crumpled tissue and old receipts aside until something sharp nipped her fingertip. She lifted the picture carefully, wincing at the soft crunch of the broken glass sliding around in the frame. She heard it break when Nora threw it into the trash—threw it like she wanted it to shatter.

The photo was scratched now, bent down the middle. The first picture Nora had taken of Gil, the last one she'd thrown away. Him and his first love. *Just married.* Gil and Blondie and Nora, there but not there, on the other side of the camera. And Suzanne herself, a mistake not yet made, the future of that ill-fated moment, just out of the frame. She bit her tongue and peeled the photo up by one crumpled corner. The glass had shivered into slivers and splinters that bit at her fingers, and soon they were spotted with scarlet, that bright ripe red welling up like tears from invisible splits in her skin. But she couldn't leave it, couldn't let go, even when the glass got slippery, even when she marred and smudged and bent the picture more. She had to take Gil and Blondie with her, the only memory she had of all of them together, because once they left the apartment where they'd always lived, when they went to Connecticut and changed her name to Westman, how would he ever find her again?

The picture finally tore free and Suzanne fell on her backside. Blood again, on her own small hands. Wracked with silent sobs. Just like the picture—shattered.

GOING TO CALIFORNIA

There was plenty of room at the ranch house. Simon went to work at once on sweepers and harvesters, always up to his elbows in something, Trouble's pale shadow at his heels. Before long, Phoebe had taken over most of the social media for Maldonado Farms. An uptick in tastings and tours and phone calls from retailers proved that whatever scheme she had was working. Suzanne—comparatively useless, as usual—spent her days on the back porch in an old rocking chair.

She and Gracie rocked the days away, side by side, with a dish of almonds or a bowl of olives between them. Theirs was an easy quietude, an unspoken understanding that some things were better left unmentioned, undisturbed. But when the mornings had ripened to afternoon or they'd traded their coffee for wine, little confessions crept out into the open and kept them company, like the one-eyed old farm cat who rarely left Gracie's lap.

"That boy's too young for you," she said, one of the last warm evenings in September. Watching Simon working in the garden below.

"Yeah," Suzanne said. "The girl is, too."

Gracie raised her eyebrows. Crow's-feet fanned out at the corners of her eyes, and her hair had, at long last, gone silver. But she still wore gold hoop earrings and lipstick like cherry cola. Clinging to youth in her own way. "Good for you," she said. Not one to pass judgment. She'd been with one man for thirty years but never married him, and when

Suzanne asked why, she shrugged and said, "What for? We wanted to be together because we wanted to be together—not because it would be a big hassle to leave."

"But you did," Suzanne said. More accusatory than she meant to be. "Leave."

"No, baby," she said. "He left me. We disagreed, about the treatment."

Suzanne picked at a splinter on the arm of her chair. "I didn't know he was sick," she said. "He never told me."

Gracie sighed. She still wore lipstick, but she had stopped smoking. Maybe the cancer had something to do with it. "He didn't tell anybody. Didn't want anybody to know. Said to me, if he couldn't die with dignity then he wanted to die alone."

Suzanne's throat tightened. Imagining the last years of his life. Wandering Little Havana, smoking again, because what did it matter? "I'm sorry."

"Don't be," Gracie said. "Live too big and you don't live long. Gil never could live small." She shook her head. "Never mind what that meant for the rest of us. But I loved him because he was like that."

Suzanne listened to the creak of the chair—a music all its own. "Me too."

"And what about you?"

"What about me?"

Gracie sipped her wine. Licked her lips. "I don't know what's chasing you. If what you want is to disappear, you can do that here. It's not so bad, being nobody." Gracie's days were quiet now, but her life was full. She had sisters and nieces and nephews. A house to keep, a ranch to run. Almonds and olives to eat, wine to drink, a one-eyed cat to warm her lap. Strays and strangers, like Suzanne. "But the Suzanne I remember, she wanted so much more."

"I wanted to be like Gil," she said. "Or like Skelly, or like you." All the somebodies she'd known, the somebodies she loved and lost and tried to cling to. "But I'm not. I tried to be normal for a while, but I'm not that, either." She was just somebody's daughter or somebody's wife—somebody's undoing, more than once. She made a life making other people's memories and smothering her own. No time left to be herself. No room. "All I've ever been good at is telling somebody else's story."

"You think that's nothing?" Gracie asked. She smiled wide enough to show her laugh lines, deepen the wrinkles around her eyes. "There is no 'somebody' until somebody tells their story. The world needs witnesses." She shook her head, sensing something still unsaid. "And you don't need the dead's permission. It's your story, too." She looked at Suzanne for a long time, then shooed the cat off her lap. "Come on," she said. "I want to show you something."

Suzanne left her wine behind and followed Gracie into the sprawling, shadowed house. The windows were always open, wind and whispers moving through the rooms. One was full of books and records, all the souvenirs of Gracie's long life on the road. Never in the spotlight, but she'd worked as many shows as any of the rest of them. Posters lined the walls, a few of Gil and the Kills' old handbills, other groups she'd toured with, been proud of, after the band disbanded. There was no way forward without Skelly—everyone saw that, even Louie. It was all he could do to keep Gil out of jail, to convince everyone as thoroughly as Nicky had convinced himself that he belonged there instead. He didn't serve long—nobody seemed to care too much if someone like Skelly saw justice—but he found God and got sober and when he got out, instead of touring clubs and theaters he toured high schools, trying and failing to scare teenagers away from the evils of sex, drugs, and rock and roll. You might beat someone to death and not even remember doing it.

What Vince thought about all that, Suzanne would have loved to know.

But the memorabilia wasn't what Gracie wanted to show her. She unlocked the closet in the far corner, which Suzanne had never noticed. Two slatted, sliding doors that moved silently on their casters. Inside were four rows of shelves stacked three deep with binders and boxes labeled in Gracie's handwriting—and Gil's. Not just *Impersonator* and *Don't Stop the Rot* and *Unholy Relics*, but other things with other names

Suzanne had never heard before. *Stone Fruit sessions.* Early demos. One labeled, intriguingly, *Phoenix.* She never thought she'd hear that melody again. Never knew where the tape went.

Woke up feeling down today
Went for a walk in what's left of the rain
And all that's left of loving you
Came crawling back again

"If he had all this," she said to Gracie, "why leave me that pile of shit in Miami?" It seemed like a red herring now, when all the while the real treasure trove was here.

"I think he knew you'd go looking for answers," Gracie said. Fingers wandering along the spines. "That you'd find your way back to yourself, but you'd have to get there on your own."

Out here there be monsters
Don'tcha hear 'em groan
Fee, fi, fo, fum
Don't let 'em getcha, darling
Come on home

The loss of him hollowed her out all over again. So many years apart, but he knew her as well as he knew himself. *Apple,* he'd said, that day at Most Wanted. *Tree.* "How do you stand it without him?" Suzanne asked. "I lost him thirty years ago but I still haven't figured it out."

"You won't," Gracie said. "You find ways to keep him alive instead."

Which reminded her of something else, something someone else had said. It was Doug's voice, wasn't it? Calling, as always, for the long-overdue vindication of Gil and the Kills. *That's the worst part. They flamed out before they got big, and if you never saw them* live—*man, you can't understand how explosive they were.* Doug could say that because he didn't know the worst parts. There were some secrets Suzanne had kept, would always keep, some that belonged to her. But there were others she was ready to release.

"My turn," she said to Gracie, and led her out of the music room, out of the house and across the yard where the Lifeboat had weighed anchor. Simon still at work in the garden. Phoebe and Trouble—well, who knew where. They'd be back. Gracie followed her in, looking closely at their things, their tiny life, the way they'd wandered. Suzanne reached around in the fridge until she found the envelope, all the way at the back. She shook the photos out and pushed them aside. They could look at those later. At the bottom, that last black cassette. The same childish hand that had labeled the photos had written on the J-card, *Idols in the Fire—Las Vegas, 1989.* The whole show as she'd shot it from the wings.

Gracie knew what she was looking at it, even if she never knew it existed. Apart from one other person, nobody did. "Where did you get this?"

"Vince," Suzanne said. "Same tape from San Antonio. It's all there." Skelly and the Jawbreaker, the Toaster and the mannequins, all the music and all the madness, all their bloody reckonings on 8mm tape. "I haven't watched it all the way through." She'd never been able to, but maybe that was changing, too. It was Phoebe's voice she heard this time—it was important, it was history. Her little piece of it. "The whole world should have been there," she said. "I want the whole world to see it."

LINER NOTES

Arielle Datz has been stuck on this trip with me since the beginning. I wrote the first version of this book ten years ago, and for a lot of those years I thought nobody but the two of us would ever read it. I didn't give up on it, mostly because she didn't give up on me. Without her trust, guidance, and bloody hard work, there would be no *Hot Wax*. To paraphrase the festival engineer, *Well, holy shit! We did it.* I'm grateful every day to have Arielle for my agent.

My editor, Tim O'Connell, somehow found the signal in the midst of all the noise I gave him. Working on *Hot Wax* together has felt like making music, electric and alive. The best creative partners (like Skelly and Gil, in their good moments) push each other to make better, deeper, more meaningful art than they could make on their own. Tim's insight and interventions have not only made this a better book but have made me a better writer. That is rare—and fucking rad.

Jack Butler, who acquired *Hot Wax* for Wildfire, has also been an invaluable member of the editorial team. He has been a tireless champion of this book and of my writing; I'm lucky to have had a chance to work with him, and now to call him a friend.

As Doug points out, a song is only as good as the production. We wanted *Hot Wax* to be a feast for all the senses, and it's thanks to everyone working behind the scenes with me that you've got this fabulous book in your hands. It's their story, too. I'm grateful to the teams at

Wildfire and S&S, who made *Hot Wax* look so incredible inside and out; to Kathy Daneman for her infinite patience and infectious enthusiasm; to Joe Thomas for helping me hold it together on the toughest days of the *Graveyard* tour; and to Georgia Pavan for being my external brain, which is no easy task.

Writing can be a lonely business, even when you have this many people to thank. Writers still need other writers to talk to about writing. But as Jiordan Castle once told me, there's a difference between "writer friends" and "friends who are also writers." I'm lucky to have a lot of friends who are also writers: Jiordan and the rest of the CLAW in Philadelphia; Courtney Maum, the Turning Pointers of 2023, and our hosts in New Mexico, who were the first people to hear any of *Hot Wax* out loud and helped it find its way; and Amy Lyons, a compassionate reader, powerful writer, and all-around marvelous human.

The people outside publishing who have supported me through the writing of this book are too many to list. For nearly two years I lived mostly out of a 2012 Honda, couch-surfing and gate-crashing my way around the country as I tried to make life as a full-time writer a reality. Like the Kill Team, I can't seem to go anywhere without sustaining some sort of grievous bodily harm, so having me for a friend also means you've probably been called at least once in case of emergency. I owe not just my life but my sanity and by extension anything intelligible I've ever written to these lifelong Emergency Contacts: Margaret and Eli, Allison and Will, Rebecca, Paige, Cary and Rachel and the Simpsons, Madison, Marcus, Liam, Justine, Garth, and Elyse.

Like the best kind of band, a family should always have each other's backs, even when they're at each other's throats. It can't be easy to have a writer in the family, but it's hard to be a writer without one. I grew up on my dad's stories of going to concerts and working security in the glory days of rock and roll in Los Angeles, and in more recent years we've been to see a lot of the old gods back onstage together: apple and tree. I owe some of my sense of adventure to my mom, who—like Suzanne—saw more of the world as a little girl than many people see in a lifetime. Since then we've seen a lot of it together; she's the kind of person who says "yes" when you ask if she wants to take a 300-mile detour into the desert to see a UFO crash site on your way to the Grand Canyon. My parents taught me not to be afraid of the world, but to be eager to go out and meet it. On all our long road trips, my brother and I shared the back seat and everything else that went along with that experience—the musical taste we were just starting to cultivate, the secret language of facemaking and eye-rolling that all siblings speak. Suzanne sure could have used an ally like that. Last but never least, my love to James and Gram, who let me take up all the time and space I need.

The family you choose is no less important than the family you're born into. Found family is the safe space at the heart of *Hot Wax*, not by accident. When you spend a few years with no place to call home, certain people become your home instead. Adam and I have spent thousands of hours in cars and hotels and deep conversation about books and music and everything else worth living for. I stole one of his best lines for the show at Wild Bucks and wrote "Minnie's Place" thinking of him. Adriana is a more kindred spirit than I ever hoped to find; our "precious likeness," as Suzanne might put it, makes me like myself more. She is my ride-or-die, the first person I'd call if I had a body to bury. Without them I'd be stranded on the side of the highway somewhere with a broken foot and five hundred records melting in the back of the car; a piece of *Hot Wax* belongs to them as much as to me.

And, of course, my deepest thanks to the people who made the music. Without it I don't think that I could write at all.

ABOUT THE TYPE

The body of this text is set in New Baskerville, which was first exhibited by John Baskerville of Birmingham in 1724. Baskerville's development of this new font family signaled a deliberate move away from the Old Style faces that were prevalent in previous centuries. ITC New Baskerville has been revived and updated twice since the dawn of the twentieth century for modern Monotype uses, and it remains a popular choice for setting continuous text due to its simple elegance and inviting legibility.

ABOUT THE AUTHOR

M. L. Rio has been an actor, a bookseller, an academic, and a music writer. She holds an MA in Shakespeare studies and a PhD in English literature. She is the author of the internationally bestselling novel *If We Were Villains*, the *USA Today* bestselling novella *Graveyard Shift*, and *Hot Wax*. She never stays in one place for long, but keeps her books, records, and four-legged sidekick in south Philadelphia.